JUDGE'S CHOICE

D1570688

JUDGE'S CHOICE

Tom & Kiki,
For your new Chalet

A DAN NEUMANN MYSTERY

Phil Rustad

Fast Dog Press • Minneapolis

Published by Fast Dog Press
www.fastdogpress.com

Editing by Patricia Morris
Cover photo by Kevin Cheung
Interior design by Dorie McClelland, www.springbookdesign.com

ISBN: 978-0-9840413-5-0

First edition
05 04 03 02 01 11 12 13 14 15

Publisher's Cataloging-in-Publication available upon request.

Books by Phil Rustad:
Dart
Alamo North Dakota
Judge's Choice

Prologue

June 1987
Anderson, Indiana

He looked into her eyes, extracting and absorbing every emotion she was feeling. He wanted to get everything he could from this experience, an act he had rehearsed in his mind many times. He had no idea why he was doing what he was doing, just that he had to do it. He never considered complications or consequences. He didn't care if he was caught. The compulsion was stronger than anything else in his life—nothing mattered as much as what he was about to do.

Three days earlier, he'd used his public persona as one of the school's brains as a harmless lure to get her to go with him into the woods. He told her he had found a patch of wild hemp growing deep in the woods and offered to share it with her if she would teach him the archaic art of hand-rolling a joint. She was always ready for a party and was more than willing to trade her expertise for a brief excursion from reality. So the two journeyed into the deepest part of the woods he knew so well, where he had recently equipped his "fort."

There, he offered her a drink, saying it was his own special "punch." Laced with Valium he'd stolen from his mother's medicine cabinet, it was just enough to make her groggy and compliant. He bound her feet and waited for her to regain her senses. He wanted her to be awake for what he had in mind.

He hadn't had any personal reason for choosing her other than she was intelligent and pretty. They weren't close friends, just acquaintances, really. He simply needed what she could provide. And it wasn't just sex.

Over the next two days he experimented on her, testing various ways of inflicting pain while not causing any real damage. Each time she screamed and writhed he became more excited. Soon he was sexually aroused and repeatedly reached orgasm, carefully collecting his discharge for removal from the site. He knew that, sooner or later, the place would be considered a crime scene.

Now, on the third day, he knew it would end. She was restrained by tape, lying on her back on the dirt floor of the hovel in the woods. He removed her gag and she started asking him what he was doing and when it would be over. She promised him that she would forget about the whole thing if he would just let her go. Realizing she was still bound, she struggled and looked at him with terror in her eyes. It was what he was waiting for.

As she slowly realized her situation, he produced the knife. Thus far, all his assaults had been in the form of simply pinching, twisting, a few burns, enough to cause real pain but nothing involving a knife. When she saw the razor sharp blade she began to scream. He didn't mind and did nothing to stop her. He enjoyed it. Her screams made him more and more excited. Each scream and moan and gasp was ecstasy to him. It was thrilling to be so in control of another person's very soul. This was the part he had dreamed about, that he had felt in his very being—that he needed to feel. This was the part he wanted to last forever.

He began to use the knife, first removing all her clothes. He cut them away slowly, revealing her in excruciating detail. When she was naked, he continued cutting on her flesh. At first she screamed in pain, but suddenly she stopped and seemed to accept her fate. She stared into his eyes, just what he wanted, and waited for the end. He had been careful to stay clear of the blood flowing from the shallow wounds. He kneeled over her, between her spread and bound legs, his erection carefully wrapped in a condom, and slid the knife, a long double-sided dagger, down between her nipples to a point below her breastbone.

"I'm really sorry this has to end. You've been so wonderful. But I have to go and you have to stay here."

The news of the end of her ordeal brought both comfort and horror to the woman as she grasped the meaning of what their separation meant for her. Her entire body stiffened and her eyes showed a level of terror she had not previously displayed. He loved it, absorbing the fear as energy, making him feel more and more alive.

He drove himself deep into her one final time and began to rhythmically pump. Hoping the knife had just been to scare her, she closed her eyes and began to respond, knowing that's what he wanted. She didn't notice that he was still holding the knife.

With the care of a surgeon opening a chest, he positioned the blade pointing toward her head and with a smooth thrust drove it through the skin under her rib cage and upward into her heart. She gasped, her eyes wide. She held his eyes as she felt her heart revolt against being sliced open by the blade. It thrashed in desperation against the blade, held steady by her assailant, simply cutting itself into pieces. He let go of the knife and watched it. The knife twitched with every beat of her heart. He touched it again with his fingertips so he could feel each heartbeat.

He released the handle again and watched as it twitched, like an external indicator of her existence. Like a primitive visual heart monitor, it moved erratically and arrhythmically, suddenly quickening, then momentarily stopping as the source of the movement tried to understand what was happening. He watched the moving handle and her eyes as her fate became clear.

As those eyes calmed with acceptance of the finality of the moment, he grasped the knife and felt the greatest rush of his young life, a feeling of total control, the knowledge that he alone literally held her life in his hand. He suddenly and unexpectedly climaxed in a hot rush he had never before experienced. He knew it would never again be as good.

But he could try.

Chapter One

The low morning sun caused Steve Holmes to squint as he drove through the gates of the Mora Municipal Airport. He had a full day planned and was pleased to see that Arnie, his company's manager and all-around do-everything guy, was already mixing the chemicals that would soon rain down on the croplands of Kanabec County. Today would consist of repeated missions, flying from the airport to the fields, applying the chemicals that kept the bugs and mold from eating crops that were intended for people and livestock, then back for another load.

Steve's company was busy enough in mid-summer to keep both his plane and the planes of his other pilots busy. One of them was Brad West, a former Air Force fighter pilot and retired airline pilot who had found a second childhood wheeling ag planes around the skies of Minnesota and the Dakotas and was already into his pre-flight routine.

Days like this—right after a front had come through stabilizing the atmosphere and promising the 48 hours without rain required by the chemicals—were few and far between. Steve would take full advantage of the weather window.

After parking his aging GMC pickup near the main hangar, Steve walked into the huge airplane garage through the open main doors and headed for his desk, which was on the side wall along with a row of file cabinets, shelves of parts, a refrigerator, and an eclectic mismatched collection of chairs arranged in a semicircle facing the open door. Parked on the far side of the hangar was Arnie's personal toy—a 1958 Cessna

172 in perfect showroom condition. The Cessna functioned as the company's only multi-seat plane, unless you counted Brad's J-3 Cub, which was only multi-seat for people under 5'8."

Sitting down at the desk, Steve pulled a job sheet from the top of the pile Arnie had set up for the day's flights. The job sheet was a report of the date, weather, license number info required by the FAA and Department of Agriculture, the GPS coordinates of the field to be worked, the products to be applied, the rates to apply the products, and the pattern he would fly to apply the products. As usual, Arnie had it all ready to go and Steve just glanced at it, got up, and walked out to his airplane.

His airplane was a mid-'70's Air Tractor sporting a big Pratt & Whitney 9-cylinder radial engine that produced 600 horsepower, more than the combined engine power of most light twins. Still, Steve loved the big yellow contradiction, a combination race car and dump truck. She had so much weight when loaded that she wallowed like an overloaded minivan in a snowstorm, but so much power when empty that she flew like a fighter. She had served him well for several years and he was filled with mixed emotions when he thought about selling her at the end of the season to trade up to a newer turboprop-powered model.

Steve climbed onto the wing and leaned into the cockpit. He flipped up a few switches, checked the responding lights, and climbed back down to do his walk-around inspection. He knew Arnie would have already filled the fuel and chemical tanks, but he believed in checking everything himself.

Steve climbed back up on the left wing, turned around to face rearward and, grabbing the center brace in front of the windscreen with his left hand, swung his left leg through the window into the cockpit, racecar-driver style. He pivoted on his left foot, swung his right in through the window, stepped on the seat, and lowered himself into his workplace. The seat had no built-in parachute like military planes do. There was no need for one in his line of work, not when you are moving at 140 miles per hour 15 feet off the ground. If something happened, there wouldn't be time or altitude to jump. Steve had lost several friends over the years and understood the risk. Those losses had made him all the more careful. He held fervently to the trite but true pilot's adage, "There are old pilots and bold pilots, but no old, bold pilots."

He reached behind his head to pluck his helmet off its hook, put it on, plugged the radio cable into its receptacle and, in the custom of every pilot over the last hundred years, leaned out the window and yelled "Clear."

The engine started to whine, then cranked over slowly. After about two complete revolutions it coughed, sputtered, and belched smoke out the giant exhaust pipes on each side of the plane. The engine bucked and complained and finally settled down. Steve released the brakes, added some power, and started to roll.

As he taxied, he reviewed the plan for the morning's mission, then tucked the paper into a pocket on the sidewall. He looked all around the sky for any unannounced traffic, even though he knew there was little chance of any so early in the day. By the time he reached the runway threshold the engine was properly warmed up. Steve tested each of the engine's dual ignition systems to be sure both were operating correctly, then keyed his microphone to announce his intentions to anyone who might be flying near the uncontrolled airport. He closed the window he had climbed in through, then with a push forward on the throttle lever the heavily laden bird rolled down runway 35, the active runway. When the airspeed indicator showed the right number, he eased the fighter-style stick back and pulled off the runway and into the summer morning sky.

Steve climbed up to about 2,700 feet, just high enough to mitigate the noise pollution he was spreading in his wake. He swung around the north edge of Mora, heading for a series of fields on the southwest side of the town. He crossed Hwy 65, skirted the west edge of town, and paralleled Hwy 65 south, crossing the northeast-facing arm of Fish Lake, flying over the Fish Lake Inn. His target for the morning was just ahead on the south side of County Road 14.

As he did with every mission, he first flew in a circle around the field to make sure no one had added any new vertical obstructions since his last visit. It was amazing how often a field he'd seen just weeks earlier would have some new tower or set of wires stretched across its end. With his visual inspection completed, he started to work.

He went through the drill of establishing baselines for his GPS system and started the application process. Steve descended rapidly, approaching his target from the west. He was careful not to drop too fast, one of the other reasons to switch to a newer turboprop plane. His old bird was carbureted just like most older cars. It relied on gravity to keep the gas flowing to the engine. He had, on occasion, descended so sharply that he put negative g-force on the airplane and starved the engine of fuel, resulting in a pilot-awakening cough from the engine and a seat cushion-sucking clench in his bowels. Not a good thing to do when rolling in on a field in a plane loaded to the max with fuel and bug spray.

As he crossed the edge of the field he hit the "On" button and began releasing the day's cocktail of bug killer and mold preventive. He settled in about ten feet above the plant tops at 130 knots indicated. The feed system for the sprayers automatically adjusted the rate of flow needed to match the wind-influenced speed. Already the day was heating and he fought the buffeting gusts that tossed his nearly 10,000-pound aircraft around like a leaf on the breeze. The pass took about thirty seconds and he released the button.

He pulled up and left into a maneuver that was sort of a half-Chandelle, half-Cuban Eight, making a climbing 45-degree turn to the left followed by a flat 225-degree turn back to the right. The result was a 180-degree turn back on the line he'd left. A little nudge to the side and he was lined up for his next pass. As he did he looked down and saw that the housing development going in on the south part of town was growing.

Two houses had begun to be built since his last visit to the field. He knew that ultimately their owners would be a problem too. When people encroached on farmland, the first time he came by he would be greeted with friendly waves and folks taking pictures. The second year they would still come out but now they would stand and stare. The third year he'd be met with shaking fists, single-finger salutes, and calls to the sheriff's department. It didn't matter that he'd been spraying the fields for decades, that he only came by three or four times a year and was only there for ten minutes. Now he was a disturbance to them.

He finished the second pass, executed the turn at the west end and lined up for pass three. He dropped over a set of wires, hit the button and cruised across the field. At the end he released, pulled up and left, and looked down at the neighborhood development again. This time he could see into a drainage ditch between two of the lots. He saw something.

He aborted the application runs, hitting the "Save" button on the system's controller so he could come back to the same place later. Pulling straight ahead, he stood the plane on its wing into a ground-reference turn so he could closely examine the ditch. Then he picked up his cellphone to call the sheriff's department and report that he'd sighted a naked body lying in a ditch.

Chapter Two

It was a hot summer day in Minneapolis and St. Paul. Hot enough to keep me indoors if you can call being in an air-conditioned garage indoors. This particular garage has three stalls and a nice woodworking shop complete with enough power tools and space to build just about anything I want to build, short of a boat.

I was giving that some thought, though—I could use two of the stalls for assembly and finishing. I've always loved the old woodies that prowl Lake Minnetonka and White Bear Lake. Maybe I could restore one of those, if I could find one. It's sort of like the boat guy's version of the car guy's dream of finding that low-mileage V-16 Packard or a '67 big-block Corvette resting in a South Dakota barn, hauling it home, and making it into a retirement account. Maybe . . . .

But that day I was working on a set of shelves. Not just shelves, shelving units, bookcases I should say, the same set I've been working on for about three years. Every time I get going on them, something comes along and halts progress. They're a long way from rebuilding a wood boat, I know, but I like the hobby and the result will look good in my basement.

My phone rang.

"Neumann," I answered.

"Dan, it's Glenn Mills."

"Hey Glenn, how you doing?"

Glenn, an old friend of mine from the Minneapolis Police

Department, was a patrol officer for about twenty years, rising to the rank of sergeant. He was happy there and put off testing up to lieutenant until he was close to retirement, not an uncommon move for street guys who want just a little more in the retirement checks. His last posting with Minneapolis was in the gang unit, a group that specializes in tracking gang activity. He had a unique ability for that since he'd been on the street so long and coordinating with other agencies. He had contacts within the community who trusted him and were willing to get him information that younger, newer cops couldn't get.

When he turned fifty-two he had thirty years in and still had his original wife, Susan, something pretty unusual for a career city cop, so he retired with a nice pension and moved north about eighty miles to a little lake called, believe it or not, Fish Lake. There are twenty-six Fish Lakes in Minnesota, but this is one of the better-known ones. Not happy with a life of endless fishing, hunting, and sitting around offering comment on how household chores should be done, he got involved in local politics, with his wife's encouragement.

For people who've spent their entire lives chasing bad guys there is only one kind of politics that matters—the sheriff's office. When the longtime sheriff decided to retire to Florida, the position was open. Usually, a rural Minnesota sheriff's position is filled from within, at least temporarily until the next election. But Kanabec County had suffered a bit from National Guard call-ups, and several other good candidates, feeling the tug of either big-city police forces or the many federal jobs that had become available in the expansion of the Department of Homeland Security after 9/11, had left. So there was no logical candidate to move into the sheriff spot. They called for a special election and Glenn ran for sheriff. Surprising everyone, including himself, he took to campaigning like a bird to flight. He won and had been the sheriff of Kanabec County, Minnesota, for three years.

"I'm doing great. The fishing is good and the weather is producing a nice crop of turkeys for this fall's hunt. How about you? I didn't wake you up, did I? You ever finish those cabinets?"

"Shelves, Glenn, as in bookshelves, or wall units since I don't own enough books to fill them. And no, I haven't finished them. I'm in the shop right now working on them. And, no, you didn't wake me up. My girl is in town from Phoenix, but she's sleeping in. I thought I'd work on the shelves, but every time I get the next step set up on one of the machines, someone calls and I'm off to save the world again. At least I know you won't make me do that."

"Don't be too sure. You don't know why I called yet."

"Whatever it is, it's better than a homicide investigation. Let me guess—you need me to pick up some parts for that antique truck you're still driving. No, that's not it. You finally decided to replace that old Model 11 shotgun and you want me to go gun shopping with you. How am I doing? Hey, how about Maria and I come up for a little fishing?"

"Well, I'd love to have you up for fishing, but I'm going to have to burst your bubble. I need some help up here and you are just the guy for the job."

"What, you got a serial mailbox vandal?"

"I wish. Dan, I've got a homicide and it's a nasty one. You know how it is out here in the country. We have about one killing per year but it's always either boyfriend/girlfriend or husband/wife, or it's a body dump from the Cities that we can figure out pretty easy. I've got trained inspectors and they're good guys. But this'n is different. Now, it's not that I don't trust my boys, it's just that this is going to be big here and I really have to deliver. What I'm looking for is a little outside oversight, to make sure I do what I should. You know my background. I never worked a homicide case past the initial scene in my whole career in the city and the ones I've had on this job have been straightforward and simple. Hell, that one last year—the woman was standing over the body with the smoking gun in her hand when my patrol guy showed up on the gunshots call, crying about how she was sorry she shot him. "What it comes down to is this: I've got a good team here but none of them have ever done a homicide like this. I won't know if these guys will be doing the right thing or blowing smoke up my ass."

I thought about what Glenn was asking. He was an experienced police officer, had thirty years on the job. But he was right about his experience. He had investigated a lot of traffic accidents, assaults, break-ins, auto thefts, and knew the city's gang population better than they knew themselves. But he had never done a homicide investigation when he was here. He had a green team and he was a fish out of water when it came to anything out of the ordinary.

"I can't offer much as far as a fee and I know you're expensive," Glenn added.

That was the furthest from my mind right then. I had already figured that if I got involved it would be pro-bono. It didn't matter. Glenn was an old friend and if I helped him it would be for a dollar a day.

"Tell me about the case. What do you have so far?"

"Man, it's bad. This morning we got a call, a crop-duster pilot saw a body in a ditch about a half mile from County Road 14. I'm out at the site right now. It's bad Dan, I'm telling ya, it's really bad," he said again.

"Define "bad," I asked.

"She was *cut up*. And I mean cut up. Whoever did this took his time and sliced her up like cold cuts. She's naked and there are cuts every-where. Not really deep cuts, just enough to hurt and bleed bad. It was almost like one of those gang things we had years ago when the South-east Asian gangs started coming to town. You know, where they would try to do "death by a thousand cuts" like their dads had seen back in the war. Her nipples were cut off, her genitals were carved up, it's unbeliev-able—like something out of a horror movie."

I could hear the tension in Glenn's voice. He'd seen a lot of hurt in his thirty years, as had I. But this amount of violence was clearly at a level that he'd never experienced before. He was choking up on the phone and he was one hard character. I was in.

"OK. Where did they take the body?"

"Coroner's on her way out. All she'll do is pronounce her dead and I could have done that. I wouldn't venture to guess on cause of death until after the autopsy. We contract with St. Paul's morgue for autopsies so it will go there after the BCA is through with the scene. They're on their way, now," Glenn said, referring to the state's Bureau of Criminal Apprehension.

"And you're still at the scene?"

"Yeah. And I truly need your help. How 'bout it?"

"Yeah. Give me the location and I'll get up there as quick as I can. OK if I bring Maria?"

"She's homicide in Arizona, right?"

"Yes. And she's only here for a few days, so I'd like to have the time with her," I said, wondering how he knew she was homicide.

"Sure, bring her. I need all the help I can get."

Glenn recited the information and I wrote it down with a carpenter's pencil on a chunk of oak molding I had handy. We signed off and I looked around for some paper. I had the address but the piece of trim I'd written it on was eight feet long and that would be a bit tough to stick in my pocket.

I went into the house to see if Maria had stirred. She and I had been seeing each other for a little over a year, after a case took me to Phoenix. Maria's a homicide investigator with the Maricopa County Sheriff's Office in Phoenix. She had caught the murder of a just-retired judge from Minnesota. I had gone to Arizona to see if the judge's killing was part of another investigation I was working. It was. We met. We clicked.

Since then, we have worked two cases together. The first one was more intellectual work; the second, more typically physical police work. In fact, she had saved my ass by shooting a bad guy. Two rounds right in the ten ring from a compact .45 at a distance of about 45 feet. Pretty nice shooting. Bad guy was dead before he hit the ground.

When that case was solved, I had asked her to marry me. Maybe it was the rush of success, maybe the realization that I was running out of time. I'd been introduced to her family in Phoenix and she'd met my family, such as it is, here in Minnesota. We'd talked about the future, where one could live in comfort year round, how long she wanted to work full time, things like that. So I popped the question. She didn't say yes. Or no. She said, "Not yet." For now, I'm taking that as an affirmative response that, someday, we'll settle down. I'm OK with that.

Maria's flight had gotten in about 8:00. When we left the airport I took Maria out for a nice dinner at an Italian place on the way home.

This was the technique I had been taught by my friend Pete Anderson. Pete was my best friend all through high school and somehow still is. He had made a fortune, first in manufacturing and more recently in North Dakota oil. Now being his best friend brought some real perks with it. We were like brothers and he gave me some advice that only a brother could give. When I started getting serious about Maria, he told me I should do what he used to do when he was traveling quite a bit on business. He said, "When you've been gone all week, or in your case, you haven't seen each other for months, the urge is to find the closest convenient flat surface and drop her on it right there. That will be her urge too, at least at first. But you'll do some real damage to your relationship if that becomes the principal focus of your relationship. At some point you are going to need to develop interpersonal skills that go beyond a quick roll in the hay.

"Do what I did all those years I was traveling. Even though, after a week on the road, the last thing you want to do is eat another restaurant meal, take her out to dinner. This gives you both a chance to get reacquainted and to talk, that's right, to talk about things that have happened since you last saw each other. This will remove the pressure to 'perform' immediately, which you will find is not always desirable when one or both of you just happens to be exhausted. Have a nice meal, talk about things, take your time, go home, and then if, and only if, things are right, find that horizontal surface. Trust me, there will be reunions when both of you will be happy to just cuddle up and get some sleep."

So that's what we had done. Maria had been working a drug case involving smuggling, not exactly unusual for the Maricopa County Sheriff's Department. But the twist was that the bad guys were using tequila shipments to move the cocaine. Mexican smuggling has gotten very sophisticated in recent years with the merger of drug operations with some military and governmental units. Mexico is rapidly descending into the chaos of a failed country, not that much different from places like Somalia where the warlords rule and the government is a joke. The police and military in Mexico are up against an adversary that is better armed and funded than they are and is without restrictions like "rules of engagement" or qualms about offering a police chief or military commander the choice of wealth or the painful and public death of his entire family. "Plomo o plata" they used to call it in Columbia—lead or silver, your choice.

Anyway, Bad Guys, Inc., I'll call them now, had acquired one of the top brands of tequila that is imported into the U.S. They were packing the real moneymaker into the trucks that were hauling the worm-killing liquid across the border. While these trucks were inspected, they were primarily the interest of the Bureau of Alcohol, Tobacco, Firearms and Explosives people, not the Drug Enforcement Administration. And the BATFE people assigned to inspect the trucks were experts in liquor, not drugs. So they did their thing—checking to make sure the booze had the proper tax stamps and such without really looking at the trucks as drug haulers.

Maria's team had gotten two people on the inside, an accomplishment that will go down in DEA history as one of the ballsiest moves ever made, and they had collected the intel necessary to take down a shipment of twelve-and-a-half tons of the white powder. It was the biggest overland coke bust in history. Only some of the ship busts have involved more of the white gold.

Maria was at the heart of it all. Fortunately, for her sake, she was not one of the undercovers, nor was she a public part of the major break in the case. Fortunately, I say, because there is sure to be retribution from the people who lost a substantial investment in the operation. Maria was ready for a few days off.

So we ate, came home to my place and crashed. I was up, not at my usual bright and snarly 6:00, but around 7:00 so I could get in a little quick work in the wood shop.

I'd made coffee so I'd have a cup for the woodwork shop, left the pot on, and started breakfast by laying out the ingredients I'd use when Maria arose. I know from experience that the smell of coffee brewing will bring my beauty down the stairs to investigate. Now, back in the kitchen putting the omelet ingredients back in the fridge, I heard a sound and looked over my shoulder to see Maria coming into the kitchen. She was wearing tight jeans, an Under Armour long-sleeve shirt and had her long black hair tied back in a ponytail.

"Good morning, Sunshine," I said.

"Good morning yourself. Thank you for a great night's sleep."

"I needed it too. It's been a crazy couple of days and I was as wrung out as you were."

"Well, I'm set to go now," she said with a wink.

I poured two travel cups of coffee as I filled her in on the call from Glenn. True cop that she is, she just said, "Yeah, let's go. It will give us some road time to talk and see the sights."

Sounded good to me. "Want a bagel for the road?" I asked. She shook her head no. I grabbed one and we headed to Mora. Little did I know what the trip would bring.

As we drove, a conversation finally developed. As expected, it was directed at the Mora murder case. Maria wanted a little background.

"Does Glenn get much in the way of homicides up here?" she asked.

"No. An occasional body drop from the Cities. But it's pretty unusual for him to have a local murder. When he does, it's almost always going to be something run-of-the-mill. This case sounds really abnormal, statistically speaking."

"I agree. Rural murders in Arizona are typically the kind of stuff you can close in forty-eight hours. In Phoenix, it might take longer just because tracking down the bad guy usually takes longer. And, of course, we have the gang-code-of-silence thing."

I nodded agreement. In urban settings, a lot of cases are solved right down to IDing the killer, then they stall. Gang threats still shut up a lot of people and it takes a reward or just the passage of time to bring a witness forward.

As I explained the condition of the body, Maria sort of drifted off and gazed out the window. I thought she was having what I called a "moment," that's when something goes "ping" in your head and you think you've heard it before. She came back.

Chapter Three

9:00 a.m.
Friday
Outside Mora, Minnesota

It took us a little over an hour to get to the site where the body had been found. I drove my GMC Denali after deciding it was too hot for a motorcycle. I know, all the bike aficionados out there will take umbrage with that statement; the truth is, I rarely ride to a crime scene. But as much as I like Maria's arms around me, I know myself well enough to understand that my head is going to be working problems other than concentrating on riding and I've always believed that most motorcycle accidents are the result of a lack of concentration on the part of the rider. You simply have to believe that every other driver on the road is out to get you so you ride in hyper-defensive mode. This works even though it's not true that *every* other driver is trying to run you off the road—only half of them are. The trouble is you don't know which half.

The real problem is visibility. Drivers don't see bikes. I wish I had a buck for every accident report I'd seen over the years that included a statement from the driver of the vehicle that hit the bike stating, "I never saw him." I could retire. What a minute, I did retire. Sort of.

So I drove my biggest and easiest-to-drive vehicle to the scene. I love the big pig, in spite of sixteen miles to the gallon. It practically drives itself. This allows time to think. Right now I was thinking about working with Glenn and staying out of the way of the BCA. I know most of the BCA people and they know me. My relationship with many of them is solid but there are a few who wouldn't be happy to see me there. It's not a competition thing, just a looking-over-their-shoulder thing. No one likes that.

As we drove I filled Maria in on what Glenn had told me. I watched her as she received the information. Her eyes were closed for long periods and she gave an occasional nod of understanding. I knew she was forming a mental picture of the crime scene.

"You think some boyfriend or ex went nuts on her?" she asked.

"That's the first place I'd go. You know these are always known-to-the-victim situations."

"So why's he asking you in?"

"Not sure. He was really and truly messed up, I can tell you that. This guy spent a lot of time on the Minneapolis streets dealing with gangs. He's no wuss. He's seen everything you and I have seen and more. This must really be bad for him to be as shook up as he is."

We talked some more about Glenn's case and then the conversation turned to personal matters. Maria's mother was ill. She had taken a fall and broken a hip. That was the start of a downhill slide. She was in a rehabilitation center and had developed an infection. Their large extended family was providing support for Mom so Maria coming to Minnesota for a few days was her chance to get away from the pressure and stress of Mom's condition for a while. Only, here she was, talking about it. I thought it was therapeutic, so I just listened.

When we got close to Mora, the county seat of Kanabec County, I turned off Hwy 65 onto Fish Lake Drive. Glenn had instructed me to go a little ways west to a street that looped south off Fish Lake Drive. Local builders were trying to develop the area into a new neighborhood. It looked like any suburban development in the Twin Cities. I guess the suburbs are moving way out. The loop was shaped like a "U" and went south, bent west, then north to hook back up with a frontage road to Hwy 65. At the curve back to the north, one street went south. It was blocked by a couple of yellow cattle gates and two sheriff's deputy cars. Off to one side of the entrance to the future neighborhood was a large sign with a drawing of the ten subdivision lots where more houses would be built. I saw the lights of two more sheriff's department and one state patrol car about 300 yards further up the undeveloped cul-de-sac.

I swung my truck toward the gates and a deputy carrying a clipboard stepped out from where he'd been leaning against his car. As I approached, I flipped on what I call my cop lights. I have the Denali rigged out with all the lights an unmarked Suburban would have—behind the grill, top of the windshield, colored flashing turn indicators—it's a package. My window was down and I held my badge case out so he could see it.

"Dan Neumann. The sheriff is expecting me." As I said this I read his name tag—Gorman. It's an old habit. I like to address officers by their names.

"He sure is," said the deputy. He gave my creds a quick look as I introduced Maria as "Maria Fernandez, Homicide." I left off the part about Arizona. She flashed her badge case as well. The deputy jotted our names and arrival time on his crime scene log and said, "I'll get the gate for you."

I called out, "Thanks, Gorman," as he hustled over and swung one of the gates open so I could drive through.

We drove down the center of what would someday be a nice neighborhood. I could envision nice houses with nice families in this nicely treed development. There would be nice summer street parties where the nice children would play nice games and nice affairs would blossom between the stay-at-home dads and moms. They would now have to be told that one nice summer evening someone had left a violently carved-up body of a young woman in a ditch between two of the lots. Nice.

I could see Glenn standing with four men just past the law enforcement vehicles. He looked good, had even dropped some weight. He was in casual clothing—jeans, a sweatshirt, no apparent sidearm. The only way to know he was with the sheriff's department was his ball cap, which was the same as the uniformed guys. It's his standard uniform. Since his election to the exalted position of sheriff, he preferred this look to the formal white-over-brown uniform with a Smokey Bear hat because it's less intimidating. He wanted people who came to see him in his office feel that they could tell him what was on their minds without feeling like they were talking to The Man. It was working for him.

Of the other cops in attendance, one was a state patrol officer in the usual maroon uniform. He looked to be about forty, in good condition, and had the high and tight haircut affected by most state troopers. The other guys were in county deputy uniforms like the guy on the gate, tan-over-brown, county-mountie outfits we city guys call them. They were a mix of ages and levels of fitness. Two seemed distracted, but one, a younger guy probably in his late twenties or early thirties, about six foot three, was standing very still, nodding to Glenn. I drove down near the other cars and pulled off the road. I popped all the windows open and shut her off. We got out and walked on over.

"Hey Dan, thanks for coming," Glenn greeted me.

"You know me—can't resist a good body dump. This is Maria Fernandez of the Maricopa County Sheriff's Office."

Glenn and Maria shook hands and Glenn gave her a smile. "I don't know what you see in this guy. I've known him since he was a dog-watch rookie and I knew he'd never make a good pimple on a sergeant's butt."

Maria jumped to my defense and said, "I'm sure I can cure his skin disorders. It's the 'always being right' thing that bothers me."

Glenn laughed and we walked over to the body. Glenn's demeanor changed instantly.

"Dan, Maria, this is Steve Schmidt of the state patrol and Deputy Nate Sheldon. Steve was in on the first response and Nate's been back in town trying to get a handle on who and what we have here."

So Nate was Glenn's up-and-coming investigator. That was good. If he was a local kid he'd know things that could really speed up an investigation. I turned to him with a "Go ahead" expression on my face. Glenn helped him out by saying, "Give Detectives Neumann and Fernandez what you have so far, Nate."

"Yes sir," he said, formally snapping to attention and clearing his throat. "This morning, about oh six hundred, Steve Holmes, a local pilot, was crop dusting the field over there." He pointed to the north. "He called the sheriff's office and reported a body in the ditch out here. That led to a radio call and brought in the responding officers, Deputy Gorman, who is now at the gate over there, and Trooper Schmidt, who was driving up Hwy 65. They about tied for the first to arrive. Trooper Schmidt secured the area. There was no reporting citizen to interview since the call came from the pilot, but I'm planning on talking with him later today. The sheriff was among the next arrivals. This was about 6:35.

"Then the sheriff called me. I was off duty so it took thirty minutes for me to get here; that was about 7:05. I came out here and was able to identify the body. She is, or was, I guess," he said, stumbling a bit with his words, "Sharon Stewart. I've known her most of my life. We were at Mora High School together. She was a year ahead of me. So I went into town to see if I could track down her last known movements."

The kid was doing well. It's not easy to see someone you know in that condition and then be professional enough to work an investigation. I nodded encouragement to him.

"She was a local resident," he said as he consulted his notes, "Sharon Stewart, 28, divorced, was seen in the Fish Lake Pub on Sunday night. That's a bar and grill located about a half-mile west of here on Fish Lake. I know Bobby, the bartender there, and it's a place I know she might go, so I called him, woke him up. The place is only a couple miles off 65 so they get a lot of going-home-from-the lake traffic on Sunday afternoons and evenings. She was seen talking with a man, not a local, who left sometime around 9:30." He looked at Glenn and said, "Bobby didn't know when Sharon left, but it was right around then too. He also didn't remember seeing them leave together or what kind of car the guy was driving."

"Any old boyfriends, ex-husband, that sort of thing?" I asked.

"Yes sir, all those things," Deputy Sheldon replied. "She had dated pretty much everyone in the area, including Bobby, the bartender from the pub. Her ex still lives here. She and her ex had a pretty physical relationship. I had a couple of calls out to their place when they were still married. Part of the divorce included a restraining order against him."

I looked at the deputy and asked, "How about you, Nate?"

He hesitated just a second, then took a breath before answering, "Yeah, me too. Like I said, she dated a lot."

"That's all stuff to check out," I said, as much to Glenn as the deputy. "OK, so she was last seen Sunday, that's five days ago now. Anyone report her missing?"

"She lived by herself in a small apartment building in town. She worked at a restaurant," Sheldon paused, consulting his notes, "over in Hinckley. I called the place and they told me she hadn't been in to work all week, but she wasn't scheduled until yesterday, so they didn't miss her until then. The manager also said that she would do that occasionally, miss work, that is, but he kept her on because she was good with the customers. Plus, he told me that he knew she didn't need a lot of money. I know that she got an inheritance from her folks when her mom passed two years ago. Her folks had a farm down near Winona that they sold to one of those sand mining companies. Didn't make her rich, but plenty of money to get by on. That was when she dumped her old man.

"He was a loser anyway, unemployed musician wannabe," he said with some derision. "She didn't need to work too much. I know she liked it, getting out and meeting people. I always thought she should be in some kind of sales job."

Maria was standing off to the side absorbing while not intruding. I wondered what she would have asked so I shot her a glance to invite her into the conversation. She responded with a cute little up-nod, saying "message received." Only two cases worked together and we're already communicating like longtime partners. What a woman.

I wanted her to jump in. She's a talented interrogator. Of course, we don't call it that anymore. Now it's called an "interview." But it's still an interrogation, even when you are talking to another investigator. There are questions that are seemingly meaningless, but that must be asked. The problem is that many investigators dismiss the "meaningless" questions and, thus, lose the opportunity to find that kernel, that one thing that breaks a case open. I hadn't heard that kernel yet. Or maybe I had, but didn't recognize it. Maybe she knew which one it was.

I nodded an understanding. "OK, someone picked her up between Sunday night and now. Has your coroner been out yet?"

"Yeah, she left just before you got here. All she said was that the victim was dead and time of death was probably early last night. She said all she's going to put on the death certificate as manner of death is "Homicide," and leave cause of death up to the medical examiner. She'll arrange transport to St. Paul."

"OK," I said. "Let's see the body."

Chapter Four

We walked about fifty yards down from where the cars were parked. I could see that they'd covered the body with one of those blue plastic tarps. It was a late effort to try to preserve a crime scene, as she'd probably been in the ditch for a while. How long we had yet to figure. The coroner thought she'd been killed the night before. She could have been dropped any time after that. If she was killed Sunday night it would have been at least four full days, an eternity as far as loss of evidence was concerned. An outdoor location with the heat, animals, and bugs would have already destroyed a lot of potential evidence. At least we didn't have that to worry about.

We stopped at the edge of the ditch next to the tarp. Glenn visibly took a breath, stepped down next to the body, and pulled back the tarp. I'd seen enough bodies in my MPD career to know that she hadn't been killed and left that morning, but she didn't look long dead.

The whole "time of death" thing that you see on TV shows is another of my bones to pick with Hollywood. They have an ME, or medical examiner, show up at a body dump and within minutes he or she has determined cause of death, manner of death, and time of death, down to the minute. Let me tell you, there's no ME in this country that's going to say that the time of death was between 10:00 and 11:00 last night on a body they found outdoors at midmorning in the summertime lying on a busted watch that read 10:30 p.m. They'll say that, based on rigor mortis, between six and twelve hours ago if it's that fresh and that they'll call you when they have cause of death, even if there are empty cartridge cases on the ground and bullet holes in the body. And that's on a body found fresh. You leave one out in the summer sun for a few days and all you'll get is "Not less than twelve hours" for how long they've been lying there. Of course, that won't get the case solved in time for the TV show's closing credits.

Although the Mora guys had seen her before, all of us still recoiled from the sight. I saw the body of a young woman who had been physically violated in as brutal a fashion as any I've seen in my years as a homicide investigator. Her naked skin was alabaster white with a multitude of knife wounds scattered uniformly over her entire surface. Think Venus de Milo with red to black cuts drawn on it. Some of the lines were up to three inches long, but most were only about an inch. Some looked like stabbing penetrations, others were simple cuts. The cuts were distributed evenly over the surface of the body and none intersected. Her eyes were black holes, probably the result of animals getting to the body after it was dumped. There were other sites on the body showing that the wildlife had wasted no time beginning the recycling process.

I looked at Maria to see how she was holding up. What I saw surprised me. While she had grimaced at first sight of the body, now she was looking at it inquisitively, sort of cocking her head like a dog does at a strange sound. Did something "ping" for her, I wondered.

There was little blood present in the area around the body. In fact, the body was unusually clean, except where the critters had been at it. This all said that she'd been killed somewhere else, then dumped in the ditch. I mentioned that to the group.

"Not too much blood. She was dumped."

It was a statement, not a question. Glenn agreed.

"Yeah, that's what I figured. I sure wish we had something that said she'd been killed in the Cities and you hotshots could take all this away."

"Not gonna happen, buddy. She's a local, she was last seen in a local bar and she's here, so she's all yours. When do you think the BCA boys will get here?"

"They said they'd send the van as soon as they could man it. I thought they'd beat you."

Which meant he'd followed procedure and called them before he called me, the correct thing to do. The BCA, Bureau of Criminal Apprehension, has the state's go-to lab and I was just an old buddy who might pitch in. As we stood there I could see what looked like a typical big white Class C recreational vehicle lumbering down the county road, typical except for the BCA logo above the windshield where the manufacturer's artwork would usually be.

We walked back out to the street where the BCA truck had parked. I wanted to talk to the lead forensic investigator.

Judy Loveless exited the passenger door of the RV's cab. She was the head of the BCA team. I knew her from previous cases. She's an experienced and thorough crime scene investigator or CSI—yeah, just like on TV—and I was glad to see her. With her on the case, I was confident we'd get everything that was available to help us solve the murder.

Chapter Five

I greeted Judy and asked, "Still riding around in this antique?"

"You know the State. We've had that new truck on request for the last two budgets and they keep saying next year. Now it's supposed to be here by the end of August, but I'm not holding my breath. What's going on here to drag you out of bed?"

I introduced her all around. She looked at Maria and gave her a little wink, like there was some kind of inside joke. I began to wonder who the joke was on. With formalities out of the way, I knew her next stop would be the body.

As we walked, Glenn had Deputy Sheldon review his notes again, which he did virtually word for word as when he'd briefed me and Maria. He had just identified the victim when we got to the body.

"Well, we'll need to seal this off as best we can," she said. She called back to her team. "Bring two EZ-Ups, and the kits for an outdoor recovery." This would be her equipment for securing and recovering a body from an outdoor situation. I gave Glenn's arm a tug.

"Let's get out of her way and let her do her job," I suggested.

Glenn said, "I'd like Nate to see this. He's been on body dumps before but this is different."

It sure is, I thought. "Good idea," I said with a nod. After Glenn told Nate to stay close but out of the way and to pay attention, Glenn, Maria, and I walked back out to the cars.

As we walked, I noticed the deputy on the gate was talking on his phone. There was not much for him to do. Crime scene security was one of those thankless duties that you only get noticed for if you screw it up.

Chapter Six

Minneapolis

She bristled with annoyance at the ringing phone. As one of Channel 7's top field reporters, Jane Vanderloo knew that the only people with that number were people who would interrupt an otherwise beautiful day with something that would require her to go somewhere, talk to people who didn't know anything, then look good for ninety seconds as she broadcast from some remote location, often in the dark, or rain, or snow, though it could go to three or more minutes if the story was big enough. She was beginning to question the move from print media to television. In spite of the good pay and the obvious impending demise of print news, she longed for mornings when she could either sleep in or go out on a story without having to worry about her looks.

Jane had been a star reporter with the Minneapolis paper for twenty years. Her beats included the usual start-up subjects for reporters—soft-touch stories about kids, local problems, park vandalism, that sort of thing. She gradually made her way up to police and crime stories. That had been her goal since J-school. She had developed great contacts within the Minneapolis PD and many suburban departments, which got her noticed by the broadcast media folks.

When her agent began receiving inquiries from TV people about Jane possibly moving their way, her initial reaction was disdain. She knew in her heart that print news was always the better format. Her father had been a well-known political reporter with a national news service and she wanted nothing less, but only covering crime. Her agent pointed out that within the next ten years it was better than 50:50 that newspapers would cease to exist. If the TV guys wanted her, she could write her own ticket while she still had the advantage, and it was better than waiting until she had to go to them.

She had the looks for it, that was certain. A great looking blond who, though she was in her late forties, still had a hot on-screen appearance with none of the flaws so many of the former red-hot talking heads had suffered with the introduction of HD cameras and TVs. And, she could "deliver," as the TV people say, on the spot, without the need for pre-written scripts or a set of questions. She was snappy and incisive off the cuff, something many talking heads couldn't begin to do.

Still, she rebelled a bit at the urgency of television. Everything was so "right now." It irked her to lose the time, brief as it often was, to nurture a story and get it just right. As a TV reporter, when the phone rang it was go right now and do right now.

She answered the phone.

"Hello," she said. She never answered with her name or gave any clue as to who she was. You never knew who might get this number.

"Hello. Ms. Vanderloo?" The caller looked at the old wrinkle-edged card in his hand. He'd saved the card for two-and-a-half years just for this opportunity. "This is Billy Gorman, Ma'am. I'm with the Kanabec County sheriff's office up in Mora. I met you at a really bad car wreck up here on I-35 a couple of years ago. Do you remember me?"

"Sure," Jane answered, although she was certain she couldn't pick Billy out of a lineup. She gave her cards to many law enforcement people in the hopes of a phone call someday. Maybe today was Billy's day. "Wha'cha got, Billy?" That was smooth, she thought. Sounds like we're old buddies.

"Well, we've had a homicide up here. A body was dropped and the sheriff is all bent out of shape about it."

Not much, Jane thought. Rural body drops were, unfortunately, not that uncommon. But, it was his dime. Let him talk. "Anything that would interest me?" she asked.

"I think so. The victim is a local girl, so I guess, that's not unusual. But the body, well, it's all cut up. Not cut apart, it's still all in one piece.

It's kind of, I mean, really weird, like vampire stuff. I overheard the sheriff saying there wasn't no blood in the body. And she's got cuts all over her."

"OK, I'm listening." Jane grabbed a notepad and started writing. This could be something if it was strange enough. Nothing TV liked better than blood, and a cut-up victim was the best. When Billy finished she asked, "Where are you?"

"Oh, I don't know if I should say. If you show up the sheriff will know I called you."

"I won't tell him. I'll say I got a hit on the radio traffic. There must have been radio calls, right? I'll say I was tipped by the radio calls."

"Yeah, there were radio calls, all right. First in was state patrol, then us. Then the sheriff had to call in the BCA and their medical examiner and crime scene folks. Plus, that other guy."

"Who's 'that other guy'?" she asked.

"Some guy the sheriff knows from when he was with MPD. Guy's a hot-shot homicide investigator named Neumann. Sheriff called him hisself. He's here now."

"Give that location again. I'm coming right up there."

This will be interesting, she thought as she hung up the phone. Aloud, she said, "Dan Neumann, hmmm. Haven't seen him in awhile. Might be able to mix a little pleasure with business."

Chapter Seven

Standing by the cars, I summed things up for Glenn. "It looks to me like you're doing just what you should. You know how this is going to go— check your two groups of suspects and push until something breaks."

I was talking about a basic fundamental premise of investigatory theory. When someone is killed, there are two groups you look at, people known to the victim and people unknown to the victim. In ninety-five-plus percent of homicides, the killer is in the first group. Husbands kill wives and vice versa, boyfriends and girlfriends, brothers and sisters, kids and parents, co-workers, neighbors, fellow church or club members. In most cases, and nearly all cases in a rural setting, the killer will be someone known to the victim. The fact that this killer was extraordinarily violent didn't change that fact. I reminded Glenn of this.

"You know as well as I do that your vic was probably done by a past or present boyfriend or her ex. You know how to do this; it's just a little crazier because of the violence."

"A *little* crazier? I don't know about that. Have you ever seen anything like that in all your years in homicide?"

"Not that bad with a knife. But there have been cases. You remember that one about ten years ago where the kid killed his old man with a pistol? He didn't just shoot him, he hit him over the head with a baseball bat about a hundred times. The guy was dead pretty quick, between the three gunshots and the first ten smacks. So what were the other hundred hits for? Just rage. Wait for the autopsy, but I'll bet you'll find this girl was gone long before this guy was done cutting. The lack of bleeding or blood at the scene indicates that."

"Yeah, you're right. Listen, I got you up here for a reason. Even if it turns out to be a run-of-the-mill case, I'd like it if you could stay involved. I like this job and I really need to nail this guy."

I noticed that Glenn didn't say "before he kills again." We both knew that in a crime of passion like this one, there was only one target, that the killer had probably gotten whatever it was out of his or her system, and that we didn't have to worry about additional bodies showing up.

Probably.

As messy as this was, it was a crime of passion like any other a cop sees in the regular passing of time. Glenn would find the guy and get himself re-elected. I was confident of that.

Chapter Eight

"This case is going to be the biggest thing that's happened out here since we tagged those fourteen meth houses two years ago," Glenn said.

Maria asked, "Fourteen meth houses?"

I said, "Yeah, Glenn here has the state record in lab shutdowns." I told the story.

Glenn's experiences on the Gang Task Force had left him with a strong aversion to everything drug related. He believes, and I have to agree with him, that the vast majority of the country's ills, as far as its youth, can be tracked to illicit drugs. Their use causes kids to drop out of school, become burglars, dealers, gangbangers, armed robbers and, finally, murderers. Like a lot of law enforcement types, he can't understand the country's tolerance of any kind of drug use. It doesn't make sense to him to go lightly on a little grass in Johnny's backpack when you know it will lead to Johnny becoming the local supplier.

Being the local supplier will lead to the need for a broader inventory, which will lead to additional customers, all of whom will need money to support their habit. This leads to burglary, assault, robbery, theft, pretty much everything bad that a teenager can get into—to say nothing of the effects of drug use on the individual drug user. Glenn considers marijuana the gateway drug. Many who want grass decriminalized say "Hey, not all pot smokers turn into violent criminals." Glenn would answer them by agreeing that not all do. "But you are looking at the wrong end of the road," he'd say. "Nearly all drug violence and drug crime and drug-destroyed lives can be tracked back to a little weed passed around at a party."

So one of the first things he did as sheriff was to eradicate the presence of methamphetamine labs in Kanabec County. He's busted so many labs that his statistics landed the county in the top tier nationally and he got a visit from Fox News, who wanted to know why there were so many meth labs in his county. He explained that there were no more than other rural counties; he just wouldn't put up with them in his county. And now there were none. He just took them more seriously than they were taken in other places. He maintained an anti-drug stance that translated down to his troops, and still does.

"You're right; this will be a big story," I said to Glenn. "You are going to have to be prepared for the press when the condition of the body gets out. They're going to be on this like a dog on a bone," I told Glenn.

"Messy, violent killings attract the press. They love blood. You know what they say—'If it bleeds, it leads,'" I said. "And there is nothing bloodier than a slasher."

Maria stopped and held up a finger in thought for a moment. "From the look of that body, there is not much blood left in it. There's got to be another site around here, one with a lot of blood in it," she said.

This is how investigations go sometimes. You just talk it out. Things come to mind and you follow them up. A blood pool was now one of the things to look for.

"I agree," Glenn said. "If she was picked up close to where she was dumped, it's unlikely that he took her far away then brought her back. There has to be a lot of blood on the ground somewhere near."

"You have any tracking dogs around here?" Maria asked.

"I've got a gal who trains them. She has a place north of town."

Glenn flipped open his phone and dialed.

"Sandy, Glenn Mills. Hey, have you got any dogs that could follow a blood trail for me?" Glenn paused.

"Yeah, I have a body and we're thinking maybe there might be a blood trail. My thinking is that the victim was picked up pretty close by and then dumped, so she was probably killed pretty close by too."

Another pause. "It was Sharon Stewart." After a short pause he said, "You know where that new housing site is south of town, just west of 65? Yeah, that's it. Head down there and I'll let the guy on the gate know you're coming."

He hung up and we started walking. When we were within earshot, he called out to the deputy on the gate and told him about the dog lady. Then we headed back to the scene.

"Nate, how's it going?" Glenn asked.

"As well as it can. That BCA lady is a little pissed that we let so many cars down the street. She said that since this is a dead end that's actually gated off, she might have been able to get a tire track. Now she is going to have to take elimination samples from every car that's been down here. She also said basically the same thing about footprints around the body."

"OK, I get it. Listen, Sandy Boomstra is coming down here with some dogs. Here's my thinking—since Sharon was probably picked up at the Fish Lake Pub and that's only a half-mile away, it doesn't make sense that the bad guy would take her very far, kill her, then bring her back. And since it doesn't look like the body has much blood in it, there must be a blood pool fairly close by. I want you to show Sandy the site and tell her what we think about the kill site being between there and the Fish Lake Pub. Then see if she can track backwards and find where it was this freak killed her. Sound all right?"

"Makes sense. I'll work with Sandy when she gets here to get her going."

"You learning anything?"

"Yeah. Don't let so many cars and people around a secluded body dump or you'll piss off the BCA investigator."

Maria and I laughed. "Smart lad," Glenn said. He turned to me. "So, now what?"

"You know the drill. Identify all her known associates—boyfriends, exes, family, co-workers, neighbors, fellow workout club members, anyone who knew her. Interview all of them for motive and alibi, and start ruling out people. In a case like this, especially one that shows such a high level of violence, it's almost always someone in that group. It will be

a jilted lover in ninety-plus percent of these cases. That leaves an unpro-
moted co-worker or a family member for the rest."

Maria added, "For family, look for some motive within the generations. Inheritance is first in those cases and you know you've got some of
that already with this vic."

I continued. "There are other kinds of control, maybe when to put a
parent into the nursing home or who would have to cut granny's grass
all summer. I remember a case where a son killed his father over twenty
bucks to go out on a Saturday night. And that wasn't in the Cities, it was
in northwest Minnesota. It's just a matter of legwork and interviews and
you know how to do that."

"Yeah, I can get them to come in and sit down. My younger guys will
know who to talk to. I wish I had your confidence on this. I've just got a
bad feeling that this isn't going to be that simple."

"They always are," I consoled him.

The fact that the victim had been seen with someone unknown to
a local bartender just before she disappeared stuck in my mind. Most
likely, she had blown the guy off and then been killed by someone she
knew. But there was a chance that she left to meet up with the unknown
guy and he killed her. If that's what happened, we'd have a real difficult
case on our hands.

The toughest crimes to solve are the crimes of random selection
where there is no connection between the criminal and the victim.
In criminal investigation we rely on patterns. People associate with
the same people over and over. Criminals do the same type of crimes
over and over. And criminals are, frankly, not too bright. Every law
enforcement type in the country has his or her own favorite dumb-
criminal story. Whether it's the bank robber who wrote the hold-up
note on a deposit slip from his own account or the guy who, like
Hansel and Gretel, dripped twenty-dollar bills, leaving a trail all the
way home from robbing the convenience store, we all have our favor-
ites. One of mine is the guy who slapped a twenty on the counter of a
store and asked for change. When the clerk opened the cash register,
he pulled a gun, declared that he was robbing the place, reached over

and grabbed the money out of the till. The clerk complied by backing up, hands up, and watched as the guy snatched seventeen dollars from the tray. The robber took the money and ran, leaving his twenty on the counter. This guy committed armed robbery and wound up with a net of minus three bucks.

So we count on two things in cases of personal crimes, that is, crimes of a personal nature. First, the bad guy is stupid. Second, the bad guy and the victim know each other. In cases of murder they almost always know each other. And in the few cases where they don't, well, let's just say, those can get to be a lot more interesting.

Chapter Nine

We watched the crime scene team process the site, looking like a collection of ancient monks intoning their chants and magical ways to discern some enlightenment from the bones and leaves that were scattered before them. As we watched, we got our personal CSI—one of Judy's people took tread prints from each of our shoes; they had finished with the vehicles.

Judy was still working the body scene. The team had covered the body and marked off an area about six feet around it. They were collecting everything they could in the area, including the topsoil. I knew from experience that they would sift through it all looking for any trace that might remain. Trace is what is unknowingly left behind by bad guys. On TV they make it look like everyone goes through life constantly shedding enough DNA to fill a crime scene van. While we all do shed some things—skin cells, hair, fibers from our clothing—it's still a matter of finding, identifying, and matching the evidence that makes it worthwhile. And finding it at a crime scene that is outdoors in the summertime and has had some time to ferment is a real trick. So Judy was taking as much of the crime scene as she could back to her lab. It would take weeks to process all of it.

I heard another vehicle approaching the gate. The dog lady. She was let through the police checkpoint and pulled her truck over just inside the cattle gates at the end of the street. Glenn, Maria, and I headed down to talk to her.

"Hey, Sandy," Glenn said.

"Hey, yourself. This sounds pretty bad."

It was a question, not a statement.

"It's as bad as it gets, Sandy. This is Dan Neumann from the Cities. He's an old cop friend of mine. And Dan's friend, Maria Fernandez. She's a homicide investigator from Phoenix. They're helping out on this case."

We shook hands. "You might not want to go down to where the body is. She's in pretty bad shape," I said.

"Going to have to. Have to give my boy a good sniff to get him started. What do you think happened?"

"We think she was picked up at the Fish Lake Pub, then killed somewhere, then left here," Glenn said, softening it as much as he could. "The theory we're working is that the killer wouldn't have taken her far and then brought her back. We're thinking that maybe your dog can get a scent and find a trail to where she was killed."

"Why don't you think she was killed here?"

I picked up the story line. I wanted to see how tough this girl was. If she was going to see the body, she'd need to be plenty tough. I made it sound as bad as I could. "She was killed by multiple stab and slash wounds. Her body was mutilated. Her nipples have been cut off, her pubic area has been slashed, her face, her breasts, in fact her entire body shows knife wounds. In addition, the animals have been at her. Her eyes are missing and there is evidence of other feeding activity. But there is little evidence of blood here, not enough for her to have been cut up here. Somewhere, probably near here, there's a blood lake."

I watched her face for reaction. She took it pretty well. I decided she could take a look and probably not add to the collection of vomit pools scattered around the body. They were starting to get ripe and the combination of aromas from the forest, the body, the puke, and the recently spread "fertilizer," read: manure, wafting in from the farm fields to the west was making this the most uniquely nauseating crime scene I'd been to in quite awhile. I was about to use an old coroner's trick and start smearing Vicks under my nose.

Sandy stiffened a bit and said, "Well, if that's what happened, we can probably track something. Nothing like a hot summer day to ripen a body and leave a trail. I'd better go down there and have a look see."

As Glenn and Maria took Sandy down to the scene, I stood and took it all in. In thirty years of police work I'd never gotten used to the sight of this sort of body. In fact, I'd never really seen this sort of murder. I'd seen bodies mutilated by horrific traffic accidents, where entire limbs or heads had been found hundreds of feet away, having been removed by the enormous forces at play when two objects, each three- or four-thousand pounds of steel, plastic, and glass, try to occupy the same space at the same time and come together with a combined closing speed over one hundred miles per hour. I'd seen what a body can look like, sort of a grotesque burned version of an inflatable sumo wrestler suit, after three or four weeks alone in a warm house during August. I'd also seen what a human head looks like after a person discharges a twelve-gauge shotgun under their own chin—really just a mask with a surprised expression and no backside. And I'd seen what a grain auger can do to an arm, if you could find it. The limb, ripped from the victim's shoulder and ground into pieces, was mixed into thousands of bushels of corn. But no one, no matter how long on the job, ever gets ready for a scene like the one I was looking at.

When one human being deliberately and purposefully slices and dices another human being with a level of violence that is completely gratuitous, there can be only one reason. Whoever did this truly wanted to hurt the victim, to cause her more pain than she'd ever known in her life. It reinforced my belief that the killer knew her and had been hurt by her. Why else would someone cause such suffering except to get back at the victim? This was personal. This was a case of payback, pure and simple. I knew in my heart of hearts that the killer was someone who believed he had been hurt by her. It had started as "I'll show her. I'll make her hurt like she hurt me," and had gotten out of hand. It had started under control and ended in complete unbridled rage.

The killer was undoubtedly male, most likely her age, probably a jilted lover drowning in anguish. He thought the only way to even things up was to hurt her. And he'd feel bad about it.

I assumed all of that from the fact that the body had been posed in a somewhat respectful manner. Yes, she was naked, which was disrespectful, but she was laid out as though sleeping, with her legs straight and arms at her side. She was down in a ditch, which offered some protection from the elements. I'm no expert on the subject, but it didn't look like a display that the psych folks talk about—bodies left in flagrantly provocative poses, usually sexual in nature. They often have "props" in the display, sometimes inserted into the body. And they are found in obviously public locales, assuring quick discovery. All this is done to satisfy the killer's need to disrespect the victim.

"Hmmm, I wonder if I should make a call," I asked myself, but decided to hold off.

It was still probably a known person. If Glenn could round up her ex and all old boyfriends and put the heat on, I knew we'd have our killer. It would just be a matter of sweating them out and seeing who cracked. They always cracked in the desperation of post-traumatic shock. When the guy realized what he'd done, when he saw the pictures of the body, he'd crack. I'd seen it too many times in the past to doubt my experience. I knew we'd get him.

But I was wrong.

Chapter Ten

Sandy, the dog handler, walked to her truck and opened a crate in the back. "Come on, Stinky," she said. "Stinky" jumped down, looking like he was right out of central casting and born to the job, a big black-and-tan Bloodhound with long droopy jowls and a sauntering gait. Sandy and Stinky walked down near the body and went to work.

"Does she think she can find it?" I asked Glenn as he walked back to me.

"She says there's a chance, said that even if the body was in a vehicle, it may have left a scent trail because it was so badly cut up. Blood has a strong scent that her dogs are trained to follow and Stinky has a shot because we haven't had any rain. Rain would have ended the search from her point of view."

I watched as the dog, his head now down and his powerful nose working the road, started pulling out line from the loops Sandy held in her hand. When he got about thirty feet out, she started walking after him, keeping the line off the ground but just slack. Stinky worked back and forth a bit but stayed in a pretty straight line with Sandy bringing up the rear. She was moving at a fast walk now, heading down the future suburban street toward the gate.

Glenn looked at me and asked, "Now what?"

"You know what to do," I repeated. "Work the case. Get the past lovers in. When you get one with an alibi problem, start working him. Show them the photos. He's going to feel bad about this and when he sees what he's done, he'll crack."

"What if the guy I'm pushing isn't the scumbag?"

I smiled inwardly. Scumbag. Glenn was old school. "You're good with people; you know when someone's lying to you. This is just like back in the day when you were on the street. But there is one other thing. Right guy or not, he's going to puke when he sees those photos. You'd better do the interviews in a rubber room."

We walked back to our vehicles. It was 10:30 and Maria and I hadn't had any breakfast, if you don't count that bagel. That's not uncommon in police work. You eat when you can whether you're working a case or a beat. Something always comes along to interrupt a normal meal schedule. Combine that with hours behind a desk or steering wheel and you can see why cops start having weight problems. Pretty much all departments now have training facilities or arrangements with local health clubs and allow their officers to frequent them while on duty. Cops need to be fit. As we age it gets harder and harder to run down perps who seem to be younger and younger. So fitness is part of the job requirements and departments encourage their people to stay in shape.

Glenn was looking slimmer than I remembered and I mentioned it.

"Yeah, down thirty-two pounds since I started this program."

"So what's the program?" I asked.

"I don't eat in restaurants anymore."

"Well, that sucks. I was just about to take you to lunch."

"I can go to lunch with you; I'll just be bringing my own from home."

"You brown bag it into restaurants? Don't they get a little huffy about that?"

"Actually, the local places have gotten used to it. I still bring them customers and I'm discreet. I sit in the corner and eat my carrots and they sell a nice meal to whoever's with me. Follow me back to the shop and we'll drop your car and go eat."

"OK with me. I have to get something in my stomach before we head back," Maria said.

We were about to get into our cars when I saw two vehicles pull up to the gate. The first was a hearse, apparently the coroner's promised transport for the body. The second was a hot Mercedes I recognized, driven by a good-looking blond. I flagged Glenn and signaled that we should wait a moment. I knew he'd want to control the situation. Glenn got out of his car and walked over to me.

"So, who's that?" he asked.

"It seems the fourth estate has arrived."

Six-foot five-inch Deputy Billy Gorman, or Little Billy, as his co-workers called him, was still on the gate when the two cars drove up. He quickly noted the coroner's vehicle on the log and lifted the gate. He'd seen the baby blue Mercedes S63 AMG behind the hearse when it turned down the cross street, wondering why the heck a fancy ride like that was approaching. He couldn't quite make out who was inside through the dark-tinted windows, just that it was a woman and she was on the phone. Some people, he thought. When she stepped out, he immediately recognized her.

"Hi, Billy," the fabulous blond said, with her hand reaching for his. "Been a long time."

"Hi, Ms. Vanderloo," Billy replied. "I wasn't sure it was you 'til you got outta the car. Pretty nice set of wheels," he observed.

"Gets me where I want to go," she replied. In truth, it was her pride and joy, a reward to herself for landing what many considered the largest reporting contract in Twin Cities' history. Even the talking heads on the 6:00 and 10:00 news didn't make what she did, much to their displeasure.

"So, Billy, what's going on out here?"

"Well, Ma'am, it's a homicide."

Yeah, I think that's why I'm here, Jane thought to herself. She knew she had to keep this discussion at Billy's level if she was going to continue to get information from him. She went with it.

"You think I could get a look?"

"Well, they didn't say to keep the press out. Why don't you make a big deal of showing me your press ID and then I'll say that I had to let you in. That way, no one will know I called you."

"Works for me," she said, as she fished her card out of her pocket.

She'd never been a purse gal, preferring pockets. It was a good excuse to never wear anything but slacks. She showed it to Billy and, reluctantly, he let her pass. He was a pretty good actor.

I watched as the deputy on the gate looked over the driver's ID, then granted her access. She looked as good as ever.

"You want me to handle this?" I asked Glenn.

"That who I think it is?" he replied.

"Looks like it. I heard she'd gotten herself a new ride. It's a hot car for a hot blond."

"Well, I don't know her," Maria said, looking at me.

"That's Jane Vanderloo. She used to be the crime reporter from the Strib. Now she's a hot number on TV. Big raise, new car, job security." I didn't mention our past relationship.

Maria gave a knowing nod, mouthing a drawn out "Right." How do women figure this stuff out so fast? I asked her to wait by the cars. Reluctantly, she agreed.

Glenn laughed. He knew the history between Jane and me. I'd been in homicide when Jane had that beat for the Strib. That's what I call the *Minneapolis Star Tribune*, the newspaper. As newspapers started losing customers to TV, then the internet, Jane jumped to TV. Anyway, over the years we wound up at many of the same crime scenes and she started working me for information, as any reporter would. We were about the same age, single, and similarly inclined. Nature took its course and we wound up in bed. It was hot and steamy for about four months, then it just stopped. I don't know why. I was still willing, but she had other plans. Since then I've affected the role of the jilted, but still friendly, ex-lover. I walked toward her.

"Well, hello old friend," she greeted me. Not exactly what you're looking for from a former intimate. I know, I'm involved, but you like to think you're still a player.

"Hi, Jane. How'd you get here so fast?"

"Just take a look at my car and you'll answer that. Tops out well over anything I'm comfortable with."

Nice dodge of my question. She knew I was asking about her source. I gave her the customary friendly shoulder hug. You know, the one where nothing important touches aside from facial cheeks, and asked, "You remember Glenn Mills? Used to work patrol in the Fourth, then moved up here to God's country and became sheriff?"

"Sure. Hi, Glenn." Another round of non-intimate intimacy. "Heard on the scanner that you had something interesting up here."

Glenn gave me the "Yeah, sure" look and asked my question again. "Must have been waiting in your car for something to happen today. I wouldn't think you'd be up this early with the late broadcast you do."

"Just lucky. I heard the BCA call go out and that piqued my curiosity."

"Not going to be much good for the 6:00 without a camera crew," Glenn added.

"They're on their way. Must have taken them longer to get going. Why don't you two fill me in while we wait."

From my point of view, she was the only one waiting. Neither Glenn nor I, or any other professional law enforcement officer for that matter, *wants* to be on the 6:00 news. Sometimes you have to be. But you don't go looking for it. As for filling her in, been there, done that, got the T-shirt. But, Glenn took the bait.

"Sure, Jane. We have a run-of-the-mill rural body dump. Someone gets whacked in the Cities, gets left up here, and we get to clean up the mess."

Glenn was willing to try to get rid of her. Me too.

I looked at Maria and could see that she was just taking us all in. She knew that law enforcement/media relationships could be complicated. She had no idea. I hoped. I motioned her to join us.

"And that's why Dan's here? Just happened to be in the neighborhood?"

If Jane had been tipped by someone up here or in the BCA office, this was our chance to find out who. She wouldn't tell us; we'd have to weasel it out of her. I helped out.

"Yep. Got an out-of-town law officer here visiting Minnesota, thinking about moving here when she gets tired of Arizona. We came up for some fishing. We were about to head out this morning when the call went out. Since we were here, I thought we should tag along."

Maria was in and played along. "Hi, Maria Fernandez," she said, extending a hand.

Jane shook Maria's hand as she looked her over, but she wasn't buying. "That's odd. The way I heard the call, the victim is local and you came up to help out. Any truth to that?"

OK, the leak is up here, I thought. Something for Glenn to work on.

"You sure you want in on this?" I asked. "It's a bad one."

"I've seen plenty of bad ones, you know that. Just give me the background and I'll handle the rest."

I looked at Glenn for approval. This was still his show. We both heard a truck and turned in time to see a 7TV truck approach the gate. No one said anything as the gate deputy went through the ID check, wrote notes in the scene log, and opened the gate.

"Why don't you go talk to Judy?" I said. I can be as helpful as the next guy.

Jane walked down the unfinished street to the crime scene, virtually unnoticed until she got within about fifteen feet of the makeshift tent. Judy Loveless noticed her, recognized her, and got up from where she'd been directing the preservation of the soil. The body was already in a bag in the back of the hearse.

"Hey, Jane," Judy offered.

"Hey, yourself. What's up? I heard there was a body dropped out here." Not really a question, more of an explanation of her presence.

"Someday, Jane, you will be on the stand explaining how you get these tips."

The two females chuckled. They shared a job, after a fashion. They were criminal investigators whose lives centered on the whys and wherefores of criminal activity. The difference was who they talked to about it. Jane talked to a camera; Judy talked to a jury.

"What fun would that be?" Jane quipped. "I heard it's a bad one."

Another statement.

Judy walked to Jane. "Yeah. It's a bad one. If I show you the body, you have to hold off on most of the information. There are a few *peculiarities* about this that we don't want out there." Out there being in the public trough. Jane knew this. It wasn't that unusual in homicide cases for the police, with the cooperation of the press, to withhold certain details about a crime in order to better the chance of prosecution. If a suspect knew the details and those details hadn't been on the 6:00 news, there was a better chance we had the right guy.

Jane said, "I understand. Keep the gory stuff quiet."

"You're going to want to after you see this."

As Jane and Judy got reacquainted, I saw Maria go over and talk to the camera crew. Two guys, one for sound, one for pictures. They looked familiar, but I didn't know their names. Maria said something to them and pointed over to Judy and Jane. The guys looked, nodded, glanced at their equipment, nodded some more, and started to smile. Maria was up to something.

A few more nods between the crew and Maria. They exchanged post-canary-cat grins. Maria had given them something to make their trip worthwhile.

Jane and Judy walked to the back of the hearse and Loveless swung open the heavy door. She pulled the pop-up gurney out a few feet to reveal a bagged body. "You might want to turn around for a minute and then take this in a little at a time," she told Jane.

Jane did as requested and looked off into the blue midsummer sky with a grin like she was playing peek-a-boo. Somewhere in the distance she could hear the sound of a plane and her head, unconsciously, cocked toward it like a dog hearing something interesting. Then she heard the buzz of a zipper behind her and her head leveled, eyes focusing straight ahead as Judy pulled it down to the victim's waist. Judy told her to turn back slowly.

As she turned, Jane saw the face of a young blond woman. Her eyes were missing, but Jane had seen that before when bodies were left outdoors in the summer. Her skin looked pale and stiff, but Jane could tell she'd been an attractive girl. Then Jane's eyes slid down the body and saw the start of the knife cuts, the missing nipples, the larger entrance wound below the rib cage. She felt her breakfast start to rise and turned away.

"You OK?" Judy asked.

Jane staggered a few feet up the side of the hearse and braced herself against it. She'd seen a lot of horror in her life, but this? Suddenly, she could take no more and violently ejected everything she'd eaten since the night before. When she was certain she'd regained her composure, she turned to go back to the end of the truck, stood, took a step, and passed out. One of the BCA techs was ready and rushed to catch her. He laid her gently on her side. Seeing the camera, Judy hollered, "Shut that goddamn thing off!"

The camera crew, no longer smiling, dutifully recorded the entire event.

I looked at Maria who was staring at Jane with a satisfied, stone "gotcha" face. Obviously, this was the plot she'd laid out for the film team. How did she know? How'd she figure out the past relationship connection so fast? I stifled a laugh.

OK, so it wasn't very nice of me to laugh at the reaction of a past girlfriend to a body that would make a Hollywood makeup artist puke. But she dumped me, remember?

We got in our vehicles and headed back into town.

Chapter Eleven

Office of the Sheriff
Kanabec County Courthouse
Mora, Minnesota

Maria and I followed Glenn back into town to his office, which was on the ground floor of a complex that looks like three building projects from three different eras. The first, the original Kanabec County Courthouse, is an old stone structure set up on a little hill overlooking, but a few blocks from, downtown Mora. Over the years, two additions were built. One bolted onto the rear of the courthouse back in the '60s, then another was more recently stuck on the south side of the first addition.

The additions are at ground level, so the original stately courthouse towers above them. It looks like someone simply bulldozed all the dirt away from one side of the hill and started adding on, sort of a lower-level growth protruding from the hill the courthouse sits on. In what looks like the first addition is the Department of Public Safety. We parked in front of an entrance that went straight into the ground floor level, which would have been the basement of the courthouse building. The sheriff's office was straight ahead.

The sheriff's office, like nearly every law enforcement office I've ever been in, holds a certain security/airlock feel in the anteroom. And they all look the same. One wall was covered with posters, some advising parents what to watch out for in their kids' bedrooms, while another advised retailers to keep an eye on those buying a long list of items that can either be used as mind-altering materials, such as paint thinner, lighter fluid, adhesives, etc., or made into something bad. Epinephrine and ammonia-based fertilizer topped the lists. Two chairs, a potted plant, and a window completed the decor. The window looked like a ticket window at a theater where you slide your money through a little tray under the window, except this window was about three-quarter-inch-thick armored glass. Without question, the rest of the wall and the door into the department were armored too. A uniformed clerk looked up as we entered and buzzed us in.

Glenn grabbed a handful of papers from an in-box and we walked down a hall to his office. It reminded me of other top-dog offices I'd visited in greater Minnesota. Simple, big enough for two visitors, lots of pictures and memorabilia. Glenn flipped through the in-box papers and, apparently seeing nothing that couldn't wait, tossed them all on his desk. Then he popped open a mini-fridge under the counter, grabbed the classic brown paper bag and we headed back out. I waved Maria into the front seat, thinking that he'd have the usual radio/computer setup squads have these days. Good tools to have, but not much space for passengers. Turned out I was wrong. It was equipped with the usual radios but not the fancier computer terminal that city cops all have. I climbed in back and asked about that.

"We have them in the patrol units. But the budget was limited and I figured I could do without since I don't have to patrol and I'm not pulling guys over at two a.m. If I'm out at a scene, there's going to be at least one of our regular cars there too, so why the expense?"

This was classic Glenn, thinking about the troops first. Get them the first-class stuff because they need it. He was right; he wouldn't be checking plates at two a.m. but his guys would be and they'd need that instant information the new systems provide. I nodded my approval.

We drove a few blocks to a place in the middle of the downtown city block area called Hazel's. Glenn pulled the car around back and parked nose out for a quick getaway, cop-style. We walked in through a back door and he led us to a booth near the rear where he could see both the front and rear of the establishment. Old cop habits die hard.

We sat and a waitress immediately came over and greeted Glenn. He introduced Maria and me. She looked at Maria, who had just opened a menu.

"I'll need a second," she said.

The waitress looked at me for my order. I love small-town cafes and I know what to say.

"Any specials today?"

"There sure are. We have the Reuben with house fries, a nice cobb salad and, of course, the roast beef sandwich."

I heard what I was looking for and answered "Roast beef sandwich."

Puzzled, Maria said, "For breakfast?"

"I had a bagel on the way up, remember?"

Maria shook her head, then said, "I'll have the farmer's special, over easy, with wheat toast and hash browns."

She nodded and left without even asking Glenn if he wanted a glass of water.

"So, aside from the occasional homicide, how's life treating you?" I asked.

"It's great, just great. The work is good. Most of it isn't near as bad as the stuff I worked in the Cities, the hours aren't killing me, and I'm in better shape than I have been in years."

"Yeah, I can see that. How'd you get on this health kick?"

"You remember Bob Hunt? He died about two years ago."

I nodded. Everyone on the force knew Bob. He was a real mover and shaker. Knew the politics, great record of felony arrests, had moved up through patrol, traffic, vice, homicide, and finally to the chief's office, where he handled public relations, something no cop wants but someone has to do. He looked like a recruiting poster at 47. Fit, worked out daily, had a tan. He was perfect for nine seconds on the evening news. He had a shot at going all the way, if not in Minneapolis, then some other major city's police force. Then, one day while out running, he dropped dead. Heart attack. Another jogger found him, called 911 on her cell, and tried to administer CPR. The paramedics said it wouldn't have helped, and the autopsy confirmed that he had complete blockage of two of his major heart arteries along with partial blockage of two others. It must have cause him some discomfort, but the people who knew him best said that he probably felt it but thought it was just a weakness he'd have to work through. His death caused a lot of people to reevaluate their own physical status.

Reaction was split into two groups, those who decided to get in shape and those who said, "See? What difference does it make?" The first group outnumbered the second about four to one. A lot of weight was lost after Bob went down.

"Yeah, I remember him. That shocked a lot of people." Including me, I thought to myself.

"If he can drop like that, anyone can. So I went in for a physical, hadn't had one in a couple of years, and my doc said I had to lose the weight. So here I am, carrots for lunch, no more restaurant food, and walking every day. I can't run with my knees, but the walking is good. I come into town and park somewhere and walk the neighborhoods. Everyone knows me and I can see how people are doing. Two birds with one stone—get out and see the people and do myself some good too."

I knew what he was talking about. Every year that went by made it a bigger challenge to stay in shape. My own fitness program includes occasional treadmill time, occasional walks, occasional workouts, occasional careful dining. The problem with this system is that it's occasional. If I'd stick to it, I'd be in shape, occasionally.

I asked, "So how is Susan handling life in the great north?"

"She likes it. I can't say she loves it, her being a city girl and everything, but she likes it and it's not that far from the Cities that she can't go and see friends or her mother once in a while. Plus, she has the space in our home for her new passion."

"What's that?"

"Scrapbooking. It's a cottage industry. There are stores full of the stuff. She found all the old pictures from our entire life together and she's making scrapbooks. Different books for different subjects. She's done two so far on my career, a couple on her family, and she has about five books worth of photos of our kids to put together once she gets that far. I figure she'll stay busy for another six or seven years if we don't run out of money first."

"Sounds like you are living right, my friend."

"Yeah, until this morning. How about you? Anything going on in your life besides writing those books on ballistics and blood spatter?" He glanced at Maria with a twinkle in his eye.

"I've got that project you interrupted this morning. I've been working on those bookcases for two years now. They're for my family room."

Our meals arrived and I paused a moment for the waitress to place it before me. It was everything I'd hoped for in a small town diner's roast beef sandwich. Two thick slices of white bread piled high open faced with sliced roast beef and smothered in dark brown gravy. On the side was a nice-sized blob of mashed potatoes and a dish of green beans for color. After the just-completed conversation on fitness and death in aging white males, I wasn't sure I would be able to eat it. That didn't stop me from trying. Maria's breakfast showed up on two plates, one with the eggs, bacon, toast, and hash browns, the other reserved for the pancakes.

"So," I went on, "I've been trying to finish this project for two years. Every time I get going on it again, I get a phone call dropping something like your case in my lap. First it was that sniper killer two years ago, then last year my buddy Pete's grandmother was killed in a burglary. Now this. I swear I'm just going to scrap them and buy a set."

Glenn laughed. "So, what do you need them for? You said you don't have enough books to fill them up." That earned a snicker from Maria.

"You ever seen those built-in wood cases, kind of like cabinets, that people have on either side of the fireplace? You can put your TV in there and all your sound gear and hide it when you have a party or something. That's what I'm trying to build. I'm going to pull back the carpeting and build them to the house, then re-lay the carpeting. They'll be permanent."

"I have a set of those in our place. But they're not so useful; can't get a flat screen into them. Not the right size."

"That's the point. I want to put a new ginormous flat screen in the family room and I want to be able to close it off when I'm not using it. So I'm building these cabinets for a specific purpose. The one that will hold the TV will sit in the corner so it can be at an angle and that will allow more room for the TV."

"Sounds like you are getting domesticated." Glenn grinned at Maria and asked, "Are you domesticating this guy?"

"Not possible," Maria answered. "I know him well enough to stay away from trying to change him."

Glenn nodded agreement. "So, you're with the Maricopa Sheriff's Office? That's a pretty big outfit with a reputation."

Maria looked at Glenn with an expression that asked where he was on her controversial boss. Most state and rural law enforcement officers, or LEOs, support her boss's strong methods. Most feds do not.

Glenn read the question in Maria's eyes and answered, "Hey, everything I've read sounds like he's doing the right thing. I especially like the pink prison outfits. Nice touch."

Maria smiled and replied, "He's got his admirers and his enemies. But he's doing a good job with his hands tied behind his back."

I chimed in, "So, how'd you find out about Maria?"

"Olson."

"Olson?"

"Yeah, Olson told me all about her. She's your, how'd he put it, your red hot chili pepper."

"Olson. You heard about Maria from Olson," I said, shaking my head. I should have figured that. Olson is the MPD's gossip central.

Olson is "Robert-don't-call-me-Bob" Olson, my last regular partner when I was full-time on the MPD. We still work together on cases when I am called in. The cases are generally tough ones that the department thinks could use my expertise in ballistic forensics. That's what had happened two years ago—there was a shooting involving an unusual type of ammunition. I got the call and wound up meeting Maria Fernandez in Phoenix. We are both committed LEOs, who have been too busy catching bad guys to have serious relationships, much less start families. Now, with her in her forties and me in my fifties, we are running out of time. We'll have to cross that bridge pretty soon if we're going to cross it at all.

Glenn replied, "He comes up fishing every once in a while. I've been getting a play-by-play running commentary of the April-August, Minnesota-Arizona, cop-sheriff's investigator relationship ever since it started. He told me she shot someone and saved your bacon on a case last Thanksgiving. That true?"

Maria just nodded. I said, "It sure is. Bad guy had already sent one my way and was drawing down on me and she put two in the ten ring just like that. Guy was out for the count before he hit the ground."

"Well, it's nice to meet a girl with a varied skill set," he said, using the modern vernacular. "Susan's not a shooter but she can fish. Usually bests me when we go and we go about once a week."

I looked at my ringing cellphone and saw "BCA" on the caller ID. I answered.

"Neumann here."

"Dan, Judy Loveless. I'm pretty much done here but I want to talk to you and the sheriff about something before I take off."

"Sure. He's here with me. We're having some lunch in town at a place called Hazel's. It's on the main drag. You want to come here or do you need us to come down there?"

"I'm starved. Order me a BLT and I'll be there in ten minutes."

I told Judy I'd even get her some chips and signed off. I told Glenn about the call.

"This should be interesting. I wonder what she wants to talk about?"

"Me too. I've known Judy for, I don't know, maybe six years. She's very good, nailed a lot of bad guys. But she's never had an on-the-scene report for me before. She usually just hauls everything off to her lab and you hear back in a few days."

I waved the waitress over to inform her that we had another person coming and gave her Judy's order of a bacon, lettuce and tomato on toasted wheat bread, kettle chips, and a Diet Pepsi. She nodded without writing anything down and headed off to the kitchen.

Chapter Twelve

In typical cop fashion we immediately returned to the previous topic.

Maria took the opportunity to excuse herself to the ladies' room. Glenn asked, "So tell me about this woman, Dan. Is this thing serious?"

Glenn has known me literally all my professional career. He knows that I, like many cops, have a divorce in my past and that I haven't had a long-term relationship since. Law enforcement work is not conducive to a normal family life. In my case, my ex had been my girlfriend all through college. We had gone to the same high school, had attended the University of Minnesota where she went for pre-law and I went for fun. I did manage to finish a worthless sociology degree with a minor in abnormal psychology. As part of the abnormal psych program, I spent some time riding around with the Minneapolis Police Department to observe people with psychological abnormalities in their natural environment. This resulted in my applying to the police academy when I graduated.

Along the way, I'd married my sweetheart. She graduated with a degree in political science—how that's a science is still beyond me—and was immediately accepted into law school. She finished her JD about the same time I got moved off dogwatch and she put her new talents to work by filing for divorce. I guess she and our parents all thought that I'd work a few years as a cop, get the Roy Rogers out of my system, and go back to school to get a real, read: marketable, education, maybe an MBA. Didn't happen that way. I was a cop and always would be a cop. Yippee-ki-yay.

"You know, I asked her to marry me."

Glenn nearly snotted his Diet Pepsi.

"Yep, asked her on the bended knee and the whole smash. It was last Christmas, after another case, the one where she had to shoot the guy. I went to Phoenix to spend the holiday with her, brought the ring, waited until I had her in the mood—wine, candles, everything. Got down on my knee and popped the question."

"So what did she say?"

"She didn't say no. She also didn't say yes. She said, 'Not yet.' She said she still had things she wanted to do professionally. Of course, my biological clock is ticking and I guess that's the next conversation she and I will have to have."

Judy Loveless came through the door, scanned the place, and found us. Not too hard in mid-morning; the place was pretty deserted. As she walked to the table the waitress delivered her lunch.

"Oh good. I haven't eaten since breakfast and that was at five-thirty."

She started right in on her BLT, taking a big bite and chasing it with some pop.

Both Glenn and I knew she wouldn't be able to talk for a few minutes, so he continued his pursuit of my domestic situation.

"So you are thinking about having children?"

That caused Judy to snort so hard I thought the BLT was going to come out of her nose. She grabbed a napkin and held it to her face. As I said, Judy and I have known each other for at least six years and we know enough about each other. She's happily married with two sons in their teens. She knows me well enough to understand the magnitude of Glenn's statement. She gasped back her composure.

"You," she choked, "getting married?" she asked, incredulous.

"No, I'm not getting married." I looked at Glenn with an expression that I hoped conveyed both contempt for his continuation of our previously private discussion and admiration for his ability to completely mess up someone's lunch. "The thought has occurred that if there's ever going to be children it's going to have to be soon."

"The gal from Arizona—Maria?"

I should have figured. I shook my head in submission. How does everyone know about this? I thought to myself. Must be Olson. I'll have to have a come-to-Jesus with him next time I see him.

I could see Maria heading back across the little restaurant toward our table. I found myself standing to hold her chair for her, something I'd never done for any other cop in my life.

I gave Judy a let-it-go look. "I'd appreciate it if you could treat it with more discretion than Olson apparently has."

"I guess that explains her behavior with Jane back there," Judy said. "She was pretty pissed off."

"Jane's a big girl; she's seen bodies before. She said so right before she puked."

Maria arrived and I slid her chair in.

Glenn laughed. "I don't know. There are bodies and there are bodies. I remember that one kid that got run over by a tank at the Fourth of July parade. That was the worst one for me."

"I had that one car versus motorcycle wreck on I-94 up in the Fourth Precinct. We had it all covered up and then somebody noticed that we'd missed the guy's leg. It was laying right out in the number two traffic lane. Looked nice and clean, like it came off a mannequin," I added.

Maria looked like she was going to tell about her worst body ever.

"Please," Judy said, holding up her hands in surrender. "I'm trying to eat lunch here."

Maria held her thoughts. I said, "Right. In your line of work, you've seen worse than we ever will."

"True, but I don't talk about it during meals. Anyway, I suppose this means you and Jane are all the way over."

That got Maria's attention. She didn't say anything but I caught her shooting a glance my way. I knew there'd be some serious talk later.

"I've been over her for a while. It was years ago and I'm the one who called it quits," I lied.

Judy shook her head. "I always had high hopes for you two. Maybe we'd get a little better treatment by the press if you were hooked up with one of them."

Glenn agreed that would have been nice. Judy got to the point of her visit.

"Listen, I wanted to talk to you about what I've found so far at the scene." She worked in small bites of the BLT and chips between her sentences.

"First off, and we won't have confirmation until the autopsy, but it looks to me like cause of death will be loss of blood. All the wounds are very small except one that may have been the coup de grâce but I don't think she had much blood left in her when she passed. It only takes 40 percent loss to cause death. On that same topic, it looks to me like there are recent needle marks on her arms."

"Drug use?" Glenn asked.

"No, I don't think so. We'll have to wait for the tox screen, but I'm going to ask for a lot of unusual tests. I think the bad guy may have been medicating her to keep her alive."

That was a chilling thought.

"Second, the condition of the body. It was cleaned very thoroughly before it was dropped. And, it looks to me as if she had been going through whatever it was for some time. That's why I think he was medicating her."

Glenn asked, "What do you mean—for some time?"

"I think, judging by the look of some of the wounds, that she had been held for at least a few days. The ligature marks on her wrists show at least a couple of days in restraint. Some of the knife wounds show signs of healing, meaning they had been inflicted a few days ago and started to recover."

I asked, "You think he was giving her painkillers?"

"Probably not. I've done a little studying of relationship killers and there is a certain type that wants their victims to feel pain. If this was a boyfriend-jilted lover sort of thing he may have wanted to cause her the same pain she had caused him. You said she had been missing since Sunday night?"

Glenn nodded.

"I think she was abducted Sunday night and held for three days before being finished off, so to speak, this morning."

"You think she was killed this morning?" I asked.

"Can't be sure. Had to be sometime when people wouldn't see the drop vehicle, so that's either last night or the night before. I know there is evidence of animals disturbing the body, but that could have happened early this morning. There's no insect activity to say she was there longer than a few hours. It's possible that she was dropped off early last night, say around 11:00 or so, it's well past twilight then, so a vehicle wouldn't have been completely out of place back there, or very early yesterday morning or today, say 5:00. It gets light here around 5:00 this time of year so a vehicle wouldn't be out of place then either."

"So, you think she was held over at least three, maybe four, days?" I asked. My mind was wrapping itself around this piece of information. Something was wrong with that timeline. If what I was thinking was correct, I knew Glenn would have a much bigger problem than I had first thought.

"That's correct. He had her for at least three days."

Glenn was starting to get it too. His face darkened as the truth of the situation became clear. This was not some typical crime of passion from an old boyfriend.

"OK, Dan, this is why I called you," Glenn said. "You know I don't have the experience to look at this and neither do my people. What does this mean—that the bad guy had her for at least three days?"

I looked at Judy and began.

"You have two possibilities. It is still most likely that it was a boyfriend or other jilted lover who started out intending to teach her a lesson. He probably never had murder in mind. He was pissed off about whatever and thought that he could even the score by threatening her, maybe roughing her up a little, and then things got out of hand."

"Out of hand how?" Glenn asked.

"He took her, something that is not too hard, especially if they knew each other, then once he had her under his control, he started slapping her around, maybe threatened her with a knife, maybe even started cutting on her. But someplace along the line he realized he couldn't just let her go. She'd go right to you. Then he'd be in real trouble. So at some point he knew he'd have to kill her to stay free. Now, how to do that? If he hadn't thought it out beforehand he'd have to do some planning. So he sits on her for a few days, finally gets his nerve up, kills her, and dumps her. He is still probably a local because killers prefer to stay in familiar areas. He knew her, he knew the area, maybe works for a road-building company or surveyor. Anyway, he dumped her here. That's your most probable suspect."

I looked back to Judy for confirmation and she nodded. Maria looked like she had something else on her mind. I nodded to her, and she said, "There is also a smaller probability that he intended to kill her all along. And I don't think he slapped her around at all. The ligature marks on her wrists and ankles indicate that she was bound, probably for the entire period. And there are no indications of any kind of physical beating, are there?" Judy shook her head. "Which might indicate that he had some kind of feelings for her. He took her, got control of her, and started threatening her, telling her how she had messed up his life and such. But she didn't react the way he thought she would and that really pushed him over the edge. The condition of the body could be a result of rage."

"Correct," I said. "If she wasn't contrite, didn't show the kind of remorse and sympathy for him that he was expecting, he may have gone off in a rage and spent two or three days torturing her to get his point across."

We all nodded and Maria asked Judy, "What did he use for bindings?"

"I'm not sure. Not rope or handcuffs. He tied her up with something, but the marks aren't familiar to me. I'll have to check the database."

Glenn said, "So my primary suspects are anyone who ever dated or had a thing with Sharon, which is going to include about half the guys between twenty and forty in the county; those who had a falling out with her, which reduces that number by about half; and, out of those guys, figure out which ones have had such poor lives that they're looking for someone to blame their personal failures on, which cuts that number in half again. That's only about two hundred and fifty guys with motive."

I knew he was kidding but the frustration of facing the next few days of interviews was already there.

Glenn sat silent for a moment.

"And who is my least probable suspect?" he asked.

"The five-percenter. If she was just a random selection, then you've got a really tough case."

Maria was clearly thinking about that angle. I looked at her wondering what was being processed and she just turned away, not ready to add it to the mix. Maybe she had an angle not yet brought up. I'd worked with enough partners to know when to leave a question un-asked.

I concluded, "You also know that most of those unknown cases are never solved. I'm hoping this doesn't hurt your election chances because if he's not in the five percent, you've got virtually no chance of catching him."

Chapter Thirteen

Judy finished her lunch as we finished the conversation. Glenn grabbed the lunch tickets and made us guests of the county and we headed out to the street. I asked Judy if there was anything else about the crime scene that was interesting to her.

"Not really. There was very little trace on the body, because it had been washed down. I'd like to locate the wash site and check it for trace. There did appear to be some trace hair on the body so I'll track that down. That's about it."

"Trace hair?" Glenn asked. "Got a color so I can get started?"

"I'm not sure it was human. Might have been animals that were near the body after it was dumped. I should be able to get a species after I look at it in the lab."

Glenn nodded. We said our goodbyes and Judy left. Glenn, Maria, and I got in his car and headed back to his office. I summed it up for him.

"You know what to do and you've got a good investigator in the Schmidt kid. Let him round up the probables and start sweating them a bit. One of them is your perp and you'll know when you get him in the room. He'll show the signs; you'll feel it. You've sweated enough guys on the street in your career to know when someone's hiding something."

"Yeah, I know. It's the 'What ifs?' that are worrying me. You know, what if it was a stranger?"

"There's nothing you can do if it was, so go ahead and treat this as you should. It's a homicide. Follow procedure and interview the likely suspects. It may take a long time but you know as well as I do that investigatory work is a grind. You just keep pushing until you break it. If that means you interview two hundred and fifty guys, then you interview two hundred and fifty guys. You do what it takes and you solve it. If you run into a roadblock or just want to talk about how it's going, call me. Especially after the forensics come back. Sometimes those reports sound like they were written in Martian. They need a little interpretation."

Maria had been sitting quietly through all of this. I had a feeling that there was something buzzing in her investigator's ear. I asked.

She didn't respond right away, just sat looking out the window watching the countryside roll by. Then she spoke. "There was one thing. Judy said there were needle marks. Could be drug use. Check around and see if she was known to use narcotics or something else. Maybe she's diabetic. But, I'm thinking about something else."

Maria looked back outside as if facing a demon from her past. Something she really didn't want to see. She turned back to us.

"Judy said it looked like the vic had been held since she was last seen Sunday night. Maybe this guy's a whacko and was keeping her alive while he had his fun with her. We should know more after the autopsy," she said, looking at me. "Make sure they screen for more than narcotics." Then she looked at Glenn. "Look for someone with medical training. Doesn't have to be a doctor, could be medic or EMT training."

We pulled into the parking lot at the county building and hopped out.

"Stay in touch. I want to know when you've caught this guy," I said as we shook hands. "And say hi to Susan."

"I will. And you bring Maria around again, next time she's in town."

"She's just getting used to Minnesotans. I still haven't sprung Scandinavian food on her."

We all laughed and I popped the door locks on my road cruiser. Maria and I climbed in, gave him a quick wave as I started it up and backed out. He headed in for what I knew was going to be a long evening.

As I drove, Maria and I each silently considered the case. Other than the extensive and exotic knife work, it had all the earmarks of a simple domestic, the kind of case we've both seen dozens of times in our careers. The vic was socially active and unattached. The bad guy was sure to be a past lover who she'd dumped, probably messily, maybe publicly. He'd then gone on to other failed relationships, lost his job, lost his place to live, his dog died, whatever. Some trigger pushed him into a state of mind that said to him, "She's the reason for all this. It's all her fault." He's thinking that if he can cause her some suffering, make her realize how bad she hurt him, maybe—and this is not as ridiculous as it sounds—he thought he could win her back by kidnapping her and educating her on the error of her ways, and his life would return to hunky dory. The women trapped in that scenario never see this point of view and that can often lead to homicide. There are case logs filled with "If only she had understood how much I loved her" that ended with death. Oftentimes, those cases ended with a murder-suicide. I always wished the jilted boyfriend would take the path of suicide-murder in those cases. But they never did.

There are plenty of cases of murder-the-former-lover then botch a suicide attempt. In those cases, I think the boyfriend just didn't have his heart in the suicide part. Again, a little practice on that, beforehand, would have made it perfect in my eyes.

When the city road crossed Highways 65 and 23, I impulsively took 23 north. Maria noticed and I said, "Let's run up to Duluth. We're halfway there and I could use a little cheesecake."

Maria smiled agreement and we went back to processing. I knew there were two conversations on the horizon, one about murder and one about an old girlfriend. I was hoping we'd have the first and she'd forget about the second.

Chapter Fourteen

Interstate 35 toward Duluth

As we drove along, I thought about the woman next to me and how we were going to deal with a girl from my past. I started to concoct scenarios that made me out as the noble law enforcement type and Jane as the evil media parasite. It's a point of view that Maria would understand.

We rode on for a while and the moment I'd been dreading arrived.

"So, you knew that reporter, huh?" Maria asked. It wasn't really a question, more of an inquiry for more data. No way to soft sell it.

"Yeah, I've known Jane for a long time. She started her reporting career about the same time I started on the job. She did a tour as a crime reporter and decided she liked it, so she stayed there. About a year ago she made a move to TV. More money, I guess."

"More money and papers are on the endangered species list. Good survival instincts, huh?"

"I guess. Look, you know how I feel about you, right? So, I'll tell you. She and I went out for a while years ago. It never amounted to anything."

Maria processed this bit of information, then asked, "How long ago?"

"I don't know. Fifteen years?" I was in courtroom mode. No more information than the answer required.

Maria was in legal mode too. "And, how long did you date?"

"About four or five months." An attempt at vagueness. I drove on.

I'm not too good at obfuscation with people I love. She would easily and correctly assume that a months-long relationship had to have a bedroom angle. She processed some more.

"Who broke it off?"

Here's where I had a quandary. I'd already said that I had broken it off. As a cop, Maria knew that some questions had to be asked more than once, just to see if you keep getting the same answer. Maria also knew as well as I did that most domestic assault cases come from relationships where a woman dumped a man and the guy had not gotten over it. It's been my experience that this is due to a fundamental difference between men and women. Women get over it; men do not. Even when a man dumps a woman, he will often have second thoughts and come back to her with regret and contrition on his lips. That doesn't mean that all's well, just that he missed the availability of familiar sex. So, here I was, trying to cool my way through this minefield, knowing that she knew how these things work as well as I do, and that I couldn't BS my way through the answer. If we were to have a future, I knew I couldn't lie to her.

"She did."

"I see," she said softly.

As a modern, sensitive, caring male, attempting to navigate this unknown and rocky shoreline, I knew that now was the time to keep my mouth shut, otherwise known as, "Next one to talk, loses."

We drove on for about ten minutes, which seemed more like an hour to me. Finally she broke the silence. "OK. I understand."

"Frankly, I knew I was busted when you set up those TV guys to shoot her reaction to the body. That was epic," I said with a smile.

"I think I sensed something between you two and that brought out the asshole in me. It was irresistible." She started to giggle.

"I mean, seriously? You told her camera guy to shoot her reaction when she saw the body? You knew what would happen. Shit, I've been in this business for over thirty years and I've never seen anything like that."

"Yeah," she said. "I suppose it was a little mean. But did you see her face? She was whiter than Mr. Clean in a blizzard."

Maria started to laugh. Her feelings of sisterhood with Jane had suddenly been overwhelmed by her years as a cop. Cops have a wicked sense of gallows humor and can be extraordinarily insensitive.

"Yeah," I said, "she was white. Right up until she puked up her guts. Man, I've never seen that kind of range. She must have put it five or six feet out there! And her face wasn't white anymore then. When she looked at you she was pure red." We shared a laugh.

We made the rest of the trip to Duluth without discussion of the case or past relationships. Fine with me. My list when I'd started the day didn't include items like "Go see body drop in Mora" or "Make old girl-friend puke at sight of butchered murder vic." And it especially didn't have a line item for "Explain past relationship to Maria." I was thinking I'd get some work done in my shop, we'd have a little breakfast, maybe catch the Twins game this evening and call it a day. As it turned out, we had a nice, relaxed tour of the harbor, dinner at Fitger's, and a pleasant drive home with the Twins on the radio. It was the start of three of the best days of my life. Funny how good and bad days can be contrasted simply by their proximity. The bad ones were just over the horizon.

Chapter Fifteen

Tuesday, July 7th
11:00 a.m.
Sheriff's Office, Kanabec County Building
Mora, Minnesota

After a long weekend punctuated by Fourth of July festivities, Maria had just one day left before I'd put her on the big bird back to Arizona. We had spent the last few days hanging around town and I needed some saddle time, so we decided to take a ride on my road bike. It's tricked out with big comfy seats, an intercom so we could talk, and Pandora for when we weren't talking. We headed up 65 and stopped in to see how Glenn was coming with his case. I figured it was 50:50 that he'd have it wrapped up.

We strolled into the sheriff's office looking like a couple of lost RUBs. That's the term hardcore riders use to describe people with a late-onset bike fetish—it stands for Rich Urban Bikers and is not a nice thing to be called by "serious" bikers. I locked our helmets to the bike. We were dressed out in our road gear looking like an ad in a Harley catalog for matching black and orange leather. I knocked on the glass and asked the uniformed clerk if Glenn was in. She gave us a thorough onceover and said she'd check. I could overhear her on the phone when she said, "Hey Glenn, you've got some guy out here with more money than sense."

Glenn came into the lobby and started laughing.

"Looks like the new and updated version of the Hells Angels are moving in to turn Mora into the next Hollister." He gave Maria a quick hug and said, "What's up?"

"We thought we'd check on how your case is coming."

Glenn's face showed disappointment. "Well, Maria, it's great to see you again, even though I'll have to have you checked for drug use or insanity since you're still hanging around with this bum. The case is another matter." He knocked on the glass and the clerk hit the door buzzer.

"Follow me. We'll talk in my office."

As we walked down the hall, I assessed Glenn's demeanor. We were four days into the murder investigation. As they say on television, the first forty-eight hours are the most critical. And most murders are solved in those forty-eight hours. If you don't have it solved by then, and I mean solved in the sense that you know what happened, not that you have the bad guy all wrapped up with a bow ready for trial, the case may wind up in your cold case file. Glenn had had time to do that and his scowl led me to believe that he either had a bad guy that was going to be politically sensitive or that he had no bad guy at all. I was hoping for politically sensitive.

So what does that mean, you may ask. They say all politics is local and nowhere is that is more true than in rural America. When the mayor's kid does something stupid like wreck his car driving drunk or a city council member gets caught fooling around with someone not his or her spouse, the local law enforcement community may be put in a position of trying to enforce the law without making the event public, keeping it under wraps, so to speak. But when the councilman winds up strangling his mistress because she thought he'd leave his wife for her, and he hasn't, and now she knows he's never going to, that can be a difficult event to sweep under the rug.

Even with his discomfort, I was hoping that Glenn had solved the crime and had discovered that it was the mayor's kid or a councilman who'd done it. He'd have some dancing to do but I knew he could handle that. After all, he was a veteran of a big city police force who had taken the sheriff's job on sort of a whim. At least it would have been solved.

We made our way into Glenn's office, peeling off the road jackets as we walked, and took seats in his comfortable chairs. He pulled a thick file off the credenza behind his desk and flopped it in front of us. Without preamble he summed up his situation.

"These are interview transcripts. I got nothing. No perp, no likely perp, no circumstantial, almost no trace, just a dead girl with no blood in her body. I'm starting to think someone's gone nuts over these goofy vampire stories that are all the rage. Except I got no bite marks on her neck for that."

I pursed my lips and looked hard at Glenn. I knew he wasn't an experienced homicide cop, like I am, but I really expected he would have this cracked by now.

"You're saying no blood in the body. That's not possible. What did the autopsy say?"

"The report's in the file. The doc said there was less than four pints, which, I think, is less than half a normal load for a woman her size. I was taught that loss of 40 percent of blood volume is fatal, and this gal had lost more than that. The ME also said there were needle marks on the inside of her elbows but no other evidence of drug use. I'm going with Maria's idea and thinking maybe this dirtbag was giving her something—either to control her or to keep her alive."

I looked at Maria. She asked, "Did they do a date rape panel or any other narcotics?"

Glenn flipped a page and said, "I hadn't looked for that before. Hmm, here it is. No alcohol or opioids but those flush out of the system pretty fast. Does test positive for high levels of caffeine and something called Phenylpropanolamine. Never heard of that stuff."

Maria had her phone at the ready. "Spell it."

Glenn did. Maria said, "It's part of the pseudoephedrine family, like you find in decongestants."

Glenn said, "Well I sure know what that stuff is. That's what you make meth out of. It's a stimulant."

Maria went on, "It says here that that it's sold by vets to control incontinence in dogs under the brand names Propalin and Proin." She looked at me.

"Did the report say anything about the quality of her blood?" Maria asked.

Glenn picked up the file and found the autopsy report. He thumbed through it and found the page with the lab results. "Says here her red blood cell count was pretty low. I s'pose that could have come from blood expanders."

We were both thinking the same thing. If the killer was keeping her alive with injections of stimulants and/or blood expanders, that took him to a whole different level of fucked up.

Blood expanders are liquids, typically plasma, that are given to trauma victims to keep them alive even though they are losing a lot of blood. The stimulants, well, they would have been *enhancing the experience* you might say. Not wanting to even consider that possibility, I shook the thought from my head.

Glenn added, "The ME said something about the murder weapon, too, the knife that administered the final death stab to the heart. He said it was a double-edged dagger, blade about six to eight inches long. It was inserted under the rib cage up into the heart itself. The heart exhibited numerous lacerations, indicating that it had been beating when the blade was inserted. You know anything about weird knives?"

"Does it say anything about the width of the blade?" I asked.

"Yeah, about three-quarters of an inch."

I pondered this. I do know a bit about bladed weapons but I'm not an expert. I guess I figure that if I'm confronted with a knife-armed enemy I'll always have a gun. Pity the fool who brings a knife to a gunfight.

"I know a guy. I'll give him a call."

Glenn nodded.

I said, "OK, this is going to sound a little patronizing but let me go ahead, all right?"

"Shoot. I got nothing to lose."

"You ran all her previous acquaintances through interviews, correct?"

"Yes. All had alibis or just didn't match up, feel-wise."

"Every possible doer—people at work, church, where she drank, who she slept with, her family, her neighbors, people at the health club, people she just passed on the street going about her life—everyone?"

"Everyone she has had contact with in the area. Of course, if it was someone passing through, I've got no way to know that."

"And the forensics and the autopsy, they were no help?"

Glenn pulled open the file again, found the autopsy report, and slid it across the table. Maria picked it up and started looking it over.

"The report says she had probably been held a total of three to four days before her death," Glenn said. "It says she died of a combination of two things. Over that time period she had been repeatedly cut, causing blood loss. The final fatal wound was a single thrust of a long double-sided blade into her heart. Her heart had literally cut itself apart as it beat against the blade. Death would have been quick. There is no way to know whether or not she was conscious at this point in the crime."

"Sexual assault?" I asked.

Maria scanned the report. "Yes, vaginal and anal. It says the condition of the assaulted areas indicates damage to those areas that is consistent with non-consensual sex. No trace of semen. There was evidence of condom usage in the form of lubricants."

Maria was looking at photos of the body. She worked in a part of the country where bad guys were more knife-oriented. They consider using a firearm less macho than a knife, though that's changing too. So she's seen victims of stabbings. But looking at her, I could see she was processing these photos as something different.

Glenn and I stopped talking and looked at Maria. She startled from her trance noticing us and I saw her blush just a little.

"What is it?" I asked. "You see something?"

"I'm not sure." She turned to Glenn. "Was there anything else in the forensics, anything unusual or unexplained?"

Glenn sat back in his chair and blinked a few times.

"Yes, there were three things. The body had been washed, which we already knew. There was evidence that it had been at least rinsed off. Second—you remember we sent my local dog gal after a blood trail? She found a spot on the edge of a parking lot about three miles away where we think the bad guy may have washed her off. There was evidence of water mixed with human blood. I sent dirt samples to the BCA but we haven't heard anything back on those yet."

Maria shook her head. That wasn't it, I thought.

"Glenn, you said there were three things?" I asked.

"Yeah. The other thing was they found hairs on the body, dog hairs from at least four different dogs. I'm thinking that's not significant because we've got lots of dogs out here. Folks don't worry about fencing and leashing their dogs. They just open the door and let 'em out. I figure that some dogs came by after the body was dumped and left their hair at the site. It must have just been picked up with the body when they bagged it."

Maria sat back in her chair. She was obviously deep in thought. I assumed she was moved by the brutality shown in the photos. I cocked an eyebrow in her direction.

"I don't know. Something about this case reminds me of something."

That's not unusual. Cops see so many cases over the years that they all start to run together. Even so, many investigators can call up memories from cases years ago. Sort of like a car salesman who remembers every car he ever sold or the teacher who remembers every student. I had a feeling that Maria was one of those who remembered every case she ever worked on. I wrapped it up.

"Well, maybe this will be a bad one for you. But these things happen. Don't let it keep you up or spoil your summer. You know as well as I do that it's still likely someone she knew. It will come out when they get drunk and start bragging about how they took care of her and whatever. We've seen it before."

"I know. It's just . . . We have a one-hundred-percent-closed rate on felonies since I've been sheriff and I hate to see that blemished."

"I can understand that."

I looked at Maria and said, "We've got to hit it if we're going to make it back for your flight."

We stood and Maria carefully, almost reverently, placed the photos back on Glenn's desk. He walked us out to the lobby.

"It's been a real pleasure seeing you again. If you connect anything, Maria, I'd sure like to hear about it."

"I'll think on it. It's probably nothing, but you know, something gets to buzzing . . . ."

We all knew that feeling. Cops get it when they've found something in an investigation that's going to be important. They just don't know what it is yet.

Glenn followed us out into the midday sun and turned his face to the sky. He was enjoying the break from his desk.

"You know, Dan, that old friend of yours has been on this from the start."

"I saw the TV report the day it happened. Delivered a story on the 6:00 news where the words "shocking" and "horrific" and "unbelievable violence" were used. She wrote it off to a local, probably drug-crazed ex. Has she been bugging you?"

"Calls every day asking for an update. Came back up here, too."

"What I want to know is how she got on it so fast."

"Either she really has someone monitoring the radio for BCA calls, or someone here called her. That's the only way she could have gotten here so fast."

A leak was something no law enforcement commander wanted to contemplate.

"Let's go with radio monitor for now."

"She get ahold of you?" Glenn asked.

"She's tried," I said, looking at Maria. "She's been calling and I've been ignoring."

Glenn gave me a "Good for you" nod of the head. "Well, keep on ignoring. You're a private citizen, you don't have to answer her."

We said our goodbyes and walked over to my bike. We put on our jackets and helmets and mounted up. After plugging in the electronics, I said "Hi-yo Silver! Away!" and we zoomed off toward a picnic spot to watch boats. We weren't even a mile away before both of us had put the vision of the slashed body out of our heads. So works the brain of a cop.

Chapter Sixteen

We cruised over to I-35 and took it up to the beautiful port city of Duluth, Minnesota. Yeah, I hear you thinking Duluth? Beautiful? That's what I said. As you crest the hill south of the city you are treated to a panoramic view of Lake Superior and the harbor. It's not a tropical palm tree view like you'd get in, say, Costa Rica or Puerto Vallarta, where you see cruise ships, blue seas, and white sand. It's an industrial view of ore docks interspersed with elevated rail lines, miniature mountains of coal, salt, and other commodities waiting to be loaded onto ships. And rust-and-white freighters, their sand-colored conveyors swinging in and out with each load of product. A view much more utilitarian, but also much more realistic, of what a working port looks like.

We descended the hill and took the exit for Canal Park, an area of the city that has become a tourist mecca in the past ten years. Shops, restaurants, hotels, and bars have taken over the formerly struggling waterfront park. It's a shame, really. People used to be able to take their families there for long weekends and now the upscale hotels price out most working folks.

We parked in a public lot and went to a sandwich shop I knew about from my previous visits called Amazing Grace. It's kind of a local landmark that specializes in homemade bread, good deli-style meats and fresh fixins. They have covered the walls with pictures of now-famous writers and musicians who, at one time or another, read or played in the place. The best part is you can wrap up a meal with a piece of unbelievable cheesecake.

We split a roast beef with provolone, sprouts, sliced avocado and chipotle mayo for Maria and a touch of horseradish for me on a fresh ciabatta roll. The monstrous sandwich was accompanied by fresh potato salad. We chased it down with designer root beer and split a slice of homemade raspberry cheesecake. This mass consumption necessitated a walk around the park before we could climb back on the bike and head home.

I always like to walk out to the end of the breakwater to see the lighthouse up close. My mind ventures back to the days of steam and sail when the lighthouse kept the ships off the shoreline. Modern GPS, radar, and autopilots take a lot of the thrill and/or risk out of it, but the lake can still take a toll in human life. Just ask Gordon Lightfoot.

As we stood at the base of the white and black lighthouse looking at Duluth's signature landmark, the lift bridge, I was struck that it was just about exactly a year earlier that we had stood on the other end of the bridge, waiting for it to lower so we could continue to pursue the guy we liked for a series of sniper murders. It was at that moment that I first considered Maria as a long-term possibility. As I mentioned earlier, law enforcement types are handicapped when it comes to relationships. We have unique work experiences that leave us jaded and cynical about our fellow man and woman.

At the end of the day, a cop has to go home to a person who has had a much more normal day. Someone who hasn't been threatened, hasn't had to defend himself physically, hasn't had to break the laws others have to observe in order to do their jobs. And, perhaps the worst as far as long-term effect, they haven't been lied to by nearly everyone they encounter during the day.

Think about it. With the exception of other cops, nearly everyone a cop deals with on the job has a good reason to lie to them. From speeders to felons to lawyers, everyone wants the cop to believe their version of the story. Often, that version is the one that will get the bad guy off, so the facts may be "massaged" a bit to fit the speaker's point of view. Load this into a thirty-year career and you can understand why cops may become just a bit difficult to get close to, which results in the high divorce rate among LEOs.

You'd think this would make other cops the logical ones to share your life with and that's true. But, as in any career, sharing a romance in the workplace is a very difficult row to hoe. I'd already had one, a long time ago. I'd tried one cop/cop relationship and that proved the rule, "Don't get your dessert where you get your bread." She wound up transferring to another precinct, saving both of us the discomfort of having to look at each other day after day.

Standing on the other side of the lift bridge with Maria last year started me thinking that maybe we could work, that a long distance relationship with a cop couldn't be any harder than what I'd tried. And it has worked pretty well. Leading right up to my stifled proposal last winter. Revisiting the locale had the desired effect on the love of my life and she snuggled close into my arm as we walked out to the lighthouse. Now, on the return walk, I was about to launch into a reprise of our relationship and try the marriage thing again when she started down a different track.

Maria suddenly stopped and looked at me with an expression of thoughtful concern that said she was about to say something important. I opened with the classic cliché, "A penny for your thoughts." I figured I could direct the conversation my way after that. I was wrong. She pulled out her phone.

"I have to make a call. This case is ringing some bells and I need to talk to someone back in Phoenix."

Not what I expected. Maria hit a speed-dial number, put the phone on speaker, and held it up between us, so I could eavesdrop.

Chapter Seventeen

Canal Park
Duluth, Minnesota

She got voice mail.

"Hello. You've reached the voice mail of Detective Bob Cassilla of the Maricopa County Sheriff's Office Homicide Investigation Department. I'm sorry I can't take your call right now, but you can leave a message. Be sure to leave the name of the case, or victim, your name, and a phone number where I can reach you. I check my voice mail frequently, but occasionally have to be in court or other places where I can't be reached. If this is urgent, dial pound 94 and another investigator will pick up. Thank you."

After the prompt, Maria said, "Bob, this is Maria. Do you remember that case we had a couple of years ago where your wife made a connection between the victim and a dog show? I'm in Minnesota and they've got a body here that reminds me of that case. Vic was a young single blond female, even sort of looks like our vic. Could you pull the files and leave them on my desk? I'll be in tomorrow morning. Thanks, babe!"

When the call was over I asked her what was up.

"I figured out what was bugging me. It's the dog hair. I'm thinking about Glenn's homicide case and there's some connection in my head with dog shows."

I looked at Maria and said "OK, what's the connection? Why dog shows?"

"We had a case three years ago in Phoenix. I didn't handle it but we all knew the particulars since it was kind of weird and it never closed.

We all talked about it. The victim was a young woman, about thirty, blond, attractive. She disappeared on a Sunday night and the body was found two-and-a-half weeks later in a shallow grave. Her body had been washed but there were traces of dog hairs. The guy I called, Bob Cassilla, has a wife who's into dogs and dog shows and he made the connection. His wife had been showing at a big dog show at WestWorld in Scottsdale the weekend the vic was reported missing. We never thought it was significant, just a coincidence. We thought the hairs had been feral dogs leaving trace when they tried to dig up the body. But we only talked about it, never followed up on it. The case is still open."

Dog hair? Dog shows? There are so many dogs near any civilized part of the planet. Digging up dead animals is what they do for a living. I shook my head in doubt, but wondered who would know about that.

I gave it about two seconds thought and it hit me. My buddy Pete Anderson has a Flat-Coated Retriever that he used to take to dog shows. It was some kind of champion, though I didn't know of what.

I pulled out my cell and hit the speed dial for Pete. I put it on speaker.

"Hey guy, how you doing?" Pete answered with his usual informal greeting.

"Doing fine. Listen, I'm doing a little long-distance investigating for a friend of mine who's now the Kanabec County sheriff. They had a body dump there a few days ago and the forensics are a little funny. The body was pretty clean but had dog hair on it."

"Dog hair?" Pete answered. "Why is that funny?"

"The BCA says that the body appeared to have been washed, as in an effort to remove evidence, but it still had some dog hair on it. The BCA investigator said that the hair was from at least four different dogs. What prompted me to call you was Maria remembered a case they had in Phoenix a few years ago and one of the investigators thought it might have had something to do with some dog show they had down there."

Pete asked, "When was the body discovered?"

"About two weeks after some dog show they have down there."

"No, I mean the body up here. Where was the body discovered?"

"It was found outside Mora."

"When, exactly, was the body found here?"

"On the 2nd."

"Hang on and I'll check the calendar."

Maria looked at me with a raised eyebrow. "He has a calendar of dog shows? Seriously?"

I covered the mic on the phone and said, "He used to go to those things all the time. He probably knows where to look one up online."

A moment later Pete was back. Maria asked her question. "You really have a calendar of dog shows?"

"Sort of. A buddy of mine who's a Realtor sends them out online to his friends. Sort of an advertising thing. Since I'm not showing my dog now, I don't print them off anymore, but it's on his website. I've got it up right here."

She gave me an eye-rolling shrug.

"There was a big show in Cambridge the 24th through the 27th," Pete said.

"A big one?"

"Yeah, it's a combined show between the Cambridge Kennel Club and the Anoka County Kennel Club. They do four days the end of June and call it the Summer Solstice show."

"Define 'big.'"

Pete said, "Number of dogs entered. A show with more than, say, a thousand dogs a day is a big show. Attracts the most spectators, vendors, best dogs, and biggest handlers, best prizes, stuff like that. Plus it will run more than the usual weekend. Maybe three, four days."

I looked at Maria and said, "You said the show in Phoenix was a big show?"

"I'll have to call down to check but I recall that it was three or four days. Bob's wife said it was one of the biggest we have in the area."

"And it was when?"

"February, I think."

"You have anything in Phoenix in February, Pete?"

"Not February, but there's a March series down there. A series is a couple of weekends in a row. Clubs will do that to attract the big shots that travel all over the country to shows. The big show in the series is in Scottsdale at that WestWorld place where they do the car auctions. I'll look up the dates."

Pete was gone again and came back saying, "Yeah, that Scottsdale show was the second weekend of March this year."

This was getting interesting, in a murder investigation sort of way. I had some new questions.

"Pete, what do you mean by big shots traveling all over the country?"

"I guess I need to give you a little background. You've heard of the AKC, right?

Pete went on to give us a quick primer on the dog show world. Who goes, who shows, how they work. He finished up with dog breeders.

"Then you have your breeder. These are people who are committed to improving their particular breed of dog. They may show as many as a half dozen dogs at the same show, in various classes. It's their hobby and their passion. They are the backbone of these shows because they are the ones who build the entries and breed the dogs that are shown."

Maria interrupted. "You mean people who run those dog mills? We've put a few of them out of business."

"No, no, Maria. Don't mix this up. Puppy mills and those awful places you see on the news have nothing to do with dog shows. In fact, the AKC actively assists in the identification and prosecution of those types of breeders all the time. No, the people who are involved in showing dogs are breeding to improve their lines. You can meet them at the dog shows, talk to them about their breed—most of them will talk your ear off as long as they aren't getting ready to go into the ring right then. And, if you're lucky, they might even let you buy one of their puppies at a later date."

"Come on," she said. "You mean to tell me that if I went to one of these shows looking for a dog, they wouldn't sell me one right there?"

"No, they wouldn't. First, it's against the rules. They could get their showing privileges suspended. Second, they will want to check your references. All these breeders have a sales contract that generally includes breeding restrictions, a medical condition guarantee, a buy-back clause that says if, for any reason whatsoever, you need to get rid of Fluffy, they'll take him back. Plus, they'll have a long questionnaire about your home and history with dogs, who your vet is, things like that, that you have to fill out before they'll even put you on a list for a dog. Many insist on visiting your home to see that it's properly set up for a dog."

"Geez, you'd think these people were selling their children."

"In many ways, that's exactly what it is. They treat their dogs like children and they are very protective. That's one of the things that is so hard to understand about the whole animal rights thing. Show dogs are better cared for than many people's kids and yet the so-called animal rights people want to stop dog shows. It's proof that they really aren't about animal rights at all; they just don't want anyone to have a pet."

We talked a little more and I asked Pete to give some thought to someone involved with dog shows killing people and rang off.

We had the last leg to cover to get home and get Maria to the airport. We talked again about the case and what each of us would do over the next few days. I could do whatever I wished, since I was "retired." Maria had a full caseload. She'd have to pull out a cold case file and get her supervisor to authorize her time on it. She was a comer in her department and I was confident she could work it out, but a rash of gang/drug killings could tie her up for weeks. We'd just have to wait and see.

My part would be to get with Pete and try to come up with some background on the whole dog show thing. If that was the string that tied it all together, it was worth pursuing. If it wasn't, it would be a waste of time. Unfortunately, there was no way of knowing which it would be until we did it.

Chapter Eighteen

Friday, 6:30 a.m., July 10
Driving north on I-35 between Minneapolis and Duluth,
Minnesota

The week had swept by quickly with plenty of distractions to keep me away from Glenn's murder case. One was a call from the director of a TV series that I'd worked on a few times who called me with a request to vet a scene for an upcoming episode.

It's one of my part-time jobs. After writing a couple of books on ballistics, I started traveling around the country as a paid expert witness, usually for the prosecution, on what happens during gunfights. That led to consulting in Hollywood. I advise movie and TV show directors, actors, and stunt people on how to properly use firearms and what is realistic in the moment of a gunfight. Most of what I consider reality still gets swept under the rug in favor of "action" but some directors at least make an effort to keep it real. I wish more would because I think the viewers, especially young males, would be less likely to go to the gun if they understood how hard it is to use them properly in the pressure cooker of a gunfight and if they saw the real results of hits on both the targets and the unintended. My experience is that there are more unintendeds hit than targets and that just makes it worse.

The TV director wanted to have the good guy, a cop, make a head shot on the bad guy at a range of around one hundred eighty feet, à la the stairway shot in the film Untouchables with Kevin Costner, only twice as far. The shot is made more complex by the need for the good guy to fire one-handed, as the FBI agent did in the Costner flick, from behind cover, with a 2-inch .38 caliber snubnosed revolver. Oh, did I mention, the good guy had been hit a few times and was wearing a lot of his own blood? Those conditions would have made this shot a challenge for Jerry Miculek, arguably the greatest revolver shooter of our time. I've seen Jerry shoot, even shot in competition against Jerry, after a fashion. He makes all the rest of us look stupid. But I'm not sure he could have made the shot.

So, I advised the director to change the shot to something more realistic. No, couldn't do that. Our hero's a hero, after all, and is expected to make the impossible shot. So, I told him to provide something for the guy to rest his arm or hand on to steady it. And to make sure he took the time to cock the hammer on the pistol. That would reduce both the amount of trigger travel and the effort required to fire and would improve the chances that the shot could be made. The director actually liked that idea. It gave him another chance for a close-up and would add a few seconds of dramatic pause. The compromise was typical of what happens in these discussions. I also committed to go to LA the day of the shooting to observe on set. I like doing that because I can make a side trip to Phoenix to see Maria and the TV company will pay the travel costs.

Meanwhile in Phoenix, Maria had dug out the case file on their unsolved murder and had sent me a copy of the coroner's report and the forensic results of the body exam. Photos showed a series of knife wounds nearly identical to those of the victim found outside Mora. It also showed contamination by dog hair, but the breeds, colors, and types of dog hair were different, just like on our vic. Coincidence? No cop believes in coincidence. I mean, it might have been, but let's not ignore it.

Pete picked me up at my house bright and snarly that morning for my personal tour of a dog show. We'd had a few phone calls over the course of the past week, but I decided the best way to understand was to actually go to one. Fortunately, one of the biggest in the area was taking place that weekend in Duluth.

I climbed into Pete's big GMC Yukon Denali and he backed out of my driveway. I love the descendants of the Chevy Suburbans that I'd known in my youth. They still look like the old buses, so much so that they are universally called Suburbans, without regard to whether they're Chevys or GMC, Tahoes or Yukons. To those of us who love them, they're Suburbans. We headed north on Hwy 100, then took I-694 east, fighting the morning rush-hour traffic until we could turn north—opposite the flood of early commuters—onto Hwy 65. We made the turn and left the morning mess behind.

We were heading up 65 to pick up Glenn. He was still nowhere on his case and had reached the point of grasping at straws. When I'd told him Pete and I were going to a Duluth dog show to see if we could find a lead he practically begged me to let him tag along. It was kind of pathetic, but I knew where he was coming from. I'd had cases where doing anything was better than sitting in my office stumped.

We rolled into the lot about 7:30 and Glenn was waiting for us. He climbed into the back seat and we were off.

Just coming out the door was Billy Gorman, the deputy who'd had the gate control job at the murder scene. He noted mentally what was going on and went back inside. "Hmm," he said to himself. "The sheriff's going off with that Minneapolis guy."

Billy walked back in to the dispatcher's desk and asked about the sheriff. He was told that Mills was going to be out of the area for a while, probably until early afternoon.

"Yeah, but where's he going? Looked like fishing to me."

"Why do you say that?" asked the dispatcher.

"Well, I saw him get into a Suburban with two guys. One was that buddy of his from the MPD—Neumann."

"They're going to the DECC in Duluth to see a dog show. Apparently this Neumann guy has some idea that our murder case is tied to dog shows so they're going to check it out."

"Yeah? Well I hope he's right cause we've got nothing so far."

Billy thanked the dispatcher and walked away wondering if Ms. Vanderloo might be interested in knowing this bit of info. He headed outside and started digging out her card.

As we approached the Sandstone exit I punched some buttons on Pete's GPS and located a coffee shop ahead. We took the next exit and stopped in for a little pick-me-up.

I had been thinking about today's mission for a while and I knew I needed a good understanding of what goes on at a dog show. When working a murder case, the investigator needs to understand motive. Motive in most cases is one of only a few possibilities. Look for motives of passion or gain, said a TV character once, and he was right. Most murders are committed by killers against persons known to them for reason of revenge, jealousy, or the possibility of some kind of gain.

"Gain" ranges from stealing the person's wallet to inheriting their fortune. It can also be a means to a reward, as in the case of someone who kills to obtain something to trade for drugs. Personally, a lifetime of law enforcement has taught me that drugs are the number one problem in our country. If you take a look at how much violent crime and how many resources are expended as a result of illicit drug use you'll be amazed. If I could somehow wipe out drug use in our country, I could save the nation about half the national budget spent on law enforcement and imprisonment.

But I doubted that drugs had anything to do with our dog show trip. In fact, I'd have been surprised if it had led to anything. We didn't think the Minnesota victim had any connection with dog shows; she didn't even own a dog. I didn't know about the Arizona vic; that was on Maria's to-do list. The only connections to dog shows were the dates and the dog hair, both of which could have been coincidental. I know, there's that word again. But if we had a serial killer on our hands and if the killer had something to do with dog shows, then his victims were selected by the killer for his reasons and by his methods. It was a stretch but it was all we had. For that reason, it was important for me to know more about dog shows.

"So tell me how this dog show thing works," Glenn asked Pete as we pulled out of the coffee shop drive-through. "I get that a bunch of dogs compete and it's kind of a beauty contest but what are the judges looking at?"

"OK, I'll start at the beginning. I used to compete in both Obedience and Conformation."

"Right. Obedience is the part with the heeling and retrieving and stuff," Glenn said.

"That's right. Obedience is the sport that tests the skills that make a dog a good member of the household. It helps teach them how to be a member of the family and what their place is in the family structure. We do things like heeling, stays, and recalls that are useful to the dog owner around the house. There is also the newer sport of Agility, which is sort of like an obstacle course for the dog. You've seen that on TV, right?" Glenn nodded.

"It has the teeter totter, tunnels, jumps, and weave poles. It's grown very popular in the U.S. But what most people see on TV is Conformation, the beauty pageant. That's both the easiest and hardest to understand."

"Why's that?"

"The idea of a beauty contest is pretty simple for most people to grasp. You line up a bunch of young women in various states of undress, have them do something to demonstrate some kind of talent, ask them a few questions and choose one. That's fine when they're all basically the same—attractive, relatively intelligent young women. It's different with dogs."

"How so?" Glenn asked.

"There are so many different breeds. Each breed of dog has been bred for generations to do different jobs. To do those jobs some dogs are small, some are big. Some are fast and sleek, some are strong and ponderous. So each breed of dog has different standards of beauty. They come in all sizes, colors, types of coats, types of heads and other features.

"So, the result is that the judges have to know the different kinds of dogs," I contributed.

"The standard for each breed of dog," Pete corrected.

"Standard," I repeated.

"Right. Each breed has a standard that describes in words what a perfect example of that breed would be. Breed standards include a physical description of the perfect dog as well as a description of the dog's movement and attitude.

"And I use the word 'dog' here generically. Boys are dogs, girls are called 'bitches' and you'll hear that word used a lot in the dog-show environment. Breed standards allow for differences between males and females, in terms of sizes mostly, but what I'm going to talk about is just generalities so we'll go with 'dogs.'"

"Got it. Even the bitches are dogs."

In the back seat, Glenn chuckled then sipped his coffee and nodded his understanding. Under his breath he said, "All dogs, even the cute ones." I stifled a snort.

"So I know there is a standard that the dog has to represent. Now, how do you judge them?" Glenn asked.

"That's the hard part for outsiders to understand. First they are judged against others of their own breed. Then, the best of each breed is judged against the other members of their group. For example, the Best of Breed herding dogs are judged against each other, producing a Group winner. The final ring is where the seven group winners compete for Best in Show. When you get to the group and Best-in-Show rings, they are judged only against the standard for their breed and not against the other dogs in the ring."

OK. Some of this was getting through to me. "How do they get to the Group and Best-in-Show rings?" I asked.

"The dog show is kind of like the NCAA basketball tournament. It's got a ladder and is an elimination game. I'll walk you through how one dog gets to the last award—Best in Show.

"First, the divisional round. That's when the dogs of one breed compete against their own breed by sex and age and a few other categories. First the boys compete by age and experience until you find the best boy dog. They start with puppies by age bracket—six to nine months, nine to twelve, twelve to eighteen. If the dog is over eighteen months old and not yet a champion, they can continue to compete in what's called the Open Class. There are also classes for other divisions, things like owner-handled, breeder-handled, and bred in America, called AmBred. Things like that. Each class produces a winner. Then all the winners compete for the Winners Dog and then Winners Bitch ribbons. That's round one. And that's where the dogs get the points to win a Championship title, so it's important.

"Round two. The Best of Breed for each breed. There are also dogs competing that have already won their championship title. We call those dogs "Specials." To get to the Best of Breed winner for the day, all the Specials, boys and girls, and the Winners Dog and Winners Bitch from today, compete against each other. This produces the Best of Breed for that day."

I said, "OK, now we have a best dog in that breed. Then what?"

"Round three—the regionals. Then the breed winners compete against the rest of the breed winners in their group. That produces the seven Group Winners. Then the finals. The seven group winners compete for Best in Show."

Glenn said, "Seems to me the same dog should win every day. It's either best or it's not."

Pete smiled and said, "It would seem so, wouldn't it? But this judging is subjective. Each judge has their own comprehension of the breed standard. Judges get reputations as 'head' judges or 'gait' judges or 'coat and color' judges. So, different dogs win. Plus, dogs are like people in a lot of ways. They have good days and bad days. A dog that struts his way to victory one day may be a little off his feed the next and loaf through the ring looking terrible. It happens."

"I think I've got that. It's kind of a pyramid scheme. Now who are the people at dog shows?" I said. "Actually, everyone and anyone. Showing dogs is one of the most egalitarian activities in the country. I've known and shown with people for years without knowing what they do for a living. I know people who are doctors, lawyers, electricians, pharmacists, government workers, teachers, judges, mechanics, anything. One time I was at an Agility trial and someone slipped and hit his head on a piece of equipment. He was cut pretty bad and someone said, "Find Kari." Now I'd known Kari for about ten years and that was when I found out she is one of the top trauma docs in the region. Keeps a sewing kit in her car. Sewed him up right there."

"You told me there are other people at these shows too, professionals."

"Yes. Most of the dogs are handled by their owners or friends of the owners but there are some that are being campaigned by professional handlers. Those people travel from show to show in a bus or RV full of dogs and grooming equipment. Some of them have other adults or even kids who go with them and help out. They show the dogs, collect their fees, and go on to the next show."

That interested me because our killer might have been active for a few years and in at least two locations. Maria was talking to a fed contact, checking out their Violent Criminal Apprehension Program, or ViCAP program, for any similar cases going back as far as it could reach. The ViCAP system had put together cases that spanned decades along with the careers of the killers they tracked down. I had a pretty good FBI contact too. I knew I'd be talking to him sooner or later, especially if we learned about any similar cases.

"So there are amateurs who show their own dogs and pros who show dogs for other people. Anyone else at these things?" Glenn asked.

"Sure. You have the club members who put on the shows. Most clubs put on one weekend of shows per year, which may be two to four days. You need a lot of volunteers to pull off one of these events. Plus you have the judges. They are people who've gone through the educational and certification process to become judges. They are the power in the ring. They are the ones who decide who wins and who doesn't."

"So, they're the ones who make people happy or piss people off?"

"You could say that. But that would make them possible victims, wouldn't it?" Pete said with a chuckle. "I've known people who would have liked to rough up a judge after a call they didn't agree with. Judging Conformation dogs can be kind of subjective. Like I said before, different judges have different hot buttons. Some like dogs toward the big end of the standard, some mid-sized. Some judges look at gait more than coat and vice versa. It can be frustrating to the handlers when you win one day and the next day a different judge doesn't even look at your dog."

"Any chance one of these guys would fit the profile?" I asked.

I'd gone over some FBI data on serial killers with Pete. Statistically, serial killers are straight white males between twenty-five and fifty years of age. Many are seemingly normal people who live openly in their communities, belong to churches, have regular jobs and such. There are a few very rare occasions, like the Atlanta Child Killer case, where the bad guy was black. Or the woman in Florida whose story they made into a movie. But nearly all serial killers are straight white males. And nearly all the victims are women.

"I don't know, Dan. It's an eclectic group. Most of the judges are over fifty and more than half are women. To become a judge, they had to have been a breeder and to have shown dogs for some time, so a lot of the handlers are kind of judges-in-training. Something else you should understand—many people who go into showing dogs are people who, for whatever reason, don't have kids. This becomes sort of their version of soccer or hockey. So it attracts a lot of older people whose kids have left, or people who never had kids."

"People who can't have kids? Like me?"

"No, you don't have kids because you frighten women." That earned an outright guffaw from Glenn.

"Although the way you and Maria are getting along, that might change," he said. "No, I'm talking about alternative lifestyles. I'd say at least thirty percent of my dog-showing friends are gay."

"That makes sense," I said.

"And that rules them out of your suspect pool."

"Not completely. There have been cases, but not many."

"Anyone else at these shows?"

"There are two other groups. There are companies called 'super-intendents.' These are outfits that handle the business of putting on a show. They are contracted by the club to prepare all the paperwork for the show—entries, catalogs, and such. Then, when it's show time, they come into town a day or two early, set up the equipment like the rings and floor matting necessary for the show, then they provide the judging record books and ribbons and collect and forward all the results to the AKC, the American Kennel Club."

I was thinking there couldn't be too many of those outfits. "How many of these companies are there?"

"I suppose there are six or seven main ones. The show we're going to is being super'd by one out of Oklahoma City. They handle most of the shows in the central and southwest U.S. Most of the shows I've been to have been super'd by the same company. I know some of the people they send to the shows."

"What do you think about them? Any chance they could be doing this?"

"I doubt it. They work as a group—come into town, stay together, leave together. Plus, the companies tend to send the same people to the same shows in the same areas year after year. That would rule out a broad area of cases. No, from what you've said you're looking for a loner."

"True enough. So, what's the last group?"

"The vendors, folks selling all manner of dog and pet products from booths at the show. They only go to the largest shows, but stay pretty regional, like I said before. I don't think the supers or the vendors fit the bill unless Maria finds that all the victims in similar cases are located in one part of the country. If you find cases east of the Mississippi or in the Northwest or New England states, there's no way he's a vendor or with a super. They just don't get around that much."

Chapter Nineteen

We rode on in silence as I tried to picture in my mind what a serial killer looked like. Over the years I'd investigated hundreds of murders and solved most of them. I held the record for a career high closing rate on homicides for the Minneapolis Police Department, and this was just another homicide, wasn't it?

My career in homicide had begun after the usual cop career path. I started in a two-man car on the "last out" shift from 10:00 p.m. to 6:00 a.m. I was in the Second Precinct, which is Northeast Minneapolis. To this day, the area is made up of ethnically based neighborhoods representing most of Eastern Europe with some Irish that spilled over from St. Paul mixed in with newer immigrant groups. We used to say, "There's a church and a bar on every block." For a new cop raring to go it was a little dull—the usual urban crime, but at a low-key level. An occasional breaking and entering that promised some action and a little drug activity, but all in all, it was, and still is, fairly tame for a big city precinct. It was, on the other hand, the location of my first officer-involved shooting.

I was about a year-and-a-half into my law enforcement career. By this time I was in a car by myself. Minneapolis, like a lot of big cities, pairs you with a veteran officer for your first six months. At that point, if it looks like you won't hurt yourself or the public, they put you in a one-man car for the balance of your probation period. You're on the street with a training officer nearby, but you present a more visible force with more cars on the street.

I was first in on a silent alarm for a break-in at an electronics store. The place had a history of break-ins because it was widely known as a source of high quality—read: expensive—electronic equipment. While running over, I shut the lights and siren off about five blocks away. You try to sneak up on the bad guys if you can. Another car, the one with my training officer, Jim, aboard, rolled in right with me. We'd communicated by radio and he took the front while I went to the back, which took just a few seconds longer. As I got out of the car, I heard Jim yell, "Drop the stuff and show me your hands!" The bad guys, who had just exited the store laden with stolen merchandise, did just that, tossing the stuff right at Jim, and taking off around to the back of the building, toward me.

I drew my firearm as I heard Jim yell, "Around the back, around the back!" I had just assumed a blocking stance as they came around the corner of the building.

What happened next takes a lot longer to tell than it did to happen. The first guy around the corner was running like a bat out of hell, arms pumping, knees lifting. He could have been at an Olympic track tryout, his form was so good. I hollered, "Freeze right there!" He did.

The second guy didn't. He passed his buddy and started to raise his right hand. I could see in the parking lot light a reflection that told me the hand had a gun in it. His hand came up and I went into automatic pilot.

At the police academy—yeah, there really is one and it's nothing like the movies—and during the eleven months I'd been on the force, I'd taken a liking to shooting. Turned out I had a bit of a knack for it and I started shooting in tactical competitions. By that night, I'd gotten myself rated as a damn good shooter in several categories. I credit that experience for getting me through the next few short seconds.

I identified myself by yelling again, assessed the threat, and took action to stop the threat. That's the proper legal verbiage for what happened. The bad guy brought his gun up and so did I. As I screamed, "Police! Drop the gun! Drop the gun!" he made the typical inexperienced mistake I'd seen many times at the range—he snapped off a shot before he had his weapon on target, hitting the ground about a foot in front of me. I aligned my weapon with the target and engaged. That's lawyereze for "I brought the gun up and started firing as fast as I could." I was carrying a .357 revolver with six rounds loaded and I emptied that thing faster than I ever had in competition. I hit the bad guy and he was, as we say, dirt. That's D-R-T, as in dead right there. I'd hit him twice in the torso, once in the left shoulder, and once (a lucky round since we are trained to shoot for the torso) right between the eyes. But in spite of all the shooting experience I'd compiled in about a year of competition, I hit him with only four of the six shots. Later, after getting through the whole "I shot somebody" experience, it dawned on me that I'd missed a man-sized target with a third of my shots from less than fifteen feet away. I practice. I'm an accomplished shooter. It was a stunning experience.

As for the shooting-someone experience, I went on the usual leave, drank a bunch, wondered why the guy didn't just stop like his buddy did, wondered why he made me shoot him, totally screwing up my life and ending his. I had counseling and therapy and a couple of weeks off. Then I went back to work. I still have an occasional nightmare about that call.

At five years, the earliest it's allowed, I took and passed the test for sergeant, which allowed me to get some experience in personnel management, as I was still in patrol and sergeants in patrol run the show. I stayed in patrol for a couple of more years, using the time to try out for and join the SWAT unit. That unit was not like what you see on TV. It's sort of an "on call" group of regular cops who have special training and skills. We work our regular assignments until the call comes. Then we get suited up all "Tommy Tactical" and head out to solve the city's problems with our unique talents. Anyway, I stayed at that until the opportunity to transfer into narcotics came along.

In the narc squad I found a home. I loved investigations and loved the proactive nature of narcotics. Patrol is like deer hunting or bobber fishing. You just kind of wait until something happens and then take care of it. In narcotics you hunt. You don't sit around waiting for something to happen, you make it happen. You set up deals, buys, takedowns, and arrests. You testify in court against some of the worst bad guys you'll ever come across. All these guys care about is getting the money and they don't care who gets hurt in the process.

It was during this time that one of the worst experiences in my career occurred. I've seen a lot of pain and suffering, but that one sticks with me even today. We had been working a case on a local gang leader who was using college kids to travel to Florida on vacation and haul his drugs back with them, a practice called "muleing." He'd even advertised in the *Minnesota Daily*, the University's paper, for kids who were going south and might want free transportation or a chance to pick up some money. Then he'd have them meet with some unsavory characters in whatever the destination city was and bring back an extra suitcase or two. Unfortunately, in this case, some other bad guys had figured out what he was up to and had robbed the mule before she got out of Miami.

The girl in question was one we'd had our eyes on for a bit. She'd come up in some research as a possible mule based upon her previous trips. She was twenty years old, smart, cute and had her whole life ahead of her. Until this scumbag got his hooks into her.

She had disappeared while on her way back from Florida. Her friends made it back and she should have too. Next we heard, she was in an emergency room in Florida the night of the last day of her trip. Then she dropped off the grid. We got a hit on her credit card when it was used in Dinkytown near the U of M about four days later. Credit card tracking was a pretty new forensic technique back in the eighties, so it often took a day or two before we were notified.

So we knew she'd come back, the signatures matched, but she hadn't shown up at her apartment building just off the U's campus. We knew there was a good chance she'd be found in the hands of the drug trafficker so we put together a raid on his ersatz headquarters in an abandoned downtown warehouse building.

The SWAT team assaulted the front of the building and I went up a back staircase, outrunning the older and somewhat fatter investigator who was with me. When I cleared the fourth floor landing and peeked into a room, I saw the girl tied naked to a chair. A gang member the size of an NFL linebacker was holding a makeshift whip in one hand and had a pistol in the other. I yelled and as he turned toward me, I shot him three times. The gang leader was also there, sitting backward on another chair facing the girl. I yelled at him to freeze and show me his hands. He slowly stood, facing me with his hands out to his sides. "OK, Mr. Cop Man. We through here anyway. You got the guy what did her. I'm a witness; I'll testify. Too late for her though. The bitch be dead."

He had a pistol tucked into his waistband and I looked at it and at him, mentally daring him to make a move. He just smiled and said, "Guess you got me."

I shot him twice in the head and he had his gun in his hand before the other cop got up to the floor. Funny thing, that shooting doesn't keep me up nights at all.

It was soon after that event that I moved into homicide. I spent the next fifteen years there, happy as a sergeant-investigator. I really got into forensics and specialized in the arcane field of ballistics and the effects of gunfire on human bodies. That led to the writing of two books on the subject. The first was on the use of wound data to determine things like the direction and distance a shooter was from the victim, including comparing the effects of different types of ammunition on human bodies. The second got into the topic of blood and other body materials, spatter pattern, and their cause by ballistic impact. Both topics are guaranteed to put you to sleep unless you happen to be the one looking for a killer.

The books put me on the map as a guest "expert," as I mentioned before, which turned out to be a pretty well-paying, though boring, gig. It also led to advising the aforementioned Hollywood types on how to correctly portray the use and effect of gunfire in movies and TV shows. That turned out to be a well-paying and really fun gig.

In my early fifties, after thirty years on the job, I had enough pension, savings, and outside income to become a part-time consultant to the Minneapolis PD. I work the cases I want and stay on their health insurance. It's a mutually beneficial relationship.

Chapter Twenty

We topped the hill at the Proctor, Minnesota, exit just south of Duluth, one of the great views on the North American continent. Granted, that's the opinion of an unapologetic Minnesotan and lover of Lake Superior. I really love it. I never get tired of it.

We drove down the steep winding hill, passing under the elevated rail lines. Upon reaching the edge of the harbor we left the interstate and turned into the new parking ramp for the DECC, the Duluth Exposition and Convention Center.

We made our way into the building, stopped at an entrance table of sorts to pay an admission fee and have our hands stamped, then walked through a set of double doors. As we walked into the show site I took in the room. The dog show was being held in a space that could easily accommodate a business trade show. It was about 500-feet long by 200-feet wide with a 40-foot ceiling supported by painted steel beams. In the center of the room stood the dog show rings, forty-foot squares sur-rounded by white expandable cross-hatched dividers with blue supports, which I knew from past talks with Pete were called "baby gates," and gray rubber mats taped down to the floor. The mats lay in a pattern that went around the perimeter of each ring with one additional mat that ran diagonally from one corner to the opposite.

At one corner of the ring at the end of one of the diagonals was an opening to allow access for dogs and their handlers. Next to the entrance was a pole with a number on it and two small tables, one inside and one outside the gates. Each outside table had a person seated in front of it, apparently doing the paperwork of the dog show. Another person stood near each gate. All of them were wearing aprons sporting the club's name, "Duluth Kennel Club" in flashy embroidered lettering. The rings were numbered 1 through 12 and were grouped in quads so each one had two sides where people could stand and watch. The perimeter of the room was lined with vendor booths.

Spectators were gathered in clusters around the edges of the rings watching the action, such as it was. In about two thirds of the rings a well-dressed person examined dogs. As a neophyte, I had no real understanding what was happening in spite of Pete's orientation lecture on the way up. In one ring, I could see German Shepherds running around the perimeter mats. In another, a judge was examining some small white dog on a table. As I looked on he went over the dog with his hands, checking the dog's teeth, ears, and rear end. Then he stood back a step and looked at the dog's proportions by measuring with hand widths the dog's height and length. I asked Pete about the process.

"The judge needs to physically examine the dogs to check the bone structure, the coat, the teeth, et cetera, to be sure the dog conforms to the standard."

"So why did he grab the dog's back end?"

"Well, these are boy dogs. Dogs have to be intact, as in not neutered. The judge has to determine that his 'equipment' is still there."

"So he feels them up?"

"Yep. Can't have none, can't have one, can't have three, gotta have two."

"And the dogs put up with that?"

"They are trained from the time they are very young to tolerate an examination. You make your vet very happy if you train your dog to show. They get used to being handled and it makes the vet's job a lot easier."

I shook my head. I was looking for someone who didn't mind grabbing dogs by the balls. Who knew?

In another ring, a photographer had set up some flowers and a placard that declared Duluth Kennel Club and the date, along with the photographer's name. He was sliding interchangeable plates into the top. One said "New Champion," another read "Major Win." A third said "Winners Bitch." I guess you get used to it.

At just that moment I was startled by a woman in a club apron standing in the ring closest to us when she loudly announced, "Open bitches, please, open bitches!" She looked like someone's grandmother. Like I said, I guess you get used to it.

Chapter Twenty-one

7:30 a.m.
Friday, July 17th
Maricopa County Sheriff's Office
Phoenix, Arizona

Detective Maria Fernandez sat staring at the computer screen on her desk. She was about to enter the information on the two cases, the one in Mora, Minnesota, and the one from outside Scottsdale, into the FBI's Violent Criminal Apprehension Program, or ViCAP system. She had never done it on her own before and was looking for a little divine guidance. She got it.

In the bowels of the Minneapolis City Hall building, some 1,200 miles to the northeast, a phone rang.

"Research," answered a voice. Maria smiled, knowing she'd gotten a hit on her first try.

"Hi, I'm looking for someone with a good chocolate chip cookie recipe," she said.

There was a just-perceptible pause before the call recipient said, "Maria! Is that you?"

Sharon Rademacher had met Maria when she had become involved in a case Neumann was investigating. Then, Maria became involved with Dan. It was Sharon who stood by Maria when another case turned into the officer-involved shooting last year. Maria was the officer. Theirs was a "sister" relationship.

Before she could answer, Sharon asked, "Where are you? Are you in town? Has that overgrown Boy Scout you're dating left you standing at the airport?"

"No, I'm here in sunny Phoenix. It's only about 110 today, so we're having a sale on hoodies."

Sharon laughed. "Ha! Well, get on a plane, honey, and come up here. It's 83 and beautiful. You could come for the weekend. We could shop till you drop and not even tell the boys."

It was Maria's turn to laugh. "I wish. Listen, Sharon, I need a favor."

"Sure, honey. Anything for you."

"Have you ever done anything with ViCAP?"

"Sure. Wha'cha need? A few pointers?"

"Yeah. I'm going to load in these two cases I'm poking around in with Dan and I've never used the thing before."

"What! Dan's got you working for him now? That guy!" Maria could feel Sharon shaking her head over the phone. "OK. What's he got you doing?"

"He's helping out a friend, a former MPD guy who's the sheriff in a little town called Mora."

"That would be Glenn. Yeah, you could say he's Dan's friend. He saved Dan's bacon once when they both went in on a domestic call. Dan was still pretty new on the force then and Glenn was already a sergeant."

"I hadn't heard about that. What happened?" Maria inquired.

"Typical domestic. He was beating on her, so she called for help. While Dan was talking to the husband, she kept getting more and more worked up. When Dan went to cuff the guy, she flipped out. Had a change of heart and decided she couldn't live without him, so she grabbed a twelve-inch butcher knife off the counter and made a charge at Dan. Glenn was right there, though, and had his nightstick ready. Flipped her arm up with his left hand, neat as could be, and gave her a little love tap right in the belly. Knocked the wind out of her and defused the situation without having to shoot anyone. They both wound up spending the night downtown."

Maria silently shook her head. How many times had she heard a similar story? A domestic is arguably the most dangerous call a cop can get. You never know if they are going to be really trying to kill each other, are just having an argument or, sometimes, just trying to get even about something. All too often, the complaining party will have a change of heart when it looks like the cops are going to take the meal ticket away. Then, anything can happen.

"Thanks, Sharon. I knew they were close, but hadn't heard about that. Sort of explains Dan's interest in this case."

"And what case is that?"

"The sheriff had what looked like a body drop, but turned out to be a local girl. After he got a look at her—the body had been abused—he called Dan. The bad guy had gone over her entire body with a knife, making little cuts along the way. Not enough to kill her, just enough to cause a lot of pain. When your BCA got the post done, the report said there was very little blood in the body.

"Anyway, we got to talking about it and I remembered a case we had a few years back. Similar condition of the body. And, in both cases, the victim was a young blond woman and the body was posed."

Sharon thought for a moment and said, "Yeah, I heard about the Mora case. It got some press down here. In fact, the reporter who broke it is a local newsie Dan used to date, way back when."

"Yeah, I met her, sort of. She showed up at the crime scene while we were there. Dan wasn't happy to see her and tried to keep her away from the scene."

"That sounds like our Danny boy. I'm surprised he didn't tell the camera crew to stand by for the Technicolor yawn."

"Well," Maria paused, wondering if she should tell Sharon. She decided she could. "I saw that coming so I did. She puked her guts up."

"That's my girl! I never did like her. Of course, her being a reporter didn't make that too likely. Never could see what Dan saw in her. Whoops! I guess I shouldn't say that to you."

"Men, right? Can't live with 'em, can't kill 'em. At least he's over her now."

"I'm not too sure about that. Are men ever over it?"

"You think he's not over her?" Maria said. "That's not the way he made it sound."

"I'm not surprised. You know men; it's got to be their idea," Sharon said. "I wouldn't worry about it, baby. You've got him plenty messed up. All he talks about is when he's going to see you again. I'm surprised he hasn't asked you to tie the knot."

"Actually, he did. Last Christmas."

"Really!" said Sharon, excitedly. "When's the date?"

"Not yet. At least, that's what I told him. I've got some things to finish here before I move to the land of everlasting winter. I hope I haven't scared him off."

"Don't worry about it, honey. Like I said, you're all he talks about. He'll stick around."

"I sure hope so. Getting a little late to start anything with anyone else."

Sharon changed the subject. "So, what's Dick Tracy got you doing, honey," she asked, using one her many nicknames for Neumann.

"I'm going to load both cases into the ViCAP system and request a search run for similar cases. I'm hoping you have done this before and can give me some pointers."

"Sure have and sure can, honey. It's a pretty good system, as long as you understand it. You know what Harry Callahan said, 'A man's got to know his limitations.'"

Maria laughed, getting the *Dirty Harry* connection.

"In this case, the woman has to know the system's limitations. Basically, you want to limit the amount of data points you load in. The system looks for comparable cases. The more details you load in there, the fewer cases will match everything, so you could miss a bunch. On the other hand, if you just ask for unsolved homicides with women as vics and knives as weapons, you're going to get a lot of junk you don't want. You have to kind of pick and choose."

Sharon and Maria started the process of filling in the blanks. Many answers were straightforward—Type of Incident Offense was "Homicide." Status was "Open." So were location, a date bracket, and weapon —"Knife." Maria entered "No" to Gang Related and Domestic. She wasn't absolutely sure about those two, but they seemed like long shots.

She also had good data for the victims: addresses, occupations, age, race, hair, and eye color. All that was simple. She cringed a bit as she entered "White," "Female," and "Blond" for both victims. The witness info was simple; there were none to either case. She had the info on the investigating officers. Finally, she entered offender info—None. They had no suspects.

Maria thanked Sharon for her help. She paused to say a little prayer before sending the information off into federal custody. Her previous interactions with ViCAP had taught her that you never could predict what would happen when you brought something to the attention of the "Beast."

The Beast was what Maria called the vast institutionalized system that is federal law enforcement. Most times you aroused it you would simply get the info you were looking for and that was that. But the Beast had other responses it could demonstrate. It could ignore you. You could send a request for info and hear nothing for weeks, or months, even after repeated requests. It was rare but a real possibility. Then there was the equal and less desirable possibility that you'll attract the interest of the Beast and find yourself crushed by its massive far-reaching arms. Oddly, this was the response Maria was looking for today. So she prayed to awaken the Beast and hit "Send."

ViCAP, which she had just queried, was a product of the Utopian dream of a paperless office. Its first version, the Automated Case System, was developed in the early '90s as a way for FBI field agents to access the massive quantities of paper that their cases generated through a computer system, thus eliminating the need to print everything and carry it with them in the field. It came online just in time to very nearly totally screw up the Oklahoma Bomber investigation. That hurdle passed, it was refined, reworked, and revised into ViCAP, a wonderful way to track and compare cases from different jurisdictions.

One of the side functions of ViCAP is to allow local law enforcement members to enter details of cases they are working and look for similar cases in other areas. Maria had entered the details of the two cases she knew of with a request for information regarding body drops and other murders where the victim was found to have been a white female, between 18 and 40, killed with a knife, possibly tortured and sexually assaulted, and the body found in a remote location. She added the probability that the body had been "cleaned" in an effort to remove possible evidence. She felt that those case features were unusual enough that if there were any matches, they could be related.

But she also knew that there was a balancing act to be danced when it came to the ViCAP.

Now it was up to the feds to get back to her with any cases that matched. She stayed for a moment to make sure the entry went through, then got up to go fill her coffee cup.

Chapter Twenty-two

Friday
The DECC
Duluth, Minnesota

Pete, Glenn, and I walked through the crowded convention center, dodging people dressed from summer casual to business formal. Pete had briefed us on what to wear to fit in, so we all wore comfortable business casual clothes. By that I mean comfortable slacks, a comfortable golf shirt with a comfortable sport coat. All that makes for a comfortable way to cover a holster. Concealing your firearm keeps everyone around you comfortable. I commented on the range of apparel.

"Yeah, you'll see it all at a dog show," Pete said. "Most handlers will be pretty dressed up but now and then you'll see someone in the ring in shorts and a golf shirt. That's usually someone who didn't expect to be in the ring that day. They wind up going in the ring to hold a dog for someone who entered three or four of the same breed and they all did well. All of a sudden they get to the Winners class and they have to take all three in but only have one back-up handler."

As I watched I noticed that, good clothes or not, these people weren't very worried about other aspects of grooming. Those showing little dogs would get right down on the floor, kneeling next to them when they "stacked," them, another word I'd picked up from Pete that meant to place the dog in its best looking pose. They would pull what looked like greasy chunks of meat from their pockets to offer to the dogs and were constantly fluffing the longhaired dogs' luxurious coats. I did notice an occasional double use of a comb or brush. The handler would finish off Fido's hair with a flourish then run the same comb through their own hair before returning it to a pocket. That gave me a shiver. Glenn commented on the kneeling.

"Man, you don't have to worry about me getting into this. My old knees could never take it," he said.

"Yeah, you should see it at outdoor shows," Pete said. "It could be raining, the ground all muddy, and these folks still get right down there. Pretty tough on the cleaning bill."

I shook my head at the concept. Actually, I thought some of the suits and dresses looked as though they hadn't seen a dry cleaner since they were purchased some years ago. Oh well.

We moved away from the show rings and toward the vendor booths. Pete said he had some people he wanted to say hi to and needed to do a little shopping. The booths ranged from very sophisticated trade show setups to a table with a sheet over it. I asked Pete about that.

"It doesn't cost too much to have a booth at a dog show, maybe one or two hundred bucks. So folks with craft businesses get right in here with the big corporations that make dog food, and national chains of stores."

"Interesting products," I said, as we passed a booth that had a bin of what looked like mummified pig ears out front. I picked one up and twirled it around.

Pete said, "That's not even close to the edge of the weird scale for products."

"Yeah," I said. "What else is here?"

"This is a big enough show to attract some of the more unusual vendors." He looked around the room and pointed. "There's a booth where the guy sells treats he makes from otherwise unwanted parts of various animals, like chew sticks made from cow esophaguses." Pete pointed out three more booths that sold products ranging from stuffed dog beds to an artist who would memorialize your pet in oils. His portraits were first class. He had several on display and they were beautiful. Another guy had an oversized booth that looked like a variety store for pet products—everything for grooming, storing, and dressing your dog. One of the busiest booths sold clothing screen printed or embroidered with dog images.

We walked out of the main arena and into a large tunnel that led to another part of the building. One side of the tunnel was lined with stacked crates for dogs and lightweight chairs and small tables where dogs were being prepared for their turn in the ring. There was a lot of noise from hair blowers and a lot of flying hair.

More booths selling all sorts of dog-related material lined the other side of the tunnel. There was a constant flow of traffic through the man-made cave going to and from the rings. Most were not walking dogs, but were pulling low carts stacked with dog crates topped by grooming tables. Sort of mobile grooming/dog storage units, all strapped together with bungee cords.

We exited the tunnel into another part of the DECC that looked like it was probably an ice rink during the winter season. The floor was the right size and, above a ten-foot wall, stadium seating ran up to the rafters. It was a familiar sight for a Minnesota native. Such multipurpose buildings exist all over the state. Even the Target Center in Minneapolis and RiverCentre in St. Paul, where the Timberwolves and Wild play, can be switched from basketball to hockey and vice versa in a matter of hours. They just lay the boards right over the ice. The floor in this room was concrete. No hockey tonight.

The room was set up similarly to the one we'd left except the rings had wall-to-wall rubber matting. The numbering system continued with rings 13 through 16. The four rings were arranged two to a side backing up to the aforementioned wall below the seats with a center aisle separating them. Exhibitors and their supporting staff, read: friends and family, had set up their dog crates and chairs in the open areas at either end of the room. Two of the rings had jumps in them. That was different and I asked Pete about it.

"This is the Obedience Trial part of the show," he replied. "These people are competing in different classes that showcase what the dog can do, as opposed to what it looks like."

I watched a dog and handler in one ring walking along as if out for a summer stroll, except the dog wasn't on a leash. He was walking in perfect position alongside the handler. As the dog moved it kept its head up, looking into the handler's face, never taking his eyes off her. In response to the judge's commands the handler turned left and right, went faster and slower. When she stopped the dog sat at her side. Then, two other people came into the ring and stood facing each other. The dog and handler started walking around them in a figure-eight pattern.

All the while the dog never took his eyes off the handler. I was fascinated. It was a keen display of teamwork.

"That is amazing, the way the dog just keeps looking at her!" I said.

"We hit the timing just right. I know that handler. She has had top dogs for years. This one was the number-one Obedience show dog in the country a few years ago. Quite a team."

While we talked, the dog and handler team moved on to other exercises. The handler left the dog sitting on one side of the ring, walked across the ring and, on a signal from the judge, called the dog. The dog came and suddenly, on only a hand signal from the handler, dropped like he had been shot. The judge gave another signal to the handler and she called the dog again, whereupon he jumped to his feet and continued his interrupted run across the ring, coming to a halt sitting right in front of the handler. I was amazed.

Pete continued. "That's a good skill to have. Let's say your dog has gone across the street to say hi to his buddy, the neighbor's cat. Now, you are a good dog owner and you've taught him to come when he's called. So you call him. Fido says bye to his friend and comes running across the street. All of a sudden, you see a car coming down the street and it and your dog are both going to be in the middle of the street at the same time. You can't stop the car, but you can stop your dog. I've actually had to use this with Sinbad on a couple of occasions."

"So, this is what you were doing at the dog shows with him?"

"This and the stuff in the first room. Sinbad is a rare dog, a double champion, Breed and Obedience. Of course, the Breed championship only took about six months. The Obedience Trial Championship, what we call an OTCH, took four years."

I nodded in wonderment.

Pete said, "There's the guy I'm looking for," and gave a head nod toward a tall man wearing tan slacks and a red golf shirt. The man was talking with a couple other guys while watching a dog in one of the rings.

"Come on, I'll introduce you."

Chapter Twenty-three

Friday, July 17th
FBI Headquarters, Washington D.C.

Annabelle Schulz sat at her desk enjoying a late morning yogurt break. It had been a quiet day for the young data analyst. Usually Fridays were quiet days, compared with Mondays, when the weekend's criminal problems seemed to land in her lap. Annabelle's job title was Field Information Support and Processing, which was a fancy way of saying that she sat in front of a computer and did her best to make sure it was doing its job. The job was data analysis—comparing information from newly solved and unsolved cases to information from old unsolved cases. The goal was to tie cases together by the similarities in data. It was one of the byproducts of the ViCAP system.

The system, initially conceived to cut down on paper, actually generated more by kicking out reports, some requiring reams of paper, comparing cases. In most cases, the compared similarities were simply coincidence, but some long-cold cases had been cracked with help from the whiz-bang computer. It could look for the smallest, seemingly insignificant details, and tie them to cases from years earlier in far distant locales.

But like all computer systems, amazing as it was, it needed human tending. Data had to be formatted in a standard manner to find those elusive similarities. People in law enforcement were still people and they used different terms and slang depending upon where they lived. A case from Texas, where a killer had used a knife as the murder weapon, needed to say "knife," not "switchblade" or "pig sticker," as some investigators were known to write.

Computers still don't have intuition so data has to be clearly spelled out. As with any search engine, the more specific the request, like the use of the term pig sticker, the more specific the answer. A request for all murders committed with a pig sticker would yield only those where the investigating officer used the words "pig sticker." And while there are a fair share of murders in Arkansas and Texas, this particular nomenclature might cause the computer to miss a similar murder in a locale where they used the word "knife."

Annabelle's job was to check all incoming search requests and alter them to fit the system's terminology. She had just finished her yogurt when a request flashed across her screen.

It was from the Maricopa County Sheriff's Office in Phoenix. Annabelle was familiar with that particular branch of law enforcement and was quick to open the file. Like most career FBI employees, she felt that the current administration's efforts to use her agency to attack the Maricopa county sheriff were misguided. While she adhered to the typical FBI belief that they could do it better, she was aware of the good work being done in Arizona against a tide of illegal immigration, drug smuggling, kidnappings, and murders. The ongoing jurisdictional battle over who got to do what was more than a little wasteful of resources in her eyes.

Annabelle looked over the case information. It covered an unsolved murder from March three years earlier. A body had been found in a roadside ditch in a rural area. The request included the victim's identity, cause of death, and other condition information. Also noted was a recent body found in Minnesota that showed similar traits. One unusual feature struck Annabelle—both bodies were nearly bloodless.

She had been waiting for a "vampire" killer since the new vampire books had become popular. Maybe this was it. She also noted that both bodies had been cleaned to remove any trace evidence. The only things found on both bodies were some animal hairs, which were probably deposited on the bodies by roaming critters .

She changed a few words, then sent it into the system. "This could be interesting," she said to the computer, wondering if her vampire theory was about to be proven true.

Chapter Twenty-four

The DECC, Friday
Duluth, Minnesota

As we walked toward the guy Pete had pointed out, he saw Pete, and a broad grin spread across his face.

"Pete Anderson! How the hell are you, buddy? What drags you out here? You finally get that new dog?"

"Dan, this is Phil Horvath, a dog-show rat if there ever was one. Phil, Dan Neumann, one of my oldest friends. We grew up together."

We shook hands. Pete introduced Glenn.

"And this is Glenn Mills, an old friend of Dan's."

Phil shook Glenn's outstretched mitt. The big man's hand swallowed up Horvath's.

"Good to meet you Dan, Glenn," he said with a nod to each of us. "What brings you and this has-been out to the show? You have a dog you're getting ready to run?" he asked Pete.

Pete said, "Dan is a Minneapolis homicide investigator and Glenn is the Kanabec County sheriff. They're working a case that might have a dog show connection. We came up to show them what a dog show looks like."

"Really? That's fascinating. Why do you think it has something to do with dog shows?"

My turn to speak. "A body was found about four days after a show in Cambridge. The only thing we have going is the timing and some dog hair that was found on the body."

"Yeah, that would tip it off, wouldn't it? You may have noticed we have plenty of dog hair here." Phil paused for a second. "Cambridge, that would have been around the end of June, right?"

"Correct," I said.

"Where was it, the body?"

"It was found in a ditch just outside Mora."

"Yeah, I saw something on TV about that. That's not too far north of Cambridge. So what is it you want to do today?"

Pete answered. "I'm trying to give these two a feel of what a show looks like and who is involved. Judges, owners, handlers, etc., anyone who would have been at the Cambridge show."

"But if you have only one body with a little hair, well, that could have come from anywhere. That's pretty thin for a connection"

"We're still doing background, but there may be a connection to another body drop. That one was in Arizona in March of '06."

"That would be the WestWorld show—big show, that one. I judged it a few years ago. They get lots of folks in from the West Coast."

"You know the shows by the dates?" I asked.

"Serious show people know their local shows by the weekend of the year. I'm an Obedience judge besides showing quite a bit, so I know the local shows and most of the big national shows. Of course, all the big-time pro handlers know the national schedule. You think it might be a serial killer?"

That was a bit of a jump. "Why do you say that?"

"Hey, I'm a big fan of crime shows and murder mysteries. If you have two crimes with the same M.O. that far apart, by date and location, you've got to be thinking serial killer. Have you tried the FBI's case-matching system?"

This was a little more help than I'd expected. Actually, one of the traits of many serial killers is that they insert themselves into the investigation. They are cop wannabes. The Atlanta Child Killer was one of them. He followed the cops around on the pretext that he was a photographer trying to cover the story. I eyed Horvath up and down.

Pete seemed to pick up my vibe. He nudged my arm and subtly shook his head. Apparently he had already ruled out this guy. I'd have to ask him about it later.

"So, personalities. What kind of people do this?" I asked, gesturing at the other people in the room.

"All kinds of folks. But I'll admit we do seem to have more than our share of unusual personalities. After all, what kind of person likes to get up at the crack of dawn, spend a couple of hours grooming a dog or two, then go into a ring where, in the span of two or three minutes, someone decides whether your dog does or does not have what it takes to be a winner? That's one of the reasons I like Obedience better than Breed."

"What's the difference?"

"You understand the basics, right? Has Pete filled you in on how championships are won?"

I nodded yes, remembering our phone conversations.

"All right. Look at it this way. All the breeds have a breed standard. But that standard is subject to interpretation. Some judges are looking at gait, or the way the dogs move, others look at the head and coat, still others at the structure. The breed handlers learn very quickly which judges are looking for what and they either groom to that judge's tendencies or just don't bother showing to the ones they know they can't win under."

We nodded in unison.

"The small fries have always believed that there has been some degree of favoritism. Since the judging is subjective, two dogs that are close in attributes could be considered relatively equal. Then it's up to the judge to pick one. Some judges have favorite colors in breeds that have more than just one color. Some like a certain size or gait. And, of course, some like certain people. Back when I started it was explained to me like this: a judge is looking over the batch of dogs in the ring for Best of Breed competition. There are three really good dogs out of about twelve or thirteen in the ring. Of the three, two are being handled by local owner-handlers, the other by a professional handler well known to the judge. Actually, that can be an advantage or a disadvantage, but most pro handlers know who doesn't like them and they would send that dog in with someone who won't offend the judge.

"But, let's say the judge knows and likes the handler. That judge also knows that handler has brought a bunch of dogs into the ring that weekend to show to that judge. Judges are generally paid by the dog, around two or three bucks a dog. So, if the handler is responsible for providing fifty or a hundred bucks in judging fees to the judge that weekend and the owner-handler represents only three bucks, it's just human nature to favor the person who provides more income. Subconsciously, that judge knows that a victory will keep that handler bringing dogs into their ring. It's not deliberate, although there have been notoriously famous cases where there were payoffs. It's no different than any other kind of competition."

Pete had never explained it quite that way. I asked, "So, that doesn't take place in Obedience?"

"I didn't say that. It's just more objective. If a dog makes a mistake in the ring, everyone in the room knows it. Here's a great example. Years ago, there was a dog in Obedience that was amazing, won the national points championship eight years out of nine that he was competing. The one year he didn't win was when the owner's husband died so she was a bit distracted. Anyway, she was showing the dog one time in the utility ring. We have an exercise called the 'directed retrieve.' The handler pivots to face one of three gloves, then sends the dog to retrieve it. The dog's job is to stay in heel position on the pivot, sit again when facing the glove, then wait until sent to the glove. Then he retrieves it and returns to his handler. In this case, the judge told the handler which glove to get, the handler pivoted but the dog didn't sit after the pivot. It's not a disqualifying mistake, but a three-point deduction at least. Well, the judge was distracted by something happening in the next ring, so he missed the no sit. He awarded the handler a perfect score of two hundred points and, of course, she also won High In Trial that day. Perfect scores are very rare. I've only seen a few in all my years of showing. The point is, we judges make mistakes and the wrong dog sometimes wins. It makes the non-winners unhappy, but we're only human."

"Ok, judges make mistakes and there can be shenanigans. But you still prefer Obedience?"

"Yes. At least it's more objective if not perfect. In Obedience, it doesn't matter what the dog looks like. Of course, the dog should still be clean and well kempt, but it's what they *do* that day in the ring that matters, not previous performances or breed standard. And every experienced handler in the room can see each dog's performance, too, so the judging has to be much more objective. Of course, the perspective is different outside the ring than in, but if you've seen a lot of runs you know what to look for. Experienced obedience handlers can pretty much predict what the scores will be."

We nodded along with the commentary.

"The best example is this: dogs are dogs. They have a tendency to do things when we don't want them to, especially if we have had them on a grooming table for two hours. Sometimes, they shit the ring. It's happened to anyone who has been doing this longer than a few shows. In Breed, if your dog poops in the ring, they have a steward clean it up. You keep showing; you might even win. In Obedience, you shit the ring and you're done for that day. It's behavior, not appearance."

Pete chuckled.

"Happen to you?" I asked.

"Like he said, it happens to everybody."

"They even changed the rules some years back to cover something Pete did." Phil said. "There is a rule we call the Pete Anderson Rule."

"What happened?"

"Pete was showing his first Flat Coat." Phil turned and looked at Pete. "What was his name?"

"Casey," Pete said.

"Yeah, Casey. Great dog. Anyway, Pete was partway through a great run when he saw that Casey was about to crap. So he asked the judge if he could take him out so he wouldn't foul the ring. It was very good etiquette by Pete, because crapping in the ring leaves all kinds of interesting smells for later dogs. The judge said OK and Pete picked up Casey and ran him out where he dropped a huge loaf. Then he came back to the ring and finished his great run. He won High In Trial that day."

Pete picked up the story from there.

"Naturally, some of the other exhibitors were a little ticked off. But the rule at the time only said that a dog that had fouled the ring couldn't be awarded a qualifying score. So when the next Obedience Advisory Committee met, the handlers petitioned the committee to rewrite the rule. Now it says that a 'dog that has fouled the ring, or was allowed to leave the ring to keep from fouling it, cannot receive a qualifying score.'"

"And the rest of us named it the Pete Anderson Rule." Phil said.

"That's how you know you have been around too long—when you have a rule named after you," Pete added.

Pete and Phil laughed at that.

Phil said, "Back to today. What exactly are you hoping to learn?"

I switched gears. "You mentioned serial killer before? How did you come to that conclusion?"

"I read a lot and have a curious nature. Plus, I remember just about everything I read. I like cop shows on TV, not the glitzy *CSI* or *Criminal Minds* stuff, but *The First 48*, real investigation kind of stuff. And I've read John Douglas's book, *Mind Hunter*. He's one of the FBI guys who developed the whole field of profiling. I'm fascinated by the whole psychotic killer thing, people who move right in and live among us, yet they have no sense of responsibility or remorse for their actions. They can do things without any feelings of empathy for their victims. Kind of like the movie *Silence of the Lambs*. The FBI guy in that movie was patterned after Douglas. He's a genius."

I had to agree. I'd heard of Douglas. He had a documented history of coming up with eerily accurate profiles of many serial killers. He did it, he said in his writings, by putting himself in their shoes, thinking the way they did. It was not without cost to him. He nearly worked himself to death and it did destroy his marriage.

"So you're a psycho-killer junkie?" I asked.

"I guess you could say that. Also, I'm a psychologist."

"What kind?"

"The run of-the-mill family counseling kind. But I'm fascinated by that kind of behavior."

I thought about his profession and made a decision to give him more information than I would normally hand over to someone not in my line of work. Or, maybe he was.

"OK, look around this room. We are looking for someone who may have abducted, tortured, and killed at least two young women. Both were in their mid-twenties, blond, attractive, about five-and-a-half feet tall. The victims were not killed immediately. We believe they were kept alive for some time before death. During that time they were sexually assaulted, physically abused and, finally, killed. The killer inflicted many small knife wounds that caused a lot of bleeding and certainly a lot of pain, then he finally killed them with one deep stabbing knife wound to the heart. Weapon was most likely a long thin-bladed double-sided knife or dagger. The bodies were then washed, we believe, to remove forensic evidence, and each was dumped in a remote location."

As I went through this litany of atrocities, I watched Horvath's face. He paled as I described the cause of death. His eyes went around the room as if seeking the person responsible. I could see he wasn't our boy.

Horvath took a deep breath. "Who could do that?" he asked rhetorically. He shook his head. "That's the problem. According to the literature, that type of person could be right here among us with little sign that he's the one. The best ones lived more or less normal lives and weren't discovered until their killing drive accelerated to a point where they were killing frequently. The history says that there is a time period between these events that shortens as the subject gains experience and confidence. Their *need* for it, as it were, begins to grow like a drug addiction, and the fact that they've gotten away with it for some time makes them think they'll never be caught. But, in the meantime, they could be standing right next to you and you'd never know. That's one of the reasons they are so dangerous. The Green River Killer was killing prostitutes, so the police made that fact known through the news. Prostitutes tend to be very good at reading people. They have to have that skill to stay alive. But this guy was so normal that girls kept getting into his car with him."

"So you think it could be anyone here?"

"Well, no. There is a very tight demographic. Heterosexual white males constitute the vast majority of killers in these cases. More than half of the people showing dogs are women. And dog shows attract a lot of people who can't or don't wish to have children. So we have a lot of people of "alternative lifestyle" you could say."

"Gays," I said.

"That's right. A higher than statistically typical number of the men and women involved in dog shows are gay. As well as straight couples who, for whatever reason, have no kids. As I said, people who can't have children, don't want children, or their kids have grown and moved out. My theory is that, like any other couple, they have a need to nurture, and owning and showing dogs takes the place of soccer, ballet, hockey, music lessons, and everything else other parents get to do with their kids."

"Got it." I said. Phil was confirming what Pete had told me. I looked around the room, observing the people. "That would eliminate a lot of people. Any other ideas?"

"Yes. When you put your case list together, you'll have a timeline. Look for a repeating period that shortens over time. Something like a first case, then, maybe six or eight years later a second, then only four years to the third, two years to the fourth, on and on until you get to one a month. Most serial killers show that tendency—they get more confident and hungrier for the experience over time. And, if he's connected with dog shows, there are records going back for years on when and where they occurred. For many people, dog shows are very stressful and that could act as a trigger to this behavior. Look for a pattern of bodies found just after dog shows. Then you can match the show up with the body."

"Always after?" Pete asked.

"Probably. Most of these people don't believe they'll be caught but they are proactive in their efforts to get away with it. If you've got one or two recent events that show the person killed after a dog show, then got the hell out of Dodge, that will be his M.O. He'll feel comfortable with it and it will be his pattern. They become very pattern-trained when the method is working for them. Historically, they only change their method when they feel police pressure and fear capture."

"Actually, we are pursuing the list thing. Any other ideas?"

"Yes, and this could be very helpful. Dog shows have paperwork. They have premium lists and judging programs and entry lists called catalogs. They contain the names of all the judges, exhibitors, registered handlers—people who would have been at that show. It will be a lot of work, but if you find the same person has been at all the shows in question, you'll have a good suspect."

I said, "All investigations are a lot of work. It's usually long hours of digging through seemingly unrelated data to find that needle in the haystack. But that judging list-catalog thing. We didn't have that before. Where can we get that?"

Phil and Pete looked at each other. "Raleigh," they said in unison.

I looked at Pete. "Raleigh?"

"Yup. That's the headquarters of the American Kennel Club. They'll have everything you need."

That was something we didn't have before—a place to start.

Chapter Twenty-five

The computer kicked out a report that included cases going back thirty years, well beyond the age of the system itself. A total of ninety-seven cases had matched enough of the data to make the first cut. Annabelle started looking them over to kick out obvious mismatches. The cases wouldn't be removed from the list, just sidelined so the investigating officer, Detective Maria Fernandez, could start with a smaller pool. This was standard procedure. Most serial killers are only tried on a few of the crimes they actually commit. Many of the set-aside cases are cleared up in the sentencing phase after the miscreant has been convicted and he's trying to avoid the needle.

She got the number of possibles down to twenty-six that looked pretty good. Then she packaged the whole file and emailed it back to Fernandez. All in all, a pretty good day's work.

MCSO
Phoenix, Arizona

Maria had just returned from a late lunch when the FBI file came in. She was anxious to see if ViCAP had uncovered any cases that might be related, but Murphy's law being what it is, as soon as the print was complete and Maria was sitting down to start the examination, she got a call from her boss. A patrol unit had been sent to a "shots fired" call. Two victims were down and dead on a street corner in one of the tougher areas the MCSO was responsible for. She wrote down the info, stood, and tucked her paddle-holstered .45 into her waistband, put on her MCSO jacket, and headed for the door. The timeline would have to wait.

Chapter Twenty-six

The DECC
Duluth, Minnesota

We strolled through the dog show with Phil as our guide. It seemed everyone in the building knew the guy. I also noticed that the crowd sort of parted as we walked along. I pointed this out to my companions.

"We do sort of stand out," Phil said. "Like I mentioned before, ours is primarily a female sport. We don't get a lot of spectators and we don't get a lot of men. I'm known to these people and Pete probably looks familiar to some of them. You two are strangers. So they are asking themselves, 'Who are the new guys?' Like a lot of activities, we tend to be a little standoffish to new people until we know who you are."

"How's that?" I asked. "Why should who I am matter?"

"Are you a judge from somewhere they haven't shown; are you someone new to the game; or are you an out-of-town lead swinger who's here to take all the points? They'll be watching to see if you stop to talk with any of the judges or professional handlers as you walk along. That might indicate that you are either a judge or high-end handler they just don't know. It might be fun to do that just to see reactions."

I could tell Phil was a bit of a gamer himself, wanting to do things just to stir up people. Of course, he was a professional observer of behavior, so maybe that was how he got his kicks. That gave me an idea.

I handed him the file I had been carrying. It contained photos of our victim. I said, "Take a look at these and tell me who could do this."

Phil stopped with his back to the wall so he didn't have to worry about someone looking over his shoulder to see what he was looking at.

He winced as he looked at the photos. He took it better than most civilians would, lingering over the general scene shots that showed the posed body and skipping quickly over the close-ups. As he looked, I added a few details about the other evidence we had—the ligature marks on the wrists and ankles, the lack of blood in the body, the sexual assault, the cleaning of the body, and the final fatal knife wound. These were details not visible in the photos. He asked a few quick questions about the victim's bio and what Glenn had done, then closed the file.

"Any candidates?" I asked.

"Oh, I wouldn't want to speculate. As I mentioned, they can live right next to you and you would have no idea."

"I'm asking you as a trained observer. You size up people for a living. Think about it. Do any of the people here fit the profile?"

Phil looked thoughtful as he gazed around the crowd. We walked on and he kept to himself. Finally he spoke.

"Why don't we sit down when we've finished our tour and I'll give you a few thoughts."

We walked on. I noticed things I hadn't seen my first time through. While most of the spectators' attention was focused in the rings, other things were happening. At one ring the judge was posing for a photo with what I presumed was the last winner. The judge was holding a ribbon and the handler was positioning the dog, which I thought I recognized as Springer Spaniel. Both the judge and handler were looking at the dog with an expression that said they expected the dog to shit gold bars at any second.

Outside the next ring, a person in a stewarding apron was lining up teams of handlers and dogs, apparently the next batch to be judged. Some of the people were ready while others were not, fussing over their clothes and the numbers they wore on their arms. Some appeared to have posses of other people helping them with brushes, squirt bottles, treats, and the armbands while other handlers were on their own—one-person operations. Just across the aisle from the ring were the grooming areas where all kinds of activities were happening. Some people were preparing dogs, as you'd expect, but others were sitting and reading a newspaper or a book. Kids were playing games on laptops, and groups of women were chatting. Some were even eating amidst all the hair and what looked like talcum powder flying around.

We made our way through what I learned was the crating area, a mishmash of dog crates, folding chairs, grooming tables, and carts carrying all the accouterment required to get a dog ready to show. Lining both sides of the room were vendor booths, with people selling everything dog-related and some things that were not. Dog food, dog treats, dog clothing and booties were displayed on racks. One booth had leashes of every color and size, collars, and harnesses. One woman sat beside a table weaving leather strips into a beautiful three-tone braid. Pete stopped and said, "Hi."

She looked up and smiled. "Pete Anderson. How are you? Been a long time. You showing again?"

Pete answered, "No, just hanging out. Can you whip me up one of my custom specials?"

"Sure, but not today. Can I send it to you?"

Pete pulled out his wallet and handed the woman $40. "Sure. You still have the address?"

"I do, unless you've moved off the lake."

"I'm still there. Thanks a bunch, Kitty."

We walked away and I said, "Two things. First, forty bucks for a dog leash?"

Pete said, "Yeah. That's a little high, I know, but she braids them out of kangaroo leather, with my custom color combination, guarantees them never to break, and knows my measurements."

"Measurements?" Glenn asked.

"Yeah, a perfect lead fits the handler and dog. Kitty knows I prefer a forty-six-inch lead."

"And that's the other thing," I said. "Her name is Kitty?"

Pete and Phil looked at each other and laughed. "Yeah," Pete said, "that's the name she goes by. Nothing phony about it. I think it might really be Kate or Kathy or something, but I've never called her anything but Kitty. She has this little business that she uses to cover her expenses showing horses. I know—horses, not dogs. She also occasionally shows dogs, but horses are her first love. And she's got an understanding husband who does all right."

I started thinking about the booths and the vendors. "So, these people are part of the dog-show scene too?"

Pete caught the connection and stopped walking. We all circled him. "I suppose they should be on your list. What do you think, Phil?"

Phil looked around, pondering the question. I could see the wheels turning in his head. Finally, he said, "Could be, but I don't think so. Vendors tend to be local. Most of these people don't go more than a couple hundred miles from home. But there are some interesting rivalries."

He looked toward a booth selling jewelry. "You see that woman there, with the necklaces and rings?" We nodded. "She had a, shall we say, a confrontation with another jeweler who had shown up at one of *her* shows. It started out with words and wound up with a knockdown drag-out, fist-swinging bitch fight."

I was amazed, and shook my head. "What was it? Some guy doing both of them?"

Phil answered, "Oh, no, nothing that complicated. It was money, pure and simple."

This time Glenn was shaking his head. "Money?"

"She thought the other person was cutting into her income."

"Can someone make that much money selling doggie necklaces?" I asked.

"Oh, yes. Some of these booths will pull in four or five thousand a weekend, net. Some of the higher-ticket stuff can bring seven, eight, or more. You work thirty weekends a year and that's a solid six-figure income."

"A hundred grand plus, in sales of doggie stuff?" I said.

"Could be two hundred grand, or more, after expenses, clear, bottom-line income," Phil said.

"But you just said most of these people don't go far from home. Are there that many shows nearby?"

"Well, you'll have to travel a little. But you can pick and choose which shows to go to. The biggest ones are the ones you'd want. They have the most spectators and, more importantly, the most exhibitors."

"Exhibitors are more important than spectators?" I asked.

"Yes. They know what they want and pay for it. The public wants a cheap souvenir for Fluffy, but a top handler will pay forty bucks for a custom lead instead of eight bucks for a store lead."

I'd just seen that.

One of the booths held a business that proclaimed itself "Greg's Scissors and More." Pete stopped there.

"I always have this guy sharpen my pocketknife when I'm at a show. This will only take a second," he said.

"Hey, Greg!"

The apparent owner of the booth was standing in the back of the booth next to a grooming table with a small poodle on it. He came over and greeted us.

"Hey, Pete! Where've you been? Haven't seen you in four or five years."

"Yeah, Sinbad retired and is enjoying couch life. I haven't been able to bring myself to get a replacement. I know if I'm going to, it'll have to be this year or next."

Pete introduced Glenn and me. We went through the hand-shaking ritual. Weber had the firm handshake of a man who worked with his hands, but he didn't really look at me. I've learned over the years to gauge people by their handshake. This was sort of an "I'm here, but I'm not challenging you" handshake. Didn't mean anything, one way or another. I gave my usual "How ya doin." Pete handed over his pocketknife for a touch-up. Greg went over to a small grinding wheel and started the work.

Glenn excused himself for a quick visit to a nearby restroom. I turned to Phil and moved to the next topic.

"So what do we do when we catch him? And how do we do that?"

"Put yourself in his shoes. You have to think like him, see the world through his eyes. You have to start prowling possible targets so you can get ahead of him and be ready for him before he strikes again. But I'll warn you: it can really screw up your mind. Some of the FBI's best profilers have only been able to do it for a short while, two or three years. Then they go back to regular duty, hopefully with their heads and families intact. That's not always the case."

Glenn returned and the knife sharpener came back and handed over Pete's knife. "On the house for an old customer like you." He looked at me and asked Pete, "So, couple of new guys to the game?"

Pete chuckled and said, "No. Glenn is sheriff of Kanabec County, and Dan is a famous Minneapolis homicide detective and writer of boring books on what bullets do to people." Pete knew I hated it when I was introduced as a cop, which is why he always did it. It never fails to change the way people look at you. Weber's eyes grew wide and he tilted his head. Like I said, never fails.

"Really! What are you guys doing here? Someone get ticked off and take out a judge?" he asked with a sparkle in his eyes.

"No," Pete said, "Nothing that exciting. How's the show going?"

"Doing great. Good show. Lots of handlers and civilians. Business is brisk."

"You can make a living sharpening knives at dog shows?" I asked.

Both Greg and Pete chuckled. "Sharpening covers lunch. Making a living is in the sales of new equipment." He looked at Pete and hesitated, as if he was letting the cat out of the bag.

Pete let him off the hook. "Go ahead, Greg. I know enough about manufacturing and marketing to know what your margins are."

"Hey, my margins are no different than any other retailer."

Pete put his hands up in surrender. "I know, I know. I'm still just a little shocked when I need new scissors."

"I have professional quality stuff," Greg said. "You do better with me than going to a beauty supply outfit." He looked at me and asked, "How about you? Need anything sharpened?"

In fact, I always carry a knife of some sort. Today, I was carrying a very sophisticated spring knife that was razor sharp. But I would never let some guy I just met do anything to its carbide ceramic blade. I said, "No." Glenn passed too.

"Well, next time you come to a show, bring something. You'll get the Pete Anderson special rate."

Pete thanked him and said, "Tell you what. When I get that new dog, I'll replace my old grooming equipment. That ought to make your weekend."

"Sure would," Greg said. "Do it soon!"

"What's with the dog?" I asked, pointing at the pooch on the table.

"Well, most shows I have a lot of stand-around time. So I do some grooming on the side."

"Greg's an excellent groomer. He used to show dogs before he got into the equipment business," Pete said.

"Some of the pro handlers bring more dogs than they can get ready," Greg said, "so they'll drop one or two off with me because they know I can do as good a job, if not better, getting them ready than they can. Helps fill in the time and adds a little money."

Pete nodded agreement and we waved our way away and headed down the aisle.

We walked, looking at the booths as we passed. One contained an artist who was finishing an oil painting of the Boxer standing on a table in front of him while its handler teased it with something so stinky I could smell it ten feet away. The dog was fixated, totally mesmerized by the possibility of getting some of the odorous stuff. He was magnificent. The painting was very good too.

The artist watched us watching him. He didn't stop, didn't make conversation, just watched out of the corner of his eye, as we commented on the quality. Not a real friendly sort. I felt the hair on the back of my neck go up.

Over the years a cop learns to pay attention to certain things—weather, your partner's mood, the moon cycle—it's true that more crazy stuff happens during full moons—and the hair on the back of your neck. It's right up there with what I call "the ping." The ping is something that clicks in your head when you come across something important to a case. You often don't realize what it is at the time, but the ping is there. If you're paying attention, you file it away for analysis later. I had both neck hair and ping with this guy. Something about him hit my red button.

We walked away and, when out of earshot, I asked about him.

"He's been around forever," Pete said.

Phil added, "Yeah, Conner Fulbright. Pretty famous animal artist. Gets a fortune for those paintings."

"What's got you interested?" Pete asked. He knows me well enough to know that I wouldn't have asked without a reason.

"Not sure, just something about him doesn't seem right. Do you know if he has any criminal history besides parking tickets and overcharging his clients?"

Neither of my dog show experts knew much else about Fulbright other than he'd been a fixture at shows for over thirty years and that they'd never seen him with anyone they'd call a friend or partner. No known wife, kids, or lovers. A loner as far as the shows were concerned. Not social but not necessarily antisocial. Hmmmm.

We walked away toward a coffee stand.

"That scissors guy. How would buying new scissors make his weekend?" Glenn asked.

"The good stuff is the same quality as those used in hair salons. A good pair of scissors will run $200 or more. If I replace my whole kit, four or five scissors, a couple brushes and combs, some other stuff, we're talking a couple grand."

"You're kidding me!" I said.

Pete shook his head. He could afford it, I knew. He'd become a very wealthy man recently and had replaced a lot of things in his life—he'd bought a new boat and a couple of new cars. He'd added an addition to and remodeled his house. He kept the same wife and son. And me, I guess.

At the coffee stand I ordered my usual black for Glenn and me, while Pete and Phil both got designer lattés. I'm still just Minnesotan enough to have a hard time paying four or five bucks for what amounts to hot milk with a few shots of really strong coffee in it. On the other hand, I have had Cuban coffee in Miami. The stuff comes in those little demi cups and is laced with so much sugar it is nearly syrup. They serve the brew for afternoon breaks to keep you going the rest of the day and, boy, does it do that. Tastes pretty good too.

We found a small table to sit at while we drank our coffee. I kept looking over the crowd, wondering who might be our target. Phil started a running monologue about the serial killers.

"According to the literature, you're looking for a white male, twenty-five to fifty, who has an otherwise normal life. In fact, some of the professional handlers might be good to look at because they sometimes take young people along as apprentices."

Having youngsters in close proximity to this kind of monster gave me a chill.

"Why is that significant?" I asked. "I would think that having possible targets around would be dangerous."

"Not until the very end stage of the game. Remember John Wayne Gacy? He worked a second job as a clown and did kids' parties. And the BTK Killer in Kansas was a Scout leader. In fact, his own kid became an Eagle Scout."

"So, what's the significance?"

"The significance is pattern. Some serial killers keep vulnerable possible targets in close proximity. That doesn't mean that those individuals are in jeopardy, it's just a pattern. And patterns are what you should look for. If you find that your last probable killings took place less than six months apart, or there are a total of seven or more killing events, you are nearing a point where anyone could be in danger. He's gotten away with it long enough to believe that he'll never be caught. And, he will have been improving, getting better at it. That also makes these cases hard to solve.

"Some of the earlier incidents may not match the current M.O. He will have been refining his methodology and improving his technique. All he wants is to get whatever his personal satisfaction is from the event. Unfortunately, the need for this fulfillment is like an addiction. It has to be fed in an increasingly frequent manner. If the killer is operating in a single area, the cases are on the local PD's radar from the beginning. But you mentioned Mora and Phoenix. If your guy is a traveler, if he's doing his handiwork in different areas, even different states, a single case will probably have been written off as a one-time thing. It will still be unsolved, but it will be cold. Only when the frequency is ramped up are the dots connected and the cases linked. That's how cases come to the attention of law enforcement when they are scattered around the country. Someone starts linking cases based on the M.O."

"How about the victims? Any guidance in that?" I asked.

"Organized serial killers will tend to pick a type, disorganized won't; they'll just take whoever they can. Do your victims have any similarities?"

"So far, with the two we know about, both are young and blond. Kind of like that girl over there," I said, pointing to a high-top table in the concessions area. There was a good looking young woman, maybe thirty, blond and fit, flirting with a young good-looking man over a cup of coffee. "You know that guy?" I asked.

Pete said, "Isn't that Hunter?"

Phil answered, "Sure is. Hunter Nelson. Pro handler. Still likes them young. In his forties and still gets the young girls. I don't know how he manages his looks. Must eat right and workout a lot."

I looked at Pete. "Do you know everybody here?"

"Not everyone. But Hunter's been around for a while."

I shook it off and said, "So if we can find a series that look like the victims were taken and killed right after one of these big dog shows, that would point to one of the people involved, maybe even someone here right now?"

"Yes. In fact, some serial killers start getting sloppy on purpose. They realize they are doing something they shouldn't, but can't help themselves. So they start looking at capture as a way out."

"Should I be worrying about suicide by cop?" I asked, making reference to the practice by some criminals of creating a situation in which a cop has no choice other than killing the guy.

"No. Most of these guys go down quietly. You can expect a peaceful surrender and long interview during which the suspect will freely admit doing the crime, maybe even speak with some pride about his technique. He'll scare you with his cold recitation of the details of each and every crime he committed. He's memorized those moments, relived them, and may have video recordings. It will be like no interview you've ever conducted."

"That would be nice. A guy who just says, 'OK, I give up.'"

"That's what most of them do. But, there is the rare bird who thinks the rules just don't apply to him and that he'll never be caught. The Ted Bundy-type. He won't go down quietly and won't give up anything in the interview. Bundy kept trading information of his crimes to push back his execution date."

Later, I'd look back on that conversation and realize that Phil had been right on every point.

Except one.

Chapter Twenty-seven

As the four men sat and discussed their ideas on the case, looking around the room for possible suspects, the crowd was watching them. While some of the women in attendance had sized them up for a variety of reasons, several men had also taken an interest in the group, Dan and Glenn in particular since they were total strangers to those involved in the fancy. And several had correctly made the law enforcement connection.

In any large group of people, you will always find individuals who have a reason to want to avoid any interaction with legal authorities. Some will have long-overdue parking tickets; some may owe back taxes. Others may have a long-ago larceny still bothering them, or maybe they had beaten their spouse that very morning. Whatever the reason, people like that were among the dog show crowd.

One was LeRoi Parmentor. A professional handler from the old south, he was showing a Havanese in ring ten. He had seen Pete walk in, and recognized Pete as a former competitor. But the two men with him had the look of cops, a look LeRoi recognized well. It was a familiarity no one in his current life knew about.

Another person who noticed the group was Frank Robinson, who was judging German Shepherds in ring four. He, too, had a reason to recognize a police officer and fear being recognized by one. He was distracted from his judging task just long enough to lose his concentration and step into the path of one of the handlers, who was running at full tilt around the ring, her attention focused solely on her dog. The resulting collision caused a brief commotion in his ring as they tumbled to the floor. The dog pivoted around to investigate, giving both parties a good sniff.

The dog's handler, a rather large woman with an impressive bosom, was apoplectic at having run into a judge. She was on the floor on top of him, her huge breasts pinning his head to the rubber mat. As she scrambled to separate herself from the judge, she apologized and asked if he was all right. Judge Robinson, in his desire to prevent the disturbance from getting any larger, quickly got back to his feet and, to his credit, said that it was his fault. He said that he was just so entranced by the quality of the class that he was mesmerized by her dog's movements. He then awarded her Best of Breed, handed out the ribbons, and retreated to the judges' lounge to sneak a sip from a hip flask he always had at the ready.

Others in the room noticed the group of four men and the sudden collision in the German Shepherd ring. Some reacted with alarm, but most found the entire episode funny. A few, however, noticed the connection between the men outside the ring and the events in the ring and had a different reaction. For some it was fear or alarm, for others it was curiosity.

For one observer, the men's appearance sparked a primal need in his soul, a need for recognition. He calmly watched as others in the room observed and interacted with them. He said to himself, "Hmmm, might have to find out, do some checking around." Was there a new challenge in his world? Did their arrival have anything to do with him?

He felt a thrill in the possibility. He knew that his ability to do whatever he wanted in the face of the challenge would prove his superiority to everyone.

Chapter Twenty-eight

At the table, we enjoyed both the coffee and Phil's dissertation on the psychosis, or lack thereof, of serial killers.

"How will the interview be so different?" I asked.

"I will guess that most of the interviews you've conducted in your career involved people who said they didn't do whatever they were being questioned about. They had alibis, excuses, or said other people did it. In most serial killer cases, once the bad guy is caught, they simply confess.

"Keep in mind that there are two primary types of serial killers. One, the sociopath, knows that what they are doing is wrong, but they can't control their erratic behavior. They have an overwhelming compulsion to commit their crimes. The second type, the psychopathic type, doesn't believe what they are doing is wrong, at least for them. They may subliminally know they are breaking the law, even confess, but they don't feel any guilt. Their behavior is extremely controlled.

"There are a few cases in history where the criminal genuinely attempts to evade capture at any cost, and when they are caught they believe they are smarter than the cops and will get off. These guys never admit their crimes and fight them to the last. A good example of this type is the Atlanta Child Killer, Wayne Williams. He's still fighting his conviction and even has the mother of at least one of his victims convinced that he is innocent, in spite of evidence that allowed a jury to convict him that got him a sentence of double life on the two counts he was tried on."

"Only two counts?" Pete asked.

"Yeah, they only tried him on two counts," I answered. "This is a prosecutor tactic. They liked him on around twenty-three counts of first-degree murder—they had that many bodies—but they only tried him on the two that had the most evidence. That way, if the suspect somehow gets off on the first trial, they have more crimes to keep trying him on. The downside is that the families of the other twenty-one victims just have to accept that he killed their family member too. Their cases are never tried, which is what happened in this case. Some of those families have bought into the 'I'm not guilty' bullshit, too."

Glenn had been processing this discussion as it developed. He had a few more questions.

"So, what should we be looking for?" Glenn asked.

"In this case, the first thing to look at is victim selection, victimology the FBI calls it. What kind of victim does the killer pick? Typically, serial killers choose women or children. Plus age, race, physical parameters like height, weight, hair, and skin color. In many cases, the victims are similar, but sometimes they are all different."

"What makes the difference?" Pete wondered.

Phil answered. "Well, it goes back to the two types of killers. The majority, the sociopaths, are what we call disorganized. They are the ones who grab prostitutes or other people off the street. They aren't really looking for a specific type, just someone they can talk into going with them—victims of opportunity. In those cases you wind up with a variety of victims. This type also leaves the most clues, since they are sloppy, to put a point to it. They just get the urge and grab whoever they can with whatever tools and materials are handy."

I asked, "So, what's the other type, the psychopath?"

"They're organized. Some are highly organized, obsessive-compulsive organized. They become masters of their craft. They learn from each victim what works and what doesn't. They are prepared, have a 'kit,' if you will, of tools and materials they need to accomplish their goal. They also tend to stick with a specific victim type. If all your vics are the same, you probably have an organized killer. Unfortunately for you,

140

those are the hardest to identify and apprehend. The guy will have been killing for years. He'll have perfected his art. The only reason you even know he's out there is that his need for it is getting the best of him. He'll start killing too frequently and, sooner or later, someone connects the dots and realizes they have a serial killer on their hands."

We looked at each other and nodded. It was what we feared.

Phil went on. "Also look at where the victims were taken—picked up in a bar, a hooker off the street, grabbed while walking in the park, et cetera."

Glenn asked, "How does where they're taken factor in? What difference does it make how the vic was taken?"

"It goes to the personality of the killer. If he is grabbing women in a park, that's more of a mugging-type approach that would indicate that the killer has self-esteem issues and doesn't believe he can get a woman to go with him voluntarily. So he grabs them. A killer who picks up women in a bar has a very high opinion of himself. He believes he can talk a woman into leaving a safe place with a complete stranger and that he can take control of her later. Of course, he may be using a little help like roofies."

"Great," I muttered. "Now I have to bring illegal drugs into the process." Roofies is the street name for Rohypnol, the date-rape drug.

"Anyway," Phil went on, "what you are hoping not to find is inconsistency in that part of the crime."

"Why's that?" Glenn asked.

"If you are trying to tie cases together, you're looking at M.O. If he's picking up some girls in a bar, some in the park, and some in the produce department at the grocery store, he's very smooth and confident. Those cases may not associate in the FBI's system."

It made sense. We all nodded understanding.

"Then you look at the cause of death and any other underlying conditions. You said that the victims are both, or all, if there are more you haven't found yet, young white women whose bodies were discovered displayed in public places. The cause of death appears to be multiple stab wounds, first many little cuts, then a final killing wound from a very specific type of blade. If there is evidence of sexual intercourse or possible sexual frenzy and no other trace left behind, other than the dog hair, and indications that he cleaned the body, then staged the drop scene, it describes a specific type of killer."

Across the room, one watcher labeled the men as they talked. He knew Phil Horvath, who was a dog show regular. And he knew Pete Anderson was a former dog show fixture, but hadn't been around for at least three or four years. "And two cops. They aren't here just to watch the show," he said to himself.

As he watched the four men, he noticed a woman watching them too. She looked familiar in a distant sort of way. "What's her interest," he asked himself.

As this visual appraisal was taking place, the dog show continued all around them. All the players and activities were in motion. A constant drone of hair dryers and conversations provided background noise. Dogs were on tables being groomed, while people were drinking coffee and eating, reading, chatting, and looking over the competition or oblivious to it. Handlers changed clothes, cut hair, brushed, and combed. Occasional cheers and applause rose from one ring or another as various winners were crowned, or rather, ribboned.

At the table, Phil Horvath continued his profile. "You're looking for a guy who's had problems in relationships with women, so he may be divorced. He's likely from a single-female-parent household, a domineering mother, has little to no self-esteem, works in a blue-collar job or lower level corporate job—not a leader or in a management position—has a history of what's called the homicidal triad—animal abuse and fire, starting as a child, and late enuresis, or bedwetting, into his teens. Back in the '70s and '80s, when profiling really started, these guys were found to prefer old Volkswagen Bugs, but those cars aren't nearly as common as they were then."

I nodded at the information, wondering what the Bug connection was.

"That's going to cover the vast majority of serial killers. But you still have some true psychotics out there. These men—they are almost always men—can be charming, attractive, and as successful in life as they are in their killings. Ted Bundy is the prime example. Although he didn't have a successful work history, he could charm women into going with him, and did many times. Only his over-the-top spontaneous killing of so many college girls in Florida did him in. He was an example of the much-harder-to-find guy. He will appear perfectly normal, have a job, may have a wife and children, has no interest in notoriety or fame, and is happy to go along living his life and committing his crimes. He does have a weakness, though. Like any addiction, he has an increasing need.

"The growing need to feel the power of control he gets from capturing, torturing, and killing his victims—it's an addiction as real as one to crack cocaine.

"These guys need more of it more frequently. Combine that with the fact that they've gotten away with it for so long and they start getting sloppy. They eventually slip up, as Bundy did, but it can take a lot of bodies to get to that point."

"How many were associated with Bundy?" I asked.

"Between thirty and sixty, very possibly more. No one really knows."

That put a blunt point on it. We had two cases we were looking at with a suspect profile that was saying we wouldn't even know about him until late in his career. I was sure there were others and they would certainly cross state lines. In fact, with Maria looking at the case in Arizona, I was thinking we were in two states already. Many states involved meant federal involvement. And if that was going to happen there was only one person I wanted to call. I'd have to check if he was back from his honeymoon yet.

Phil had to get back to his dog, so he gave me his card and headed off.

Pete and I returned our attention to the show. Pete provided a running explanation so I saw that after ribbons were awarded, another breed of dog started the process again, first with the male puppies, then male adults. The different varieties of males and females within each breed were judged, and the other classes like Bred by Exhibitor and American Bred, each produced a winner.

Since we weren't planning to stay all day, Pete explained that when all the winning dogs were reduced to Winners Dog, the process would be repeated with the females, followed by the "Specials," the dogs, male and female, who had already won championships.

They entered the ring to compete against the Winners Dog and Winners Bitch in the Best of Breed ring. From them, the final winning example of each breed would be selected. The process would go on through all the breeds, lasting all day until the Group Rings selected the best from each group. Those seven dogs then competed for Best In Show, the top dog. At least the top dog at that show on that day. Tomorrow would likely produce a different "Top Dog."

As he finished that part of the tutorial, Greg, the guy from the scissors booth came over with a cup of coffee.

"Mind if I join you?" he asked.

"No problem," Pete replied. "Taking a little break?"

"Have to. Stand on this concrete all day, pretty soon your feet are screaming at you."

Although I had some things I wanted to discuss with Glenn while they were fresh in my mind, they would have to wait with the civilian at the table. Pete understood and changed the subject to the show.

"How's attendance been? I've heard entries are down," Pete asked.

"True, but the more casual exhibitors aren't my main customers. Most of my business is serious handlers like you. But, spectator attendance matters. I do sell a lot of merchandise to them."

"And that's been enough?"

"Yeah. I've got a theory about that. Taking the family to a dog show is a pretty low-impact day out, money-wise. Most shows don't even charge admission and those that do, well, it's only five bucks each or so, and kids are free. That's a lot cheaper than a ballgame or a trip to a movie. So people bring the kids here. Works for me, because they buy stuff."

Pete asked about some of the different personalities at the show. Greg was sort of a gossip central, knowing who was handling which dog, who was on the rise and who needed some new prospects, who was sleeping with whom, all the little things that lie under the surface of any close-knit group of people. After another coffee sipping break, Greg turned to me.

"So, you and Glenn are cops, right?"

"I'm sort of retired. Glenn is the sheriff of Kanabec County."

"Can either of you give a guy some advice about picking out a gun?"

Glenn looked at me, knowing it was a subject I could talk about all day and excused himself to use the restroom. Pete also left, saying he wanted to talk to someone.

"Anyone," he said over his shoulder. I guess they'd heard me talk about guns enough.

"Firearm selection is a very personal thing," I told Greg. "It all comes down to what works for you. A pistol has to fit you properly in order to be easy to use. How much shooting experience do you have?"

"Not much. I volunteer with my local police department on what they call a Community Emergency Response Team, so I know a lot of cops and have shot at the range with them. Some of them have told me that I could be a good shooter if I practiced."

I'd heard of CERT teams. They're people who live in the area and have skills useful to the police in times of emergency. Their skill sets include SCUBA diving, rock climbing, radio expertise, trauma care, things like that. I asked Greg what his CERT skill was.

"Well, everyone is trained on search-and-rescue and triage in case of a high casualty event like a tornado. But everyone also needs a kind of specialty. You can guess what mine is. Take a look around," he said with a wave of his hands. "I'm the guy they call when they have an animal problem. It might be a house fire and the fire department has rescued some pets, or a cat lady gets reported and they need someone to help with the cats. That's my primary job on the team. But I've picked up some radio skills over the years and can help out with that too."

Greg's work with his local PD made me more comfortable in our gun discussion. "Do you have a permit?"

"Just got my purchase permit. I figure I'll pick out a gun, get comfortable with it, and then get the carry permit. That's why I'm asking. There are so many brands and types and calibers, to say nothing about price ranges, I don't know which way to go."

"If you're going to carry, you need to practice. Carrying a firearm presumes a lot of responsibility. You have to know the law and have proficiency with your weapon. For that reason, I generally tell people to go with a nine millimeter. That's the most common caliber, so it's the cheapest to shoot. You'll want to make sure to go to the range at least every two months or so."

"Two months?" Greg said with surprise. "The cops I know only qualify twice a year."

"Yes, and I disagree with that. Even though ninety-five percent will never draw their weapon in the line of duty, that doesn't mean they shouldn't be proficient. Personally, I shoot every month and go through around 8,000 to 10,000 rounds per year. But I shoot in competition too."

"Wow, you are the right guy to talk to. So what do you carry?"

"Depends on what I'm doing, where I'm going. If I expect a high probability that I'll need it, I usually carry a .45 caliber high-capacity gun, like a Springfield XDM. That's not practical for everyday carry though. It's just too big and clunky. Most people carry a compact semi-automatic nine or a small hammerless revolver, .38 or .32 caliber. Since nearly all states have carry laws now, the manufacturers have come up with literally hundreds of guns to choose from. That's why you need to try them out and see what fits your hand the best and shoots the best for you."

"OK, I get that. But, what do you carry daily?" he asked again.

"Most often, I carry a CAB 9c, nine-millimeter compact. It's a little spendy but worth it. Absolutely reliable and accurate, once it's in service."

"What do you mean by 'in service'?" Weber asked.

"It's like any piece of finely built equipment. It has a break-in period. To make it reliable you've got to run a lot of rounds . . . ." I could see that Greg was distracted by activity near his booth.

He said, "Well, gotta go. Thanks for the advice," and left the table. I watched as he trotted back to his booth. Glenn came back to the table, looking relieved that I was sitting alone. Soon after, Pete rejoined us. None of us noticed the approach of another player in our world.

Jane Vanderloo sauntered up. "Hello boys," she said.

Across the room, a killer watched as the attractive woman approached the table and sat down with the three men. He observed the interaction among the foursome and could see that they knew each other. He wondered what the relationships were. He decided some research was in order.

Chapter Twenty-nine

I looked at Jane and shook my head. "And just what are you doing here? Your station send you up to do a human interest story on the dog show?"

Pete helped out, saying, "There are much bigger shows right in the Cities. You could have saved the mileage. Slow news day?"

"No, I'm investigating a murder. Something you might consider doing yourself," she said, baiting me.

I looked at Pete and Glenn. Glenn folded his arms across his chest, stroked his chin, and looked off at one of the show rings, watching the handlers primp and fuss over their charges. Pete, who knew Jane because of our aforementioned relationship, rolled his eyes, looking off in the same direction. I received the message: I was on my own.

"OK, I'm trapped. Go ahead and ask, but I'll tell you up front, I've got no answers."

"Sure you do. You just don't recognize them. I'll help you. Let's start with 'Why are you here?'"

"Pete is looking for a new dog. You remember Sinbad, his Flat-Coated Retriever? Well, he's getting old and Pete doesn't like to be without a dog, so he's here scouting."

"And Sheriff Mills is along as a consultant?"

"No, Glenn just wanted to get out of the office for a while. You know how it is."

"Sure I do. That's why I'm here too. Nothing like a run up to Duluth, one of my favorite cities, for a little sightseeing and lunch."

When we were dating we would run to Duluth for a quick hot couple of days. She'd told me that she had never thought of Duluth as a "vacation" spot prior to our visits. I, too, associated Duluth with Jane. Until Maria.

We three guys just looked at each other. I was thinking about how to work this to our advantage. Jane was much more than another pretty face. She was a skilled investigative reporter with a track record of getting people to talk about things they didn't want to discuss with the police. But we were the police. We could do the same thing to her.

"Jane," I asked, "What exactly do you know about the case?"

"I know that you had a murder near Mora that is unsolved. And, I know the body was mutilated. You made sure of that."

"Yeah, I apologize for that. I was a little cranked up." First thing was to offer an olive branch and calm the waters that had been stirred up by Maria that first day. I'm sometimes accused of impulsive and counterproductive actions. That's true, but I didn't do it that time. Maria certainly had tuned into my signals, though. Anyway, Jane dumped me; remember?

"Apology accepted. I don't really have anything you probably don't have. All I know is that the poor woman who was killed in Mora was a local girl and you don't have any leads. You've pretty much ruled out any locals as the killer, so you have to broaden your possibilities. I don't know why you're at this dog show. I can presume you think there's some connection, maybe even that your killer might be here."

As she spelled out her view of the story, Glenn and I looked at each other. She must have a source within his department. Why else would she be here? I decided to dive in.

"Jane, we think the person who killed the woman in Mora might be a serial killer. He may have killed another victim in Arizona, near Scottsdale. We are working a theory that since both bodies were found just after major dog shows had been held nearby, it might be a connection."

"To say nothing of the fact that several types of dog hair were found on the body in Mora," she said. Again, I looked at Glenn. There was smoke coming out of his ears. Sure, she may have gotten that info from a BCA contact, but . . . I was sure he'd have an answer to his leak problem before nightfall.

I countered. "Both bodies were found outdoors in hot climates where feral dogs are not unknown. I think that's just coincidental."

That might have been the wrong thing to say. Jane had heard me say many times that nothing is coincidental. She reminded me of that with a skeptical look.

Without acknowledging her look, I said, "We are putting together a list of possible killings that might involve the same guy. So far, it doesn't appear that he is targeting dog show participants, just locals near the shows. I say that only because if he was targeting dog show people it would have been noticed."

"True. How many cases do you have so far?"

"Just the two right now."

"OK. I understand why you and the sheriff are here," she said, with a nod to Glenn. "But why is Pete here? Is he some kind of dog show expert?" Jane knew that Pete is my best friend.

"I told you. He's looking for a new dog. And, yes, he knows about dog shows." I went on to describe Pete's background. Jane was surprised to learn that Pete was more than a typical Minnesota businessman. The discussion went on for a few minutes but the important stuff was already on the table. Jane had a few ideas that we'd already ruled out. We didn't tell her that.

We reached a working agreement. In return for constant updates on what she was discovering, we agreed to keep her in the loop and give her exclusive access to any arrests we made. It was the kind of deal reporters love. They get access and only have to give up information they think we already have. Happens all the time.

We finished our coffee, stood and said goodbye, and began strolling toward the door, past more rings, exhibitors, spectators, and vendors. As we walked, I took in the entire scene again—sort of a controlled chaos of activity with some people grooming, some in the rings, some talking, some sleeping. I still didn't get it. Why do people do this? I wondered.

We stopped outside a ring where German Shorthaired Pointers were being judged. At least that's what I thought they were. To tell the truth, all I knew was they were some kind of hunting dog, the same as a friend's family had in North Dakota. A group of three dogs that looked about the same to me went in the ring, were judged, and were back out in about six minutes. I asked Pete.

"In and out just like that? I mean, it wouldn't be such a big deal to get short-haired dogs ready but some of these people have been working on their dogs for hours. All that for six minutes? What's the draw?"

Pete stopped and looked around. "I suppose this looks like the whole thing to you, but it's much more. First off, it's very egalitarian. There are people here from every walk of life. Right now I can see people who are teachers, construction workers, office folks, MDs, attorneys, a judge, an electrician, pharmacist, real estate agent, salesman, everything you can think off. None of that matters here; all are equal, brought together by a common love of dogs.

"Think about it in terms you understand. You're a car guy. Not the hard-core Minnesota Street Rod weekend club member who works that show every year, but you understand that kind of commitment. So you know why people go to a Saturday night, or even Thursday night, car show in a strip mall's parking lot.

"You get there about 6:00, pull your folding chairs out of the trunk, pop the hood, and sit around talking cars with your buddies. It's the same thing for dog people. And it's not all here at the show. I'll give you an example.

"A few years ago Carol and I were at a show in Wausau, Wisconsin. Saturday evening, we went to dinner with four friends. One couple was from Chicago, the other two were judges, one from Duluth and one from Cleveland. The server was making small talk and asked if we were from the area. Carol spoke up and told the server that we were friends and announced where everyone was from and that we get together about once a month for dinner.

"That was true and it was a way to look at our sport that I'd never considered before. It's truly a social activity. Sure, there are a few people who make a living at it, or from it if you're the guy selling supplies or if you are the superintendent. But pretty much everyone else is there for the social aspect."

I nodded as Pete went on.

"Look at it this way. At a juried car show where trophies are being awarded, the cars are only being judged for a few minutes. Same with us. But car guys will get their rides parked hours before, spend the whole morning polishing, adjusting, touching up, then hold their breath while the judge is there. After, they take off and go shopping at the booths, looking for that one something that will make their car more authentic or faster or cooler. It's pretty much the same for us. Just a bunch of people who share an interest and enjoy being around each other."

It made sense. Now, as I scanned the room I saw the commonality of people who shared a hobby, an activity that gave them community, travel, and a sense of accomplishment, as well as a four-legged friend who was always glad when they got home. I was beginnning to get it.

My ability to solve crimes, sometimes crimes that hadn't been solved by top detectives in our department as well as other law enforcement agencies, is strongly centered on my ability to read people. I don't know how I developed it or how to teach it to someone else; it's just a gift. I wondered if I'd seen, met, perhaps even spoken to a psychopathic serial killer that day and not read him correctly. Could I have met an individual who, almost casually, could lure a woman into a situation that resulted in her capture, torture, sexual assault, and death and not had a ping in my head or felt the hair on the back of my neck go up? Those "tells" had never failed me before. Could he be that good? Or, maybe we were totally on the wrong track.

When there's real evil near, sometimes I can feel it across a room, almost like an aura that's invisible to everyone else. My buzz gets louder as I get nearer the individual. I didn't get it that day, except for the artist; I'd had a pretty good hit on him. That was based on the look he gave me. He had something going on that he was hiding. I'd put him on the list. We should be able to match him up with locations of other victims. Pete and Phil said he was famous and received high prices for his work. Fame and money equal easy to track.

We walked out of the DECC. Just as we hit the door I looked back and saw Jane smiling and talking to that handler guy, Hunter something, over by the coffee stand. The guy gets around, I thought.

We walked in silence out to the parking ramp. Mentally, I reviewed what had learned. No standout suspect; could be anyone. In fact, serial killers are nuts and the press is ever vigilant. And Glenn's got a leak in his office.

I thought I'd handled Jane's surprise appearance well. We'd worked together on cases in the past and I was confident this case would be no different.

Wrong.

Chapter Thirty

Inside the DECC, the killer watched the three men leave. He also saw the woman who had sat down with them go around to some of the people the men had talked to. He was blessed with a fantastic memory, especially for faces. Just another of his gifts, he thought. Was he born with it or did he pick it up later, he wondered as he watched her. He knew he had received "gifts" from many of his subjects. Maybe his incredible memory was yet another one.

He turned back to the dog on his grooming table. A Rough Collie was standing tall, waiting for the man's attention. It was a handsome animal, but not the familiar sable color like Lassie of television fame. He was a blue merle, black and tan. That meant the dog was primarily gray—which animal people call blue—and white with swirls of black dancing around his body and a black patch on his head. His legs were white with tan patches and with a few black freckles for character. There were patches of tan fur on the sides of the dog's muzzle, and on his eyebrows, or points, as the dog show folks called them. His long puffy tail ended in the preferred white paintbrush tip.

Many owners and handlers came to him for his artistic grooming abilities. He knew the standards for all the breeds that require maximum skill and was a magician in sculpting the perfect dog out of a mountain of unkempt hair. Not just the obvious ones, like Poodles and Shi Tzus, but the more subtle breeds like Schnauzers. His skill was using brushes, combs, scissors, and other less-known materials to create the perfect example of whatever breed he was working on. His greatest talent wasn't in highlighting a dog's best features; it was in hiding the less-than-perfect ones. He could create an illusion of something out of nothing or redirect the judge's eye away from an offending fault. His attention to detail created many champions out of dogs who otherwise would not have come close to that goal.

The Collie's head was excellent. It looked carved from a block with perfectly aligned top planes, the top of the skull and the top of the muzzle. They had to be perfectly parallel with just the right amount of break between them at the eyes. And they were, thanks to his ministrations. He had worked the dog's head with a very fine pin brush and stripping comb usually reserved for Terrier breeds. His work was the quality of Michelangelo working in marble, he thought.

He turned his attention to the Collie's ears. One ear was the head's only flaw. "Hmm, one of your radar dishes is a bit higher than the other," he said aloud.

The ears should be close together on the head with a high reach to the sky and nice, evenly bent forward tips. The Collie's ears were perfect except for one tip. The right ear folded just right while the other was not down quite far enough. It made matters worse that the offending ear was the dog's left, the side more visible to the judge in the ring.

"Have to fix that," he said to his salon subject. The dog stood motionless, accustomed to long periods of personal attention. He'd been receiving such treatment since he was eight weeks old.

He reached into his grooming kit for a small bottle that contained a slightly gooey dark substance. He dabbed his right index finger into the goop, then screwed the top back on the bottle, set it down, and started rubbing the adhesive between his finger and thumb. When he had massaged it to the right feel he rubbed the adhesive into the beautiful black hair on the top and inside of the tip of the offending ear. Then he cleaned his hands and took out secret weapon number two, a bottle of finely ground tungsten powder that he sprinkled on the top of the ear. He carefully worked it down through the fur into the adhesive. He repeated the process on the underside of the ear leather, finishing the job with a very fine comb that straightened and separated every hair. He released the ear and stood back to look at his work.

"Perfect, as usual," he said aloud. The ears were exactly even, perfect set and tip. He was the best groomer in the building and had proven it once again.

As he worked, it finally came to him. She was a reporter. He'd seen her on television when he was in the area. She was obviously interested in whatever the cops were interested in and he thought he knew what the men were interested in. That made her very attractive.

When she came to him, as he knew she would, his story was ready.

Chapter Thirty-one

Sunday, July 19th
The DECC
Duluth, Minnesota

He'd had two days to think about the challenge that had been laid down. After Friday's visit by the three men, he knew he had to react. No, not react. React is what someone on the defensive did. He wasn't on the defensive; he was in control. He could do anything he wanted. He was master of the universe.

He'd done a little research on the players he'd met Friday. Most interesting was the reporter. She, as he guessed, was following up on the same investigation as the three men. When she got to his booth he'd asked her why she wasn't with them, or at least trailing them around with her microphone. He turned on the charm and she responded. Like a lot of people who have plenty of charm of their own, she was susceptible to his kind of coy, teasing banter. She told him she had received a tip about the case, that there may be a serial killer involved and that it was a very big story. Then, she let it slip that she and the cop who knew so much about guns had once been involved. That bit of information intrigued him.

"Former girlfriend," he whispered.

That was all he needed to know.

Once he reached his decision, sometime in the middle of Friday night's sleep, he stopped tossing and turning. From the time he started his experiments, as he called them, he had been at peace with himself. No longer did he suffer from long nights awake, wondering why he couldn't attract women, why he couldn't have a "normal" relationship with a woman. He finally realized that as long as he harbored what he called his "needs," he would subliminally focus them on whatever woman he was involved with and she would, sooner or later, become uncomfortable with the vibe he was sending. Women were very intuitive that way, he realized. They could pick up on the subliminal, the non-verbal, communication, even though he tried hard not to reveal his innermost thoughts. For a time he could hide his urges from the women he met, but if the relationship went long enough, his true nature would sneak out, scaring the woman off. So he had developed a way to satisfy himself by granting those attentions to other women, away from the ones he was trying to live a normal life with.

The women in his life were divided into two groups: those who received all the kindness, love, consideration, and benefits of being in a relationship with a modern caring, sensitive man, and those who became an outlet for the underlying needs. It was a good balance, he thought.

Although he didn't know it, the killer fit into an FBI profile rather nicely. The profile was that of the psychopathic serial killer like Ted Bundy. He was charming, attractive, and intelligent. He was also completely disconnected from any feelings whatsoever for the humanity of his victims. They were mere subjects in his experiments. And, like many of his ilk, he had a deep passion that was unfulfilled. He craved a sense of order in his life.

FBI files are filled with serial killer profiles that say the killer had joined, or attempted to join, organizations that had structure and authority, primarily police, military, or security forces. He was no different. He'd applied for police training when he graduated high school and was turned down due to a lack of a college degree. He applied to the Army but flunked the induction physical due to a slight heart murmur and was classified as "unfit for military service." So he went to college and, through a fluke of his childhood, became involved with dog shows and discovered it to be the perfect cover for his experiments.

He knew that what he was doing was considered wrong by society, that it was illegal and violated the social mores of others. But those rules didn't apply to him. It was his way of compensating, dealing with his own feelings in a way that would hurt the fewest people while allowing him to live a relatively normal life.

Once a woman was in his control, she was just an outlet for his anger and lust. He knew he couldn't expect a woman in any kind of normal relationship to let him do what he had to do to the others. He was protecting them and their families as well as protecting himself. If a few strangers had to die each year, it was a small price to pay for his "normal" life.

He had never competed in school sports or even joined bowling leagues or softball teams as he aged. His professional schedule didn't allow for it. Between the necessary travel and dealing with clients, he had no time for that kind of competition. But he loved the thrill of a challenge. It was one of the things he enjoyed most about his "hobby." There was a fantastic thrill in the selection process, the pursuit, the capture, and of course, the experimentation that followed. There was even a certain satisfaction in the steps involved in preparing the bodies for disposal. He enjoyed the entire process. It gave him a feeling of complete control of his life, something he had lacked before he started his experiments.

He knew he was looking at an even bigger challenge. He had spent two evenings researching Dan Neumann. "Thank goodness for Google," he'd said several times. He'd learned that Dan had a long and distinguished career with the Minneapolis Police Department, reaching the position as its top homicide investigator, and that Neumann was indeed a firearms expert. He had ordered Neumann's books on forensic ballistics from Amazon, which he hoped would be waiting for him when he got home. But he already knew the guy was an opponent of the first water, a challenge to be emulated and defeated.

By the time Best In Show was announced at 5:15 on Saturday afternoon, he had decided on a course of action. His need was, by then, compelling.

But the exhilarating anticipation was nearly more than he could stand. He knew from experience that thinking about it would make it that much more fulfilling. So he thought about it.

A lot.

Chapter Thirty-two

Maria arrived at work a bit late. Her morning schedule had been interrupted by a call from her Minnesota connection, as she now called Dan, and what she thought was going to be an early morning arrival at the office had turned into a late one. She didn't mind; it had been a tough weekend.

She had spent most of Friday night working the late afternoon shooting site, then the balance of the weekend working the case. They had a suspect almost immediately, picked him up about 4:00 a.m. Saturday, put him on ice while the crime scene info came in and follow-up interviews took place, then sweated him until he cracked. A typical thoughtless shooting solved in that magical forty-eight-hour period and put to bed, at least as far as the investigators were concerned.

Oddly, the TV shows seemed to always get it wrong. Granted, they have a one-hour time period, forty-two minutes, really, to get everything done. But the crime scene collection of data usually takes six to ten hours, interviews with witnesses another three or four, but that's usually done while the crime scene is being processed. Add a day for an autopsy and a day to run down the bad guy so you can talk to him and that's pretty much the whole forty-eight hours. In the weekend's case they were lucky. There were three eyewitnesses, one of whom was willing to identify the shooter, and the shooter had, as they so often do, run to the familiarity, security, and comfort of home, making for an easy pickup. After that, it was a matter of a good interview.

Over the years talented cops realized that the less confrontational they were with a subject, the better their chances of getting at the truth. Haul a guy into a room, sit him down at a table, and start haranguing him with incriminating statements and he'll immediately go defensive and clam up, or worse, ask for a lawyer. Once that happens the chance of a confession is nearly zero.

Good interviewers start with a few comfort issues. They ask the subject "Are you thirsty?" "Need a smoke?" "Something to eat?" They get the subject comfortable with the situation. Then they let him sit for an hour or two, alone in a brightly lit room with no TV, no magazines, no phone, no radio, nothing but his thoughts on why he's there.

After a suitable period of time for introspection, the cops come back as if they've only been gone a few minutes. Maria was great at it. Usually she'd say something like "Sorry about that. Had to take a phone call." The bad guy would look at her, wondering how a phone call could last what felt to him like days and she'd again make him comfortable, then start with innocuous questions like "Where were you?" "Who were you with?" "Did you know the victim?" She'd give the subject a chance to make some statements that were contrary to other information she had. Her technique was very subtle, allowing the subject to feel as if things were going his way and she was buying everything he had to say. She also played on her youthful good looks, implying to the subject that she was new at interviewing and throwing in a giggle or flip of her long dark hair every once in a while, maybe get him talking about his car, as she had in this case, to give the impression that she was either falling for the guy's rap or was just not too smart. The technique was especially effective with suspects who were Latino, like her. After letting him tie up all the loose ends in what he thought was a bulletproof story, she'd start throwing curveballs at him.

"Now Alejandro, you said that you were at the cantina on South Pecos at the time of the shooting, right?" she had asked.

"I sure was. I was with some of my homies. They'll tell you."

"Yeah, I did get a chance to talk to three of your friends whose names you gave me. But one of them said he wasn't there, so he couldn't alibi you."

"So he forgot, or maybe I forgot. We are always together, so maybe I just thought he was there."

"Yes, but if he forgot, or maybe you did, what else might you have forgotten? Anyway, it's not that important. You said you didn't know the boy who got shot, correct?"

"You're right, mama. I didn't know that homie from shit. Why would I want to do him?"

"Well, that's what I was wondering. So I did some more checking and one of his friends said that the victim had met you last week, that the victim had accidentally bumped his car into your car in the parking lot at Rodrigo's. His friend said that the guy had waited for you so he could make it right with you about the car. It's hard for me to believe that you wouldn't remember someone who had hit your beautiful car."

And so on. She went at him with inconsistencies and holes in his story, jumping around from where he was to where did he get a gun, to the car, to the dead guy, to his girlfriend, to his job, to what did he do with the gun, to his dog—confusing him by intentionally reading an occasional fact incorrectly and getting him to fill in the blanks until she had him locked up tight. When people are being pummeled with incorrect information they want to fix it. It's human nature. The first response is to correct the error. Don't give them time to think of a convincing lie; make them answer with their first thought. He wouldn't even know what was happening while it was happening. Only after, when he was sitting in his cell, did he wonder, "How'd that bitch figure all that out?"

So, after a good night's sleep, she was back at work on Sunday morning. She looked at the printout on her desk and thought, "OK, that's today's job as long as no one else gets shot, knifed, run over, or beaten to death." She started by going through the information on possible similar cases and weeding out ones that she thought were long shots to be connected to their murders, which included setting aside cases that involved additional weapons such as guns, or some kind of strangulation in addition to the knife wounds. That didn't mean they wouldn't be added in later, but for now she was going with the cases with the most similar M.O.

Next, she sifted through the dates of the body discoveries, estimated the dates of death, and began creating a timeline. Going with the possibility of the dog show connection, she numbered each of those dates with the corresponding number of the previous weekend of the year. Her plan was to compare the estimated date of death to any dog shows held nearby on the previous weekend. It was a long clerical exercise, but such exercises are an important part of good police work.

When she finished she had eight good matches. In every case the victim was a white female in her mid-twenties to early thirties, between 5'2" and 5'7", not a runway model but not overweight. Each one was also blond. It was an exact type. Each victim had been tortured with an exceptionally sharp-bladed weapon, the weapon that was also the probable murder weapon when they were finally dispatched. All showed signs of sexual assault. Although no semen was found with any of the victims, a lubricant was, indicating use of a condom. All the bodies showed massive loss of blood, had been thoroughly washed, and then left in remote areas not far from their last known whereabouts.

Oddly, three different medical examiners had noted that the pubic areas of their victims had been recently shaved or waxed, possibly after they were kidnapped. The ME on the earliest case had found the shave job to be sloppy, with nicks and cuts inconsistent with the careful shave one would expect a young woman to give herself. The other two MEs had noted that the area had been waxed. Maria saw this connection and had an idea. She made a note to call each ME with a question.

Using a large whiteboard, Maria laid out her timeline. She put each case on the line along with a date. Then she went to her newly acquired dog show calendar and began looking for nearby shows that had been held around the time the bodies were discovered. When she was done she had a timeline that stretched back almost twelve years and covered deaths in eight states. All eight bodies had dog shows in close time proximity, but five of them looked like the time of death was actually before the weekend of the local show. In three of those cases, the bodies had been found before the show took place; in the other two they were found after the show, as they had in the Minnesota and Arizona cases.

That would mean the killer arrived in the vicinity early, selected his victim, had his fun, then dumped the body before going to the show, which was inconsistent with what Maria knew of serial killers. And she knew quite a bit, having attended two four-day courses on serial killers put on by the FBI.

Maria knew from the evidence that they were dealing with a highly organized killer. In every case there were signs of organization, from the similarities of the knife wounds to the remote areas where the bodies were found, to the cleaning of the bodies. Some settings were rural, others urban. Some of the victims were country girls, some city.

Another FBI key was a triggering event, also called a stressor. If her theory were true, the dog shows could be the stressors. If that was the case, then why kill before a dog show? That would leave the killer in the area while there was a possibility the body could be found.

Maria now knew there was a definite connection to dog shows but also knew that an organized killer wouldn't be so arrogant as to kill then stay in the area, so there had to be another answer. She thought for a while, then called Pete with a question.

Chapter Thirty-three

10:30 a.m.
Sunday, July 19th
Robbinsdale, Minnesota

It was action day. I had to do something that was against my nature as a cop, but necessary in this case. If I wanted to stay involved in the case, I'd have to bite the bullet and make the call. It's not that I don't like the guy I was calling. In fact, I like him quite a bit. But I viscerally hate his organization.

Will Sanford has been a friend and "Brother in Blue," in a manner of speaking, for about ten years. He was involved in a case I worked years ago and we'd hit it off as well as two competitors could. It's hard for people outside of law enforcement to understand the relationship, so I'll try to put it into business terms.

Imagine you own a small local software outfit and your company makes a breakthrough with a new product that you are confident will be a market shaker. Let's call it "Net Surfer Golden Delicious." But, to really make things take off you have to bring in the biggest player in the field, a company that could help you or just as easily take your discovery and leave you crushed along the side of the orchard. Let's call that company "Johnny Appleseed." There are no patents, no trademarks; you just have to trust in good faith that they will keep you in the game. In fact, you already had experience being crushed by the behemoth and it wasn't fun. Just because you later had an acceptable experience with the giant didn't make you any less apprehensive about calling the giant in again. Especially when the giant's name is the Federal Bureau of Investigation.

I'd called Maria earlier that morning and, after the usual expressions of mutual loneliness and talk about our next get-together she told me she was starting on the ViCAP search results. She would be going over the cases to find the most likely matches, but a quick glance told her there were more than a few, spread throughout several states. The one sure result we could look forward to was that her inquiry and its results would wind up on another desk today, a desk in the Hoover Building in D.C.

The FB and I, as it is sometimes referred to by other law enforcement agencies—and frankly, that's one of the nicer references; others include the feebs, the federales, those fucking feds, or just "them"—is that big company you have to call that might just leave you crushed on the side of a road, figuratively speaking. I don't mean that they would actually take physical action to put a competitor out of business, although that might be easier to deal with; they just have a manner about them that says "OK, little brother, *we'll* take it from here," and then all your hard work, your suspects, your whole case and the credit go off to feddie-land and you never see them again, except on television when the bad guys are busted, then you'll see some federal spokesperson make that last TV stand-up for the purpose of assuring the population that there is nothing to be concerned about, "We" are here to protect you. They are the original Men in Black.

That said, I knew I had to make the first move. I've always believed that a strong defense has to be proactive and this was going to be the first move in a chess game called "Whose case is it?" I wanted it to be mine, though I knew I'd settle for just staying involved.

It was Sunday afternoon, a day for baseball and summer picnics, not homicide investigations. That's why I wanted to do it then. The Men in Black work 24/7 and there was a chance I could be benched by tomorrow morning. No reason to wait. I dialed the phone.

"Hey Dan, how are you?" the guy on the other end said. Apparently his caller ID was working fine.

"Great, Will, just great. How was the honeymoon?"

Will is the guy I mentioned earlier who was out of town. But all good things come to an end and there are few things as good as a honeymoon. At least that's what I've heard.

"It was great. Two weeks away. Got to see a part of the country neither of us had ever been to. I tell you, if the SAC position in Anchorage opens up, I might go for it."

"So tell me about it. All I knew was you were going someplace north."

"Yeah, that was the plan. We wanted to really get away for a while. We had to tell the office where we were, but I figured that if I told you the details you'd either call me for updates or show up. Molly didn't want that."

"I'll bet you didn't either. Listen, if it wasn't for me calling you, there wouldn't be a Mrs. Sanford."

"I know and I'll be forever in your debt, even though you did get me shot in the process."

"Hey, I didn't write the plan and I certainly didn't tell you to walk on out there to see if anyone would start shooting."

"True enough. Worked out pretty well after all, didn't it?"

"Sure did, for both you and Pete. You got the girl, Pete got the money. All I got was cold. So, Molly heading back to Bismarck?"

Will laughed and said, "Eventually. Her boss told her to get back when she could. I guess the good karma of all those busts the Bureau made after that little episode is still flowing. She has a couple of days unless I can think of a way to keep her here. We'll be living apart until we can find a way to get the same assignment, maybe something back at Quantico or D.C. So what's been happening around here while we were gone?"

"Funny you should ask. I know you don't need another wife, so I'm hoping this doesn't go that direction for you, but Maria and I have stumbled into what we think is a serial killer case."

"Really?" I could almost see him perk up. "I think I'd like to hear about it."

So I told him. As with the case last winter that ended with his meeting the lovely Special Agent Molly Foss of the Bismarck, North Dakota, office of the FB and I, and his getting shot in a gunfight that wrapped up that case, this was a case that I knew the feds would be coming into. Will and I have a history and I knew he'd keep me in the game. Will's reaction was all business.

"That sure sounds like a serial case. The similarities are there to draw a line to a single unsub."

Unsub is fédérale talk for an "unknown subject." In fact, it's one of the few things they get right on that TV show about profiling. Most of the rest of it's Hollywood.

"As we speak, Maria is combing through a report she got back from your people on Friday. She sent an information request for similar cases to the ViCAP system. When the list of similar cases came back with so many hits, I got a little concerned that Maria might be getting a phone call with a "Send us your data, and thanks for the effort" message from D.C."

"You're right to be concerned. I'm sure your list is in someone's in-basket right now and they just haven't gotten to it yet. As soon as they do they'll assign it to the Investigative Services Unit."

Investigative Services is what the Feds call their profiling unit. It is chock-full of very smart people, all of whom have at least ten years' field experience before they can even apply to the unit, then they undergo extensive training in the psychological aspects of criminal identification. They have an amazing track record of successful arrests and prosecutions. Their success has almost been enough to help the unit overcome its previous designation of Behavioral Sciences Unit, which was quite logically known inside and outside of the FBI as the "BS Unit."

"Of course, being assigned doesn't mean you'll hear anything anytime soon. Those guys always have full plates. It could be awhile before they can get to your case, so we have a little time."

"We" was what I wanted to hear. "Well, I'm not waiting. I'm calling, in a spirit of mutual support and the new, kinder, more sensitive post-911 age of law enforcement interservice cooperation, to invite you to the party."

"Yeah, and if you believe that, I've got a lake place in Phoenix I'd like to sell you," Will replied.

We both laughed.

"Hey, this might be a way to keep Molly here for a while," Will said.

"How's that?"

"She's been through the profiling training at Quantico. One of her projected career tracks is to get to Investigative Services. I may be able to talk her boss into letting her stay here to work the case."

"Sweet. And we could use the help. See what you can do."

"Will do. In the meantime, why don't you have Maria send whatever she has and I'll get Molly on it."

"Got it. I'll call you when she has something to send."

Chapter Thirty-four

6:00 p.m.
Sunday
Duluth, Minnesota

The killer finished his stay in Duluth doing what everyone else in the dog show business did—cleaning, packing, and getting ready for the next show. He was fastidious, with a packing order that would do a military planner proud. "A place for everything and everything in its place," he repeated as he worked.

The show superintendent's crew was hard at work, rolling and stacking the rubber mats on carts that would soon be on a truck to Oklahoma City. There, they would be placed in a machine much like a car wash, which would grab the loose end and pull it through a set of rollers that would wash both sides of each mat in an attempt to remove all the scent, hair, dried urine, and whatever else was present from the weekend's dog traffic. After a pass under blow nozzles, they were rolled back up and placed on the truck for shipping to the next show.

The practice produced a fairly clean mat but the blowers were incapable of rendering the mats completely dry so they would still be wet when they were unrolled at the next show. Having the undersides wet was an unplanned benefit if the mats were rolled out onto bare concrete, the typical floor in a dog show venue. The still-wet rubber mats would form sort of a bond with the flat smoothness of the bare concrete, which would prevent them from slipping around during the show. It worked well unless the next show was in a northern climate such as Minneapolis in winter when they'd arrive as four-foot-long, sixty-pound frozen cylinders that would have to be coaxed into unrolling and left to thaw overnight. Invariably it resulted in matted rings that looked like they were covered in corrugated fiberglass.

Others on the crew were collecting all the other accouterments needed for the show—ring tables and signs, and the baby gates that formed the ring dividers. One collected all the paper used by the judges and the show secretary to tabulate and record the results. Once it was processed in Oklahoma City it would be forwarded to the AKC headquarters in Raleigh.

The rapidly emptying convention center was a flurry of packing and moving, and participants thinking about the weekend's successes and failures. Some were gossiping about dogs and their handlers while others were still steaming about the judging. Those who had finished championships would now consider retiring their dogs to lives of luxury and couch potatoing. Others, both finished and not, would decide to abandon Conformation competition and go on to the parts of the sport that held more appeal for them—Obedience, Agility, Tracking, Herding, and others. For those exhibitors, Conformation was just a starting point, an opportunity to bring a young dog to the show, take him in the ring and give him treats. This not-so-serious segment of Conformation believed there could be no better conditioning for a young dog who was headed to sports where no treats were allowed in the competition ring.

Most of the dogs would continue to compete in Conformation. Their owners and handlers had high hopes for either their dogs or themselves, envisioning a win at the Westminster Kennel Club show or the AKC's Eukanuba National Championship. For an owner, it would bring prestige and recognition beyond compare. For a handler, it would mean a big jump in income.

One man was returning to a different kind of competition. The killer had his setup all tucked away in his RV and was ready to head out. But he had one last task to perform before leaving.

His RV, a forty-two-footer, had been built as a "toy hauler." The rig was a combination camper and garage, the kind that afforded the outdoor sports lover an opportunity to bring along his "toys"—4-wheelers, motorcycles, etc., wherever he went. It worked well for setting up a grooming shop at dog shows, isolating all the loose hair from the rest of the RV.

The garage space walls were lined with cabinets stocked with all the supplies needed to make little Foo Foo beautiful. A sink along one wall was big enough to bathe all but the largest breeds. An oversized grooming table completed the little shop on wheels.

Hidden in a cabinet was the padded plastic-covered table that mounted onto the grooming table. The table had a pedal-powered lift that allowed the operator to raise and lower it like a barber's chair to the optimal height for the job at hand. A typical vertical arm on one end had a slip lead hanging from it that would be placed around a dog's neck to encourage it to stay in place while being worked on. The show dogs were accustomed to the restraint.

The custom tabletop held a few hidden features that came in handy if the other kind of subject was reluctant to stay in place and needed some restraint as well.

He checked his supplies, making sure he had everything ready for his upcoming adventure. All was in place. Finally, he checked his favorite instrument—an authentic Fairbairn Sykes fighting knife.

The knife fit his needs perfectly. A simple, utilitarian tool, it was designed to do a job and do it well. It was developed in China in the early '40s by a British Police Commander who had been trained in both English and Chinese hand-to-hand combat.

At twelve inches, it was small enough to conceal, should that be necessary. There was also a shorter version, designed to be strapped to the forearm under a shirtsleeve. He had one of those, too, but found the shorter blade to be less effective for his needs.

He held the knife up to a light, admiring its form. It was no ornamental showpiece. The entire knife was black except the edges of the razor-sharp blade. The hilt was roughly stamped out of black-painted steel and the grip was cast from black-painted cheap pot metal, but the parting line of the mold could still be clearly seen. The entire assembly was held together with a 5/16" nut screwed into the tang of the blade, forming a crude pommel. It was ugly, but it worked. He slid the blade back into the sheath and placed it in the appropriate drawer. Then he took out his phone.

Chapter Thirty-five

Sunday
Phoenix, Arizona

It had taken all day and all the energy she'd had after yesterday's murder case, but Maria had the files sorted and divided the way she preferred. Her eyes were getting blurry and she'd reached a point she knew too well, the point beyond which she was incompetent. She carefully stacked the files in chronological order and picked them up for the short walk back to her file cabinet.

About two steps into the journey her jacket caught on the corner of a desk as she rounded a turn. The files, the product of an entire day's work and organization, slipped from her grasp and spilled to the floor. A stream of English and Spanish profanity flew out of her mouth in one long unpunctuated run-on sentence.

With her hands on her head and a mournful wail of "Madre Mia" she scanned the floor. Pages were scattered randomly in a ten-foot circle. Since it had all come from the FBI and had been printed just two days earlier, the pages looked the same. Even the photos.

The photos. Maria knew that all were marked with a date and case number code, so sorting would not be difficult, just tedious. She scooped up the pages and began the process, first separating the copy from the photos, then the individual cases.

Each photo had two code numbers, one for the case and the other for the date. Fortunately, Maria had created a key so she knew which case was which. She started to lay the photos in piles on a conference table in case-date order. As she did, she had her first real chance to examine them in detail. That's when Maria started to see the absolute similarities in the wounds.

Crime scene photographers are trained crime scene investigators. They are taught to use a series of steps in all their investigations. As a result, the photos looked like they could all have been shot by the same person.

There were full-torso shots, front and back, of each victim. Pictures of the breasts, arms, necks, buttocks, and pubic areas were all from similar angles and framing. Maria started re-sorting by the subject matter of the photo and the date of the case. The results were startling.

Her table had eight columns of photos. The bottom row was the full frontal shots. Each one had a column of photos rising above it depicting a different angle or body feature—rows of left arms, of right breasts, of rear torsos, etc. Maria noticed that the neatness and sophistication of each column improved over time. The earliest photos showed some sloppiness while the newest ones showed very clean and orderly cuts.

"Oh, my God," she said. There was no question. The columns of photos clearly showed that the killer had to be one person.

"Yes!" Maria felt the rush investigators get when they find that needle in the haystack. She knew it was one person. And she knew they'd get him.

Chapter Thirty-six

Sunday
Jane's home
Minneapolis, Minnesota

She had answered the phone with her usual cheerfulness, even though she was tired from a weekend of work and exercise. Work was work but the exercise, a way to stave off the effects of aging, was a necessary evil. She worked with a narcissistic focus to keep her youthful looks and trim body, knowing how important it was to her career. Younger versions of herself kept trying to claw their way into her business.

It was a continual battle. She knew colleagues—she couldn't really call them friends—who'd been moved aside when HD cameras took over. There was no hiding even a few wrinkles from them. And television always added pounds to everyone's appearance. If she wanted to make the next move up the ladder, she had to be smarter and better looking. New York was her goal. It would have to be one of the big older networks, not Fox. Her political views wouldn't keep her off Fox; like most reporters, she had none to call her own, just took on the views of the network she worked for. No, the issue was the Fox profile. The women Fox hired had 140-plus IQs and were lawyers with trial experience and beauty pageant looks. Jane had the IQ but not the JD. She could have competed in pageants years ago but didn't. All she'd ever wanted was to be a reporter. TV was an accident.

The voice on the other end of the phone line promised her the reward she'd hoped for from all the shoe leather she'd used and all the dog hair she'd ingested at the dog show, the jackpot that could, if she played the opportunity right, move her up a rung or two in her field, maybe all the way to New York. Along with the money and prestige would come the recognition she craved, the power to frame her own agenda would help her do whatever she wished, both professionally and privately. She dressed quickly, jumped in her car, and drove north.

She found him in a horseshoe booth in the corner of the lounge, sitting in the dark. Moving with the confidence of an accomplished predator, she maneuvered to the table in a zigzag pattern, taking care not to let anyone see her face. The last thing she needed was to be recognized and have the meeting interrupted. He was seated half facing the room and half the wall, sort of casually watching the room but not obviously interested in anything in particular. He motioned her into the booth. She slid in as the server came by. As she ordered a Tanqueray gin and tonic she noticed that he turned away until the server left. Anonymity was fine with her. Deep Throat's lack of identity hadn't hurt Woodward's reputation and may have enhanced it.

He started talking, slowly at first, then with more and more detail. She wrote down nothing, trusting her amazing memory. He talked about his life and all the people he had met as he traveled the country in his big RV. She ordered another drink, as did he. About halfway through it she noticed she was getting quite a buzz on. As the minutes went by, she was following his lead in the conversation. Soon she followed him out of the room. She climbed up into the RV for the promised tour and said goodbye to reality.

Chapter Thirty-seven

Tuesday, July 21st
Outside Mora, Minnesota

By 2:00 a.m. he'd finished the grooming and was readying the body for deposit, as he called it. He had wrapped her in a brand new sheet that he'd washed several times. As with the other deposits, he'd use the sheet only once, then destroy it. He carried the body to his vehicle and gently set it up on the passenger seat, belting it in to look like a sleeping woman who'd had a few too many that night. He was confident he could convince any officer if he was pulled over. He had read that trick had worked for at least one of the other fellows in his line of work. Now for a little added panache.

He drove back to the familiar spot and unloaded the body, carefully laying it out as close to the exact position as he could recall, and posed the limbs as he had done the last time. He had to go with memory as he had no pictures; flash photography was a no-no at body deposit sites.

"There, that will fuck them up a bit," he said aloud. He returned to his vehicle and drove back to his RV, loaded the car on the trailer he hauled behind his RV, and headed for home.

As he drove he thought about his latest experiment. She was older than his previous subjects. He had believed his focus on younger women, somewhere between twenty and thirty, was natural, since they had the most to offer. They were the most beautiful, the liveliest, and most responsive. They delivered the best experiences to him in their fear, their resistance to him, and finally their submission to the inevitable.

He also believed that he drew from them some of their life experiences, their talents, and abilities. If that were true, the older, more mature, more worldly women would have something uniquely theirs to give. This one surely had.

She had aroused from the drug-induced dream-state with apprehension but also with curiosity. She seemed to become immediately aware of her circumstances but was not overwhelmed with fear. In his research, he had learned that she had done a stint in the Army when women in combat roles was just beginning. He knew there were widespread sexual assaults at the time, nearly all of them unreported until years later, and wondered if she had suffered that fate too. If so, it would have prepared her well to resist what was about to happen to her.

She began asking him questions about his background, education, and life experiences. She sounded like she was going to write his life story, a thought that interested him for a moment but he quickly dismissed. It would have led to the end of his freedom.

She then started telling him about herself. He knew she had no immediate family, but she had a cat. She made the mistake of lying to him, saying she had a daughter in high school for whom she was the sole provider. He knew what she was doing.

He knew a lot about police work and the recommended methods to help hostages stay alive. All the classes he'd attended recommended that hostages, especially female hostages, try to establish a bond with their captors and tell their captors about themselves, personal details about their lives, including their dreams for the future. When there is enough time, it almost always works to establish a bond of humanity with their captor. In fact, the longer the event goes on, the greater the chances that the captive will survive. Unfortunately for Jane, the target of all her psychological "Please like me" bonding not only had a short schedule but he recognized what she was doing. In the end, she received the same attention he had always delivered.

"Fun game to play," he said to himself as he drove away. "Certainly better than some brainless coed or waitress. Might have to try another one of them."

One day of ecstasy was all he could afford. After all, he had a life and a schedule to get on with. The last experiment had been unplanned, or rather, unscheduled, a reaction to seeing the three people at the show on Friday. His routine was now refined to the point where he could almost write a schedule for the next couple of years. He knew his activity was becoming more frequent and he should be concerned about his impulsiveness.

He'd studied past serial killers and the methods used to catch them and knew that increasing frequency would draw more law enforcement attention. But he also knew that he was good at what he did and could practice his craft with impunity anywhere in the country. And he couldn't help himself. It had become an addiction. Like any addict, he needed more frequent and more intense highs as time went along and the latest one had been better than all of the others.

She had been a more challenging catch, as he knew she would be. In spite of a manner and charm that allowed him to pick up women anywhere in the country, he knew she would be wary. His usual method was to dress right, flash his big smile, show a little cash at the bar, let them take the initiative, then offer a little excitement. They were willing to take a walk and see what the night might bring. The night brought him the thrill of control and pain. Not his pain, of course, the thrill of their pain, and the thrill of seeing the recognition in their eyes as it became clear to them that he was in control of their very existence, that he could bring them pain or pleasure, and that he was the only one who would decide which. The sexual release was the most intense after they understood. He was willing to share that release with them. He just wasn't willing to share it with the police.

With Jane, he knew he would have to suppress his alter ego or inner self, whatever it was that had often triggered a woman to reject him when it revealed itself. He had learned to control himself during the "acquisition phase" of the exercise with a typical victim but he knew it would have to be completely undetectable with Jane.

His effort paid off and she had become his. Women, even intelligent, wary, suspecting women, succumbed to his ability to calm their fears and lower their natural defenses. It was his greatest weapon, a gift, he believed, that also justified his actions. Why else would he have such ability? It was officially sanctioned from nature, or God, or The Force, whatever, in his eyes.

As he drove he reviewed the past few days in his head and why he had performed the last experiment. Certainly, the need was there but it had only been a couple of weeks since the last one. His mental schedule told him that he wouldn't be experimenting again for at least three months.

It was something about those three at the dog show. When he first saw them he pegged two of them as cops. He'd thought for years that, sooner or later, the end game would come because some cop got lucky, a witness that he hadn't noticed would have seen him or his vehicle, or maybe he'd slip up and leave some kind of trace behind. He knew from his research and his job that evidence would be found if one looked hard enough. He'd asked others at the dog show about their conversations with the four men, in a curiosity sort of way, first asking about Pete's return. It was normal to wonder if a past participant was getting back into the game. When it was confirmed that the other two were cops, and that Pete was educating them about dog shows, he'd become obsessed to learn more.

The sheriff was from the town where he'd left his previous subject, so it made sense that he would be interested. The cop was a Minneapolis homicide investigator, but he was a specialist in ballistic forensics, not serial killings. Why was he with the sheriff and Pete?

One handler, who had a reputation as an expert eavesdropper, had overheard the two talking with Phil Horvath, the Obedience handler and judge, about serial killers. He learned that Horvath was a psychologist and knew a lot about serial killers. As his conversation with this new source of information went on, he began to realize that the men were trying to learn about him. That got his heart going.

As he went about the routine of cleaning and grooming, he could easily see the special treatment he'd given her body. He'd made a personal challenge to his opponent. His careful handiwork was obvious to him, but would it be seen by those who were challenging him? It was so subtle he thought it might be missed. Oh well, if they're that stupid, all the better for me, he thought.

But he hoped they would see it. What fun was a little old-fashioned competition if the other guy didn't even know he was in the game?

Chapter Thirty-eight

Tuesday, July 21st
MCSO
Phoenix, Arizona

Maria's calculations of the timeline had ground to a halt. She'd left a message for Pete Anderson when she'd been unable to reach him the day before. Then another homicide had interfered with finishing the timeline. It was fairly straightforward; she had him under arrest in thirty-two hours, and he sang like a big canary.

Back at her whiteboard, she returned to the game of phone tag. Pete had returned her call Tuesday morning. She tagged him back. He surprised her by calling back in four minutes.

"Hey Maria. How you doing?"

"Doing great. Enjoying a nice warm Arizona summer—about one-twenty today. How is it up in winter wonderland?"

"Beautiful! When are you going to figure out that one-twenty is not right for anyone and spend your summers up here so Dan can spend his winters down there?"

"Hey, Dan's welcome anytime. He's retired, mostly, but I still have a job to do. He can come here anytime he wants. In fact, my mama was asking about him at Sunday dinner this week."

Pete thought that would be a sight he'd pay to see. His lifelong buddy, rough-and-tough Dan sitting down for Sunday dinner with a large, boisterous Mexican-American family in Phoenix. It would happen if Dan got his way on the marriage thing.

"I got your message last night. Sorry I was out all day. So what can I help you with?"

"I've been putting together a timeline for cases that might match up with Dan's case. I found eight good matches, as far as the victimology, that go back about twelve years. The match criteria are the same victim profile as far as type and cause of death, then matching them with nearby dog shows plus or minus a week of the estimated time of death. Here's the weird thing."

Pete interrupted. "The weird thing? Like slicing and dicing young women isn't the weird thing?"

"Yeah, I know. But we have to look at the similarities in weird events to find the differences in weird events. Interesting way to make a living, isn't it?"

"Sure is. What's the weird thing."

"In five of the cases it looks like the victim was taken and killed before the dog show. Some of the victims were still found after, a couple actually during the dog-show dates. But the estimated time of death was before or during the show."

"So why is that weird? I would think that backs up the case, proving the guy was in the area when the crime occurred."

"My training says that this would not be his M.O. He should want to clear out as soon as he drops the body. He is a highly organized killer and he knows that the more miles he can put between himself and his victim the better off he'll be. To still be in the area, and in at least one case where the victim disappeared before the show and was believed to have been killed after, means he must have still had her with him while at the show. That's inconsistent with a highly organized personality. They are not risk takers. There have been cases where killers have held onto bodies or body parts while appearing to live normal lives, but they are the scatterbrained, unorganized types. I think this guy would dump the bodies as soon as he is done with them."

"OK, give me your dates and I'll look at it. He paused and thought. Maria could hear him scratching his bearded chin. Finally, he said, "There are some," he paused, "inconsistencies with the AKC calendar."

"What kind of inconsistencies"

"Well, you know that the shows dates are based on a numbered week-end system, right?"

"Yes, that's what I'm using."

"Well, the weekends aren't always the same."

"What do you mean?"

"AKC doesn't always start the numbering system on the first weekend of the year. If the first of January lands on a Thursday, Friday, Saturday, or Sunday, they don't start the numbering with that weekend. They'll start it the following weekend instead. For example, this year the first was on a Friday, so the weekend numbering began with weekend one landing on the ninth and tenth. Last year the first was on Thursday, so weekend one was the third and fourth. Everything gets shifted back a week about half the time."

"That's consistent with what I found. Five of my matching events seem to be before or during the show weekend."

"I'll bet those are shift years. I have a copy of the AKC's weekend chart for the past few years. I'll scan it and email it to you. You'll be able to match it up with your odd weekends and see if those were shift years."

"Thanks, Pete. I knew there was something like that and that you'd be the guy to figure it out."

Fifteen minutes later, using Pete's chart, Maria had a new list. Pete's calendar didn't go back as far as the earliest of her cases, but she quickly figured out how to extrapolate the system for the earlier years. All eight cases she was looking at showed that the victims had been taken and killed after a major dog show had been held in the vicinity.

Maria was finishing this accounting task when she got a call from the ME who had performed the autopsy on the third victim. She had queried all of the MEs about an unusual physical characteristic they may or may not have found on the victim they autopsied.

"Dr. Kelly, I'm working a possible serial killer case. The reason I called was about a case you had four years ago involving a murdered woman."

"Yes, I got your message and pulled the file before I called. I have it right there."

"Great. You noted that the victim's pubic area had been waxed."

Maria could hear the doctor rifling through the file. He came back on the line.

"That's correct. I noted that the victim's pubic area had been waxed and it looked to me as if the hair removal had been recent, perhaps just prior to death. There was evidence of skin irritation. Hmmm."

The conversation went on a few more minutes until Maria had the answer she was looking for.

"Thank you, Doctor. If you'd like to notify the investigating officer on the case that I'm putting together a list of similar cases, it's all right with me. If we can find this guy, we'll be able to close out a bunch of cases in one arrest."

"I'll do that," the doctor replied and hung up.

Chapter Thirty-nine

8:14 a.m.
Tuesday, July 21st
Mora, Minnesota

"Sheriff, I think you'd better come out here."

The radio call came from Roy Holder, one of Sheriff Glenn Mills' older deputies. He was calling from the road that accessed the new housing development on the south side of town, the one where Sharon Stewart's body had been found. The development, which had been named "Whispering Meadows," now had a new name. As will happen in smaller communities, the locals were already calling it a variety of less than complimentary names such as Screaming Meadows, A View to a Kill, and The Drop Zone. The developer was apoplectic. Glenn had issued a department-wide directive that prohibited the use of anything other than the area's correct legal description, with the threat of suspension without pay for anyone who violated his edict. So far no one had.

"What's up, Roy?"

"Not sure I should talk about it over the air, Sheriff. But you might want to call your buddy in the Cities again, and that gal from the BCA," he said.

"Oh, shit," Mills muttered, then said, "I'm on my way." As he walked out to his car he pondered the possibilities. Someone could have desecrated the crime scene. People took local crime personally and they would try to erase it from the community's collective memory. He was sure that was it. Roy had been on the job a long time and he was part of that collective memory. By the time he left the parking lot he had decided Roy was probably over-reacting.

He was wrong.

When he got there he could see Holder's patrol car parked near where the Stewart woman had been found. Further down the street was a work van with the business title "Kanabec County Surveying" lettered on the side. Two guys in work clothes and reflective vests held hard hats in their hands as they stood by the van. Holder was half sitting on his cruiser's left rear quarter panel. His eyes were lowered and his arms were crossed. He was slowly shaking his head as if refusing to accept something. Glenn parked next to him and got out of his car.

"OK, Roy. Whatcha got?"

Deputy Holder looked up and Glenn could see tears in his eyes. Roy was a thirty-two-year veteran of the force, with time off for service in the first Gulf War. He'd been one of the first in on the ground when coalition forces reached the remains of the Iraqi Republican Guard tank units that had been decimated by 120mm cannon fire from US M1A1 Abrams tanks that had "reached out and touched someone." He'd been on the "Highway of Death" to see the results of impact of 30mm depleted uranium rounds delivered via the GAU 8 rotary cannons of A-10 Warthogs on armored and unarmored vehicles and human flesh, charred bodies frozen in grotesque poses. No clothing, no hair. No eyes. He'd seen a lot of death. Yet in spite of his experience, something had moved him to tears. Now Glenn was worried.

"Over here, Sheriff," Roy said. "I covered her up. After the ass-chewing we all got on the last one, I figured I'd better."

"Cover her up?" Glenn asked. "Oh, no."

The two walked over to the drainage ditch between two lots, the same ditch where Sharon Stewart's cut-up body had lain. Glenn gently pulled the tarp back and saw a body in what looked like the exact same place and posed exactly the same as Sharon's. She even looked like Stewart. Glenn took a quick breath as recognition hit him and he blinked his eyes in disbelief.

"Oh my God," he exclaimed. He rolled his head on his big shoulders and looked skyward for guidance. But he doubted he would be receiving any divine assistance with this. He did need assistance, though.

Holder said, "I don't know who she is, Sheriff. Not from around here, I don't think."

Mill's head swung from side to side in disbelief. "No, she's not from around here." He pulled the tarp back over her and turned away.

"Those two made the call," Holder said, indicating the two-man survey crew. "I caught it and came out here. They're here to survey for another home to be built. They saw the body, called it in, and waited. I don't know if they'll be selling any more lots soon," Holder added. Glenn nodded his understanding. It was going to be hard to sell lots in a neighborhood where naked mutilated bodies of murdered women kept dropping in. He pulled out his cellphone.

First he called his office, instructing his assistant to call all the players from the first case back in. That included the BCA Investigator and the Ramsey County Coroner's office. Then he hit the speed dial for Dan.

Chapter Forty

My phone rang as I was cleaning up from a late breakfast. I'd been on the phone pretty late the night before with Maria talking about our future, her parents, serial killers, my next trip to Arizona, her research on our serial killer, the usual stuff two people in love discuss. So I was a little behind the curve that morning. I grabbed my cellphone and saw it was Glenn.

"Hey, Glenn! You get it figured out?"

"No. I've got another one."

There was only one thing "another one" could refer to. I stiffened at the news.

"Tell me about it."

"Looks the same as the other one, blond, cut-up, same ditch, same pose. Gotta be the same guy. Any chance you can come up?"

"Yeah, I'm going to want to do that anyway. Listen, we both know this was going to go federal sooner or later. I've briefed a guy I know we can trust. I'll call him and bring him along."

"If he's all right by you that's good enough for me. I need all the help I can get. Bring him."

We rang off and I spun through the numbers in my phone. When I found Will Sanford's, I hit "Dial."

"Sanford," he answered with his usual clipped efficiency.

"Hey, Will. How's it going?"

"Been back just two days and I'm ready to leave again. How you doing, Dan?"

"I'm not sure. Just got a call from my buddy, the sheriff in Mora."

"Let me guess. He figured this thing out. It was a local guy and you don't want my help now."

"Not quite. He's got another body."

"Not good. I sent an inquiry to Quantico yesterday, but haven't heard anything back yet. Not that I'd expect to. I figured a couple of days, if not weeks, before anything shows up. I'm sure they've got a lot on their plates. Does the sheriff think it's the same guy?"

"He thinks so. But, you know how it is. He's probably just seeing things into it. I'm heading up there. You want to come along? And any chance Molly could come along?"

"I'll have to clear it with Bismarck and the local SAC," he said, referring to the Special Agent in Charge, "but I think I can get her for you. And, of course, I'll have to assign myself since I am best equipped for liaison with the locals, a rowdy and untrained bunch who, nevertheless, can, like the blind pigs they are, occasionally find an acorn in the forest."

"Great. Do you want me to pick you up or will you be using one of the helicopters your loyal subjects have so graciously provided for you?"

"You're going up there right now?"

"Yes. Glenn Mills called from the crime scene. He's got BCA on the way. I'd like to see the vic before they take her away."

"Me too. Seeing the scene still beats photos no matter how many and how good the photographer. OK, I'll get Molly tuned up and we'll go from here. What's the location?"

I gave Will the info and we said our goodbyes. I checked my email and saw that Maria had sent her report. While it printed, I closed up the house. I grabbed the papers, jumped into my Suburban and headed north again.

Chapter Forty-one

11:14 a.m.
Tuesday
Outside Mora, Minnesota

I pushed the limit driving north. Not too much, though; the vic was already dead. But I wanted to get there before the BCA started processing the scene. There is a freshness that is lost as the minutes tick by. I needed that first fresh impression.

Glenn had said that the body was posed exactly like the first one. I doubted he was comparing it to a picture. He was looking into his memory, and at this point he was seeing bodies in his sleep. I thought he was just overreacting. Probably.

I rolled into the scene and took a moment to gather my thoughts. This time, I noticed that the vehicles were parked well away from the crime scene and that the locals had already set up one of those quick portable tents over the body. Keeping the sun off her was a good idea in the summer heat. Many people who don't experience Minnesota summers think that, in light of our winters, summers must be pretty mild. I, on the other hand, think that summers in places like Arizona, Florida, and south Texas, should be about 160 degrees. That's what they'd have to be to have the same temperature spread that we do. A typical Minnesota year will see a range from around -15 or lower to the high 90s, like it was that day. That's over 110 degrees from top to bottom. To be fair, those southern winter getaways would have to peak out around a buck and a half. Let's see their AC bills then.

Glenn met me on the road.

"This is pretty bad, Dan. Two drops in as many weeks and the M.O. is the same. I was really hoping your traveling serial killer idea was going to pan out. Now it looks like this guy is in my lap."

"Don't know that yet, Glenn. Let's take a look."

I took a step and Glenn blocked my way. "Dan, there's something I haven't told you." He paused. "About the victim." Glenn was staring into my eyes. He was looking at me with an expression I'd seen a thousand times. It was a face cops saved for those moments when they have to deliver the "bad news," the news that a family member has been injured or killed. It's a part of law enforcement work that all cops have to deal with during their careers. Some are better at it than others. But all have to do it. I put my hands on my hips and braced myself.

"Dan, it's Jane Vanderloo."

I felt my knees weaken as the breath was sucked from my lungs. I looked toward the tent and could see part of a leg from under the tarp. Glenn grabbed my arm to steady me and hold me back. He knew my first reaction would be to run over. And he knew that I needed to process the news before I saw her. We stood transfixed for what seemed like a long time as I tried to wrap my head around his words.

Someone I knew had become the killer's most recent victim. She was someone I'd once had a deep, intimate relationship with. That relationship still played a certain important part in my life experience.

She had been here when the first victim had been found. Within seconds the wheels started turning in my head. Did her presence here play a part in getting her killed? Or could it have been random?

You've heard me say it before: there's no such thing as coincidence in a criminal investigation. Jane's murder and being left in the same spot was not random. Something she'd done had selected her for death. Or was it something we'd done? Or didn't do.

"OK," I said, looking at Glenn. "I'm ready. Let's go."

"Dan, you don't have to do this."

I looked at Glenn. I knew he was trying to protect me. And he was right; I didn't have to do it. But I had to and he knew it. I gave him a look and shook his hand off my arm.

We walked over to the tent. I made my way close to the body and pulled back the tarp. It was Jane and, just as Glenn had said, she was posed in exactly the same pose as the first victim, or at least as exactly as I could remember. We'd know more once we compared this scene to photos from the first one.

I turned away. I didn't need to look long. I didn't want her image burned into my psyche as others had been. I wanted to remember her as the intelligent, beautiful, vivacious woman she'd been. I felt a fire begin to burn in my soul. I wanted this guy. I *needed* this guy.

I heard the crunch of tires on gravel and looked over to see Will and Molly pulling in.

"Glenn, tell your guys to let them in. It's the FBI guy I told you about."

"Looks like two of them" Glenn observed as he waved at his man on the roadblock.

"Yeah, he's a Special Agent out of the Cities. His wife is a trained profiler."

"She's a fed, too?" he asked.

"Yeah, I introduced them." That wasn't quite right, but it was close enough.

"I'll bet that makes for interesting table talk at dinner. Kind of like what you and Maria must have."

"Don't know yet. They just got back from their honeymoon."

Will and Molly walked up, creds in hand as the feds always do. They want everyone to know that Uncle Feddie is here and all will be right in the world. Even though I knew this pair wouldn't affect that typical Fed attitude, they still played the role. It's part of their culture.

"Will, Molly, this is Sheriff Glenn Mills. Glenn, Will Sanford and his wife, Molly." I left off Molly's last name since I didn't know what she was going to go by. She filled in the blank.

"Molly Foss, Sheriff," Molly said as she shook his hand.

"Will, the victim is Jane Vanderloo," I said. I knew that he knew her too.

"From Channel 7?" Will asked.

"Yes. And she was investigating the first murder. She was here at the crime scene after the first body was found."

I noticed Molly had an odd look on her face. Once again, the ping had struck.

I hadn't known Molly long enough to know how well her ping worked. In fact, I doubted Will knew. Working with the same partner for years, you get to know their ping so well it's like it hits both of you at the same time. Not so with new partners.

Usually it's subtle, in the background, easy to ignore. I know that there have been plenty of times the ping has sounded and I missed it. I was too focused on the obvious. Later, the obvious turns out to be irrelevant and the ping held the answer all along.

As I looked at Molly I got the feeling that she'd been pinged hard. She had something to say. Will saw it too and asked, "Something, Molly?"

Molly pondered for a moment, probably deciding whether or not to stick her neck out, then said, "Dan, you said she showed up here when the first body was found, right?"

I nodded. "Correct."

"This is pretty far out of the Cities. Any idea how she knew to come here?"

Glenn kicked at the dirt road beneath his shoes. "No, but I've been thinking about that. Or, had been thinking about that." He looked at me. "I guess I let it go when I got tied up with other business."

It's easy to drop balls in an investigation. New information comes along and suddenly you're off on a new trail like a dog with his nose to the ground. In Glenn's case, he had a whole county to take care of. Other, less urgent things, get left behind. Sometimes forever. I nodded to Glenn. "Any ideas?" I asked.

"Yeah, it's pretty clear that she had to have been tipped. That means someone in my department must have dropped a dime," he said, using the old-school reference to a pay phone call. I used to think we should change it to "dropped a quarter" but now I think we should say "Hit the speed dial" or some such, since pay phones are pretty much extinct.

We all considered what it meant. Most likely, Jane had been contacted by someone within Glenn's office, which brought her to the first body drop. Now, only days after we'd all been at the dog show in Duluth, she was dead in the same manner as the first victim. Why?

"Will told me you two went to Duluth last Friday to see a dog show. Is that correct?" Molly said in strict, formal federal-eze.

Glenn and I nodded agreement. "She showed up there, too," I said. Then Glenn smacked his forehead with a "Doh!" sound and shook his big head. We all knew what he was thinking. Whoever tipped Jane about the body had also tipped her about our trip to Duluth. "I'll find out who did it right now!" He stormed off with his phone in his hand.

The big BCA crime scene RV lumbered in as Glenn contacted his office. We could hear him lighting someone's ass on fire. With his experience as a Minneapolis street cop, he was good at it. I'll bet his staff had never seen that side of him before.

We lucked out. I saw Judy Loveless was back to process the scene. Having the same investigator is a big plus in a case where you think you have a single perpetrator. She could use her training and experience to mentally compare the two events and find parallels another investigator might miss.

She got out of the crime scene RV with her camera bag, setting it on the step and digging into it as I walked over to her.

"Judy, before you start, I need to tell you who the vic is."

She looked up from her bag and gave me a curious look. Her look darkened as she saw the pain in my eyes. "Who is it?" she whispered.

"It's Jane Vanderloo."

Judy looked away, out into space, as she dealt with the information. After what seemed like forever, she looked back and I knew she was prepared to do her job. I gave her a nod and turned away.

She got right to work with her camera.

While the BCA team did their job, I reviewed the case for Will and Molly. I started with Glenn's first case and followed the timeline through my conversation with Maria the previous night. That the bodies had been cleaned except for the dog hair seemed to interest Molly. I covered the dog show possibilities and what Maria had come up with from the Fed's ViCAP system as far as possible additional cases.

"So, now Maria is putting together a timeline including the possible cases and comparing that to the dog show information. She's looking for any overlap in persons who were at most or all of the dog shows that are related to the body drops. It's going to take some time to come up with a list."

Molly answered for the FBI contingent.

"I think we can help on that. Nothing like sheer horsepower when it comes to tracking down details like those."

I saw Judy waving us over to the body. I alerted the others and started walking. I hung back from the scene, not wanting to see any more than I had to.

Viewing bodies has never been a part of the job that I enjoy or even find interesting the way most CSIs do. To me they are just a reminder of the sick and twisted minds of some of our so-called fellow humans. You can still read or see interviews on television with people who believe that this type of behavior is just the result of poor childhood nutrition or an abusive home environment. I disagree. I've seen enough of it to know that there is evil in this world. Some people's heads just don't work right and they are capable of acts beyond the imagination of normal minds. They have no empathy for their fellow human beings and can kill with no more regret than stepping on a bug. To kill with a knife is to kill in a very intimate, intensely emotional, personal way. When you are dealing with someone who holds that perspective on reality, it's tough to know how to catch them.

"It sure looks the same to me," Judy said. "I've taken photos and I brought along the file from last time so I can do some comparisons. Why don't you folks go get some lunch or something while I do that. Should take about an hour, maybe less."

Even though we'd all just seen a horrible crime scene, we were all cops. And cops know to take a lunch break when the opportunity presents itself. There may not be another chance. We got into Glenn's car and headed for Hazel's.

Chapter Forty-two

Judy Loveless was having mixed feelings. She was sure the scene she was processing was the work of the same individual who killed the woman in the previous case. But, aside from knowing the victim, there was something different here. She couldn't quite put her finger on it, but something in her gut told her to be very attentive to the scene.

Crime scene investigators are a unique sort. They have to be able to carefully and scientifically process a scene that often includes whole human bodies and other relevant evidence. In her career, Judy had processed scenes with deaths and injuries that were the result of gunshots, knives, auto accidents, falls from buildings and, in one case, a man who somehow fell out of an airplane. She'd seen the results from wild animal attacks, fires, chemical exposures, impacts from large moving objects such as trucks or agricultural equipment, ligature strangulation, severe beatings, and even natural causes. Not all were ruled crimes, but they had to be treated as if they were, just in case. But this case, with its parallels to the earlier one, had her in a quandary.

She carefully took photos of the knife wounds, knowing that if the cases were linked, the wounds would be critical when they went to court. Anytime you are trying to prove a suspect repeated his crime, the defense will try to prove, by showing differences in the evidence, that one was done by someone else. Perhaps a copycat. As she shot the multiple photos with a high-end Nikon digital camera, she felt something was different. A copycat killer would be easy to prove if the wounds were different so she took extreme close-ups of individual wounds, full torso shots she could map the wounds on, and a full in-situ shot, showing exactly how the body was found. When she completed her work, she turned the site over to her assistant and headed to the BCA Mobile Crime Lab.

Inside the converted RV she popped the photo card from the camera and inserted it into her computer, which was hooked to a high-definition printer. She selected the photos she wanted to work with and hit the "Print" button. As the printer did its work she dug out the photo file from the first case. She laid the first set on the left side of the truck's only table and the new photos, as they came off the printer, on the right. Then she started studying them.

It took about twenty minutes for it to hit her. The new victim had not been held and tortured for days. Jane's wounds were all fresh, which was consistent with her being taken Sunday night and killed within a twenty-four-hour time frame. Second, there were minor differences in the knife wounds on Jane. And the differences weren't on all the cuts, just some of them. She had the close-ups side by side and could see that some of the cuts on Jane overlapped slightly older cuts, as though the killer had gone back over the same area that had been, to the untrained eye, already worked, in spite of her belief that Jane had been held only a few hours before being killed. She carefully checked the first victim's photos and couldn't find a single overlapping cut, but the second one had many, though they were all on the victim's front torso area from just beneath the breasts down to the pubic area. The arms, legs, neck, head, and the complete dorsal, or backside of the victims, looked identical.

She took the torso shot of the second victim and started looking for a pattern in the overlapping cuts, literally connecting the dots. It took another twelve minutes, but after four tries, using a new copy of the photo each time, she saw the pattern.

Chapter Forty-three

Glenn was still on his carrot kick. The rest of us were eating more typical Midwestern-diner fare, ranging from a hamburger for me to a Cobb salad for the bride. Will had a tuna melt and all agreed we'd come back to Hazel's if the opportunity presented itself.

We settled up with the restaurant, Will and Molly getting the fed-required receipts, and loaded back into Glenn's car. The trip back to the crime scene was a quiet observational journey. I guess everyone noticed that I had just picked at my burger and fries. I had no real appetite, which was unusual. Glenn tried to take our minds off the murder by telling us all about the current fishing prospects.

"It's a bit tougher now in mid-summer. You have to get out at sunup or sundown and that's pretty early or late, depending on if you are a morning or night person."

"I'd vote for nighttime" Will said.

"Dan doesn't have to vote. He don't fish," Glenn said, giving me a sideways glance in the passenger seat.

"Hey, I've fished. I used to own a boat, you will recall."

"Yeah, I remember your boat. It would be great for fishing if you wanted to troll at about forty knots. The only thing that boat was good for was booze cruising or chasing women."

"Chasing women?" Molly asked innocently. "That sounds about right."

"Will, what have you been filling this poor girl's head with? You know I am in a committed relationship," I said.

"Sure, now. Keep in mind I knew you P.M."

"What's P.M.?" Glenn asked.

"Pre-Maria. He was a definite threat in a target-rich environment before Maria came along and tamed him."

"OK, I'll give you that. But I'm a settled-down kind of guy now."

The banter continued until we reached the road into the housing development. Then we got quiet.

Judy Loveless came out of the BCA truck at the sound of our arrival. She had a somber look on her face.

"Folks, I found something that may be the strangest thing I've seen in eight years on this job. I don't think this is going to make your day," she said to me as she motioned us into the truck. We followed her lead and found ourselves standing around a small table in the front of the equipment-filled box. She sat down and pulled out some pictures.

"These are pictures of the wounds from the first case. As you can see they are placed with near precision separation, forming a latticed pattern on the victim. In fact, they are present over nearly the entirety of the victim's surface."

We could all see the pattern and definition of the wounds. It reminded me of a hound's-tooth check jacket I have. I may never wear that jacket again. I decided I should have had a beer with my burger. Judy produced another photograph.

"This is the pattern on the second victim. While it is almost identical, and I believe the wounds were made by the same weapon, there are differences. Here, on the torso, some wounds overlap. At first I thought that perhaps the killer had just gotten sloppy in his work, but the overlapping cuts form another pattern. It took a few tries but I found the pattern.

She pulled a fresh photo of Jane's torso and, using a black marking pen, she connected the sites of the unique wounds, like a kid doing a connect-the-dots picture. As she did, letters appeared. When she finished we all stood there stunned into dead silence. Finally, Molly said it for all of us.

"Oh my God, Dan!"

The letters spelled out

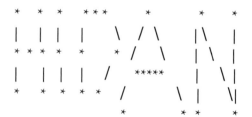

HI DAN

Chapter Forty-four

With over thirty years in law enforcement, I'd heard of cases in which criminals had issued personal challenges to the people who were trying to catch them. I'd heard of it, but it is so rare that I'd never experienced it. In the thousands of cases I've worked, no one had ever plainly and clearly flipped me the bird. I very nearly lost the little lunch I had eaten.

Molly saw what was happening and quickly stepped in.

"Dan, sit down right here," she said, pulling over a chair. As the person in the room with the most psychological training, she took over explaining the meaning of what we were looking at.

"This is actually good news. We now know that the killer knows who you are and that you are on the case. The most logical explanation is that he was at the dog show last Friday and saw you there. This is a personal challenge, which means that he doesn't believe you can catch him."

"That's great, Molly. He goes out and kills a friend of mine, a former girlfriend of mine, slices her up like this to send me a message?"

"I don't accept that Ms. Vanderloo is dead solely as a method of delivering his message. I think he was due to kill again anyway. Do you have that timeline Maria came up with?"

"Yeah, it's in my folder." I dug through the file folder and came out with Maria's list of possible associated crimes by date. The timeline started twenty years ago and showed eight cases. There was a list of bullet points that Molly reviewed and shared. She began her explanation.

"You see here that Maria found eight similar cases. No doubt there are more, but the eight she found are enough to show his pattern. Maria also notes here that the cause of death is absolutely the same—extreme blood loss caused by numerous non-lethal knife wounds ending with a single thrust of a double-edged weapon from under the front of the rib cage upward into the heart.

"All the victims were female, between twenty-three and thirty-two, between five two and five seven. All were blond." Molly paused, then said, "Here's an interesting note—she says that there were three victims whose pubic areas were shaved or waxed just prior to death and she believes the killer did it. She checked with the coroners on those cases and found that those three victims were not natural blonds. She further checked with the investigating officers who reported that family members and close associates reported that shaving the pubic area was not typical behavior. One reports that a boyfriend stated that the victim in that case would never shave that area; he'd asked her to and she'd refused.

"So it looks like he has a penchant for natural blonds and if they turn out not to be, he shaved or waxed the area to make them appear that way. Here's the most important part as far as you are concerned, Dan. The timeline shows an increasing frequency. This is common in these cases."

She looked into my eyes. "I believe that he would have killed again anyway, because it was part of his increasing frequency. He is helping us by making this personal. You can't let it be personal to you. This is evidence, nothing more. And it's evidence that will help us catch him."

"Nice try, Molly. Those may be the facts but I'm still the guy with his name carved into a dead woman's body."

Chapter Forty-five

Will turned to Judy and said, "This is now a federal case. All evidence you find here will be turned over to the Bureau as soon as I can get a team here. If any of this leaks," he said with a glance toward Glenn, "there will be hell to pay."

We all nodded. Everyone in the truck knew the consequences of leaked evidence. In this case, with an intelligent killer who was confident in his methods, he would change his M.O. to throw us a curve. One of the most famous, or infamous, examples was the Atlanta Child Killer case. In that case, someone from the Atlanta Police Department leaked that they had recovered fiber and hair from several of the bodies. The fiber was specific to a type of carpeting used in car interiors. After that, the killer started throwing the bodies into the rivers around Atlanta.

The FBI profilers assigned to that case had actually predicted that change after the news leak, but profiling was so new then that no one believed them. Ultimately, it was that call by the profilers that resulted in staking out the bridges over the Chattahoochee River and, on the last night of the stakeout, the man who was finally tried and convicted of the murders was caught when he threw a body off a bridge. But he wasn't convicted for killing any of the boys that were thrown in the river. As the killer correctly determined from the news reports, throwing the bodies into the river removed the hair and fiber evidence from the bodies.

Judy nodded her understanding. She'd had to turn over cases to the feds before. In this case, she didn't mind.

"You can have it. I've got the case file from the first one right here too: you can have it all. All I've thought about since the one two weeks ago was what the press would do with it. As soon as they find out the bodies lost so much blood, well, you know what they'll call this guy?"

We all shook our heads.

"He'll be the 'Vampire Killer' and you'll wind up with a pile of copy-cats. I can see the headlines—Bloodless Body found in Minneapolis, Count mounts as 'Count' is still loose, Blood Killer Sucking Police Budgets Dry. You can have him."

Again, we shook our heads at Judy's insight. She was right; the press would love this guy. Then Molly made it worse.

"There's another factor here. Ms. Vanderloo was a celebrity. There's no way we're going to be able to keep her death out of the press. And they're going to want a cause, other than another simple homicide. It's not going to take them long to notice her body was found in Mora, where another female was recently found dead. If anything about the cause of death or the term 'serial killer' or, God forbid, 'vampire,' gets out, you'll have reporters from all over the world on the next plane here. There'll be a stampede to Mora and we won't be able to keep it from becoming a circus."

We nodded our understanding. "What can we do?" Glenn asked.

"As I said, this is now a federal case," Will said. "Any compromise of information will be treated in the harshest terms available. Our office will prepare a press release that will state the cause of death was a stab wound. That's the truth. And we'll talk with Ms. Vanderloo's employers. I'll guarantee them first shot on anything we come up with and threaten them with obstruction if they leak."

"I'll have a word with everyone in my department," Glenn said. I was sure it would be more than just a word. He'd threaten them, then tell them how important they were to a successful conclusion to the case. Then he'd threaten them again, just for good measure. By the time he was done none of them would recall even being at the scene of the crimes.

There would also be at least one other conversation between Glenn and one of his people. He would figure out who had tipped Jane the first time, and then again last Friday. That person was in for the ass-chewing of his or her life, topped off with living with the fact that his news contact was now a victim.

We trooped back out into the hot summer sun. The body had been wrapped and was ready to go to St. Paul for the autopsy, although that might change now with Big Brother on the case. I asked Will how he wanted to handle it.

"I'll inform the SAC that you asked for our assistance. The fact that Maria has a similar case and that the others are spread all over the country will justify our entry. It will probably be assigned a Major Case number in D.C."

I nodded. Major Cases get special treatment by the Men in Black. Others included the aforementioned Atlanta Child Killer and the 9/11 attacks. Important cases draw the attention of the giant in a big way. But it can be a two-edged sword for the agents involved. If you are the one to solve a major case, the career rewards can be great. But screw one up and you'll be investigating illegal seal harvesting in Barrow, Alaska.

One of the key guys on the Atlanta case received both a letter of commendation and an official reprimand from the Director of the FB and I within a week's period. The letter of commendation was for his work solving the case and assisting with the trial strategy, which resulted in the conviction. The letter of reprimand was for allowing an answer he'd given a reporter regarding the probability that the suspect would be convicted to be printed as a quote. Like all good reporters, one had asked the FBI guy if he thought the suspect was guilty. The Special Agent gave the only acceptable answer, which was "He fits the profile. If it does turn out to be him, I think he looks pretty good for a good percentage of the killings." This was at the end of an interview that his bosses had authorized with a magazine reporter and, in fact, had ordered him to do in spite of his reluctance. The reporter then took the statement completely out of context and it was picked up by newspapers that ignored the guy's qualifier and produced headlines like "FBI Man says suspect guilty." That's what you get for cooperating with the press. That's why I usually don't.

Outside in the heat Will asked, "Dan, can you get Maria up here for a task force meeting? I think we need to get started on this as soon as we can and she's going to be needed for the associated case study she did."

I thought for a moment. It was Tuesday afternoon. She'd have to get approval from her boss. He was a guy who was always willing to go the extra mile to solve a case, and the one in Scottsdale was still open on his desk. But he had had his differences with Big Brother over the years, political differences that had been magnified in recent times. Still, I thought he'd look at this as a way to show the feddies that his people were as good as any out there. So, assuming his approval, I figured the earliest I could get Maria to Minnesota would be Wednesday night. That meant Thursday for the first task force meeting. And it was likely that we wouldn't get everything done in one day, so Maria would have to stay over the weekend. Tough for me, but I was willing to make sacrifices in the name of justice.

"I'll see. I think the quickest would be by tomorrow night. Maybe we could have dinner with you and Molly and talk about a game plan."

"Good idea. And let her boss know that the Bureau will pick up the tab for travel and overtime."

"That'll soften the blow. Sounds good."

Chapter Forty-six

Tuesday
Maricopa County Sheriff's Office
Phoenix, Arizona

Maria answered the phone on the third ring, a bit slow for her.

"Homicide. Fernandez," she said.

My usual greeting would be something like "Hey, mamacita. I got some time to keel, so you want to check out a body I found in my bedroom this morning?" said with my best Cheech Marin accent. But even the prospect of a few days with Maria couldn't block out the shock of the morning's events.

I said, "Hey, how you doing?"

"You all right?" she asked. I should have expected that she would sense the tension and shock I was feeling. It's not sexist to realize that an intimate would immediately read that.

I stumbled on the words but told her we had another body, that the feds were requesting her presence and that I needed her in Minnesota as soon as possible.

"Can you come up here right away? Will and Molly are on board now. Will says he wants both of us on the interjurisdictional team. He wants to see what you have and said that the feds will pay for your travel if you can get free."

"The feds are going to do us a favor?" she asked, referring to her department. The tension between the FBI and her boss was well known to all.

"That's what he said. If you can make it, he wants to get together for dinner tomorrow night and go over everything, then start a task force investigation on Thursday."

"OK. I'll have the rest of the information on the dog shows in question from the AKC by tomorrow morning. I've got a pretty-well-defined timeline with locations and such. Pete had the key to that with the shifting of the AKC calendar from year to year. Give me a minute to check with my boss and I'll call you back."

She hung up. I walked over to some shade away from the crime scene and started thinking about what all I'd have to get done by the next day. I was doing a better job of keeping my house visitor-ready, but still there were last-minute details I needed to see to, like clean towels and sheets. And a stop at the grocery store. Funny how domesticated I'd become.

I also had a few thoughts about telling Maria who this newest victim was. My first thought was to wait until she got here. But I knew that was wrong. She'd blow up if I just dropped it on her at the meeting. And there was the news angle. As soon as the media heard it was Jane, the story would go national. I envisioned Maria sitting in the boarding area at the airport, watching the thirty-minute national news loop repeating itself ad nauseum and seeing the story. I decided I'd better tell her now and get it over with. My phone rang.

"Hey baby. That was quick."

"Sure was. I got through to my boss and he cleared it with the sheriff. I called travel and I'm on the late morning flight. It gets me up there about 4:00 in the afternoon tomorrow. That all right?"

"You bet. I'll be waiting at the gate."

"I'll see you there."

Before I could ring off she said, "Hey, what's going on?"

"What do you mean?" I tried to evade. Silence

"OK." I said. "There's one more thing I think I should tell you right now."

Maria must have sensed the caution in my voice. She answered with a long drawn out, "OK. I'm listening."

"Maria, the victim is Jane Vanderloo, the reporter. Do you remember her? She was at the first crime scene."

I'll admit that question was stupid on my part. Of course she remembered Jane, probably had a file on her by then. So, I guess I figured she'd say something like "Yeah, I remember her," or words to that effect. I was wrong.

"Oh my God! Dan, victim selection is very important in serial killer cases. Sure, there's a slim chance this is coincidence, but very slim. There's only one reason the killer would pick her and that's to get to *you*."

"That's pretty much what Molly said, and she's been to the FBI's serial killer training classes."

"Well, so have I, the short course, anyway. And Molly's right. These guys are very picky about who they choose. They have to satisfy the killer's specific needs. Your ex-girlfriend is the vic. I'm sorry to say that's why she was chosen. Oh, Dan! I'm so sorry."

"It gets worse. He carved a message, a greeting to me, into her. It's not obvious but he cut the words "Hi Dan" into her belly. Judy Loveless discovered it. I guess that makes it personal."

Maria was quiet for a moment. I thought maybe I'd lost the signal. Then she said, "Dan, I know this must be tearing at you, but it's really a plus for our team. If he's singled you out as his opponent, he'll do other things to try to connect with you. You may have talked to him when you, Glenn, and Pete went to the dog show. Think about who you talked to and how they struck you. Did you get a feeling on any of them? Don't answer right now, just think about. This guy's already been in front of you."

"OK. Email your flight info and I'll meet you at the gate."

One of the few remaining perks for a law-enforcement type is that we can still meet incoming visitors at the arrival gates without having to be a traveler ourselves. You have to call ahead, identify your department and what flight you're meeting, and check-in through the airport P.D. to get a gate pass, but that's all simpler than standing in line at the baggage carousels. If you are known to the airport guys, and I am, you can even leave your car out front in the Police Car Only area. I walked over to Will, who was talking on his phone. He looked at me and signaled the question thumbs up or down. I gave him a thumbs up. He nodded his understanding.

"That's correct. And I have it confirmed. The representative of the MCSO will be available. I'll need to hold the first team meeting on Thursday to go over the case histories and start the process. Nine o'clock sound good?"

He listened, then said,

"OK, we're set. You'll talk with D.C. and get them on board?"

Another pause.

"Got it. See you Thursday."

He hung up and looked at me.

"When will Maria get here?"

"She's cleared and on the afternoon flight tomorrow that gets in at 4:00. I told her we'd have dinner with you and Molly to set the ground rules and get a head start on your 'Team,'" I said, making quotation marks in the air. Did I say I'm a bit skeptical when the big boys get involved?

"Good. I want you two on this all the way. We'll supply background and feet on the ground in the other locations. I want to put together a formal list of the cases Maria believes are related and reopen those. We can take a fresh look at the files with the local investigating officers and re-interview witnesses, analyze evidence, you know the routine. If D.C. agrees with our findings, we'll have a Major Case and that will get us the horsepower to run this guy down. It's pretty clear that he's in the end stages of his run. He's already killing with more frequency. So if we don't get him, there's going to be a big body count in the next few months. Molly says it's now or never. He'll kill another eight or ten, plus maybe a mass killing before he implodes and either calls us or pops himself."

Will was referring to the tendency for these guys to up the ante as they become more and more addicted to the thrill of control. A quick definition is needed here. A mass murderer is defined as a guy who kills a bunch of people all at once as opposed to a serial killer, a guy who kills over time. Several famous mass murderers turned out to be serial killers who had reached a point where their frequency rate became more than one at a time. Ted Bundy was one of them. He had killed many women before the January 1978 invasion of a sorority house in Florida where he moved himself into that killer elite status of serial killer turned mass murderer. His final tally has been estimated at between forty and four hundred; no one really knows. And now no one will ever know. After more than ten years of appeals, that animal was finally put down in 1989.

I thought our guy had killed more than enough. None of us wanted to even consider "between forty and four hundred."

I told the group what Maria had said about the connection to me and Molly agreed. Glenn and I looked at each other and tried to discern who we talked to at the dog show that could have been a vicious serial killer. Both of us just shook our heads. It would take some work. We agreed to meet at the new FBI offices in the Minneapolis suburb of Brooklyn Center in two days. Hopefully, I'd have some insight by then.

Chapter Forty-seven

When I joined the MPD, I was at a point in my life where I wasn't into guns any more than any other typical Minnesota kid who'd done some pheasant or deer hunting. I'd taken the usual Department of Natural Resources firearm safety class, gone out after game in the fall, and done a little shooting. As for the hunting itself, my preference was pheasant hunting. Both duck hunting and deer hunting involve sitting for hours in a blind waiting for the game to come to you. That's not my nature, which is to go after whatever I want. I liked pheasant hunting simply because it's active—you go after the game. But by the time I started classes at the U the only handgun shooting I'd done was with a friend's dad's guns and that experience was less than satisfactory. We took several handguns with us to the shotgun warm-up range on a friend's farm and had at it. We couldn't hit a bull in the butt with a bass fiddle. Looking back, I'm a little surprised we didn't hurt ourselves.

But back to the police department. I spent some time on the range with other cops, men and women. It was there that I received my first introduction into proper handgun shooting. In just a couple of trips to the police range I learned about grip, sight picture and front sight, breathing, and the most important thing—trigger control. Ask any competitive shooter and they'll tell you that shooting is 80 percent trigger control. Knowing how to squeeze a trigger and when the exact moment is right to squeeze the trigger without moving the gun off target, plus the ability to re-engage, is what shooting is all about. Turned out I had a bit of a knack for it, after a fashion. And, even more important, I liked it. It was fun.

When Maria and I worked our first case together I saw that she was super smart, a hard worker, insightful investigator, and a competitive shooter. Pile on her good looks and it was a match made at the PD range.

Ah, Maria. My new soulmate. Now I understood what Leonard Bernstein was writing about. She was at that moment heading to the airport with her bikini for my hot tub and files for my murder case. What could be better? When it comes to cop love, it's the best thing I've ever experienced.

We needed to talk more about the marriage thing. I could live in the land of eternal summer—summers in Minnesota, winters in Arizona. We'd have to have something up here on a lake though, I thought. Midsummer in Phoenix is a cast-iron bitch. I was thinking I could sell the Robbinsdale house and find a nice place, maybe one that already has bookshelves.

Chapter Forty-eight

I picked up Maria more or less on time at 4:15 and we drove west to Edina, the suburb I grew up in. It's an interesting mix of middle to upper-middle class homes and businesses, including the world's first enclosed shopping mall. The mall, called Southdale, is modestly sized by today's standards, and it's a fraction of the size of its legacy, the Mall of America, a town unto itself located in Bloomington, just across the highway from the airport. Personally, I still prefer Southdale. I've only been inside "The Mall" a handful of times, usually to meet someone who thought that a combination shopping mall, restaurant center, and indoor amusement park would be a convenient place to rendezvous. It's not.

We drove up France Avenue from Interstate 494 to a small independent restaurant I favored. It has kind of a British pub atmosphere, good food, reasonable drink prices and, most important, quiet. Too many large chain restaurants are simply too noisy for a conversation and the ones that are quiet enough have tables so packed together that eavesdropping is an issue. We parked near the front door in the almost vacant parking lot and headed inside.

As expected, we were first to arrive. I'd told the others, Will, Molly, and Pete, to show up around 5:30. That would allow for a delayed flight or give Maria and me a little private time. Bingo on number two.

I checked in with the reception desk and told them we had friends who'd be along in about forty-five minutes. We headed to the bar, grabbed a high-top table, and ordered a couple of beers and a plate of buffalo wings. I like spicy food but over the time we've been together, I've learned that Maria can put away bites that would have melted the inside of my mouth like cellophane tossed into a campfire. We each ordered different sauces.

"So, how's Mom?" I started.

"Doing well," Maria replied. "Her blood pressure has settled down since she quit smoking. It's weird. You nag someone about something for years and finally a near-death experience convinces them that lighting money on fire is bad for their health."

"Good. Glad to hear it." I really like Maria's mom. We caught up on her family and mine, a process that takes her a lot longer. We were about halfway through the wings and our second round of beers when the rest of the group walked in.

Will led the way with Molly trailing and Pete bringing up the rear. We grabbed our beers and wings and headed up front to meet them. I don't mind eating in the bar. In fact, I usually prefer it, but this get-together needed a bit of privacy and quiet so I'd told the front desk gal to save us something in the back corner. She led us to a round table with five chairs away from other diners. Will and I grabbed the chairs that had their backs to the wall and let us face the crowd, the windows, and doors, of course.

"Hey, Maria," Pete said. "How are things in Phoenix?"

"Same old, same old," Maria replied. "They kill 'em and I find 'em. Nothing as interesting as what we're here for."

That brought the subject at hand to the surface rather quickly. Molly was seated next to Maria and Molly quickly took the lead. "We have eight cases going back twelve years. All the victims' estimated dates of death line up with the presence of a dog show being nearby. The forensic data shows an increasing level of professionalism in the killings with the bodies being increasingly neater, if that's an acceptable thing to say, and less trace present at each body dump site." Molly was holding a copy of Maria's file that I'd provided yesterday.

"I'm especially impressed with the 'blond' thing you nailed. That really tightens the victimology profile. But we'll go over all the technical stuff tomorrow. I want to talk to Pete tonight about the whole dog show world and if he has any thoughts."

Pete looked uncomfortable. He'd told me that he wasn't sure he could add anything to our conversation. I'd told him to just come along and enjoy dinner. His wife, Anne, was out of town. She writes cookbooks and has enough fans—read: book sales—that her publisher sends her on book-release tours. Her latest book was on desserts and Pete said he had spent the last two years fighting her requests for taste testing. Like most of us, he's battling his waistline as he ages. She told him to do what the taste-testers do—just chew it up and spit it out. He told me he's too Norwegian—read: cheap—to waste good food that way.

He looked at Molly in response to her statement. "I know the dog show world and I know the people who show around here. But it sounds like the person you're looking for might be from anywhere. I don't know where to begin and I sure wouldn't point you at anyone unless I was sure."

"That's perfect, Pete," Molly said. "We aren't really expecting you to solve this. Just tell us about the show process, the people, the history, things that you are sure about."

Molly proved to be a skillful interviewer. As dinner progressed she quizzed Pete about how people become involved in the sport of showing dogs, how people move into their various roles, and become handlers, breeders, and judges. She guided him through a maze of questions about specific people and learned how handlers learn their trade and how people decide what breed to show. She asked how people generally travel to shows—drive or fly, where they stay—hotels or RV parks—and where they eat—restaurants or cook for themselves. All of the answers determine an individual's ability and opportunity to take captives and torture them to death. I listened as she quizzed Pete about the superintendents and the vendors.

"I really think that the superintendents are the least likely. They are too busy and have too many people with them. They have a lot of work to do and are busy the entire time from setup to tear down. Their only downtime would be during the show and, even then, they are somewhat busy. Plus they travel as a group."

We all nodded understanding as he went on.

"And the vendors are usually regional. If you go to a lot of shows in your home area, you'll see the same vendors at those shows, but they just don't travel that far. They don't need to. Maria's list has shows from here to Ohio to Arizona and I can't think of one vendor who would go to that combination of shows. One vendor I know is a local guy, a Realtor who works with my sister-in-law. His wife makes custom leashes. They go as far as Cleveland for the big IX show in December, probably because it's so big, and they'll go down to Kansas City, but that's because she has relatives there. So about half the country is all they travel and they go farther than anyone else I know. Even the supers are pretty regional. The center of the country is serviced by an outfit in Oklahoma City; the eastern part of the country is taken care of by a couple of East Coast companies, same on the West Coast. None of them go to all the shows in question. It's got to be a handler or a judge. They're the only ones who cover that much ground."

Everyone seemed convinced by that. And Maria had identified at least four individuals, judges and handlers, who had been at all of the eight shows in question. We would learn about them tomorrow.

Chapter Forty-nine

Thursday, July 23rd
7:32 am
Robbinsdale, Minnesota

I had the coffeemaker roaring in full song by the time Maria came down the stairs for breakfast. She was wearing work clothes, which means slacks, blouse, a loose jacket and comfortable shoes, attractive but practical. She looked like any other professional woman on her way to the office for casual Friday, or Thursday, as was the case. It was supposed to be hot that day, so the jacket might have been optional had she not needed a way to hide a weapon.

We had a light breakfast and headed up to the new FBI building. The feebs had erected a monument to federal law enforcement on a site previously occupied by a Cracker Barrel restaurant. The location was just off I-694, part of the interstate loop that runs around the Twin Cities. It has a great view of the highway, which, I'm sure, the restaurant people thought would make for good traffic. But it's a bit hard to get to off the exit in that area and travelers, fickle as they can be, ignored the place. That might explain it. Or it might have been that Minnesotans don't have a taste for grits or even know what sweet tea is.

The fed's new building will eventually have everything they need to fight crime and terrorism for the next hundred years. It even has a vehicle-stopping fence that's rumored to have run about a million dollars.

The old feeb digs were in downtown Minneapolis in an attractive, if typical, high-rise office building a block south of the east end of the Nicollet Mall. While it is a prestigious office location if you are, say, an insurance company, it doesn't offer some of the security requirements needed by the modern FBI. And, like all federal law enforcement buildings nationwide, it's a target for any whack job, foreign or domestic, who thinks blowing up a federal building would accomplish whatever their own cause du jour is. If someone had parked a truck bomb, à la Timothy McVeigh, outside the downtown place, they'd have taken out three or four other buildings too. Given what I know about the fed's concern for their own image (they really hate being called Famous But Incompetent), I'm confident the new place is as much to prevent that as any other reason.

We cleared the gate and were directed to a visitors' parking area. After locking our firearms in my Suburban's center console, we walked to the building, not really knowing if we'd be on this case after the meeting. Uncle Feddie can be like a benevolent relative who takes an interest in your life, if it suits him. Today, we thought it would. Clearly, we had a serial killer at work, and clearly, the killer had struck in multiple states. That alone would make the case federal. But it was a puzzler, to me at least. I knew that federal interest would be tempered by federal feelings as to whether or not the case could be solved. I'd seen cases I thought should go federal that hadn't and cases that I thought should remain local that had gone federal.

Molly was waiting in the lobby and got us past the front desk. The usual accouterments were present: receptionist desk, American flag, and the great big seal of the F, B and I. They made sure there was no doubt in anyone's mind where they were. The thought that always occurred to me when entering feddieland came from Rod Serling's opening to that great TV show: "You're traveling through another dimension, a dimension not only of sight and sound but of mind; a journey into a wondrous land whose boundaries are that of imagination. That's the signpost up ahead—your next stop, the Federal Zone!"

As we rode the elevator to the third floor, I wondered again who this person was and why he had made it so personal. The fire began to burn hotter.

Chapter Fifty

Minneapolis, Summer of 1979

Nearly every law enforcement type who's been on the job for a career's length of time, say at least ten years, has at least one case that changed their life, a case that could destroy them emotionally if they allow it. And it's not always a case involving one person doing violent damage to another. It can be a particularly bad traffic accident, a house fire, a kid who was walking down railroad tracks, whatever. The one thing they all have in common is that someone died in a particularly horrific fashion. That sight will burn into your brain and give you nightmares for the rest of your life. Mine came at about the five-year mark.

When I was relatively new to the job of homicide detective, we had a case in Minneapolis that started the initial fire in me. It was my first professional encounter with a new class of criminal—the child killer. I didn't catch the case when it opened, only after there were already three victims and the news coverage was ramping up. The condition of the bodies had leaked to the newsies and that made it front page material.

The kids had been tortured and raped before being killed in horrific fashion. The bodies—at least we thought they were already dead—had then been dismembered and thrown in trash dumpsters like leftovers from a grocery store's butcher department. You can only imagine how much pressure news like that will put on a department. No city wants to be home to a child killer and the political nature of the chief's job in a city like Minneapolis requires that he or she be able to point to progress and, ultimately, a solution to the case, a solution that means no more children will be in danger.

I was brought on board when the mayor announced that he'd authorized the chief to form a task force of homicide specialists to stop this horrifying killer. He threw out the number thirty in answer to a reporter's question about how many cops were assigned to the case. That was more than the total number of homicide investigators on the force so all of us, plus some street-savvy uniforms, were brought together to work on the cases full time, overtime be damned, until it was solved. We did.

I was more than happy to be put on the task force. One of the victims was the daughter of a high school friend, a girl I'd dated. We'd gone our separate ways, but when I heard about the loss of her daughter, a young girl who, if things had gone differently, could have been my own daughter, I was all in on the case.

As is usually the case with crazies, the guy was an unorganized opportunistic killer who would simply grab a kid when the chance presented itself. He had snatched the kids, mostly little girls but a couple of boys too, from playgrounds and ball fields, on their walks home from school or, in one case, from a piano lesson. Some kids were black but most were white. So he was showing no particular target type, more just targets of opportunity. I thought that was the key but most of my fellow officers on the case thought there was no key.

Going with my thought, I talked the captain into letting me use a decoy. Keep in mind that this was in the early '70s before political correctness had settled in and the idea of standing a six-year-old on a street corner under the watchful gaze of a half-dozen cops seemed like a good idea. It wasn't.

One of the guys on the team had a brother with a nine-year-old daughter who looked like a six-year-old. She would be our bait. Patty was very mentally mature for her years and convinced us at her briefing that she had the psychological stamina to both understand what we were asking of her and the ability to pull it off. We dressed her up like the kids who had been murdered and put her to work, asking her to walk up and down streets similar to ones where kids had been grabbed. No luck. We stood her on a street corner in some of the seamier parts of town and all we got were a couple of pimps we busted for trying to talk her into a career in personal services. We had her play on swing sets in several parks where kids had been taken. No hits. The bad guy did grab two other kids while we were working my idea.

Finally, at the end of one of the walk-home scenarios, the team broke up and the kid's dad went to get her. She was gone.

We put out the radio calls and had over thirty patrol cars in the area in less than a minute. We closed off twelve square blocks and stopped every moving vehicle therein and found nothing. Then we got a call from a hardware store. The manager had a kid there who was lost. He held her until we got there and her dad took her home. That was the end of bait patrol. But not the end of the killer. The fire grew.

A cop's life while involved in an investigation like this does not stop. I still had other cases to work. I was driving to the office from the scene of the latest body discovery and, quite randomly, got the first call to investigate a noisy neighbor. Actually, the call wasn't for me, it was for the nearest patrol car, but I was closer and I felt the need to do something in "law enforcement" that day, so I stopped to see if the officers needed any help.

As I drove up to the scene in a very nice neighborhood in South Minneapolis, I saw a little girl about eight or nine running across a yard. She was naked and screaming. I dumped the car into park and ran to her, yelling that I was a policeman and that she should stop. She was, understandably, scared to death and not inclined to stop for anyone. As I got closer I saw she was bleeding from stab wounds to her . . . well, rest assured that it was something I still have nightmares about.

The patrol unit assigned rolled up as I was wrapping the girl in my jacket. I scooped her up and carried her to the squad, telling the patrol officer to call for backup and an ambulance. Then I set the little girl down and asked her what had happened and who had hurt her.

She was remarkably cognizant of what was going on. She said she had been walking home and that a man had grabbed her and put her in his car. I asked where the man was now and she pointed to a house two doors down. There was a rather dumpy looking white male, about five foot nine, balding, overweight, standing in front of the house. I could see something flash in his hand and thought it might be a knife. She said that he was the man who had kidnapped her. I didn't need anything after that. I yelled to the patrol cop to send all the backup down there and I took off running.

As soon as I took my first step toward him, the guy disappeared. The fire in my gut was burning at full rage. I knew he was the child killer and I knew he was going to be stopped. I was fully focused and thinking about my high school girlfriend's daughter and what the animal had done to her—not the best state of mind when pursuing a murder suspect into his own lair.

My head was not thinking of anything but running the guy down and putting him away, praying silently that he'd give me a reason to go to guns. I had my .357 Colt Python revolver out and was fully tactical— my hearing shut off, my vision cut down to the tunnel in front of me. I charged across the neatly mowed yard and took the front steps two at a time. I didn't even feel the door as I threw a shoulder and busted though it into a clean, well-kept living room. It was empty

I saw a trail of bloody drips on the polished oak floor running from the front door, where I'd last seen the suspect, going back to the kitchen. I slowed slightly and followed the trail like some modern day pursuer of a horror version of Hansel and Gretel. The trail continued to a rear door where I had to make a decision. Did he go back outside or downstairs? I asked myself. I hadn't heard a door slam, but I'm not sure I would have heard anything at that point. I chose the stairs into a dark basement.

Catching my breath for a moment, I found and flipped on the light switch. Nothing. I yelled "Minneapolis Police! Come out now or I'm coming down shooting." Still nothing. It was decision time.

Did I really want to head down those stairs into a dark unfamiliar basement that very probably contained a killer armed with, at the very least, a big knife? I knew from training and experience that in tight quarters a knife in the hands of someone who knew what to do with it is every bit as lethal as my .357 Magnum six-shooter. My prey drive over-rode the caution button and I charged down the stairs.

As I turned the corner into a family room I noticed an odor. It was not an unfamiliar smell; I remembered it from my youth. It was the odor of deer camp after the hunt, the smell of gutted deer and entrails and blood—the strong, coppery smell of blood that ten thousand years of evolution has trained us to seek, yet in a contemporary setting, we subliminally know we should be wary of. It was no problem that day. Ten thousand years of evolutionary hunt drive was in full force and I pursued the source of the odor.

I burst across the family room and peeked into the mechanical room. I knew that was where the suspect would be because that was where the laundry sink was. He'd need a sink to wash up his foul mess and keep it from creeping up the stairs and invading his seemingly normal life above ground. What I saw can't be described as anything less than a scene from Hollywood's most disturbing horror show.

There was a stainless-steel table that looked like it had come from a restaurant kitchen, complete with a magnetic knife rack holding an assortment of bladed tools. There was a large bucket under one corner of the table and I noticed that the table was raised slightly on the corner opposite the to facilitate easy drainage of whatever fluids were on the table.

Beyond the table I saw a clothesline, like many people have in their basement laundry room. Only this one wasn't drying ladies' underwear or some other unmentionable that the homeowner didn't want hanging outside. It held skins, skins drying like salmon on a sun rack in western Alaska.

Finally, I saw the man, cowering in the corner. My firearm moved to position on its own, no conscience effort on my part, coming to rest with the front sight covering the shaking man's forehead. All it would take was 2.7 pounds of pressure against the finely tuned trigger and I could send a 130-grain jacketed hollow point bullet into space at a speed of 1,410 feet per second. He wouldn't even know it happened. At that range the bullet would rip out his brain stem before his mind could process the flash. His consciousness would end like throwing a light switch. It would have been merciful, really. I would end the terror caused by the puking scumbag, an action that would bring a huge sigh of relief to the whole city and save the people of Minnesota the cost and trauma of trying him, convicting him, and paying to confine and "counsel" him for the rest of his worthless life. Just one little tug.

Chapter Fifty-one

The newest fire was building as we walked to the conference room. What did the SOB believe that carving his message into Jane would accomplish, other than to just plain piss me off?

Will was waiting in a conference room. I've been in several FBI field offices, but Minneapolis is a regional office so it's one of the big ones. We entered a nicely appointed room with the usual large table, comfy swivel chairs, and electronic gizmos that make all sorts of video presentations and communication possible.

Already present were two other FBI agents who were introduced as Orv Kingman and Sheri Broughton. Glenn had driven down from Mora. In spite of his 30-plus years on the MPD, Glenn looked as nervous as a chicken at a barbeque. He was a bit apprehensive about dealing with Big Blue. I smiled as I waved at him across the table. We sat and waited for the proceedings to commence. Orv Kingman stood and took the podium at the head of the table.

"Good morning and welcome to the first meeting of the Midwest Interdepartmental Homicide Investigation Team. We'll call the team MIHIT, or My Hit, from this point forward. This case has been assigned a Major Case number by the Bureau. As such, we have the resources necessary to pursue it wherever it takes us within the United States. I know everyone has been introduced. I just want to review areas of expertise and assignments.

"Will Sanford has been assigned as the team leader. He will oversee and coordinate the team's efforts as well as handle communication with Bureau headquarters."

That's nice, I thought. With Will in charge, we should be kept in the game.

"I have been assigned as special agent for communications," Orv said. "My responsibilities will be here at the Minneapolis regional field office as a resource person. Anything you need while out in the field, just call me. Special Agent Broughton is a specialist in data analysis. She has experience working serial crime operations and has a special talent for seeing the connections between criminal events the rest of us might miss. Special Agent Foss has been through the Bureau's school for fieldwork on serial crimes. That classwork is a prerequisite for taking the full-blown profiling curriculum should Special Agent Foss choose to apply for that later in her career. From what I've heard, she has a knack for it."

Molly blushed. I'd only known her for about seven months but Molly had proven to be a very down-to-earth type. Receiving this somewhat backward praise—"She has a knack for it" but it's too early in her career to go for it full time—provided a bit of embarrassment. Kingman went on.

"Also with us is Detective Maria Fernandez of the Maricopa County Sheriff's Office. She is an experienced homicide investigator and has been working on the connections between the two Minnesota cases and a similar case in Arizona several years ago."

He was almost polite to a member of the department headed by a sworn enemy of the Bureau. Nice.

"Next is Sheriff Glenn Mills of Kanabec County. His department is investigating two similar cases just outside Mora, the county seat and location of the Kanabec County Sheriff's Office."

Nothing like starting a job by being introduced as the guy closest to the crime who hadn't figured it out yet. Any wonder why we don't get along?

"And, finally, we have Dan Neumann from the Minneapolis Police Department. I think we all know that he is a renowned homicide investigator who has unlimited expertise in exotic firearms, forensic ballistics, and almost always gets his man or woman."

Almost, I thought. I wondered if Kingman was referring to the case a few years ago that came to a head just before the feds were going to come in. There had been a series of killings using a firearm no one could identify. In the course of the case, two acquitted bank robbery/murder suspects, a defense attorney, and a judge were all shot to death with the unknown weapon. The attorney and judge were shot outside Minnesota, which brought it to federal attention. Then, at the last minute, the prime suspect was killed in an accident. Or was he? The feds wouldn't be dredging up that one failure of mine, would they? Sure they would. Besides, I knew who did it. At least I thought I knew. It happens—you don't always get the doer.

"That's the team. I'd like Special Agent Broughton to start out with what she has on related cases."

Sheri Broughton took the podium. She was dressed in typical fed attire, a conservative blue business suit, though with slacks instead of a skirt, white shirt, small bow tie at her neck and auburn hair somewhat severely pulled back into a bun on the back of her head. She looked like a well-dressed middle-school English teacher.

"Good morning. In your packet you'll find the section on related crimes." We all flipped open our binders to the section she referenced, to carry the schoolteacher thing a bit further. "These are the cases we believe have been committed by the same individual. The victimology corresponds to the three cases we are listing as primaries. Those would be the two bodies found outside Mora, Minnesota, and the body found in Arizona. Sheriff's Investigator Fernandez has been very helpful in putting together the original data request that we processed at headquarters. She then went through the data to cross reference with the AKC dog-show calendar and came up with a list of possible associated crimes going back twelve years. This list was then processed by the Bureau, producing the final list."

OK, so I'm overly sensitive to the treatment, but she was calling Maria a clerk typist, not that there's anything wrong with that line of work. But, come on. I knew that the "processed by the Bureau" list I was looking at was exactly the same as the one Maria had put together, because I'd seen it. I guess it isn't official until big brother gives it the once-over. Oh well.

Broughton went on. "Detective Fernandez also added an interesting twist by observing that the unsub has a predilection for blonds, natural blonds. Of the eight cases identified by Fernandez, she discovered that three of the victims had had their pubic areas defoliated, apparently just prior to death. She checked with the medical examiners involved with each case and discovered that those three victims were not natural blonds, but had colored their hair. The non-blond pubic area apparently destroyed the unsub's desired victim profile. I believe that the unsub shaved the victims to support his fantasy, which requires a natural blond victim."

Chapter Fifty-two

Friday, July 24th
On I-94 between Fargo and Bismarck, North Dakota

The killer enjoyed driving. He'd had to do a lot of it in his work, both in his profession and his avocation. The miles ticked by and the view changed constantly. Contrary to the opinions of those who'd never set foot in the immense middle section of the continent, it is not all a vast flat region of farm fields and hick towns. The land rolls and the highway undulates both up and down and side to side, like some endless anaconda slithering through the countryside. Each rise turned the page on the scenery and each bend was there to accommodate some geological variance left by retreating glaciers about 10,000 years ago. Every mile was new.

He was on his way to another show, another opportunity, as he liked to view it. Normally, he would make a little money and have a little fun. This weekend was just for fun and he knew what fun he'd be having. It was the only reason he was heading to Bismarck. The show was superfluous to his need. He recognized that the need was taking priority but he didn't care. He knew they'd never catch him. They didn't have the smarts, as his mother used to say.

His mother used to say a lot of things. She told him exactly how to live his life, whether it was the way he wanted to or not. She ruled over him, guided him, criticized him. She made sure he knew that he was a mistake. She hadn't planned to have him. She wanted to be alone with his father for a few more years before having children, but the father had apparently not received the script. After marrying, he'd become an abusive alcoholic. Thinking about his mother, he wondered if dear old dad ever had a chance. She could have driven the pope to drink. So one night after getting a load on and slapping the bitch around a little, he impregnated her and left, never to be seen or heard from again.

He'd grown up in that environment. His mother never trusted him, never said a kind word, never showed any affection toward him. She tolerated his presence only because, in his eyes, she could rule over him. He lived in the basement of their modest home in central Indiana, keeping to himself out of fear and loathing of the woman upstairs.

She had recovered from the departure of his father well, marrying again and producing a daughter. That stepfather had also disappeared after a bender that followed another fight with his mother and another appearance by the local police. The killer thought his stepdad was only looking out for himself when he left, that he was bailing on an admittedly bad relationship. The killer thought the man had tried, showing some interest in the son he'd inherited. But his mother's reaction to the man's attempt to be a father figure in the boy's life only led to his mother stepping in and accusing the man of meddling in business that was not his. The fight that followed left the house again without an adult male presence for the boy to look up to. At five years old, all he had was a tyrannical mother, a half-sister, and a life of fear and confusion.

His confusion was compounded as he grew older and had to deal with a bout of bed-wetting that further humiliated him. When his mother discovered wet sheets, she'd lock him in the basement for two days. He quickly learned to wash them himself after she went to work. It was his first experience at adapting to overcome an unpleasant situation.

As he grew he developed a fascination with imprisoning little animals. When his mother discovered he had dissected the neighbor's cat, she locked him away for a week. When his half-sister told their mother that he'd been looking at her in the bathroom, she called child protection and had him removed from the home.

It hadn't gone quite the way his sister had portrayed it. At ages 12 and 10, they'd had the usual curiosity about their differing anatomies. One afternoon, before their mother got home from work, they'd gotten inquisitive about each other and started removing clothing in an effort to learn more. He found the experience unsettling and when they were comparing genitalia, he touched her. She touched him in return and the result was a raging erection that surprised them both. He couldn't control it and a moment later had climaxed in her hand. They both reacted with confused apprehension and fled in different directions. He hurriedly dressed and cleaned up the emission while she retreated to her room, got dressed, and cried. When their mother got home, she intuited that something had happened and questioned the girl until she told the story of her brother peeping into the bathroom.

His foster parents used the foster system as a source of income. There were three other kids in the home already and, as the newcomer, he was ostracized. He retracted into a shell, determined to do whatever he had to to avoid attention. He focused on schoolwork, didn't participate in clubs or sports, and made few friends, all the while battling the demon inside him that was demanding he do something to show the world that he was in control. He created a world for himself in which he could control everything.

When he was fourteen, a do-gooder social worker decided he should go back to his mother. He didn't care. He still hated her but hated the foster parents more. At least he'd get back his freedom.

He went to the classes he chose, got the grades he desired, talked to the people he chose to talk to. It all culminated with the first kill in the woods after his senior year.

Driving to Bismarck, he was in total control. He knew that he could do whatever he wished and they could not do a thing about it. They'd look for him, try to collect evidence to prosecute him, try to catch him in the act. They would fail. He was too smart and too careful. He even knew how to throw them off the trail. He'd prove it.

Chapter Fifty-three

We'd spent the rest of Thursday reviewing the evidence of the eight older cases we believed to be related to the three new ones. The blond hair thing was amazing. When we looked at the victims' pre-death photos, they were close to being sisters. All were in the 5'3" to 5'7" range, between 22 and 34 years old, about 110 to 135 pounds. All had average features; none were what you'd call model beautiful and none were homely. They were average American girls—the kind of girls who would go out on a weekend night looking for some excitement. They had found it.

The victimology, the profiles of the victims, were very similar from the first case we had identified from years earlier to the first victim found in Mora. The most recent was different. She had been selected for her relationship with me. She was 5'6", 127 lbs., and a natural blond. But she was 48 years old, though she didn't look it. Molly and Maria believed she was a message.

The sophistication of the crimes improved with time and the killer's experience. In the earliest case, at least twelve years ago, the body had been found partially buried in a clumsy attempt to conceal it. The ME on the case estimated the girl had been killed about a month before the body was found. There was little in the file regarding any other forensic trace. DNA as evidence was relatively new back them and tracking animal species from hair was unknown. The notes said the body had been "disturbed" by animals. I knew that meant "eaten," at least partially.

As the timeline progressed, the killer moved toward using binders like electric cord or even rope. Those materials left distinct marks on the bodies. We believed he graduated to using regular handcuffs and occasionally duct tape. Case number three (we had numbered them by date order) was the first with a shaved pubic area. The shave was unprofessional and the ME noted nicks and cuts. Cases six and eight also had bare areas, but the hair had been removed by waxing in a very experienced way. I made a note to add "Knows how to wax" in the killer's profile. We believed the quality of the job indicated he had prepared for the procedure by practicing. There were no guesses as to whom he practiced on. Maybe himself.

All the evidence led us to a profile of the serial killer. He would be between his late thirties and fifty, old for a previously unknown serial killer. But that was consistent with him being a traveler. They are the hardest to catch because their travels separate the victims and don't lead law enforcement to believe a serial killer is at work. He may also look unnaturally young, as he continued to take young women as victims. The average age had crept up over the years but the first Mora victim was only twenty-eight so he still had the ability to entice a woman possibly twenty years younger to go with him. That gave me an idea I'd have to follow up on. He would have a history of at least two of the serial triad—bedwetting, animal abuse, and arson. I'd heard about this combination of traits before but still couldn't really understand what those three things had to do with one another.

He would be an extremely organized killer. That meant that he was a planner. He would have all the tools he needed readily at hand. He would have a place to carry out the torture and murders and his postmortem cleansing of the bodies. Molly and Maria believed that he'd be very organized in his public life as well. He might have a "normal" relationship with a woman, possibly even have a family. He would be an upstanding member of his community, probably doing volunteer work with kids or at a church.

And, in the manner of others before him, he would probably try to become involved in the case by talking to police investigators or acting as a reporter.

Finally, he had something to do with dog shows. He would be someone who was right at home in that environment, traveling to dog shows all across the country, participating in his own yet-to-be-determined way, then indulging his need to kill before leaving town.

We spent Friday morning compiling a list of players who had been at all of the shows in the time proximity of the murders. We had to consider the judges, the professional handlers, and the casual hobby handlers. As the meeting went on, the list got shorter and shorter until we had it down to seven people. All fit the profile—white males between 34 and 50 leading outwardly normal lives. That's about all we had.

The group of unsubs (there's that FBIeeze again) included two types: judges and professional handlers. The judges were Frank Robinson (not the ballplayer), Mickey Jefferson, and Harold Slatowski. The handlers were LeRoi Parmentor, Bobby James, Hunter Nelson, and Stanford Smithson.

We called Phil Horvath, the handler-judge-psychologist, in to see if he knew anyone on the list and, if so, we hoped he could give us a little insight into who they were. Turned out, he knew them all. He agreed to come over to the FBI building.

"Yeah, I know all these characters," he said after we'd filled him in. "They are all pretty common fixtures at shows. They actually made it to every show you're looking at?"

Will explained. "Yes. These men were at every show after which we have an unsolved homicide that fits our profile. We're hoping you can fill in the blanks about personalities, backgrounds, and any traits that our people could use to either keep them on the list or eliminate them as suspects."

"Well, from what I've heard from Dan on the topic, I don't know if I can eliminate any of them. They all live seemingly normal lives, some have families and kids, some don't, I just don't know."

Molly had the most experience with profiling. She said, "Phil, just tell us anything you know about them and let us decide if it's helpful or not. You never know what little, apparently insignificant, thing might give insight into their character."

So Phil started in. "The judges are all well known. They work a lot of shows, which, I guess, is logical, since they got through your screening as being present at all the shows in question. Frank is from New Jersey. He's a Terrier breeder, four or five different kinds over the years, known to be very particular about those breeds as far as what he's looking for. He's done both Westminster and the big AKC National show, which makes him well respected or connected or both."

Will asked, "This guy is a dog breeder and they let him judge the dogs he's bred?"

"Not exactly," Phil answered. "To be an AKC Conformation judge, you have to have bred a number of champions. It shows you know what they are supposed to look like. It's the same with the handlers. Most of them have bred dogs. Now they make a living showing their own and other people's dogs."

Molly asked, "How about their personal lives? Are these guys married, have children, or have hobbies outside of showing dogs?"

Phil looked over the list. "Let's see. I know Frank is married. So are Harry, Hunter, and LeRoi. Stanford has a partner he's been with for years. Mickey's single at the moment. I don't know about Bobby."

"What do you mean by 'partner'?" Molly inquired.

"Stan's gay. He's been with his partner George for as long as I've known him. Over twenty years."

Molly looked at the team. "I'd say take him off the list. He's completely out of the profile." She looked at Phil. "This type of crime, especially against female victims, never involves a homosexual killer. It's always a straight male."

"You're absolutely sure?" Will asked Molly.

"As sure as the profiling methodology allows. It could be a homosexual female, but the nature of the crime, the sexual assault, pretty much rules that out."

Phil said, "Then you'd better take Bobby James off the list, too. He's as gay as they come. His real name is Roberto Jimenez, by the way."

"You sure he's gay?" asked Kingman.

"I should know. I am too."

The group looked at each other. I have pretty good "gaydar," but it hadn't gone off with Phil. I asked, "That seems like a statistically higher than normal concentration. I'm looking at seven names of dog showing guys here, plus you makes eight, and you're saying three of you are gay. That's almost forty percent. Is that right?"

Phil said, "It's a pretty small statistical sample, but the sport does attract a lot of people who don't, for whatever reason, have children."

Molly spoke up, "Well, sexual orientation stats aside, we can rule out Stan and Bobby. So we're down to five. Let's look at them."

And so the discussion went on. Sheri Broughton ran the remaining group through the FBI's system. It turned out that one judge and two handlers had some small-potatoes criminal background. Mickey Jefferson had two minor busts for possession of marijuana, and LeRoi was a serial speeder, with a half dozen or more tickets per year for as long as the records went back. Hunter Nelson had a minor conviction for arson when he was sixteen. That one caught Molly's eye.

"Arson is part of the serial killer triad," she said. "Serial killers almost always have a history of at least two of the following three things—arson, cruelty to small animals, and enuresis, or bedwetting."

I asked, "Do you have a picture of this Hunter guy?"

Broughton nodded and dug it out of the file. When she flipped it right side up she looked at it and let out of low "Whoa" under her breath. She passed it around. When it came to me I understood. Though his bio said he was forty-eight, he didn't look it. He was about five feet ten inches tall with blondish hair showing just a touch of silver at the temples. His skin was unnaturally youthful. The guy looked about thirty years old.

"Any way to check his medical records?" I asked.

"Not without a warrant. Kinda looks like he's had a little tightening, doesn't it?" Will answered.

Kingman looked pensive, rubbed his big chin and said, "There might be a way." I knew he was referring to the changes in warrant requirements since passage of the National Security Act—post 9/11. A lot of privacy had been lost in that one. "You think that moves him to the top of the list?" he asked the group.

Molly replied, "It could. There are other factors. We need more background on his personal life—family, occupation, etc. That will tell us if he fills in enough blanks to deserve attention."

Kingman nodded, indicating he'd find that information.

The meeting broke up for the weekend and Maria I headed to my place for a day and a half of non-police work. She was booked on the last plane to Phoenix Sunday evening. She made the plane but I wish she hadn't gone.

Chapter Fifty-four

Saturday afternoon, July 25th
Bismarck, North Dakota

He was at a city park with one of his smaller dogs, enjoying the warm summer sun on the northern plains. A strong breeze was blowing from the west, as there almost always was in North Dakota. He had dressed in what he believed was correct for someone who was about thirty, and pulled off the look with aplomb. Wearing khaki cargo shorts, a Ralph Lauren polo in a nice sky blue, and sockless topsiders, he would have fit in on any college campus. He topped off the look with a Gatsby cap to keep the sun out of his eyes. He was gorgeous.

This would be the trail-breaker. If they were somehow able to connect him with other dog shows, this would be his alibi. He looked around for a target. In North Dakota, finding the correct type would not be much of a challenge. Not like, say, Arizona, where he'd had to really search. Fortunately, there were plenty of transplanted Germans and Scandinavians whose granddaughters and great-granddaughters fit the bill. That made it easy, once he'd deduced where they hung out. After that it was turn on the usual charm and have his "secret potion" standing by. In the Peace Garden State there were blonds galore. All he had to do was interview a few and make a selection. So easy.

He perused the park, looking for a target. Finally, he had a chance with one, but she was too busy to sit and talk. He spoke with a nurse on her way home from work. She revealed that she had to be back at the hospital that evening and that simply would not fit his schedule. He wanted a couple of uninterrupted days, so he let her pass.

A nearby park-side pub with outdoor seating offered possibilities. He saw a possible target having a drink in the late afternoon sunshine. He put the dog back in his nearby RV and went over to start the process.

"Jennifer?" he said, as he approached her. She looked up and he startled. "I'm sorry. I thought you were someone else."

"That's all right. Who's Jennifer?" she asked.

"I'm really sorry to disturb you. You look so much like an old friend from Duluth. I'm just passing through on my way west and thought serendipity had somehow cast me together with a woman I once had a crush on in college."

"Sorry. I go to NDSU, right up the road." She was charmed by his looks and self-effacing manner. He looked kind of Hollywood, with an approachable natural openness. And he was blushing. How many men blush these days, she asked herself.

"Are you going to continue looking for Jennifer or can you sit down?" she asked.

"No, just stopped off for a drink and dinner." He sat facing her, the right direction.

She said her name was Monica. She was a grad student home for the summer. She was living with her parents, but they were at the family's lake place and weren't expected back until next weekend. Perfect. She looked at her phone and shook her head.

"Well, I just found out that my girlfriend can't make it," she said. "One of her kids came down with something, so I guess I'll just have my drink and take off."

They looked at each other for a moment and he said, "Well, if you change your mind, I hate to eat alone."

She glanced around the room, coyly weighing her options. What the heck, she thought. He's here, it's a public place, and I have to eat, Why not?

"OK, let's go," she said, "but it's Dutch, OK?"

"OK. What's Dutch?"

"You're not from around here, are you?" He shook his head. "It's when we split the bill."

"Oh, that's fair. We'll be Dutch."

She laughed at his misuse of the term and rose just as the waitress brought her drink. She dropped a five-dollar bill on the table, picked up her drink, and they headed toward the dining room.

Over dinner she learned that he was single, lived and worked in Ohio as a teacher, and had been in Bismarck for a dog show.

"Oh, I saw that on TV. They said it was at the Civic Center."

"Right, the convention center. Big show. People from all over the country."

"Why were you at the show?"

"I judge dog shows. Actually, I should say I'm a dog-show person. Mostly, I show dogs myself, but this weekend I'm one of the judges."

"A dog-show judge? That's cool. Can you make any money doing that?"

"Not really. People who do it love the sport. It's a way to put some-thing back into the sport. It's not dying out or anything, but if no one was judging, you couldn't have a show. I get paid a small fee and expenses."

"Makes sense. So they bring you in for the shows and you get a trip out of it."

"That's about it."

"You're here from Ohio. That's a long way to come just to judge dogs. I suppose you flew in."

"Usually I would. They fly the judges in, but it's summer, I'm off work, and this show is in the middle of a series of shows. So, I'm on a dog show vacation. I drove my RV. It saves the club money and I can just go on to the next show."

They had a nice conversation over dinner. The topic of dog shows blended into how dogs are shown and what different breeds he showed. When he said he had a star Bichon Frise he was campaigning she asked, "What's a Bichon Frise? And what does campaigning mean?"

"Bichons are small white dogs with really puffy hair. Did you see the movie Coming to America with Eddie Murphy?"

"Yes, very funny."

Remember the little dog the family owned, the family with the burger joint and the daughter Eddie wound up with?"

"Sure. Oh that was a, what did you say, Bitchen Frizzy?"

"Pretty close, that's what a lot of people call them."

"Oh, I've always loved that dog. So cute."

"He's all that. He's doing very well in the shows and I think I have a chance to take him to the AKC Championships and Westminster this year."

"I'd love to see him. Do you have him here?"

"Right out in the RV. I could show him to you after we're finished, if you'd like."

They finished eating, he got his check and paid with cash. She paid hers and they walked out to the parking lot. When they reached his RV he said, "Just give me a second to get everyone put away or they'll jump all over you."

She could hear some barking from inside the RV. He went inside, readied himself, and called out.

"OK, come on in. She climbed up the steps into the darkened RV and he slipped the bag over her head before she knew he was there. Inside the bag was a chloroform-soaked rag—old school, but effective. She struggled for a moment and was out.

"That's the way it works," he said to himself. "If more men knew what chick magnets dogs are, there wouldn't be any strays in the country. Every shelter and pound would be empty."

The Bichon Frise, or as he liked to call them, bitchy frizzy, was almost too cute a chick magnet for his purposes. He wanted to attract women one at a time and they seemed to flow to him in groups. That's why he'd changed his method to just telling them about the dog. He really had one, but it was better if going to see it was the woman's idea, rather than his. If she was reluctant to enter the RV, he could bring the dog out. It made it more natural looking in case anyone was watching.

Driving to the family house was easy. He parked the RV in a WalMart lot. She was coming around by then, so he administered the Rohypnol to keep her compliant. Satisfied that she'd give him no trouble, he went outside and unhooked the little SUV and loaded Monica inside for her last trip home. He was going to do this one right in the house and prepared everything with that in mind. He was wearing all new clothing that would be destroyed after the event. He had gloves for him and cuffs for her.

When they arrived at the address he had gotten from her driver's license, he saw that he'd lucked out by selecting a woman whose childhood home had an attached garage. He took her keys to the front door, went in, found the service door to the garage, opened the garage door, and drove the car inside.

Walking her up the steps from the garage, all he had to do was guide her in. She was almost too compliant. Not much fun where there's no resistance. But he knew she'd be coming around soon. He stripped her and trussed her up in the bed, making ready for his fun. That's when he heard the door.

After quickly covering her he looked down the hall and saw a late-middle-aged man and woman come in. Instantly, he knew they were her parents. In the brief time he'd had with her, and his quick perusal of the house, he'd seen family pictures. He recognized them as Bob and Sally, according to the inscription on the golf trophies. He arranged the bedcoverings to hide the restraints and stepped out into the hall to greet them.

"Hi Bob, Sally. I'm not sure if you remember me, but I go to NDSU with Monica. We met back in Fargo." He put out his hand in welcome. Mom and Dad were perplexed. He went on.

"I was in town and had lunch with Monica but afterward, she seemed to be a little sick to her stomach. So I brought her home. She's sleeping." He led them down the hallway to the bedroom. As he stepped down the hallway, the killer slipped his hand into his pocket. His fingers felt the familiar comfort of the Gerber spring knife. With practiced skill, he pulled it out and concealed it in his hand, just in case.

The father's radar had been squawking at him since the man introduced himself as a friend of Monica's. He was very close to his daughter and knew all her friends. Still, she could have met someone new. But the man said that they'd met in Fargo. They hadn't been to Fargo in all the time Monica was going to grad school there.

The killer sensed the father's growing distrust and silently flicked open the knife's razor sharp three-inch blade. He gripped it in his fist with the blade pointing down from the heel of his hand, not in the pointing position typical of TV knife fights. While he wasn't what would be called an expert knife fighter, he had studied the art and had taken a few classes. He knew what had to happen next and was prepared to exercise his greatest advantage—surprise.

As they entered the bedroom, the killer stepped aside, letting the father see his daughter in the bed. She let out a low moan and rolled to one side revealing the restraint on her wrist. Monica's father reacted as any father would, turning to confront the man who was obviously planning to harm his precious daughter. As he turned to confront him, the killer raised his left hand high. The man had no choice but to instinctively follow the motion of the killer's hand, and as he did, he raised his chin exposing his vulnerable throat. The killer threw a quick right cross, not aiming for the man's chin, but just below. Bob sensed the motion and reacted as anyone would, raising his chin and turning his head to the right to dodge the blow, which made him more vulnerable to the path of the razor-sharp steel. The blade of the knife contacted the man's neck just below his left ear, catching the carotid artery. As it traveled under his chin it found nothing but soft tissue to slow its crossing, opening up the man's throat in one sudden slash. Blood shot from the wound as if someone had yanked a gas pump handle from the side of a car.

The woman froze, aghast at the sight of her husband's life force flooding the floor beneath her. The killer looked at her with a smirk on his lips and said, "What a mess" as he watched the man slip to his knees, clutching his throat as if that could stem the flow. The killer snatched a lamp off the dresser and smashed it over her head.

The killer knew that knife wounds took time to have effect, many minutes in most cases, but this one was of a type that the recipient couldn't ignore. There was no attempt to stop him now, no way the man could put up a fight or even a defense, should additional damage be the killer's intent. It wasn't. He was content to stand and watch and the man died without understanding.

The killer looked at the unconscious woman and said, out loud now, for he was in his element, "You're not too bad for mid-fifties, are you? Your daughter could have grown old looking as good as you and would have made someone happy for a long, long time. Now, you both get to make me happy."

"Hmm, two. Never thought about that before," he mused. "This will be interesting."

Chapter Fifty-five

Monday, July 27th
Robbinsdale Minnesota

My phone rang as I was finishing putting the breakfast bowl in the dishwasher. I'm an early riser all year, but in the summer, I'm up by 5:30 and have finished my morning exercises, ablutions, and breakfast by 7:00. Still, it was a bit early for a phone call. I figured it wasn't Maria, who'd flown home the night before after a great weekend that included fishing and a grilled feast at Pete's house on the lake. She didn't get home until near midnight. It was only 5:00 a.m. in Phoenix and the only phone call she'd be up for was a homicide call.

"Dan, glad I caught you," Will said when I picked up. "Can you come up here right away?"

I knew "up here" meant his office. I answered, "Give me five minutes to get out of here and I'm ready. Formal wear?"

"No, whatever you've got on. We may have another case."

I rang off and got myself out the door in record time. I rode my street bike up to Brooklyn Park, got through the main gate and passed on the visitor's lot, opting for the motorcycle lot right up close to the FBI's new building. I have a big placard for it that says, "Believe it or not, this is an official police vehicle." Every city cop in Minneapolis knows what my bikes look like but I was in feddieland. I hoped it would still be there when I got back.

I rushed through the usual check-in in the FBI's entry and met Will as he was coming out to get me. He filled me in.

"This morning, the police department in Mandan, North Dakota, got a call on a body drop. They checked it out and somebody up there realized it matched the info notification we'd sent out last week. They contacted our office in Bismarck, which is right next door to Mandan, and Bismarck sent a team over. We're waiting for their report now."

We entered the conference room and I saw that Orv Kingman and Sheri Broughton were already there. Kingman was on the phone. Will asked, "Anything yet?"

Broughton answered, "Preliminary report says the cause of death looks the same. Knife wounds over the entire body and loss of blood. We're still waiting for an ID on the victim."

Kingman put down the phone and said, "The victim's name is Monica Walstad. She's described on her North Dakota driver's license as twenty-seven years old, blond, five foot five inches and 122 pounds. License shows she lived in Bismarck. They're doing further background now."

I knew they'd be looking for more information such as where she worked, relationships, known associates, habits, criminal background check, anything that could give us a clue as to how she came to be where she was. Which prompted me to ask, "Where'd they find her?"

Broughton answered, "In an alley behind an all-you-can-eat buffet. The ME is on the scene and estimates at least twelve to eighteen hours since time of death. She must have been killed yesterday and dropped this morning."

"OK," I said. "Anyone know if there was a dog show somewhere around there this past weekend?"

Kingman answered this time. "I asked the local Special Agent about that. He's checking."

As if cued, the phone rang. Kingman picked it up.

"Kingman." Pause. "Yes." Another pause. I don't like listening to one side of a conversation. Especially when I know the room is equipped with VOX. "All right. Keep on that background check." He hung up.

"The local paper confirmed there was a large dog show there this weekend. The Bismarck Kennel Club held their annual three-day show."

I asked, "When will we get photos?"

Everyone in the room looked at me. They all knew what I was driving at. If this was our boy, maybe there was another message.

"And see if someone up there can get one of those show catalogs from the kennel club," Will added, breaking the tension. Will wanted to see if any of our targeted individuals had been at the Bismarck show.

Will and I stepped out and down the hall to a break room for some coffee and a mental rest. We both knew that this was a bad dream that couldn't be stopped simply by waking up. We had to find this guy and take him down. Another body, one in North Dakota, was just adding to a score that would continue to rise until we figured out who it was. We also knew that some serial killers were never caught, never stopped. The crimes stopped, but for what reason? Did the bad guy get busted for something else? Did he get hit by a bus? Did he just get over it, like the big guy named Edmund Kemper out in California?

Big Ed, a classic serial killer who was one of the models for modern profiling, killed his mother one fine Easter morning. As with many serial killers of women, he'd had a rough childhood, raised by an overbearing, domineering mother who constantly told him he'd amount to nothing. After killing his mother and a friend of hers who had come to the house for Easter dinner, he took a ride in his car, called the police, and turned himself in. His demon had been exorcised. I didn't think that would happen in our case.

We picked up our coffee and sat down.

I shook my head. "Man, I don't know where I'm going with this."

"Neither do I. Still, it's a murder investigation. We can get this guy."

"Yeah, but another victim. I don't know how I'm going to sleep if this keeps up."

I startled as Will slammed his hand down on the table.

"Hey! This isn't about you and it isn't on you," Will shouted. "It's on him. He's doing the deeds, not you. He's kidnapping and killing those women, not you. You can't feel like you own this or you'll *lose your perspective.*"

It was a rare display of emotion from a man I'd known for years. I shook my head, trying to clear my thoughts.

"I don't know, man. I look at Molly—she really fits the profile, you know—and I think of someone doing this to her and I just don't know. We've got to stop him."

"You're right about that," Will replied. "But you are doing everything you can. You have the biggest and most powerful investigative organization on the planet behind you. We will get him! Come on. Let's go back and see what they found."

Chapter Fifty-six

The team, including Molly, was gathered around the table looking at photos of the newest victim. She had been a very attractive young woman. Now she was dead.

The body was like the rest—white. Not Caucasian white, but a Halloween white, punk rocker white, Goth white, like the kids who make themselves up with black nail polish and hair and pale white skin. *Night of the Living Dead* white. She had the same knife marks all over her body. I looked at the photos, trying to see if there were any cuts overlapping. There were.

On the small of her back the killer had crisscrossed some cuts. Molly had already found the spot on the small of her back and made several copies of that photo, which she was trying to decipher. On the third try she got "#35." There were more crossed dots on her buttocks. Molly worked on that area until she came up with the word "DAN." In between, she found the numeral "4." All told, it spelled out "#35 4 DAN." Thirty-five for Dan. I looked at Will and said, "Still think this isn't on me?"

Molly kept looking at the photos. The look on her face said something wasn't right.

Broughton had a phone tucked under her chin. She was talking with the Bismarck PD and taking notes. "OK, got it." She paused. "Yeah, as soon as you can find out who she is, call us."

She hung up. "The Bismarck PD is going to the girl's home to notify her parents. They are also tracking down a Rose Roddick, who is with the Bismarck Kennel Club. If we can get her on the phone we should be able to see if one or more of our suspects were there."

Will looked at the team and his watch and said, "Let's take a break for lunch. Everyone back here at 1300, unless you're called. Sheri, you stay here and stand by the phone. What do you want for lunch? I'll send something back."

We broke up and I went with Will to his office. He made a quick phone call to order Broughton's lunch and then we just sat there, transfixed. What should we do next?

My cellphone broke the spell. I answered it.

"Neumann," I said. "No, I'm not available for that. In fact, I won't be available for anything for the next week or so." I listened and said, "Come on, Ole, you know how to handle this. If you need someone to backup the ballistic forensics, I'll be available and untainted for testimony." I hung up.

Will looked at me expectantly. "MPD," I said. "They have a case for me. As you heard, I'm not available."

"What was it? Might be more fun than this," Will said.

"Shooting last night in south Minneapolis. Looks like a murder-suicide, but they are having their doubts. Could have been a double homicide made to look like a murder-suicide. They've got good people; they don't need me for that."

"Who called?"

"Olson. I think he's just looking for someone to talk to. He gets lonely when the Twins are losing."

My old partner is a diehard Twins fan. They were having the worst season since they went from worst to first in '91. Maybe next year . . .

Will got up and said, "We're not accomplishing anything here. Let's go eat."

Chapter Fifty-seven

Tuesday, July 28th

The killer thought contentedly about the last event. It was too short, but he'd had to get back to his regular job. You can only take so much time off, he said to himself. He'd held the same job for nearly twenty years and it was a good job. Working for a city was one of the last good jobs in America, he often reminded himself. Regular pay raises, good medical, good pension plan, and, plenty of time off for dog shows. All in all, he couldn't think of a better arrangement.

Of course, if he hit the lottery, that would change things. He could go on the road full time. Just go to shows, traveling in a newer RV. He'd seen one with a slide-out lower storage shelf so big it held a car. The car in the video he'd seen had been a low-slung German sports car. Wouldn't that be something? How easily could he pick up his targets with a hot car? The life of leisure. They would never catch him.

He'd arrived home late on Monday. It's a long drive from Bismarck, North Dakota, to anywhere. It took him about 18 hours. No problem. He made drives like that all year round. His big RV, even though it was a few years older than he wished, was still very comfortable. He could buy a new one. New ones were going for great prices. His mother had left him quite a bit of money when she'd "disappeared." That's one they'll never find, he'd often thought. Deep inside, he'd wanted to leave her right in the middle of the village square, maybe in the arms of the Civil War hero who silently stood watch astride his mighty steed. But he knew better than to draw attention to himself. He overcame that compulsion and she was where no one could reach her. He hoped she was in hell after all the things she'd put him through.

He had mused as he drove, enjoying the moment. Over the years he'd come to appreciate the virtue of patience. So impatient, people today are, he thought, chuckling at his use of "Yoda syntax." He knew that the greatest pleasure was in the waiting, the anticipation, and the game. He was playing a great game and had to keep it going. There was no end-game, just a question of how high the score would go.

He'd needed the drive to come down from a place he'd never been. How dare she die on him, deprive him of his final victory? What the hell had happened? He thought he had the process perfected. Sure, the arrival of her parents was unplanned, but not a completely unforeseen possibility. He always had contingency plans, fallbacks and cutouts to allow him to complete his experiments. He had known going to her house was a risk, but some risk was part of the fun. At least he'd had her mother to finish off and he got some thrill out of that. She did look a bit like his mother.

He was still musing in his office, but popped to attention when the chief stuck his head in past the logotype that identified the office as that of the city's "Community Relations Officer" and asked, "How's that new school vandalism program coming?" The project was one he'd been formulating for about three months. He'd created a game that used a table-sized layout of a city park, complete with ball diamonds, swing sets, basketball hoops, even trash cans. The idea was to have kids pre-vandalism age, second through fourth grade, play the game. They'd be in charge of the park and were given a budget for new playground equipment that also had to cover repairs. There were cards describing some bad thing that had happened over the weekend. They would turn a card and learn that a storm had knocked over trees or someone had set the climbing wall on fire. Then they had to fund repairs out of their bank. The kids that had tried it so far had learned some lessons in real-ity. There was no money left for a new water slide because of the money needed for the repairs and cleanup. The game was about ready to go.

"I think I can turn it over to the DARE officers now. It's been playing pretty well since I made the last refinements. The kids are learning that it's expensive to replace things."

"Great," the chief replied. "I'd like to bring it up at the next city council meeting. I'll let you know when the agenda is set."

"Sounds good, Chief. I'll be there."

The chief disappeared down the hall. "Yup," the killer thought, as he straightened his tie and sat back down. "It's good to be in law enforcement."

Chapter Fifty-eight

Tuesday, July 27th
FBI Headquarters, Minneapolis

Over lunch we decided that Pete could help with deciphering the dog show catalog, if we could get one, so we called him in. He was getting checked in through security when we got back from lunch. We walked into the conference room in time for a phone call from Bismarck. Sheri Broughton was talking when we came in. She saw us and hit a switch to put her on the "box."

"That's right, Mrs. Roddick. We're assisting the Bismarck Police Department with an investigation."

"Oh my," came a tinny voice from the speaker in the middle of the table. "Has this something to do with that girl they found this morning?"

"Yes. If you could send us a catalog from last weekend's show, it would be helpful."

"A show catalog? That's odd. How would that help you?"

"Well, we don't know. We're just looking at everything."

"You know, I heard that there were some of your FBI people at the show in Duluth. They were there checking up on some of the judges. We thought it had to do with tax evasion or perhaps someone had rigged the winners in some of the big shows, like they did years ago."

I looked at Pete and mouthed, "Rigged?" Pete nodded.

Will caught our exchange and whispered, "Seriously?"

Pete whispered, "There's a lot of money at stake in the biggest shows, the national championships. Fifty thousand dollars to the winner. Back in the '80s, some judges were suspended for taking what amounted to bribes."

"That could interest us," Will said. "But not today."

Orv Kingman walked in with a phone in his ear and nodded to Broughton.

Sheri went evasively on. "Yes, we have a few things we are checking out. Can I get a catalog from you or is there someone else I should call?"

"Well, I have one," the woman said, "but I don't know how I'd get it to you right away. You know, the mail takes three to four days from here to the Cities, and he's already come by today."

"That's all right. An agent from our Bismarck office is on his way to your house right now. He should be there soon. You can give it to him and he'll send an electronic copy to us and return your copy to you." Over the speaker we heard a doorbell ring. Kingman again nodded at Broughton. The timing was impressive.

Mrs. Roddick said, "There's the bell now. That's remarkable. I'd better answer it."

"That's our agent. His name is Eric Stewart. You can give it to him and he'll bring it back to you." She hung up.

I looked at Will and said, "You guys are amazing."

"The difficult we do immediately, the impossible takes just a moment longer," he announced with typical Bureau pride.

Thirty minutes later we had copies of the catalog, along with a computer report. The report was the result of a scanning program that reviewed the catalog looking for specific names. It had found two. Hunter Nelson and Mickey Jefferson.

I looked at Pete and asked, "What do you think?"

"I'm a little surprised. It's a small show, not that many people go, even though it's three days. It's a great show to go to, but expensive because of the travel. That doesn't affect the pros too much. They'll go because it's what they do for a living. And the show needs judges, just fewer of them. I suppose the thing to do would be to find out how they got there and when they left."

Pete picked up the catalog sheets. They'd been assembled into plastic spiral binders, and found the page he was looking for. He said, "Call this guy," he said, pointing to a name. "He was in charge of Judge's Hospitality. He can tell you if Mickey or Hunter drove or flew in for the show and where they stayed. And, you can call this guy," he said pointing to another name. "He was in charge of RV reservations. He'll know who stayed onsite in an RV."

Broughton and Kingman hit the phones. Will waved Molly, Pete, and me out into the hallway and we followed him to his office.

"OK, Pete. What should I know about these two?"

"I know Mickey pretty well. His name on the list surprises me, but I guess it fits, too, doesn't it? Every time you see one of these guys arrested on TV, they talk to his neighbors and they all say, 'Gee, he seemed like such a nice guy, member of the church men's group, Boy Scout leader, volunteered at the senior center.' I guess that's part of the cover, huh?"

"It's not really a cover," Molly said. "It's their nature. They appear normal, in some ways overly normal to everyone in their everyday life. It's their alter ego that is the dangerous part. As I said, they are very smart and they can easily move throughout society; they just have no regard for their fellow human beings."

"OK," Pete said, accepting the description. "Mickey is a normal guy. I've had drinks with him a few times. He has a wife and a couple of kids. I think he works in the court system somehow or with the cops where he lives. Something in law enforcement."

"That fits, too," Molly said. "Often, these people will have attempted to get into law enforcement at some time in their lives. They will have applied for a job as a police officer or with the sheriff's department and been turned down, usually for not passing the psychological screening that's part of the process. Sometimes they do get jobs in law enforcement, but that's rare."

"What about the other guy," I asked, "Nelson?"

"Well, he'd be my choice," Pete said. "I know that he's had some run-ins with parents of some of the junior handlers in the past."

Will asked, "What's a junior handler?"

"Kids get involved with the sport through their parents or other family members or 4-H. Like most things kids do, most of them try it and go on to other activities, but some really like it. I've seen them showing in Obedience and Agility at very young ages. One young local girl, only three-and-a-half, titled a dog at an Agility trial here awhile back."

"Three-and-a-half?" I asked. "How could a kid that young train a dog?"

"She didn't. The dog was her mother's and already had some titles. But she showed the dog and finished a title at that age. It was quite a story. Anyway, kids get involved in Conformation with someone and the ones that take to it want to do it all summer. So, some of the big handlers take these kids on the road and sort of mentor them while having them do a lot of the grunt work like bathing and grooming the dogs, feeding and picking up after them."

"So, this Nelson had a run-in with parents?"

"Yeah, the word was that he was hitting on the girls. They were teenagers and some of them . . . well, you know how the kids look these days; they look pretty mature in a physical way. One of the girls told her parents that he was sneaking peeks at her when she was changing clothes or bathing. After that came out, another girl who had worked with him a couple years earlier said that he'd molested her. Nothing ever came of it, legally, but he doesn't have many people willing to send their daughters out with him anymore."

"When did this take place?" Molly wanted to know.

"About four or five years ago," Pete said.

"How does that work as far as the event timeline?" Will asked.

Molly thought for a moment then said, "Doesn't really make sense. If he's the guy, he was already killing girls by then. Unless he was starting to lose control of his impulses. If he was, those girls were in mortal danger." She looked at Pete. "Do you remember the girls, what they looked like?"

"The girl who made the first complaint was about seventeen years old, physically mature, about five foot five and blond. I think the one who made the molestation complaint was blond, too."

"That works. What does this guy do for a living?" Will asked.

Pete thought for second, scratching his head. "I'm not sure. Let me call a guy I know." He walked down the hall for privacy.

Will, Molly, and I looked at each other, wondering if Nelson could be our boy. He had been in all the right spots and he seemed to like young blonds.

Pete came back to us and said, "I called a friend who's a pro handler and knows both Hunter and Mickey well. He said He said Mickey is a court reporter and Hunter works for the police department in his city as some kind of public information officer. He's not a regular cop, but works for the force."

Molly summed up our thoughts. "He's our boy."

Will said, "I'll get Kingman to find out what the guy drives and get a BOLO out on him now."

Chapter Fifty-nine

We went back into the conference room. We told Broughton what we knew. She perked right up.

"Great," She said. "We've got him now!"

"I'm not 100 percent sure. It's a great coincidence, but you know how coincidences go," Molly said.

We all nodded.

Sheri Broughton broke the tension. "So, what's our next step?"

"Good question," Will said. "Pete, are there any big shows coming up where this guy will probably be? Hopefully, something not too far away."

Pete nodded. "This coming weekend, one of the biggest of the year. Right here in town. The St. Croix Valley Kennel Club Show. It's out at the Washington County Fairgrounds. I'd bet Nelson will be there."

"OK, preliminary plan for observation. Then I want ideas to improve it." We all nodded.

Will went on. "The show is this weekend. First, we have to determine if Nelson is coming. How can we do that?"

Pete said, "The show starts on Thursday, it's a four-day show. The superintendent for the show will have the catalogues printed by now. Right now they will be loading them on a truck to drive up here tomorrow to set up the rings on Wednesday and get ready for Thursday morning. But they don't release the catalogs until the first day of the show. They're supposed to keep secret who's coming so people don't stay home rather than show against a dog they know they can't beat. Absent entries means lower points, so they do everything they can to get all the entered dogs to show up."

Will asked Pete, "What's the name of the company?"

Pete said, "Onofrio Dog Shows; you know, like the actor."

Will looked at Kingman and nodded. Kingman left the room. Will said, "We'll have someone in that company's office in Oklahoma City within thirty minutes. He'll get a copy."

I bowed my head and said, "Once again, I am awed by the power of the fed."

Molly chuckled. Will smiled and said, "By now, you should know— the only thing we can't do is what we don't want to do."

It turned out to take less than the predicted thirty minutes. In twenty-eight, we had a copy of the upcoming show's catalog, sent as an electronic file from the show superintendent. Pete looked it over. In the back was a list of licensed handlers who would be at the show. "Here he is."

"Now, this doesn't necessarily mean that he'll be here on Thursday," Pete said. "It just means that he is listed as the handler on at least one dog that is entered this weekend. The first two days are what we call 'specialties,' shows that are limited to one specific breed. The big show starts on Saturday."

Sheri Broughton's phone rang and she picked it up. She listened for a moment, taking notes as her face drained of color. We all knew she was getting some very bad news. Finally, she said, "Send the report as soon as you have anything. And the autopsy reports, too." She hung up and looked at the group.

"He's upped the ante."

Chapter Sixty

I had just zeroed in on the plural—autopsy reports—when Sheri said, "That was our investigating agent in Bismarck. He said that the Bismarck officer sent to notify the vic's family found a second crime scene. There was no answer at the door, so he walked around the house and checked the doors. He found them all locked, but was able to see in a bedroom window. He saw what looked to be a body in the house. He forced the door to check the victim and found that there were two victims, both dead. He called it in and we sent a team.

"Our agent said he's never seen a scene like it. They've tentatively identified the two victims as the Walstad girl's parents." She was struggling for words to describe the scene. "The father, Robert Walstad according to ID found on site, was found on the bed in the master bedroom. But, the mother, Sally's, whereabouts weren't readily obvious. She was eventually found underneath him in the bed.

"The man's throat appeared to have been cut. There was pool of blood in the doorway to one of the other bedrooms, it looked like the daughter's room. He said the blood was, quote, massive and it had been disturbed. There was a drag line to the master bedroom. So that may be where the father had fallen. His blood-soaked clothing was found in the clothes hamper."

Sheri paused, took a deep breath and continued. "The woman may have been tortured in a manner consistent with our killer's M.O. The body shows many knife cuts, but they are bigger than previous victims.

When they separated the bodies they discovered the woman's nipples had been removed and the man's penis was missing. There was also a chair in the room with traces of duct tape on the arms and a urine stain on the cushion. No blood was found on the chair.

"A quick check found one neighbor who said he'd been sort of keeping an eye on the place since he knew that the girl was there alone and the parents were out of town. They weren't expected back until late Sunday evening. The ME stated that the male victim had been dead at least 36 hours, indicating that the parents must have returned home Saturday evening.

"Preliminary thinking by the local team is that the parents came home, interrupting whatever the killer was doing to the daughter. The killer dealt with the father by slashing his throat. Then he captured the mother. The daughter may have been tied up in the chair while the mother was tortured and killed. Bismarck SAC is on the scene and has ordered a top-level crime scene processing by the Bureau's people." She stopped and took a drink from her water glass. Then she stood and excused herself.

Chapter Sixty-one

We were all lost in thought at how to identify this animal. I had a thought.

"How big is the father?"

Molly grabbed Sheri's notes. "DMV records say five-foot-eight. One hundred and sixty-eight pounds."

"Then he's not necessarily a big guy."

"Good idea, Dan. If the dad had been over two-fifty, it would have limited the size of the killer to someone who could have moved that body," Will said.

Molly continued to peruse the report. She startled and popped her head up, stopping everyone's heart for a moment.

"Wait a second. How did the local PD identify the victim so fast? The report said she was naked."

That was a puzzler. Molly picked up the phone and called. There was a lot of back and forth and then she hung up.

"They said the girl's driver's license was found under the body. The killer must have placed it there."

"That means he wanted a quick identification. He didn't leave it there by accident," Will said.

Molly added, "He wanted the girl ID'd so they would find the parents. He wants us to know that it's him. He's going over the edge. He's personalized the contest by naming Dan and he's upped the ante by saying that no one can catch him. He's about to blow. This could turn really ugly really fast."

The phone rang again. Molly took the call and put it on speaker. It was the Bismarck agent who was at the autopsy of the daughter, Monica Walstad. He had a report that stopped us in our tracks.

"Here's what the ME has preliminarily. Cause of death is asphyxiation. The knife wounds to the body seem to be post-mortem. Significantly, there is no large penetrating wound to the heart as was present in the previously associated cases and blood volume in the body seemed to be normal."

The agent continued, "I asked the ME about it and he had an idea. I had the Bismarck PD check the house for one of those breathing machines in the girl's bedroom and they found one. The ME said that shows the girl had a nocturnal breathing problem, sleep apnea, very unusual for someone as fit as she was, but not impossible. He also said he ran what he called a date-rape panel to look for the presence of any narcotics and it tested positive for Rohypnol. The ME says that, although it's very unusual, a too-high dose of Rohypnol can cause a person with a sleep apnea problem to simply choke out and die. That's what it looks like to him. So he's calling the manner of death a homicide."

"That's it," Molly blurted. She had spent a lot of time looking at the photos of the victim. "The knife wounds are in disarray compared to the other victims. There's no order to them other than the message. They're just scattered around and there are crossed wounds in areas away from the message."

"Is that significant?" I asked.

"I'm sure it is," she said. "If the girl died on her own she denied the killer the pleasure of killing her. He may strike again soon!"

Will said, "What about the mother?"

"She'll calm him down for a moment, but it won't last. I think we should expect him to make a play for another victim soon."

"That's going to make this weekend even more significant," Will said.

Sheri came back into the room with her phone in her ear. She signed off and said, "When the local office found that the parents were dead, they immediately put it on the local media, asking if anyone knew where they or the daughter had been the last few days. They got a couple of calls. The victim was last seen Saturday morning when she had a late brunch with a friend. She was at a little restaurant next to a city park. They're sending agents to interview the staff."

We began planning for the weekend's local dog show. There would be over thirty agents assigned to general surveillance and shadowing the prime targets. Plus communication and transportation people. The plan started to come together.

About two hours into it, Sheri's phone rang. She spoke for a moment and hung up. "Bismarck reports that the girl was having lunch with a man, early thirties, blond hair, average height, fit, no marks or tats. They left together."

Molly said, "That pretty much describes Nelson."

Will said, "Let's go over the plan again."

We spent the rest of the day planning while dodging the ever-increasing interest of the press, not an easy thing to do if you want everyone alive and the bad guy convictable. Our focus was on Hunter Nelson. He was present in Bismarck and the other locations, had the right background, had the history with the juniors, and fit the description of the man seen with the Bismarck victim. We tried to predict where he would go on his off hours while at the upcoming dog show. Pete was invaluable for this. He really knew the dog show people inside and out. The plan came together and we dispersed to prepare to execute it.

Chapter Sixty-two

Wednesday morning, July 29th

A plan evolved that featured using Molly as bait. She'd be available to Nelson at any of the local bars he might visit or we could follow him out of town after the show Sunday to see if he stopped somewhere to troll for a victim. We had plenty of resources—equipment, weapons, communications, bodies. The only thing we lacked was prescience. We simply didn't know what was going to happen.

Fortunately for me, the plan included having Maria with us as an unfamiliar face who could provide close-in support without tipping anyone off. She made arrangements to get to Minnesota as fast as she could.

After one last briefing to bring Maria up to speed, we'd head out to the Washington County Fairgrounds in Lake Elmo, just east of the Twin Cities metro area, for a few quiet days of stakeout observation. At least, that was the plan . . . until the story broke.

My TV fired up at the usual 5:30 and the local news channel greeted me with the story of a serial killer in our midst. Not only had the state suffered its second weird killing of a female, but the second victim had been a local celebrity. As I flipped through the channels the reporters were all digging, but without results. I knew that wouldn't last. By noon, a law enforcement official would be standing in front of cameras. There were only two candidates for that job, a representative from the FBI or Glenn Mills.

Glenn was the obvious choice since both bodies had been found in his jurisdiction. He could hold them off for a little while with the clichéd response of not being at liberty to discuss an ongoing investigation. That would simply divert the reporters to other sources. They'd know the BCA was in on the investigation so they'd hit their contacts there. They'd know Jane had reported on the first killing, so they'd dig into the background she did for that and start playing the tape of her report nonstop. They'd call other political contacts with oversight of law enforcement in the state who, in turn, would call their contacts, which, in turn, would generate another whole round of phone calls from legislators' aides to collect information. This was the news industry's version of an "All Hands" drill on a Navy ship. Everyone had a job and everyone would do it.

At 5:45, my phone rang. "Dan, it's Will. Have you seen the news?"

"Sure have. It's killing my appetite. How's this affect us?"

"Don't know yet. Not sure how D.C. is going to want to play it."

I guess I should have figured on that. The FBI doesn't take a shit without considering the political and publicity implications. "So, what are the possibilities?"

"Two that I can see. Ignore it or go public, announce that we're on the case. The latter is my best guess. That way we can control the flow of info and still try to go through with our plan. In any case, the ante's been upped significantly. We'll have a lot of people at the dog show this weekend. There's been no connection made by the press to the dog show angle, so we're still off the screen on that. But if that gets out, it won't be the vampire killer, it will be something else. Hell, I'm half-tempted to release the vampire thing just to blow them off the track of the dog show."

I chuckled. It's always hard for non-LEOs to understand how law enforcement officers can see humor in the course of all the horror they endure, but we can. We have to. It's the only way to cope.

"There's a third way. A red herring we could throw at the press." I said.

"Yeah, what's that?"

"Glenn. We could lay some B.S. out there about how it's still local in Glenn's area and feed him enough to keep the press focused on Mora and off our backs for a few more days. He'd have to be out front, though, instead of your fine fellows."

I could hear the gears in Will's head grinding. Would the feebs want

268

to put someone else out front as a decoy? That would help the case but take them out of the spotlight. That could be attractive to them in the event the guy gets away. Not their fault. Hmmm.

"I'll present it and let you know."

We finished our conversation with a confirmation of our noon meeting. From there we'd head to the site of the dog show. If there was a press conference, Will would handle it. I was to stay in the background, which was just fine with me.

I finished up around the house and, at the appointed hour, drove to the airport and picked up Maria. While it would be nice to say that we had a reunion typical of separated lovers, we're cops first and our personal business would have to wait. We talked about the case. It took about thirty minutes to get from the airport to the FBI building. During the drive the only non-law enforcement stuff was a quick kiss when she got into the car.

Will had a conference room set up for us and we reviewed the case and plan quickly. Molly was the bait. Normally, it could be a very dangerous position to put someone in. But Molly was an experienced agent who could definitely handle herself. Maria would cover Molly as she trolled for Hunter Nelson. Molly had his file so she'd be able to make herself familiar with, and available to, him. After the quick lunch meeting, we split up into groups and headed to the Washington County Fairgrounds to look the place over.

I had called Pete to see if he could join us as a tour guide. He met us there after the hour-long drive from his place on Lake Minnetonka.

Pete got out of his ride du jour, a 2014 Cadillac CTS-V coupe. It's a nasty near-black thing with a beautiful black and grey leather interior. It has red pinstriping and about 650 horsepower. The cognoscenti call it a four-door Corvette. It's some kind of special model and they only built a couple hundred of them, so it has a number—35, I think. Anyway, since Pete hit it big in North Dakota he's turned into kind of a car nut and has a storage building full of neat old cars. This one isn't old so he doesn't mind driving it, at least a little bit. He let me drive it once and it scared the crap out of me.

"Ah, another beautiful August day in Minnesota," he said by way of greeting. It was about 80 degrees with a low humidity. You just never know about August in Minnesota. Could be eighty, could be one hundred, or sixty-five and overcast. A haze limited visibility to about three or four miles under the cloudless sky and there was no breeze. Not bad. I was glad the weather was great. I want Maria to want to be here, and eventually live here.

Pete, Glenn, and I started walking toward an area where people were setting up the show. Basically, it was the same as I'd seen in Duluth, just outdoors. I was generally familiar with the fairgrounds. All Minnesota county fairgrounds are pretty much the same. The only differences are size and whether or not they have a racetrack. Washington County was on the large size. No real racetrack, just sort of dirt bike track that had been hollowed out of a low spot on the south end. It functions as both a motocross track and catch basin for the water produced by summer thunderstorms. Standard steel pole barns were scattered around for everything from poultry judging, craft displays, 4-H projects, and baked goods. The pole barns varied in age, but not in design. They were all about sixty feet across and two hundred feet long. Red wooden barns stand on the north end for whatever animals might be in residence. There is a campground with baths for RVers and shacks for the food vendors.

An open pavilion lay across the ersatz street where the main judging of the show would take place. The covered pavilion, with its asphalt underlayment, would shield the people and dogs from the hot summer sun. The show rings were set up partly under the pavilion's roof and extended out into the sunshine. We headed there from the parking area. On the way we passed through a partly covered, partly exposed area that was full of vendors. I heard my name called out.

Chapter Sixty-three

Wednesday
Washington County Fairgrounds
Lake Elmo, Minnesota

I looked toward the sound and saw the scissors salesman I'd met in Duluth waving at me. Pete and I headed over to his booth, which was in a state of setting-up disarray. I gave him a wave.

"Hey, how you doing?" I said, with a bit of wise guy in my voice.

"Doing great. Weather like this, who could complain? That's always a problem with this show. It's a crapshoot. I've been here when it's beautiful like this and when there's a thunderstorm or even tornadoes. I'll be happy if we get a couple of nice days before it gets nasty."

Pete agreed and they reminisced about a particularly bad thunderstorm that had occurred some years earlier when Pete was still in the game.

I scanned the sky, knowing that the weather was the least of my problems. The scissors guy went on.

"Hey, you remember talking about carry guns in Duluth? Well, I followed your advice and bought a CAB 9C. Haven't had much time to practice with it yet, but I will."

I vaguely remembered our conversation in Duluth. Right now, all I wanted to do was finish my recon sweep. I mumbled a quick, "Be sure to break it in," as I scanned the area for our target. What I heard next broke the spell.

"Are you guys here about the serial killer?"

Pete and I looked at each other, then at the scissors guy, whose name, I then remembered, was Greg something. The fact that he had his name embroidered on his shirt might have helped too. "What do you mean, serial killer, Greg?" I asked.

"It was on the news this morning. They said that some woman had been killed last week and that it was the same guy who had killed another woman after the Cambridge shows last month. They said she was a TV reporter who had been investigating the first murder."

The guy seemed pretty interested and I recalled that he was on a citizen's response team with his local PD back wherever he lived. I took a chance.

"Yeah, we're checking out some leads. Listen, you go to a lot of these shows. If you had to pick someone to be a little off-center, who would it be?"

"Oh shit, I don't know. We've got more than our share of oddballs in this game, don't we Pete? The radio said the FBI is on the case. I suppose you've got a profiler and everything, huh? Those folks are pretty good. I'd listen to whatever they tell you."

I asked, "How much do you know about profiling?"

Greg smiled and said, "I've read everything out there on serial killers. Fascinating stuff. Got interested when that TV show about profiling came on. Of course, when I read the books by real profilers, I found out that most of the stuff on the TV show is baloney. Those guys are real sick wackos."

I was wondering how I'd made it through all my years in law enforcement without developing the fascination for serial killers that seemed to be turning up all around me. First, Phil Horvath and now this Greg guy. Maybe it's the TV show. Of course, I know plenty of cops, pretty much all of them, who have little to no interest in ballistics, so maybe I'm the oddball.

"OK. So based upon your research, who would fit the classic mold?"

Greg laughed, "My research? Hah! I don't want to get anyone in trouble, but there are a couple guys who check off a lot of the boxes. I don't know; I don't want to hazard a guess. You know, if I pick someone and I'm wrong, you could spend a lot of time looking at the wrong guy."

I nodded. "Well, keep us in mind if you see anything," I said, handing him my card.

"Yeah," he replied. "And if you need any help, you know, undercover or surveillance, that kind of stuff, call me. I'm here all the time and no one will suspect I'm watching."

Good point. "Deal," I said, shaking his hand. Pete and I walked away.

After a reasonable distance, I shook my head and said, "Everywhere we turn we find closet profilers."

"It's the TV show." Pete said. "Carol loves that show." I rolled my eyes.

We got over to what I took as the main showing area, a long pavilion that was basically a thirty-foot-wide roof with a twenty-foot-wide asphalt-paved floor. The show rings were set up on each side of the pavilion using the standard white lattice baby gates running to a three-row split-rail fence. Pete said, "This area will be crowded with exhibitors getting ready to show. They drag their crates on carts in here to prep their dogs for the ring. Spectators are restricted from this area. It just gets too crowded."

I was surprised. It was a fairly large area. "This will be too packed to allow spectators? How many dogs are here at one time?"

Pete chuckled. "It's not just the one dog and one handler. It's the cart, which has anywhere from one to six crates on it, a grooming table mounted on top and the posse of helpers that fluff and primp the dogs just before they go in the ring. There's a lot of prep work at the last moment.

"For the first class, the prime handler will take a dog in, get judged, and come out. That takes about three minutes per dog. If that dog wins, then that dog has to be ready to go back in to compete against the other winners, so he has to be kept ready to go. If that dog came in second, he still might have to go back for Reserve Winners, which is second-best winner, so he has to be kept ring-ready too. If he's third or lower, it's back in the box and the handler takes in the next dog for the next class.

"In the Winners round, if a handler has two dogs to take in, they'll take the one they want to win and hand the other dog off to the backup handler. They all go in, do their thing, and the Winners Dog is chosen. Then, that second-place dog we talked about before might have to come back in for picking Reserve."

I thought I had learned all the dog-show terminology. "What's Reserve?" I asked.

"Reserve is second place for the points. If it turns out that the dog that just won the points is somehow ineligible or gets disqualified, the second-place dog will get the points. It almost never happens, so we call it the 'Kiss your Sister' award."

We both chuckled at that. Pete went on. "That's it for the boys. Then, they do it all over for the girls and once again for Best of Breed. There's a lot of scrambling, changing arm-band numbers with rubber bands flying everywhere, handing off of dogs, and getting the dogs ready to go. It all happens very fast; there's no waiting. When the ring steward calls your number you must be ready to go. After Best of Breed you pack everything up and haul it back to your grooming area."

I thought about what sounded like organized chaos for a moment and said, "So, there's little chance our bad guy will have time for any nasty behavior during the show, right?"

"I don't know how he could. If he's a judge or a handler, he's busy. It's got to be after hours that he's making his move."

That jibed with what Molly had said—the show was the trigger. He might make a selection during the show, maybe arrange a rendezvous, but he wouldn't take a victim until the show was over. Not enough time available for his idea of fun and games.

After a thorough stroll around the area, we reported back by phone to Will, who said he'd finished scouting observation points where our primary target, Nelson, could be watched during the days to come. Other agents had been scoping out the three local bars where we expected Nelson would spend his free time looking for a victim. One group of feebs predicted he'd just make a stop in and not spend time, not wanting to become memorable, but another group said he'd want to be familiar with the lay of the land. Some thought he'd want to wait until Sunday to even go near any place there might be show people, but someone else said he's so smooth that he can be known in a bar and still get away with it. No consensus.

Will said, "OK, you two can head home. We'll all be out here tomorrow and nothing will probably happen for a couple of days. We'll keep surveillance on Nelson around the clock until he makes a move. I don't expect anything until Sunday."

Chapter Sixty-four

Sunday afternoon, February 2, 2015
Lake Elmo, Minnesota

Pete and I strolled the grounds toward the end of the last day of the show. Pete stopped and spoke with folks he knew, congratulated them on points wins and commiserated with those who felt they'd been wronged. I guess it's like that in every sport. A ball called a strike, a foot on the sideline that was missed and the touchdown scored, a hand-guarding foul in the closing moments of a basketball game where none had been called for the first forty-six minutes. While many major sports now have instant replay, it would never happen at a dog show. How closely does the dog in the ring match the breed standard? That was purely the subjective opinion of the judge apparently. I guess that's why they call it judging.

Pete was distracted by an acquaintance and wandered away. The show's participants were completing their tasks for the day, varied as they were. Handlers stacked and pushed their equipment back to their "home base," the superintendent's crew tore down the paper sheets and the numbered poles they were attached to, club members gathered up the candy baskets and other materials, the stones and bricks that were used as paperweights, all the things that apparently kept a dog show moving.

I noticed what, at first, I thought were worms curled on the concrete aprons of the rings as they would have been after a rainstorm. It surprised me since there had been no rain for several days. Looking closer, I saw they were discarded rubber bands, hundreds of them. Exhibitors used the rubber bands to hold the dog's entry number on their arms. They lay cast off and forgotten along with an occasional paper armband, neither worth keeping for reuse or a scrapbook page commemorating a victory. The odd detritus of a large dog show. I shook the sight from my eyes.

I found Pete and we headed over to the FBI's command vehicle, an RV full of communication equipment disguised as an RV full of dog-show people. As we walked, I reflected. Would tonight or tomorrow bring us the head of the killer or would he strike again? Would he be able to slip through the huge FBI net or would he sense its presence and not attempt to take another victim? Or would he collect another Best-In-Show ribbon and just head home, leaving us like the curled rubber bands kicked to the curb?

The past four days had passed without incident. Each day Nelson had shown up, directed the grooming of the dogs in his care, assigned dogs to each of his three assistants, showed the dogs his clients had paid a bit more to have him handle personally, and won his share of ribbons. Each day had started early and ended late, including a visit to one of three local watering holes after his Friday afternoon trip to the Best-In-Show ring. Nelson didn't win but apparently had plenty to celebrate. Pete said it was a perfectly normal weekend at a major dog show.

At the end of each day, most of the exhibitors went home, since most were local folks. The pros and out-of-towners repaired to their RVs to work on the dogs for the next day.

In one of our tutorials I had asked Pete why someone would bathe and groom a dog that had just been bathed and groomed the day before. He said it was part of the sport.

"Personally, I think it's sort of a compulsive behavior," he'd said. "Especially the Poodle people. They re-cut their dogs' hair all the time, almost as it's growing. The show superintendents take that into account when they put the schedule together. They know that it takes longer to get the coated dogs ready so you usually see the shorthaired dogs earlier in the day. But even with the extra time, they'll come running up to the ring at the last second with a brush in one hand and scissors in the other. And, that's not just the Poodle people, that's Goldens, Shih Tzus, Setters, all kinds of long-coat dogs."

Apparently when the clipping and brushing were done, it was time for the humans to party. A couple of the undercover agents complained that the parties got bigger and noisier throughout the weekend.

The press coverage had died out after the first couple of days when nothing else was forthcoming from the task force and no more bodies had been discovered. The FBI had kept a lid on the North Dakota killings by having the local cops release a massaged version of the truth so that the connection to the Minnesota murders had escaped the press thus far. There was a tribute piece on Channel 7 about Jane, but even that was more like a newspaper obit than coverage of the case. The dog show had gone on and the weather stayed nice, which, I was told, was unusual for the event.

Chapter Sixty-five

Sunday evening

Molly was set to "deploy"—I love the feebs' use of tac talk—to whatever bar it looked like Nelson was heading for. We'd try to get her in there before him, so he could "find" her, not the other way around. She would position herself near an empty barstool and look as inviting as possible. Maria would also be in the bar but they'd pretend to not know each other. Maria would be there for surveillance only. She'd be wired up with two-way comms out to a Suburban where Will, two other FBI communication specialists, and I would be waiting. We had it all planned out—foolproof and no danger to anyone.

In order to build a case against Nelson, we had to let him go to a certain point in his plan before we initiated ours. We had to take the guy in the act, with all his gear prepared, in order to show he had intent to do another victim. That meant that he not only had to have a conversation with Molly, but he had to pick her up, take her to his vehicle, and then to wherever he had planned to have his fun with her.

To provide some protection, Molly had been given a pill to take before she started drinking anything. It's an experimental drug that's supposed to block the effects of Rohypnol. Someone figured out that opiates can be blocked by taking Narcon before or after exposure to drugs like heroin and OxyContin so, they thought, why not come up with something to block roofies? But, like I said, it's experimental. The pill has to be taken just prior to exposure. Molly even tested it so she would know what the experience felt like. She also ingested

Rohypnol without the blocking agent so she'd know what that felt like, just in case.

The feds also sewed a tracking homer into her clothing. It had a fairly good range of about a mile. The final measure was another tracking homer she actually would swallow just before her encounter. This had a shorter range, only a couple hundred feet. The thought was that the beacon in her clothing could be removed, but the one she swallowed could not. But, we'd be close enough to swoop in if her clothes were removed and dumped someplace.

We were ready.

We thought.

Chapter Sixty-six

The FBI command vehicle was parked in a corner of the campground, which was part of the fairgrounds. To help with the disguise, they'd rolled out the sunshade and set up a dog exercise pen. Of course, the FBI, being the FBI, had also assigned an agent to "pen pick-up" and "shade roll-up" in the case of a quick drive-off in pursuit—one guy, probably with a fresh JD degree, whose only job was to hit a switch and grab a fence. Who says we don't have enough money?

Anyone visiting the vehicle was instructed to wear casual clothes and park far away so the cars would be scattered randomly around the area and not look like we were having a party. Will was in touch with the people watching each of the bars we expected Nelson to visit before leaving town. Four cars were ready to provide a loose tail as soon as he left the fairground.

Glenn had joined us for what we hoped would be the capture of a serial killer. Molly was waiting in a car equidistant to all three bars. All was set to roll. We sat and waited for something to happen.

I reflected on the possibility that we were looking at the wrong man. Will had people covering Nelson and would try to discern where he was headed in time to get agents and Molly into the place ahead of the prime suspect. If Nelson headed home, we'd tail him at least 200 miles, handing off coverage to other FBI assets as he drove south. Oddly, we hoped he would attempt to strike. If he did, we'd be ready. But, what if . . .? In truth, "he" was still unknown.

Waiting is the toughest part of an operation. We thought we knew who the bad guy was, we knew what he'd done, we knew what he was going to do. I could practically feel the cuffs snapping around his wrists. But nothing was happening. During the wait we had to be careful not to drink too much coffee or smoke too many cigarettes—if I smoked, that is. Murphy's law, being what it is, the call would come while you were in the john or burning a heater. The minutes dragged on and I had to fight the urge to look at my watch or the twelve-inch clock the feddies had so thoughtfully hung on the wall of the RV. Every time a radio peeped or a phone buzzed I jumped. I just hoped I'd have a little adrenaline left when it finally went down.

Another radio peeped. Will listened, then turned to us and said, "He's on the move."

We all waited expectantly for more details, but the minutes went by. The call had come from a parking lot near the show site. All we knew was he had gone to his car and was hooking it up to his big RV. He hadn't left the parking lot. Finally, Will held his finger to the receiver bud in his ear. "The RV is rolling now. It's turning toward town," he said. "Let's go."

We quickly stepped out to the cars. I rode with Will; Glenn rode with another unit. As we moved toward Lake Elmo, Will got more updates. Finally, we had a target—the St. Croix Inn.

The St. Croix Inn was an institution known widely for its great food. It also had a large bar that would be busy on that last evening of a summer weekend. It was the bar we hoped Nelson would choose. It had the best layout for surreptitious observation of Molly. Will told me Molly was in position. That meant Maria was too, since she was riding in Molly's car. Once inside, they'd separate and be strangers to each other.

We rolled into the parking lot and left the car facing out near an exit, poised for a quick getaway in case we had to pursue Nelson. We saw Nelson parking his RV, which was towing his car, in the large back lot reserved for vehicles with trailers, a common parking lot feature in Minnesota. We paused so we wouldn't reach the door at the same time. After literally counting to fifteen, once Nelson disappeared into the bar, we went in.

Our eyes adjusted to the dim lights quickly and we saw Molly at the bar and Maria seated at a table with an FBI guy in the corner. The feeb was there to keep Maria company and prospective suitors away. She needed to be free to observe Molly and provide cover when required. Neither of us gave any sign of recognition as Will and I made our way to a table across the floor from Maria.

Will and I scanned the room and identified three more federal agents at a table near the bar. Their job was to observe Molly's drink and make sure Nelson didn't put anything in it. If he did, they had a signal they'd flash to Molly so she'd know to pop the antidote before she drank any of it. Everyone was in place. We waited for Nelson to make his move.

When you're in a state of hyper-attention and have "gone tactical," like we were, you can develop tunnel vision and become over-focused on your target and miss other things that are going on around you. Will and I were both guilty of this when I felt a hand slap my back and heard, "Hey, Dan! How you doing?"

I jerked around to see Greg Weber, the scissors vendor, standing behind me. Will looked over expectantly as we both hoped the guy would just keep on walking, but he pulled out a chair and sat down.

I made introductions that explained Greg's connection with the dog shows and left out Will's employer, just saying he was an old friend. Greg shook Will's hand and said, "I'm a little surprised to see you here, Dan. Kind of out of your normal territory, isn't it?"

OK, he had my attention. "And how would you know what my territory is?" I jabbed back with a smile on my face. The last thing I wanted was to draw attention to myself.

"Well, just a guess. I know you live on the other side of the Cities. It said so in your book."

That surprised me. "You read one of my books?" I asked.

"Sure. After you gave me that advice on a gun, I checked you out a little and found out about your books. Fascinating stuff. Makes me want to take some classes and maybe help my local PD out with investigations."

I explained to Will, "Greg works with his local PD on their Citizen's Emergency Response Team, handling pet issues during emergencies."

"Yeah, that's what I get called for. But I've been thinking that if I had more training in CSI stuff, I could provide more services. Plus, I would get called for more interesting stuff than grabbing a couple dogs or cats that have been pulled out of a house fire or a car wreck. It'd be cool to get to go to crime scenes and help collect evidence. I'm already a pretty good photographer. I could do that, too.

Will was looking at me with a gaze that would have done a wife proud. It was a "Make him go away" look if I ever saw one. I had two choices. I could tell Greg what we were doing there and that we needed privacy or I could lie. I didn't think telling him the truth would get rid of him. He was obviously a cop wannabe and hanging around during a stakeout would be right on his bucket list. So I went with a lie.

"Hey Greg, it's good to see you again. But Will and I are working on a problem he's having at work and it's kind of private. Can you excuse us?"

"No problem," he said as he stood and reached for our hands with a big smile. "I've got some other folks I need to go see anyway." We shook hands all around and he said, "Good luck with your problem. If anyone can help you, Dan's the man." He headed over to a table where a couple of other vendors from the show were seated and plopped down in an empty chair.

"What was that?" Will asked. "Who is that guy and why is he your asshole buddy?"

"He's the guy from the dog show I told you about when we were at dinner. Pete knows him and introduced us in Duluth. Runs a booth that sells and sharpens scissors, apparently a busy activity at a dog show. Pete stopped and had his pocketknife sharpened. They talked about Pete getting back into showing and it sounded like a new set of scissors would set him back a year's tuition at St. Olaf." I shook my head and wrote him off as white noise, trying to get back to the job at hand. Will shook his head and asked, "What was that about gun recommendations?"

"In Duluth he said he was looking for a carry gun. You know me, get me talking firearms and I'm going to have an opinion. I told him to get a CAB 9C like I carry. Glenn and I talked to him when we were doing recon on Wednesday. He asked if we were working the serial killer case and volunteered to do inside surveillance. He's a wannabe."

"Well, if he just keeps his distance he'll be helping us now," Will said with a nod of his head toward the bar. I looked and saw Hunter Nelson taking a seat one stool down from Molly. "Here we go," I said quietly.

Chapter Sixty-seven

As we watched, Molly demonstrated acting skills worthy of a Hollywood Oscar winner. For a cop, working undercover often requires the ability to assume a personality that is generally diametrically opposed to the cop's real morals, but otherwise quite close to the cop's real nature. There are some cops who are naturals at it. I've always thought that meant that those cops could have gone either way when it came to law and order.

Indeed, any cop has to be able to go beyond the moral restrictions that societies place upon themselves. Cops have to be willing to use force, even violent and lethal levels of force, to do their jobs. This trait can show in their personalities and make them a little unapproachable in normal situations where civilians are present. That's why most cops prefer cop bars, cop friends, and cop parties. Molly had to look not only approachable but weak enough to be good victim material. She had to look "blond" colloquially, not to put too fine a point on it. She was doing great.

Hunter Nelson had entered the room and scanned it with a practiced eye. I watched through the distraction of the scissors guy as he nodded to other acquaintances in the room, shook off a few invitations of a seat or a drink, and continued until he had taken in the entire venue. As his gaze passed Molly, she threw him a sideways glance, just enough to let him know she'd seen him. He headed her way.

Nelson struck up a conversation with Molly. While we couldn't hear them, I knew that Maria was listening electronically. I looked over at Maria and saw her holding a finger to her ear, concentrating on the conversation while she looked over a menu. The FBI guy with her was entranced by the baseball game on the television hanging on the wall behind Maria's head. They looked like a couple that had years behind them—her choosing dinner, him watching the game.

The banter went on for nearly an hour before Molly excused herself to go to the bathroom. It was her opportunity to take the pill that was supposed to block the date-rape drug. I was nursing my second non-alcoholic beer, its taste becoming stale and flat, and munching on bar pretzels and peanuts, with one eye on the bar and one on the TV. The Twins were up 4-3 in the top of the eighth but the Tigers had driven the Twins starter from the game and they were into the questionable bullpen.

Will was more interested in Molly's return, which had yet to occur. His phone rang and he took a moment to look at it, wondering who could be calling him. I looked at him, wondering the same thing and expecting an answer like "Headquarters." The feebs like to keep track of operations in real time, even it means interrupting the field operators at a critical moment. That's who it was. Will made a quick report, basically that we were all sitting on our hands waiting for something to happen when I looked over to the bar and noticed that Nelson was gone. I flagged Will to get his attention and pointed. He looked toward the bar. No Nelson and no Molly.

I saw Maria hustling toward the back and jumped up and ran over to follow. When I caught up to her she was looking toward the back hall. I asked her if she'd seen or heard anything. She said she'd heard Molly say, "Hey, what are you doing back here?" but that she'd lost the audio signal. Will was on his radio as we all ran outside. No sign of Molly or Nelson. Glenn hollered and pointed and we all turned to see an RV rolling out of the parking lot.

"Is that Nelson?" I asked.

Will looked at one of his guys, who was nodding. The fed said, "Yeah, I think so."

Will put the word out and we scrambled to our cars. Within seconds there were four vehicles racing after the RV.

Will and I were in the back seat of a blacked-out Suburban. Will said,

"We should pull him over now while we know he's in the driver's seat. If we rush the vehicle we can keep him separated from her."

Personally, I was glad he wasn't suggesting the use of firepower to separate Nelson and Molly. If we knew she was in the rear of the RV we could, basically, saw the vehicle in half with automatic weapons fire. That was a standard procedure for the Bureau's Hostage Rescue Team, or HRT. It would keep him from going to the rear of the coach as we approached. It was an effective method but it only works if you know for certain where the hostage is. We didn't know where in the coach Molly was so weapons fire of any kind was a bad idea. Besides, modern RVs are packed with exterior cameras and we didn't want him to know where we were coming from, to say nothing about when. While I was thinking, the feds put a plan into action.

As we crested a small rise the lead chase cars could see the road was clear ahead and smoothly accelerated past the RV like they were just folks on their way home. With a few more quick messages on the secure radios, the next two trail cars closed up around the RV's rear and the lead cars executed a sliding turn to block the road. The agents in those two cars were out of their vehicles in a flash with M-4s and pistols drawn. The RV eased off the roadway and stopped on the shoulder.

Two agents rushed the windshield and held their weapons on Nelson as two others quickly entered the coach. By now, Will and I were on foot running up the road and I could see Nelson being pulled out of the driver's seat. We stepped around to the curbside of the coach in time to see Nelson flying out the door, hands cuffed behind his back. An agent on the shoulder caught him, spun him to face toward the RV, then slammed him into it. Nelson muttered an obscenity that was muffled by the sound of his chest hitting the RV. Two agents emerged from the coach and said, "Pull the lower storage panels. She's not inside."

"Who's not inside?" asked Nelson. "What are you doing?"

Will answered Nelson. "You're under arrest for multiple kidnapping and murder counts in a variety of states to be enumerated in an indictment. You'd do yourself some good here by telling us where you hid Agent Foss."

"Agent Foss? Who's Agent Foss?" asked Nelson. "What's going on here?"

Will took Nelson by the arm and led him around to the rear of one of the Suburbans. He popped the liftgate and it rose with a near silent hydraulic hiss. Nelson sat on the ledge as Will started explaining the facts of life and death to him.

"Hunter, here's where we are. We know that there has been a killer on the loose for at least the past twelve years. Said killer has been operating in the areas where large dog shows have just taken place, meaning that the person has some connection with dog shows. We know from the show records that you were present for each and every one of the shows near the location where a body was found. We know you have a thing for young girls. We know you work with law enforcement types. We know you were just hitting on a blond in the bar—Agent Foss—an attractive woman who fits the profile of your preferred victim and who was in the bar undercover to attract the killer. We saw her leave and you follow her to the back of the bar, where you did something to overpower her and take her hostage. Now, I'm going to ask you this one time only, where . . . is . . . she?"

I saw Will lean in close to Nelson's face as he delivered the question. His voice was stone cold and his eyes had the menace of a predator about to strike.

"I haven't done anything! I don't know what you're talking about!" Nelson screamed.

The other agents finished their search of Nelson's RV and came up empty for Molly. They did find a complete collection of dog grooming equipment, and a pretty good collection of porn, most of it young girls. Other than that and the dozen or so dogs, their barking adding to the general chaos of the night, no one was in there.

Glenn stepped in and said, "Check the basement."

"Basement?" The team leader asked.

"Sure, big coaches like this have a lot of storage space under the main floor. You can get to it by pulling the side doors up, like on a bus. It's a big enough space to hide a person."

One by one they pulled open the doors—nothing.

I looked back at Nelson and Will. Nelson was frozen in fear. Will looked as though he was ready to shoot Nelson in places that would guarantee an answer.

I grabbed Will and said, "Listen, Molly's not here. That means she's somewhere else. We've got to find her."

Will's eyes clicked open as the realization hit him.

Chapter Sixty-five

Sunday evening

FBI Agent Molly Foss woke with a throbbing headache. The pain seemed to be in sync with the rumbling she felt, forcing her to choose between focusing on the headache or that she was in a moving vehicle. She slowly cracked an eye to take in her surroundings. It was dark, but she could see that she was in a vehicle, more specifically, a room that was moving, an RV. It was moving slowly over fairly even ground. She couldn't tell if it was on a street or in a parking lot. Molly glanced around the moving room and heard a radio voice say "It's 7:45 on Sunday evening," and made a mental note of the time—1945. Although the windows were covered by shades, there was enough of a gap around the edges for her to see that it was still light outside. Silently she repeated "1945."

Cautiously, Molly assessed her situation. She was bound hand and foot, hands together above her head and feet tied separately to something, her legs apart. She appraised her physical condition, starting at her head and working her way down to her toes. All seemed fine except for her head, which was throbbing from a blow she'd received in the back hallway of the St. Croix Inn. That moment started to come back to her. As she had made her way to the Ladies Room, she kept one eye on Hunter Nelson in case he followed her. He did not. She pushed open the bathroom door and was startled to see a man standing there. At the sight of a man in the Ladies' Room she blurted out, "What are you doing here?" In that fraction of a second, before she could do or say anything to Maria via radio, he grabbed her arm, spun her and hit her with something. That was when the lights went out.

Gradually, the feeling returned to her limbs. She could hear the man singing along with the radio in the front of the RV. He has a good voice, she thought. His singing would cover any noises she might make as she tested her restraints, she thought. That was also when she realized she was covered with a sheet. Underneath it, she was naked.

I watched as Will recovered quickly from his rage toward Nelson for not having Molly. He quickly went back into FBI mode and radioed out the information that Agent Foss was not present in the RV. All units were to monitor the homing beacon frequency for the beeper sewn into Molly's clothes. He ordered an immediate search and the various units raced off in different directions. If there's one thing the feds know how to do, it's search, I thought.

Molly listened as the RV rolled to a stop. She heard the engine sounds power down, but not completely die away. "Must be a generator," she thought. The coach rocked slightly in rhythm with footsteps as the man walked back to the room where she was being held. In the dim light she couldn't see his face, only his back as he worked at a counter. Finally, he turned and spoke to her.

"Hello Agent Foss, I'm Greg Weber," he said to Molly. "Or should I say Mrs. Sanford? Didn't expect to see me tonight, did you?"

Molly couldn't help but gasp. Greg Weber was known to be one of the dog show people, one of the vendors. But he wasn't on any of the suspect lists they'd developed. He was completely off the radar screen, but suddenly, with total clarity, she knew where their mistake occurred.

"It's all right. You can talk to me," he said. He carefully lifted the sheet and looked at her smooth taut skin. "You must work out quite a bit to stay in such good shape. I'm sure your day job is mostly sitting at a desk." He took a long hungry look at her then said, "Yes, you are special."

Molly felt a primal chill flash through her body but said nothing, just looked at the man she had been trying to identify for the past three weeks. How could he know who I am, she wondered.

He dropped the sheet back over her and answered her silent question. "In your profiling attempt, did you include a trait about reading minds?" he asked. "I can, you know. I'm reading yours right now. You're wondering how I could know who you are. You're wondering because I haven't been visible in the investigation. You know that I know who Dan Neumann is and who Sheriff Mills is, but how could I know you and your husband? It's OK. I'll tell you. It's because I'm a professional. I'm not your run-of-the-mill grab-a-girl-here-or-there type of individual. I research. I know that Dan and your new husband are old friends. I know that Dan is responsible for you meeting Special Agent Sanford. I know what you and he look like because I take the time needed to do things right. And, I know that you just got back from a honeymoon in Alaska. Didn't think I'd get that one, did you?" he said with smile that was almost friendly.

No, Molly thought, I sure didn't. Her mind was now in high gear. She'd overcome the fear of the moment and was analyzing the situation. He must have access to some law enforcement data system, she surmised.

"Figure out who I am yet?" he taunted. "I'm a law enforcement nightmare. Because I know everything you do and you don't know shit about me. But I'll tell you. In fact, I'll tell you anything you want to know."

He slowly paced around the room, his eyes never leaving her, like a cat examining a mouse he was about to turn into a game.

"Why? Because we both know that your conversations with me will be the last you will ever have with anyone. I will be that last person you have any interaction with. I will be the one who keeps you alive, who speaks with you, who touches you and caresses you. And, you may as well know right now, I will be the one who brings you experiences you never expected. I will show you how much pain a person can endure and not die. You'll want to, but I'm not going to let you. You already know the routine. You know I can and will keep you alive throughout this experience. At some point you'll try to make friends with me, thinking that may spare you the ecstasy and the agony, but it won't. I'll let you believe that it will, but it won't. And, finally, you'll beg me to end it."

He produced a small scalpel, a skin knife, the type surgeons use to begin a procedure, and moved it through her field of vision, turning it to reflect the bright overhead lights. "Shall we start?"

Molly tensed, feeling the fear return. She tried willing herself to relax but failed. She knew she would have to get through this first encounter if she was to escape and survive. She closed her eyes and tried to breathe deeply through the gag.

"No, no," he said. "You must open your eyes. If you don't, I will make it most uncomfortable for you."

She complied and saw that he had set the blade down. "See? That wasn't so bad. That was just for practice, sort of a warm-up for the real thing. We can't start that until you've had a little something that will, shall we say, heighten the experience?" He disappeared near her hands and manipulated her arm, then she felt a cold sensation in her arm. She twisted her head as far as she could and saw, for the first time, that he had installed an IV shunt in her right arm. He was removing a needle from it. "Just that little something," he said again. "It will make you more sensitive to what we are going to do."

He placed the spent syringe on a tray and looked under the sheet once again. She sensed him taking a deep breath and watched his eyes roll up into his head. "Oh yes. You will be so good," he said, drawing out every word in anticipation. His calm returned and he looked straight into her eyes and said, "One last thing. I promise I won't cut you while you have the gag in. It's not that I'm worried about your ability to breathe. I just want you to be able to scream."

Molly's eyes snapped shut as she tried, without success, to block the last statement. She heard him shuffle around the room, then leave. The RV's engine fired up and she felt movement. Once again, she pushed down the panic that was trying to take over her body. She had to be professional, to focus on something. She began to think about how they had missed this obvious choice.

The team had been looking at people who participated in dog shows. They looked at the exhibitors, the judges, and the professional handlers. They looked at the various club officers and the professional superintendents. But they had given only a cursory look at the vendors.

The entire category of participants existed in the background. In all the team's meetings, it was as if the vendors didn't show up. They were there all the time, but were invisible. Suddenly, Greg Weber made a lot of sense. He was present, familiar with the system, traveled alone in an RV, would not be noticed at nearby bars. But she didn't know anything about his background, his profile. She had two goals now. First, to secure her own freedom; and second, to learn as much about Weber as she could before she broke free.

Molly knew that in order to break free she would have to secure Weber's confidence. He had to be confident that she was broken and unable to resist. Right now, that wouldn't take any acting. She was securely tied to the table at three points—her feet were secured separately to the table sides and her hands were bound above her head by light rope, maybe sash or drapery cord. It would take time for her to work her way free from the restraints, but it was time she wasn't sure she had.

Chapter Sixty-nine

The tiny transmitter sewn into the hem of Molly's slacks produced a signal that, under ideal conditions, would have allowed the FBI to track her location up to a mile away for up to four hours. The device had been activated just before Molly entered the bar. It would only transmit for another two hours and fifteen minutes.

I stood by a car with Will, looking at the RV the feds had zeroed in on. It had taken forty-three minutes and only happened because the feds had, in typical federal overkill, brought a dozen receivers. They were sure Molly's transponder was inside. But the RV wasn't the one we thought we'd find.

It belonged to LeRoi Parmentor, professional dog handler and serial speeder. I didn't know if that was part of the serial killer profile or not. The feds were focused on the rear of the coach, where they were getting a strong signal from the transponder. The assault team was ready to go in.

Will gave the signal and the next thirty seconds were a combination ballet and train wreck, a balance of choreography and violence. The coach had two doors, one by the driver's seat and one about halfway back along the passenger's side. Both doors were breached by the simple expedient of opening them. The team poured into the coach yelling, "Federal agents! Federal agents! Get down on the floor! Show me your hands!" No shots were fired.

Two minutes later the team leader came out of the coach and walked over to Will. "No sign of Agent Foss. I'm pretty sure we were set up."

"What do you mean?" I asked.

Will shook his head and asked, "Where's the transponder?"

The team leader said, "We're still looking for it. I've got the signal, but we can't find it in the coach."

The assault team leader had learned from the first coach. He motioned to his guys and they started pulling up the side panels. One, armed with the radio finder, located the signal's source in the rear compartment. Will and I rushed in to see that they'd found a brown paper grocery bag. Will grabbed the bag and pulled out Molly's clothes. He looked desperately around the scene.

There was no sign of Molly.

Chapter Seventy

After only about fifteen minutes of movement, Molly felt the RV stop. She was brightly awake, as though she'd had a triple espresso. She wondered if that was because of the injection. Weber came back into the compartment.

Greg Weber was in his glory. He was in control. He had a woman, and not just any woman—an FBI agent, an adversary, and the wife of another of his adversaries. To top it off, she was a friend of his chief adversary. He could feel the power coming to him through her. He examined her as she lay on the medical table he'd installed in the back of his RV for his "experiments." It was moderately comfortable with a lightly cushioned top covered by a removable rubber-lined sheet. He had rigged it with restraint tie points at the ankles and above the head. Long ago he'd determined that a woman felt more vulnerable with her hands tied above her head than secured at her sides, so that was the position he preferred.

"This is a little unfair, isn't it?" he asked conversationally as he removed the gag from Molly's mouth. "After all, you know who I am and what I'm doing, so there's not really a surprise in it for you. All my other subjects believed with all their hearts that they would survive my ministrations and were, therefore, much more willing to go along with what I asked of them."

Molly tried to engage him. "You're right about that, of course. You're taking a pretty big risk. You know that, right?"

"Oh, I know. By the way, you weren't my target tonight. Actually, I had no specific target tonight, though I would have gladly taken Dan's girlfriend, Maria. That would have been the pièce de résistance," he said, drawing it out and rolling the "r" with what he thought was a proper French accent. "I was just looking for someone who would fill the need, just a target of opportunity. When I saw you, you were too much of an opportunity to pass up."

Molly knew she had to keep him talking. "Why take me at all? You know that right now, hundreds of federal agents are looking for you. Why take that risk?"

"I had to, of course, because of Dan. *He* picked you, chose you. Dan set you up in front of me like some kind of unreachable piece of fruit, just a bit too high on the tree for me to grab. But I did grab you and now I have you right where I've had so many others. He must have known I'd take the bait, you being so beautiful and intelligent." He paused. "And blond."

He paused as he checked her bindings. "Did your profile include that, Agent Foss? Did you know that I prefer intelligent women? I tried the dumb ones. They're easier to obtain but they just lay there and blubber and pray and beg. Do you know how demeaning that is? Not just to themselves, but to me. It's demeaning to me. Catching them is like rounding up sheep for the slaughter.

"A co-worker and I were talking about another fellow whose wife seemed to stray from time to time. He told me that the poor fellow said that his wife was a beautiful and responsive woman who just needed something to do. When the kids got into school she was left home, bored, and that was no fun. So she'd get herself picked up and laid. He said that her problem wasn't that she was looking for sex, she got plenty of that at home. Her problem was that she was looking for something to do, someone to talk to. And when she ran out of things to say, she'd take off her clothes. Apparently, she didn't have much to say.

"That's the trouble with stupid women. They don't have anything to say. They can't comprehend what is happening to them. I get no rush from that. No, for me to truly absorb another individual, they *have to understand* what's happening. They have to anticipate the things that I'm going to do and resist, then surrender. They have to give themselves to me completely at the moment that we become one. That's the only way it works for me."

Molly thought hard. Her profile training had been the short course, the first step of many. True FBI profilers have years of experience to shape their thinking. And they aren't usually dealing with the unsub directly until after the arrest is made. Certainly they were not talking to him from the position of being a hostage and potential next victim. She had to drive the conversation her way and find a way out.

Molly said, "I'll resist. You know that. But I'll never surrender. You know that too, right? I'll never cooperate with you, no matter what you do to me. You'll be left with nothing. You may as well just kill me right now and get it over with. That's your best chance for escape."

Weber looked at her with a blank expression. Molly thought she might have gone too far, pushed him off the edge. She thought he might kill her, just as she asked. His smile returned.

"Oh, no," he said. "You're not going to get off that easy. I have big plans for us. We're going to have a lot of fun." He started to smile. "Oh, yes. This will be so fun. You think you can stay ahead of me, maybe get my trust, get loose, *get away*," he said, stretching the phrase out in a tantalizing sneer. He leaned in close. She could smell his breath, feel it on her cheek and ear.

"You'll come around. But remember this conversation. Remember it for when you have reached that point, the point where you are ready to die, to ask me for mercy. You'll get there. They all do. They start out thinking they can outsmart me and pretty soon they are making small talk and trying to get me to feel them up, to rub them and squeeze them and put my fingers into them." He walked around the table, apparently occupied with his preparations. He became very matter-of-fact.

"They fake orgasms. Maybe they're real; they do a good job of it. I don't know or care. All I know is that drives me toward *the big finish*," he said with touch of bravado.

Molly looked at him silently. She saw the intensity in his wide eyes, the flush of blood in his cheeks. She was well and truly afraid.

She said, "You know that I believe I'll survive this and I believe that you probably won't. Tell me your story. Tell me why you do what you do so that, in case I'm right, I can explain you to others. I can write a paper about you—maybe even a book. I can lift your legend into FBI history as one of the great ones."

Molly knew from studying cases like Ted Bundy that the smartest, longest practicing serial killers reacted well to the promise of intellectual immortality, the thought that they would live on forever in the files and lore of the FBI. Weber's face showed that he was warming to the idea. Then he shook his head.

"Oh, I don't think I'll need any help from you. I think I'm pretty well assured a place in FBI history right now. The only question is where?"

"Come on, Greg. Tell me about it. What happened? When did you realize you had a calling? I know you've been doing this a long time, a lot longer than others of your craft. You've been doing this for at least twelve years that I know of, but it didn't come to the Bureau's attention until recently."

Weber knew she was stalling, trying to get him to waste time, time he didn't have if he was going to get clear of the area.

By taking an FBI agent he realized that the current game was up. He'd have to go through an identity change. He'd planned for it. His plan included getting to his safe house. He'd had a premonition that he might need a fallback position in case he had to hit the reset button. He had bought a house using a pseudonym, and set it up as his safe house. He didn't know why he did it at the time. Like so much else in his life, he had just done it and found out later why. Clearly, some previous experiment participant had planted the idea in his brain. He had used it a few times for "extended stay guests." And he wanted nothing more than to take Molly Foss there and have at her.

"We will get away," he said.

Who knows, he thought, maybe Will and Dan and Maria will show up and I can have some fun with them too?

He stopped and looked into Molly's eyes. "You're very smart. You know what's going to happen and you aren't the least bit frightened, are you?"

"I'm plenty frightened," Molly snapped. "But I'm curious too," she said, regaining her composure. "I want to know how your world works. Maybe you're the one who has it right and the rest of us are all just drones coasting through lives that could be so much more."

Weber chuckled. She was so full of shit. She thought she could escape or stall until a rescue was mounted. He knew that would never happen. They'd have to find him first and he'd made sure that couldn't happen. He told her so.

"Let me ask you this. Do you think that your husband and Dan will come to your rescue? Or maybe you think you can slip your bonds and get away? I suppose that's possible," he said, giving her a bit of what he thought would be hope. "But you've noticed, haven't you, that you're naked under that sheet?"

Molly couldn't suppress a shiver. The killer stood back and continued.

"Wonder where your clothes are? Think I'm keeping those as a souvenir of our meeting? Not a chance. I know a thing or two about how the FBI works. I work in law enforcement too. I know you probably had a signal beacon in your clothes someplace. And, while that would have been a great souvenir, I simply couldn't have it lying around. So when I stripped you—you are a magnificent example of our species, by the way, perhaps the most beautiful woman I've ever had, or rather, will have had. Even a natural blond, which I'm sure you know by now is my preference. The subtle birthmark on your left breast, well, that's just the one imperfection to make the whole perfect. It was all I could do to keep from having you right then. But I have found that the anticipation just makes it better."

Molly felt a shiver as she saw his eyes roll up into his head as he contemplated that thought, then roll back down to land on her.

"In any case, your clothes aren't here. I put them in another RV, one belonging to a handler—a fine fellow who by now is explaining to your co-workers that you are not there and that he has no idea how your clothes, including the beacon, got in his RV."

He raised the sheet again to gaze at her. "Amazing how perfect your tan lines are. Even after a honeymoon in Alaska where, I'm sure, you didn't do too much sunbathing. I suppose it would have been too much to ask for you to have gone to the Bahamas or somewhere you could have increased the definition of those lines. It is summertime, after all, and I suppose going north had a certain 'out-of-the-way' appeal." He dropped the sheet and leaned close to whisper, "I particularly like the three sharp triangles of pale whiteness, one over each breast and the one over your magnificent blond tuft. They *will* make wonderful souvenirs."

Weber focused on Molly's eyes as he delivered that bit of information. He saw her fight her natural reaction of surprise to no avail. He felt the beginnings of despair and fear in her heart, began to feel power he knew would soon come to him. It had started.

Nothing could stop him.

Chapter Seventy-one

At LeRoi Parmentor's RV, the scene was at a standstill. Parmentor had been brought out of the coach in cuffs and seated on a nearby picnic table bench, where he was interrogated by another FBI team member. The Minneapolis Division Special Agent in Charge had shown up and taken over the operation. One of the team members had placed a call after Will blew up when it became clear that Molly was missing. Like any good law enforcement organization, the feds knew that there had to be separation between the investigators and the case. With Molly missing, Will could no longer be the agent in charge on the case. One of the division's top interrogators was working over Parmentor. He stopped, said something to an agent nearby, and walked over to the SAC, who was talking with us.

"This guy has no idea how that bag of clothes got in his rig. I've got a list of everywhere this coach has been for the past three hours and it includes a restaurant and a gas station, either of which could have been when the clothes were put into his RV. Both are within a probable area for someone who had left the bar. I think the guy grabbed Agent Foss, stripped her, and stuffed her clothing in this guy's rig to send us off course."

The SAC looked at Will and said, "All right, this is our case from here on out. Agent Sanford, you and your non-federal people are hereby relieved. This is now a kidnapping of a federal officer and it will be investigated by federal authorities. I'm advising you and your friends that you are officially off this case. You are considered family of the victim and will be treated as such. Go find a place to lay low, let us know where you are in case we need to talk to you, and just stay out of the way." He didn't wait for a response, just turned and walked away.

Will and I looked at each other. We knew we were in, with or without federal sanction. The SAC was a pretty new guy to the area and didn't really know Will and certainly didn't know me or my reputation with his organization or he would have known there was no way I would accept all his "the feds are large and in charge" crap. Will knew enough not to say anything within earshot of the boss man. We just locked eyes for about three seconds, exchanged curt nods, and walked to his car.

While we walked, I called Maria, who was still at the bar. "Hey, babe. What's going on there?"

"It's nuts. We had the place locked down and the FBI were processing everyone out so they could leave when things went crazy."

"What happened?"

One of the feds got a phone call about a minute ago and did some kind of hand signal to all his buddies. Then they announced that everyone not a fed was off the case. Glenn tried to ask one guy he's friendly with but all the guy would say is that it's now a federal kidnapping case and we are all off the team. What happened out there?"

I quickly gave Maria the basics, saying that I'd elaborate later. I didn't know what the fed's eavesdropping capabilities were, but I know that they can listen in on just about any conversation they want to. I didn't want them privy to whatever it was we were going to do.

"OK, here's what I want you to do. Get Glenn's attention and get both of you out of there. The feds will be happy to see you leave. Tell them you're going home. Then meet us down the street at the Perkins restaurant in Stillwater. We'll be there in a few minutes. We'll talk there."

Ten minutes later we were in the back party room of the Stillwater restaurant. After a quick order of coffee all around, we settled into our problem. Will started the discussion.

"She has the other transponder on her. She swallowed it about eight o'clock. But it has a very limited range, so it's imperative we figure out who took her."

Glenn said, "We locked down that place just as soon as she disappeared. Everyone in there was checked out and cleared. It had to be someone who left before we closed the doors."

I asked, "Does that place have cameras?"

"Yes, we checked on that when we recon'd the bar," Will answered. "But it'll take hours to find them and review them. Molly will be out of reach by then."

I said, "We've got to figure out who left just before Molly went to the Ladies' Room. Who was there and left? It has to be someone from the dog shows, so that rules out most of the people in the bar. C'mon, people! We've been working these guys for a month. Who's missing?"

Chapter Seventy-two

Weber's RV

Molly lay on the table, dismayed that her clothes had been planted somewhere to throw off the search. He was smarter than anyone had given him credit for. But she was smart too. And she was far from desperate. She had training and skills if she could just employ them. Now what? she thought.

Weber watched her regain her composure. This one will take some time to break; all the more fun, he thought. He picked up a long dagger and showed it to Molly. "Do you know what this is?"

He held the knife before her and turned it, making sure she could see the perfect blade. "It was invented by two guys in the Shanghai Municipal Police back in the 1930s. One was named Fairbairn, and the other was Sykes. It's a Fairbairn-Sykes fighting knife. For some reason, it became known as a Fairbairn knife, which kind of leaves Sykes out in the cold, fame wise. Anyway, those two guys learned knife fighting from the Chinese and developed the knife to maximize the techniques.

"Fairbairn later wrote a book on the topic in which he said"—Weber affected an English accent—"and I quote, 'In close-quarters fighting there is no more deadly weapon than the knife. In choosing a knife there are two important factors to bear in mind: balance and keenness. The hilt should fit easily in your hand, and the blade should not be so heavy that it tends to drag the hilt from your fingers in a loose grip.'" As he spoke, he manipulated the knife through the air, the light flashing off the blade. He continued, "'It is essential that the blade have a sharp stabbing point and good cutting edges, because an artery torn through—as against a clean cut—tends to contract and stop bleeding. If a main artery is cleanly severed, the wounded man will quickly lose consciousness and die.'" His eyes flashed with the last phrase.

"This one is authentic, made by The Wilkinson Sword Company during World War II for the British SAS. I keep it quite sharp. Well, of course I do; that's what I do." He grinned at her as he held the knife close to his own eyes, admiring its simplicity. "Quite an accomplishment, really. Previous to this design, knives were either for stabbing or slashing. While slashing is an effective combat technique, a bleeding wound generally takes quite a while to render the recipient *hors de combat*. But a pure stabbing design has an unfortunate tendency to stick, shall we say, in the adversary. In that case, you are pretty much out of luck and out a weapon if you haven't hit some immediately fatal location. This design, with its narrow double-sided blade has the advantage of being able to pass between things like ribs and gristle without becoming entangled in such a way that it can't be removed."

Despite her best efforts, Molly's fear level rose. Weber was in his element and giving a grand performance. Unfortunately, she knew the ending to his version of the play. She needed to write her own ending and willed herself to calm.

"Would you like to know how I came upon this particular methodology for my experiments?" Molly nodded, too frightened to speak. "It wasn't overnight; I'll tell you that."

Weber proceeded to recite his entire career to Molly. How he had started by dispatching his high school classmate and the thrill he felt with that moment. How recapturing that moment became his life's ultimate goal. How he had changed his process over the years, finally settling upon women in their late twenties or early thirties, blonds, and always women who were fit.

"Fat girls just don't seem to last as long," he said.

He reflected on how he had tried to go into law enforcement and was rejected. So he went into the next best thing by joining the Citizens Emergency Response Team.

"That was sort of a catharsis for me. I was able to spend time with law enforcement folks, learn about them, how they thought, how they investigated crimes. I've used that information to make sure that I don't make any mistakes."

The monologue began to fascinate Molly. She was again becoming what she had trained to be—an FBI agent. Her fear receded as the profiler in her took over. Even in her current circumstance she could start crawling around inside Weber's head. She asked, "How did you get involved with dog shows?"

"That's right, you haven't had a chance to do any background on me, have you? My mother, God bless her dearly departed soul, she was the one. She showed dogs, Shetland Sheepdogs to be precise, and she would drag me and Sis to the shows with her. This was when I was very young, you know. I didn't have any choice. But what red-blooded American boy wouldn't want to spend his summer weekends, and much of the rest of the year, too, sitting around a dog show with no one else his age to talk to or play with except his sister? My mother always said that I'd enjoy it more if I got into something like Junior Showmanship or Obedience, just so I had something to do while I was there, but nothing ever really appealed to me. Until the day I met Barney."

Molly had to ask. "Who's Barney?"

"Barney was my mentor in the scissors business. He had a nice trade going, selling an occasional pair of shears or sharpening an old pair. But he was a knife guy from way back. I met him when I was fourteen. My *mother*," the word dripped with sarcasm, "was still dragging me to dog shows and, truth be told, I was pretty good at it. Won lots of junior classes, finished a slew of championships for my mother's clients. I was doing OK. But there's way too much free time at a show for a fourteen-year-old. I started hanging around with Barney. He educated me about knives. Scissors too, but knives were his true love.

"I'd had dreams—premonitions, really—of what my life was going to be. I knew that I was different, that somehow I had been chosen to correct the world's ills. I could see what was wrong with this world, and I knew it was up to me to change things."

"What's wrong with this world?" Molly asked.

"I don't expect you to understand. You're one of them, part of the problem. All the problems in this world can be traced to you and those like you, like the women I choose . . . like my mother!" His voice rose, growing stronger as he ranted. Molly knew she could push him only so far before he'd turn on her, so she backed off. She just nodded.

"Do you know what my mother did to me? Of course not. You never even considered me a suspect or a *person of interest*," he said with a sneer. "Person of Interest, that's a hoot. You know what the street cops call a person of interest? Do you! A suspect! A doer, a scumbag, a bad guy. You federal agents with your unsubs and crap like that. You really think you can find someone who is smarter than you? Don't you realize how lucky you are that criminals are stupid?

"Not me, though, huh? Any guess what my IQ is? Want to take a shot at that? When you run into someone like me, you're lost. I can operate at my own whim right under your noses and you don't even consider me as a potential adversary. Hah! You're a bunch of accountants and lawyers, two professions with no imagination or insight, I couldn't have picked better."

Molly chose her words carefully, thinking there was one direction the conversation could go that might give her a chance. Over beers and dinner with Maria and Dan, she had heard about Dan's interactions with Weber. At the time, none of it registered. But in hindsight it all made sense. She knew what she had to do. She didn't like it because of the danger it was sure to bring others, but knew she had to do it. "What about Dan? You seem to understand him better than I do."

Weber paused, then smiled and nodded. "Dan. Now he's different. He's better than the rest of you idiots. You know, he's the only one who might be able to keep up with me intellectually. I studied his career and it parallels mine in many ways—always the best, always the one blamed when things were out of anyone's control, and the one willing to take the biggest risk for the biggest reward. Yes, Dan and I have a lot in common. I even bought the same kind of gun he carries." He drew a CAR 9C from a waistband holster and held it out for Molly to see. She rolled the dice.

"But you can never be Dan. He's on the side of law and you're a criminal."

Weber's countenance darkened as his head swiveled back to face Molly. He said slowly, "I believe you'd find that there are very few differences between lawmen and the so-called unlawful over history."

"Even so, how will you be remembered? As the equal to a great man or as a common killer?"

Weber exploded. "That's where you are wrong!" he shouted. He whirled and leaned in close to Molly's face. His faced was flushed red and he was panting.

Suddenly, he calmed. His face returned to normal and his breathing slowed. He leaned in close and stuck out his tongue and licked her lips, smiled, and whispered, "I believe that you will find that I'm a most *uncommon* killer."

Molly felt terror with those words. She willed herself to stay calm and focus on her mission. She knew that escape was her first goal.

"I should have been Dan," he said, matter of factly. "I could have been, if anyone would have given me a chance. I applied for the military. They said my test scores weren't 'right.' They never explained what 'right' was, but I knew. I scored too high and they wouldn't let me in. I was too smart, too imaginative for them. They want drones who will follow orders without question, who only kill on command, not with creativity and flair. Same thing with the police. How could someone with a 150-plus IQ not pass an application exam to be a cop? It was all bullshit. So I tricked them at their own game. I joined the CERTs and got the chance to work with them. They taught me all about investigation techniques, forensics, and interview methods. I've worked all my life to be Dan and now I've got my chance."

He paused and his face brightened with realization. "And, you know what? *You* are going to help me. *You* are the perfect bait to draw him in." He took a deep breath and sighed. "I shall become Dan. Just like I become all my partners. I absorb them into my soul, into my very being. Everything about them, everything that makes them who they are becomes mine."

He turned to her and cocked his head, saying in a gentler voice, "You don't see that now but you will when it happens to you."

Molly pushed the line. "What do you mean 'absorb' them. You just torture and kill them."

"Ha," Weber laughed. "You have no idea. None of them did either. But they give themselves to me, freely. They give all that they ever were or ever would be. You know, there was one who was a helicopter pilot. Afterward, I had the strangest dream that I could fly a helicopter. So I went to a flight school and took a trial flight. I was a natural; the instructor said so. He asked me how many hours of flight time I had. He didn't believe me when I told him that I'd never even been in a helicopter before. That was how I discovered the gift. Everything my partners have, they give to me. I *absorb* them. It's the only way for them to stay alive. They live within me. When I take Dan, I'll become him and have everything he has."

Chapter Seventy-three

Perkins Restaurant
Stillwater, Minnesota

"We're missing something here. Rather, somebody," Will said.

I shook my head and stared ahead. A sliver of light was coming from the kitchen and I saw a sous chef dicing onions. It hit me like an Acme safe falling on Wile E. Coyote. Cuts, knives.

"Greg Weber."

Looks flew around the group. Glenn broke the spell.

"The scissors guy, yeah, he was there. I saw you talking to him."

"He was there just before Molly disappeared," I said. "He stopped and talked to us, then went off to talk to someone else. Was he there when you cleared the place?"

Everyone looked around the table. No one could remember seeing Weber after the lockdown. Will grabbed his phone.

"This is Special Agent Will Sanford. I need a complete background on a Greg Weber." He looked at me and said, "Address."

I was digging through the vendors list in the dog show catalog. It included what they sold and their home addresses.

"Anderson, Indiana. Have them check with the local PD. He's on their CERT team," I said.

Will relayed the information. The person on the other end of the line came back with a vehicle description. Weber drove a 2007 Winnebago Journey that towed a Honda CRV. We had tag numbers and colors. Will hung up.

Glenn said, "Will, give me that info and I'll put it out."

"What do you mean—out?" Will asked.

"As a county sheriff, I can put out a statewide, through my office. I'll be sure it's a straight up 'Be on the Lookout—locate, observe, and report only.' That, and notify us, of course."

I said, "Good. Tell them it's a possible abduction. That'll keep anyone from attempting a stop." I knew that a local LEO would react differently to that description of the situation compared to a stolen vehicle or even a possible robbery suspect. They would understand that an abduction could go violent in a New York second. They'd back off and message us while doing everything they could not to lose the guy.

I said, "Get that out, Glenn." Within two minutes his office had the info and put out the bulletin.

I asked Will if he was sure the FBI would get back to him when they had something.

Will said, "The person I called will call me back when they get more data. He'll keep us in the loop. In the meantime, let's split up and start searching. Dan, which way do you think he'd go?"

I laid out a search pattern for our three vehicles. Maria would come with me; Glenn and Will would each ride alone. We agreed that no one would approach Weber alone. We'd call the rest of the team in and go from there. There was one last item I addressed.

"Weber is armed. He's got a CAR 9C. He talked about it. But, something he said . . . ." I trailed off. There was something he said that I'd heard but it hadn't registered with me. A ping? What was it? Maybe it would come to me.

We headed out to our cars, praying we'd find Molly in time.

Chapter Seventy-four

Molly was walking a tightrope. She had to keep Weber talking and get him to want to do something he might not want to do. She needed a few minutes alone.

"Greg, why did you choose me? You know you can't have Dan without killing him. And you can't kill Dan without killing Maria first. She won't let you. So why did you pick me instead of her?"

"Good, Agent Foss. Good. You're learning. You're beginning to understand what I must do. Obviously, I must first take Detective Fernandez. You were just irresistible."

"How so?"

"I saw what was going on, even if that idiot Nelson could not. I knew who you were because I do my homework."

His words gave Molly a shiver. How much homework had he done? She asked.

"Your homework?"

"I'll explain." Weber smugly turned a chair around and swung a leg over it to sit on it backwards facing Molly as she lay on her back on the table. As he leaned into the chair back, he ran his eyes over Molly's form beneath the sheet. He felt the fire start to rise inside and reminded himself mentally to slow down, to not just take her right that second, as satisfying as that would be. He knew it would be better the longer he waited.

Weber reached out and, casually, circled Molly's nearest nipple with his fingertip, smiling as it popped to attention under the sheet. "When

Dan came to the Duluth show, I immediately knew that he was the one, the one who would either destroy me or make me whole. So I researched him and the other guy who came with him, Glenn. I already knew Pete Anderson, so no interest there. I have access to the database research engines in my police department, so I can get all the info you or any other cop can. I found that Glenn is basically a retired street cop so I knew he wouldn't be a threat. And his wife is a typical housewife in her sixties. No threat or satisfaction there.

"Later, you folks got into the picture. By that I mean the FBI. After Ms. Vanderloo made my acquaintance, you got involved. There was a news conference. Agent Sanford was introduced as the Agent in Charge of the investigation. I saw Dan standing in the background, trying hard as he could to hide in plain sight." Weber chuckled. "That brought Will Sanford to my attention. And you."

Weber spun the chair and pulled open a cabinet that contained a laptop PC. "I'm on satellite. I can research anywhere in North America," he said with satisfaction.

"I found that Will is a typical FBI wonk, except for his somewhat-frowned-upon relationship with Dan. Plus, he had just married you, so he was distracted. I checked you out, too. You are a threat. You've had profile training and are an up-and-coming star with the Bureau. And, as you may know, I find women of your type to be most provocative.

"And I studied Maria—another rising star. I knew immediately that she is the key to Dan. When I have her, he will come to me."

Molly saw her opening and took it. "But, why me? Why not Maria . . . or both of us?"

She saw a light spark in his eyes and went on. "You know I'll be rescued and you'll be caught. If you're going to go out, which is definitely a possibility, why not make your last party the best? Maria and I could take you places you've never even thought of. Think of it—two of us at the same time. Take us away and make it last."

Weber felt his heart jump. Yes, he thought. He felt himself begin to pant. Two. Both Maria, who he had to have, and Molly, who he had wanted so bad that he'd risked his whole plan just to take her. Two at once. He could barter with them for experiences he'd never had, trading that for turning his knife attentions to the other. Previous women offered to do things but there was no one else to turn his bloody intentions to. Now he could. The possibilities were endless.

Molly saw his reaction, too. She knew that what he did next would decide her fate. Either he'd bite on the option she gave him or not. If not, she would go down in history as another victim.

Chapter Seventy-five

The search

Maria and I headed toward Stillwater on the chance that Weber had chosen anonymity among people. The others went south and west toward St. Paul. We were in constant radio contact.

Will went through the motions of notifying his supervisor about the possibility of Greg Weber being the culprit, but leaving out the fact that our team was still on the job. All over Washington County RVs were being checked out by local law enforcement but none had the Indiana plates we were looking for.

One rig, the right make and color, towing a Honda CRV with a solid blue license plate, was tailed for fifteen minutes as our team was called in. The locals were having no problem keeping us in the loop while taking their time notifying father fed. When we got close enough we found that it had Montana plates, which are the same blue as Indiana. The team decided that it was too close a coincidence to just let go, so we waited until the rig was caught at a traffic light in Woodbury to make a felony stop and search. The feds were doing their own thing by then, all but ignoring us. We had Glenn's badge for authority, our three cars plus two Woodbury cops and were able to block the RV in and storm the door. We found an older couple from Bozeman who were on their way to the Wisconsin Dells for a vacation. It took about forty-five long minutes, lost minutes in the search.

We all knew that Molly's very existence was dependent upon our finding her and the longer it took, the worse her chances were. Will was, quite naturally, becoming desperate.

Weber's RV

Molly watched as Weber became frantic. He was searching the RV, for what, she did not know. He began haranguing her for information on where he could find Maria, what they would be doing, where they would be searching for him. She didn't know, had no idea. She didn't know the area and the plan didn't include her getting captured. But she knew it was her only chance to guide him into a trap.

"I think they will be looking for this RV by now."

"Not this RV. I'm not a suspect. But, you're right, they'll be on the road looking for Nelson's rig, or LeRoi's," he said with a chuckle. "I'd love to have seen that. Especially LeRoi, the old fuck. Teach him to owe me money."

He climbed onto the chair facing her again. "Again, you've pointed out my advantage. I'm simply smarter than all of you. That's not surprising. None of you law enforcement types are all that bright. The Green River killer ran his string to over twenty years before they got him, and he was operating in only one area. And he was nowhere near my IQ."

He produced the dagger with the skill of a street corner sleight-of-hand operator and flicked it within a millimeter of her nose. "Where is Maria?"

Molly had no idea and told him so. He slowly peeled down the sheet and pressed the tip of the blade against her left nipple. "Don't make this hard. If you tell me, I promise I'll go easy on you. After all, it's Maria I have to have. Who knows? You might even survive."

Molly gasped as her thoughts raced. She stammered, "She wasn't involved in the pursuit team. She was only briefed-in on the stakeout. If that's broken up, she would go back to Dan's house."

"Why? She's an experienced investigator. No, I think you're lying, Molly."

Molly's fear was rising but she tried to control her voice. "No, that was the brief. OK, maybe she wouldn't go to Dan's, especially if he's not there. But she's not FBI. If there is a pursuit, she won't be on it. I think she would go to the comm center."

A look of peace came over his face. "Thank you, Molly. That wasn't so hard, was it?" Weber turned away for a moment and she watched his hand reach out toward the head of the table. What she heard made her quickly inhale and exhale deeply twice, then gulp as much air as she could hold.

Weber turned back with a hissing anesthesiology mask in his hand. He placed the mask over her face and she struggled for a moment against the cold gas, then relaxed herself to appear to pass out.

Weber waited a few seconds, then removed the mask. He knew he couldn't leave it on her. He'd lost a subject that way once; apparently the gas had been too much for her and she died while he was away. What a waste, he recalled. He checked Molly's bindings, the cuffs on her ankles and the rope securing her hands above her head. Finding them satisfactory he said, "Now, don't do anything stupid while I'm gone."

Chapter Seventy-six

Weber's RV

Molly felt herself coming around. The "examination room" of the RV was spinning when she opened her eyes. She took a deep breath and concentrated on her state of mind. "Wake up, wake up, wake up," she told herself. She slowly started to regain some clarity to her senses. She tried her eyes again and the room had stopped spinning. It was still a bit out of focus, but improving steadily as she looked around.

Her deep breaths had prepared her for the gas by allowing her to hold her breath as she feigned unconsciousness. Even so, some of the gas had gotten into her system and she had to purge it now to make her move.

Slowly, she began to saw away at her bindings.

In preparing for her assignment, Molly took into consideration that operations rarely go perfectly. So as a backup, she had the FBI specialist who had supplied the swallowable transponder apply something new in the way of "James Bond" equipment to her person. She had been given a special manicure.

Instead of the usual acrylics, micro-razors were applied to the three middle fingers of both hands. The blades, which with polish looked like normal nails, could be used to cut an attacker or, as she was doing now, used to saw through rope bindings.

Molly listened for the radio, trying to estimate how long she'd been out. No sound. No way of guessing when he'd be back; she knew she had to work fast. Weber could return at any moment. She felt her fingers working at the rope around her wrist, could feel the fibers begin to fray and, finally, she felt the bindings begin to loosen.

Then she heard the sound of a vehicle outside.

She tried one hand to see if it was free. Just about. She sawed more frantically as she heard a car door shut. Her hand slipped free. Quickly now, she loosened the other hand, but there was no time to work on the cuffs holding her ankles. As she replaced the bindings around her wrists, trying to make them look tight, she took deep breaths, trying to clear her body of the remainder of whatever drug Weber had given her before he left. She knew there would be only one chance for her plan to work. She felt the RV rock as he mounted the entrance steps.

Weber came into the room and looked at Molly, who pretended to be drowsy and still half out of it. "Ah, here we are. Did we have a nice nap?"

Molly rolled her head and looked at him with half-open eyes. She let a little drool roll out of her mouth and down her cheek. She held her hands together as if they were still tied. She whispered, "Water."

Weber went on. "You were right. I went back to the area just south of the bar and there is a control post set up. The place is crawling with federal agents. No sign of Dan, no Maria, no Will. I think they must be out looking for Hunter Nelson, don't you?"

Again, Molly whispered, "Water."

"What's that? Do you have something new for me. A little something that might speed us along our journey? That's what I'm looking for. Maria will join us. Maybe Dan, too, if the opportunity presents itself, then we'll all head home. Not my old home, of course. Can't ever go back there. But a place I've set aside for just this sort of moment. This event needs some planning and time to mature and no better place than at home. You should feel honored. I've only taken three guests home over the years. They were all special and made the experience last a long time. Over four months in one case."

One last time, she tried it. "Water," she mumbled.

Weber leaned over and put his head close to hers. As he did, he lifted the sheet with his hand to expose her breasts. His focus was there as he said, "What's that?"

Molly tensed her core muscles as she slipped out of the severed bonds. With all the strength she could muster, she balled her hands into fists and brought both hands around her head, her elbows extending as she did, adding speed to the swing. Weber felt the movement and began to turn toward her. Her fists caught Weber high on his temple. She felt a slight crack as the thinnest portion of his skull fractured, stunning him. She grabbed his head and immediately twisted and tilted his neck.

Breaking a human neck is much harder than they make it look in the movies. There is a technique taught by Special Forces schools and spy agencies where the killer attacks the victim from the rear, simultaneously grabbing the victim's chin and hair and twisting. Even with that perfect approach, the amount of strength necessary is more than all but the largest, strongest, and best trained can supply. Molly didn't have a hope of breaking Weber's neck, but she wanted to stun him, long enough to give her a chance to get out of the cuffs binding her ankles. Pushing his head toward her feet, she did a half situp and drove her right thumb into his left eye.

He hadn't seen it coming. At the moment of impact, Weber was still focused on Molly's breasts. The initial blow stunned him enough that he collapsed onto Molly's chest and belly with a whomp of exhaled breath. He had just opened his eyes when her second blow blinded him. His knees buckled and he collapsed toward the floor.

She quickly grabbed him so he wouldn't slide off onto the floor, taking with him any chance of escape. She bent over him and reached for his pockets, feeling for the keys to the ankle cuffs. Fortune smiled and she found them in the first pocket she reached. Good thing, she thought; reaching the other pockets would have been tricky. She pushed his limp body and saw his head hit the corner of a table before it hit the floor. She went to work on the cuffs holding her ankles. In a flash, she was loose.

She hopped off the table, grabbing the cuff that had held her right ankle. It was open, but still attached to the table. She pulled his left hand up and snapped it into the cuff to hold him. Then she ran into the bedroom of the RV, rifling the first drawer she came to searching for clothing.

Her FBI training took over. She was now the primary witness in a multiple homicide case. While the movies would portray her as valiantly arresting the bad guy and waiting for the cavalry to come over the horizon or shooting it out with him ala Jodi Foster in *Silence of the Lambs*, her training told her to escape. They knew who he was and where he was. They would come back with plenty of people and weapons. She'd run out naked if she had to, if Weber showed any sign of regaining consciousness. The only thing in her mind right then was escape, and Weber was beginning to moan.

She yanked out a sweatshirt and a pair of jeans. As she headed for the door, she saw her own shoes, so she grabbed them then popped the door, jumped to the ground, and ran like never before.

Weber grabbed his head with his free hand, looking a lot like a cartoon character who had been hit with a frying pan. He literally saw stars. As his senses returned he put it together and realized where he was and what he had been doing. He looked at his cuffed wrist. He shook his head clear and looked around the RV.

"What happened?" he asked himself. He looked at the table and saw the frayed bindings. With a cold blast of realization his mind cleared enough to tell him that his prisoner was gone.

Mumbling a thanks to himself for his commitment to redundancy, he slid open a drawer on the table and located a spare handcuff key. He moved as quickly as he could to the door, opened it, and looked outside. No Molly. In an instant he knew what he had to do. Escape.

As soon as she was out of sight of the RV, Molly stopped to put on the clothes, cringing as she slid her legs into the jeans and pulled on the sweatshirt. Then she put on her shoes. She had always been a runner and although these shoes weren't ideal, they were better than the spike heels the FBI profiler had advised her to wear as part of her "pick me up" disguise. She had argued that the more comfortable shoes would be typical of those worn by a woman out for a quick drink and some company on a Sunday evening in Minnesota.

Grateful to her father for teaching her how to use her inner sense of direction, she looked up for a quick fix and decided to head east on the assumption that, sooner or later, she'd run into one of the north-south roads that paralleled the St. Croix River. From there she could hitch a ride and contact the team.

Molly popped out of the woods and found herself right where she'd hoped. A two-lane state highway was about fifty feet in front of her. She trotted up to the shoulder and waited, thinking that she'd flag down the first vehicle to come along.

Chapter Seventy-seven

Weber had practiced a quick getaway in case it was ever needed, even though he never thought a catastrophic failure of one of his plans could ever occur. His sense of thoroughness, though, had driven him to be prepared. He always kept everything packed and ready to go. All he had to do was hook his car to the rear of his RV and then he would haul ass. Molly was out there someplace but there was nothing he could do about that. He had to put miles between himself and those who would soon be hunting him. He finished the hookup, jumped into the front seat of the RV, and started toward the highway.

He had hidden the RV in an unmarked access road he'd found with Google Earth. It looked like a field access road, but ran through a copse of trees that provided perfect cover. There was evidence that local high schoolers were familiar with the spot. Trash, including empty beer cans and condom wrappers, were scattered around the site and Weber hoped that other tire tracks would help cover his own. He had parked the rig facing out, as he always did, and was glad he did because he knew that minutes mattered. He pulled out to the two-lane highway and headed south.

Dan's Suburban

Maria and I had gone east to a well-used state highway and were headed south, the direction I had guessed Weber would go. It would take him to the interstate, his fastest route away from us. Maria was apoplectic. She thought Molly's capture was all on her. It wasn't but I understood her point of view.

"Dan, oh God, Dan. What are we going to do?"

"We're going to find her and get her out of this. You are going to calm down. I need you to be Detective Fernandez right now, not a freaked-out friend worrying about something that is not her fault."

"If he kills her I'll hunt his bum ass down and feed it to the wolves."

"That's my girl. Now, let's get to work." I turned right onto Stagecoach Road, heading for I-94.

Molly watched for traffic. It was late on a Sunday evening and she knew traffic would be scarce. The moon provided just enough light so she could size up a vehicle before exposing herself. She knew she wasn't far from Weber's RV and didn't want to step out into the traffic lane in front of him. She first heard, then saw a vehicle speeding south. It didn't look like the small SUV she'd seen when she ran from Weber's RV but rather a large vehicle so she took her chance and stepped out, frantically waving her arms. The vehicle flashed by but she knew the driver had seen her because she heard the engine straining as the vehicle braked and the rear window lit up with flashing lights. She started running toward it.

I couldn't believe my eyes. There, at the side of the road was a woman waving her arms. I was going too fast to stop before I passed her. I hit the police flashers and the brakes. Our momentum took us just over the crest of a hill. Maria jumped from the car as I racked it into "Park," and jumped out, running back up the hill to meet a charging Molly Foss.

"Molly!" Maria shouted. "Molly, are you all right?"

When she realized it was Maria running toward her, with me close behind, Molly broke down. All the cool law enforcement officer toughness she had been carrying disappeared and she collapsed into Maria's arms. I was right on Maria's heels and wrapped my long arms around both women, easing them onto the shoulder and down onto the ground.

Weber just about ran off the road when he came over the hill and saw the three people he most wanted sitting on the side of the road. Instantly, he saw three possible outcomes to this chance encounter.

His first impulse was to stop and try to capture all three, but he knew that that would be impossible. Neumann and Fernandez were sure to be armed and while he might have been able to take out one, he couldn't take both. He could run them over. He steered the RV toward them. His RV was big enough and heavy enough that it would surely kill all three. But they were far enough off the roadway that he might not be able to keep the 50,000-pound bus and the SUV it was towing on the road. If he wound up in the ditch, that would be as much as a confession. At the last possible moment he wrenched the RV back onto the roadway and missed the sitting ducks. He passed close enough to see the look of recognition in Dan's eyes.

"That's him!" Molly shouted, as the huge bus passed them by. I already knew and was hitting the speed dial. I yelled, "Car! Now!" We were scrambling for the Suburban when Will answered.

"Will, just listen. We've got Molly. She looks fine but we just found her so I don't know for sure. We are on Stagecoach, north of Tenth." There was a pause and Dan shouted, "Will, shut up! Weber just went past us in his RV. He's going south on Stagecoach. When he gets to I-94 he'll probably head east. We need to block him. Get your folks to handle that. We're in pursuit."

I had reached the driver's seat of my Sub so I tossed the phone to Maria and dropped the Sub into drive. The 6.2 liter engine roared with the pleasure of having its four-hundred horses set free. The Sub launched itself in pursuit of Weber's RV. I hit the full lights and siren. I turned to the women in the back seat and said, "I've got a back-up piece in a holster in the center console." Maria pulled my holstered Springfield XDM 40 out of the console, pulled the pistol from the holster, pulled the slide back to check the chamber—hot—and slid it back into the paddle-style holster which she gave to Molly, who slipped it into her waistband.

Even with lights and siren wailing, I had to be careful. With the road's curves and hills and many side entrances, there was a good chance I would come upon a slower vehicle. And the chances were about 99:1 that the vehicle would be smaller than my Sub. I didn't want this to end in a collision with a minivan full of children.

I knew that if Will was getting through to anyone, roadblocks would be set up on I-94 in both directions from the Stagecoach entrance. As I approached the ramps, I could see a state patrol squad on the overpass above the interstate. I slowed and opened my window.

Flashing my shield, I asked the trooper, "When did you get here?"

"About twenty seconds ago."

"You see anybody, any vehicles as you approached?"

"Yeah, there was a Subaru wagon headed down the ramp to go east."

"Which way did you come from?"

The trooper pointed east. "From the river. Headed up here, turned, and stopped."

"You didn't see anyone heading west or south?"

"Couldn't see west, I was coming up the ramp. There was plenty of weekend traffic on the highway and I was overtaking, so I don't know if anyone I saw down there was entering from here or already on the highway." He pointed south and said, "Pretty hard to see anyone going that way."

I looked ahead and nodded. There was a sharp rise just south of the highway that crested within a quarter mile. Anyone going that way would be out of sight within seconds.

"Molly, out of the car."

Both women gave me a look that Medusa would have envied. I didn't even bother to argue. "OK, you're in. But you stay in the car if we catch up to him."

Another look. I gave up. "All right," I capitulated. I thanked the trooper and hit the gas.

I looked in the mirror at Maria and Molly in the back seat and said, "I'm guessing south. If he went east or west, we'll get him. If he doubles back, we'll get him. The only way open is south." The women nodded and we raced down the county road.

Chapter Seventy-eight

Weber had cruised over the interstate connection without a thought of turning onto it. He knew that's what law enforcement would expect him to do—to run for the state line. He also knew that state lines meant nothing when it came to capturing a serial killer. The feds were already on the case and the only line that would stop them was the Canadian border. That, too, was out of the question. Those passages to freedom would be locked up tight long before he could get to one. His only chance for escape was to bolt to one of three hiding places he'd had the foresight to prepare, tap into his hidden resources, and assume the alternative identity he'd spent years establishing.

"I'm not a common killer," he said to himself. He'd known for years that this day might come. No one pulls off the "perfect" crime. He recalled a TV interview he'd seen with an aging Alfred Hitchcock. The interviewer asked if anyone could ever commit the perfect crime. The suspenseful sage replied, "Certainly. The perfect crime is the crime that is never detected. A crime, no matter how trivial, that is never detected is perfect." By that definition, Weber knew that his crimes were not perfect, no matter how well they'd been committed.

Many of them had been detected. Oh my, how they'd been detected. Part of the fun was watching the media react to the discovery of one of his experiments. Some were discovered immediately but a few had yet to be found. Those produced a kind of disappointment. While he didn't want to be caught, he could hardly bear the times no one had found his subjects. He'd hidden them too well. That's why, over the years, he got better at placement—secure enough when he needed to go there, populated enough that the body would be found the next day.

The exception was his mother, who he both didn't want found and couldn't have found. His life had begun when she had "gone to Iceland to live with a maiden aunt." Finding her would create some tough questions.

He drove south and soon found himself in the town of Afton, a river town on the St. Croix.

Good, he thought, as he slowed to the reduced speed limit. There was sure to be marine and RV dealers. There was no place better to hide for a bit while the local search died down. He knew from his police department experience that searches spread out with time as the possibility grows that a fugitive has slipped through their net.

He spied a marine dealer right on the river with a huge parking lot filled mostly with small cruisers and sailboats on one side and RVs on the other. He was able to pull around the back row of RVs into an open slot. In a flash he was out the door disconnecting the SUV. He threw the heavy tow rig into the up position and looked around to make sure no one was watching. He got into the SUV and backed it around the rear of a large storage building, stashing it between the building and some overgrown lilac bushes.

He stepped out and entered the building through an unlocked rear door. As he scouted the building he began planning his next moves.

Although it was getting dark outside, an exit sign inside the building provided enough light to permit walking around without tripping on all the junk that was stashed in the building. Boat seats, outboard motors, and sailboat masts created an obstacle course. Tires were piled along the walls and a half dozen boat trailers were stacked in front of an overhead doorway. Two older RVs were parked near one end of the building and a thirty-foot day cruiser sat on blocks on one side of the barn. It would take awhile to learn all the nooks and crannies he could hide in.

There were windows, a row on either side about five feet above the floor. They were eighteen inches high and four feet wide and tilted outward. "Possible exit," he noted aloud, and a good place to observe the parking lot. He pulled a worktable over and set one of the discarded boat seats on it. He opened the bag of provisions he thought he might need through the evening and spread the contents—bottled water, crackers, sliced cheese, cuffs, tape, pepper spray, rope—within easy reach. His shiny new CAB 9c pistol was secure in the stiff new leather of his belt holster. His Fairbairn was tucked into its scabbard, strapped to his waist, ready for quick deployment.

He climbed up onto the makeshift perch and watched the lot.

Chapter Seventy-nine

I eased off the gas and we entered the bucolic little river town of Afton. I've always had a soft spot for Afton from my days boating on the St. Croix River. It's got a great little ice cream place, and like most river towns, a somewhat colorful history. I was trying to remember everything about it.

As we slowed and entered the town, I looked around, trying to put myself in Weber's shoes. If he came through here, what would he do? He could roll right through but I had a hunch he was nearby.

I started thinking out loud, hoping my passengers could provide the insight that seemed to be escaping me. I pulled into the parking lot of a little café.

"OK," I said. "Coffee and analysis." We all bailed out of the Sub and headed inside.

With fresh coffee all around, I said, "OK, I'm guessing he passed on getting on the interstate and came south. Will he keep running or pull off and try to hide?"

No sudden insights were forthcoming. Maria finally said, "He's got to keep going. He knows we saw him and he knows we're on his ass."

Molly spoke up. "I don't think so. He works with his local PD. He knows that we'll do everything we can to shut off all routes of escape. He also knows that the longer he stays out of sight, the better his chances will be to slip away because we'll have to dilute our resources as we stretch out our net."

I agreed. "I think you're right. This guy is really smart, Maria. He's not going to spook like a typical scumbag. He's got nerve. He's got to have a helluva nerve to have grabbed you," I said to Molly.

Molly had settled down enormously since we picked her up. She was breathing normally and had her usual calm, thoughtful visage. She was deep inside herself searching for some scrap of information on Weber that would help us find him. She gazed out the window.

"Dan, I don't know if this will help or just piss you off, but I'm going to say it anyway." We all leaned in close.

"He's fixated on you. Somehow, you represent everything he thinks he should be, could have been, if only his life had gone differently. He told me as much when he had me."

OK, this is war, I thought.

I said, "What, exactly, do you mean by fixated?"

"Like a lot of serial killers, he has a fascination with law enforcement. He told me he'd applied to be a cop. That didn't work so he joined the CERT team. There's no psychological test for that, just the usual background security checks. He passed that because he, likely, has no record at all. Not even a speeding ticket."

Maria spoke up. "What else did he say about Dan?"

"He said that he would 'become' Dan. That, if he could capture Maria, and, maybe, you, Dan, he'd be able to become you. He told me that he's learned, from what he calls his 'experiments,' how to take a person's soul into his own and become that person. He said that's what's kept him from getting caught all these years, the fact that he can 'become' other people.

"In fact, I'm sure he thinks he can get away and assume some other personality and go on with his life. He told me he has a safe house. He'll have to completely disassociate with all his past, and I think he can do it. He'll go underground for a while, then start over, sort of like his own witness protection program."

We shook our collective heads at that one.

"So, what's he going to do?" I asked.

Molly replied, "He's got the immediate problem of staying away from us, and a longer-term one, getting Maria, then you. For now, he needs to duck the search. I think he'll lay low and let the heat die down. That may be days or a couple of weeks. He'll be hiding deep until an opportunity presents itself for him to grab Maria. He still wants to be you, *needs* to be you. I don't think he'll run off without exhausting the possibilities of getting you and 'taking over your soul.'"

I've tracked some pretty crazy dudes over the years, but nothing like that. Clearly, to me at least, our only option was to track him and get him off the street.

"OK, I agree. He'll hole up somewhere. But where? He's got to know we'll check any usual spots—campgrounds, parks, WalMarts, places where he could try to fit in or hide. He can't just stash it in a garage. He's driving a forty-foot RV towing a car. How hard is that to hide?"

"Plenty," Maria said.

"Yeah, plenty," I agreed. "So that's where we've got him. If he can't get out of sight, he's got to hide in plain sight."

That thought bounced around our collective heads for a moment, then I had it. "He's got to hide in plain sight. That means he's got to park someplace where his RV won't look out of place. And, you're right, Molly. He can't go to the usual places because we'll look there. So, where else?"

They looked at me and waited. "How about a repair yard?" I asked.

"Perfect," Molly said. Maria nodded her agreement. "So how do we find an RV repair yard around here?"

"Simple." I knew the answer and told them. "The same guys who work on RVs work on boats. There are only two major marine dealers in this town. We'll park out of sight and scope each one out on foot. Maria, call Will and get a report. Then tell him what we're doing."

We each took one last slurp of coffee and I dropped a twenty on the table as we headed out to the Sub. We had already gone pretty much through town, which was fine. The two marine dealers were located on the river at each end of town. It was a good bet that Weber had gotten to the south one before he'd made his decision, *if* he'd made the decision. I parked behind a copse of trees and we got out.

"OK. Here's the plan. We split up and recon the yard looking for his RV. Everyone clear on what it looks like?"

Nodding heads.

"Remember—no engagement even if he's outside in the open. We're going to do this right and that means bringing in Will and Glenn. Even if that means Will decides to bring in the whole F, B and fucking I."

I got a look from Molly that promised a later conversation, but she nodded and we split up.

The Marina

In the pole barn, Weber was nodding off. How could he be sleepy, he wondered. It promised to be one of the most exciting nights of his life and he didn't want to sleep through it.

He heard a car approach and saw it drive into the yard and park near a sailboat. A middle-aged couple got out and walked over to the sailboat, engaged in an animated discussion. Weber chuckled to himself.

"Somebody's getting a new asshole," he said. As he watched, the man climbed a tall ladder to reach the gunnel of the boat, which was about twelve feet above the ground. He stepped into the boat and produced a flashlight. Weber watched as he shone the light around the boat, obviously looking for something. He found it and tossed it down to the woman. Another round of mutual disrespect ensued as he climbed back down the ladder. "A little entertainment, free with the accommodations. Thank you," he said, as the car drove off.

He had thought hard and decided the cops would focus on Wisconsin and decided to give it until about 3:30 in the morning before he'd move on. Their adrenaline rush would soon wear off, he thought. Then the cops would all be heading home, dog-tired and depressed at being defeated.

He told himself, "Just a little longer and I'll be out of here. Maybe a quick trip across town to Dan's house." The idea stirred him and brought new energy to his body. "Yes," he whispered. "I'll go pay them a little visit. They'll never expect that!"

Chapter Eighty

South end of Afton, Minnesota

We gathered back at my Sub. No joy on Weber's RV. The search had taken thirty-five minutes. Now what, I wondered. My phone rang.

"Yeah, Will." I said, recognizing the number. "We're in Afton, the south end of town. We've done a foot search here and come up blank. If he's here the next best place for him to hole up will be the other marine dealer, on the north end of town." I listened. "OK. We'll meet you up there. We're trying to stay out of sight and do a recon for the RV and the car. If we find the car we've got him. If the RV's here but the car's gone, we'll know what he's driving." I listened again and said, "Keep coming into town. At the bottom of the hill Stagecoach will merge with St. Croix. Keep going a couple blocks until you get to the Catfish Bar Café on the left side. Park there; we'll meet you."

We got back into the Sub and headed to the café. I saw Will turning into the parking lot. We parked next to each other, facing out.

Will jumped from his car and got to my Sub before Molly could get out. He helped her then wrapped his arms around her, stammering, "Are you all right, are you all right?" Both of them broke down and slid down to the ground next to my rig.

Glenn had been riding with Will and walked over to where Maria and I were standing, watching the reunion. Maria put an arm around my waist and looked up at me. "You know, you can be pretty amazing at times," she said.

"This had nothing to do with me. Molly got herself out of that mess all by herself. We were just lucky."

We all watched Will and Molly for a minute, then Maria said, "OK, there'll be time for the lovey dovey stuff later. We've got a very bad guy to catch."

The pair rose and I said, "OK, what's the plan?"

"First off, I've called in the troops," Will said. I don't know how long it will take them to get here, but I'm thinking we have about 15 minutes until we're buried. With that in mind, I think Glenn should go up to the north side and block all traffic on the road. When my guys get here he can vector back."

There was general agreement from everyone except Glenn, who naturally wanted in. I cut him off.

"Glenn, you are the only one here with what can pass as jurisdiction. Try to really block the road with civilians so the FBI guys have to sort that out and come up with a plan before they come down here. Keep them off our back for a few minutes and if he's here, we'll smoke this guy out." Reluctantly, he agreed.

I had expected Will to have a problem with my plan to do this alone. After all, the FBI is expert at digging bad guys out of hiding holes. I guess taking a guy's wife can change his opinion on tactical planning.

"There's another marine dealer about two blocks east and a block north of here. I used to boat here a lot so I know the layout. There's a main building with a large paved lot in front of it. I doubt Weber will be there. A little further along, there are two buildings that are used for repairs and storage." I drew the scene out in the air with my hands. "There's a grass parking area and a storage area north of those buildings. In winter, they store the boats there, so there are big wooden cradles scattered around. Right now it'll probably have some boats and RVs that are in waiting to be serviced. If I were Weber, that's where I'd hide. I'd be in the car, ready to roar if I spotted anyone. If he's not there, he could still be in the RV, although that doesn't make sense. Or he could be in a building. If he is, it means he's willing to fight.

"We'll split into pairs, try to encircle both buildings and get a look at the grass parking lot. If the car's there, we can check that out first just by looking in the windows. If both the car and RV are there, he's probably still here and hiding, so we don't want to tip him to our presence. So, be quiet. Keep your phones on but make sure your ringer is off. When we're in position, I'll call you," I said, pointing to Will. "Questions?"

There were none, so we checked our phones and headed down the street looking for all the world like two couples out for separate strolls. Glenn trudged up the street toward the intersection he would be blocking.

The storage building

Weber sat on top of the table and nodded off. Once, he startled so violently he nearly fell off the table. "That would be just great," he whispered conversationally. "Fall off the table and kill myself, save everyone the trouble." He readjusted his position and stretched. "I'd better eat something." He popped a couple crackers with cheese and drank half the bottle of water. Stretching again, he looked outside.

It was darker outside and that meant darker inside. The one exit light was doing its best but it was red, like the battle lamp on a ship's bridge. Pretty soon there would only be enough light to see out the windows. "Good," he said. For Greg Weber, darker was always better. He functioned well in its secretive cloak, moved through its shadows silently and fearlessly. He loved the dark. It gave him confidence.

Once, before he became a creature of the dark, he bought a set of night-vision goggles. They were wonderful. He'd gone out stalking women with them and found the tactical advantage of seeing in the dark was inestimable. One night when he was prowling, the batteries ran down. At first, he panicked as most people would. Slowly, he removed the goggles and stood still. Within seconds, his eyes adjusted. Not as much as he would have liked, but they adjusted quite a bit. He began to see without the goggles. He wondered if it was another gift from one of his girls. Maybe one of them had extraordinary night vision. Oh, how he wished he knew for certain if he'd gotten it from one of them. It would have even been better to know which one.

He took one last look out into the darkness. Nothing. "Well," he chuckled to himself, "That's what you get when you hire lawyers and accountants to do a cop's job."

Chapter Eighty-one

Dan's group

As we approached the parking area, we were fighting the mosquitoes and the darkness. I had a Surefire tactical flashlight but using it was out of the question. We skirted the buildings and moved around to the rear to check out the parking area. From our side I could see a line of RVs. That would be a perfect place to stash one, I thought. Maria must have had the same idea because she had ducked behind a thick bush and, using her phone for light, checking her notebook for the plate info on Weber's rig. She pointed and whispered excitedly, "I think that's it."

I looked along her line and, sure enough, I saw what could be Weber's RV or its twin. We needed to check the plate. I called Will and filled him in. He said he and Molly would stay where they were and give over watch while I snuck in and checked the plate. Maria stayed in our position, drew her pistol, and covered me from there.

I worked my way over to the RV and got a look at the plate. Bingo. I gave Maria the high sign. Now, where was the SUV?

This time, Will hit gold. The little light from the dock area was just enough for him to see a deflection in the ground indicating a vehicle had recently driven on the grass. Moving around some trees, he spotted the Honda. He drew his weapon and crept up to the side of the car. It took a bit of slinking, but he was able to determine that the car was empty.

Weber was near, either in the RV or maybe in one of the buildings. After communicating our finds, we withdrew a block to the west to formulate a plan.

Inside the building

Weber nodded in and out of sleep. Suddenly, he startled, snapped his eyes open and sat up straight. He looked around the darkened storage building, searching for . . . what? He felt something. The hair on the back of his neck twitched, then stood at attention. He listened hard, thought he heard the hissing of a snake. Someone was out there; he just knew it. It was another gift from one of his girls, a woman's intuition.

They had located him and were closing in. As he silently slid onto the floor he said, "Time to get ready."

The Parking Lot

We decided he must be in one of the buildings. He wasn't in the car and why would he hole up in the RV? That was an inferior vehicle for escape. So he must be in one of the buildings. Still, we couldn't just leave it at our backs and risk him coming out guns up. We had to deal with it somehow.

A straight-on assault with our little group was lunacy. The RV's thin walls wouldn't stop any kind of fire so we couldn't sneak up to it and take the door like you could on a house of other building. If he started shooting through the walls, he'd take out whoever was at or near the door. So I crept up and checked the two doors by lightly pulling the handles. Both were locked. I pulled my pocketknife, flicked it open, and cut the valve stems off the tires. No easy job that. But it would at least slow him down if he ran. In the meantime, we'd have to keep an eye on it until we located him.

I returned to the group and we laid out our plan. Given what she'd learned in training, Molly didn't think he'd put up a fight. He'd give up, be taken in, and tell his stories. That's what we wanted.

Unsaid was that all our training was screaming in our heads that we should call in the reserves and wait the guy out. We knew it, we knew it was protocol, it was smarter, it was the better part of valor. We just didn't care. We all, each one of us, wanted this guy as only a cop can want a doer.

We decided to split up, surround the building, and enter. We would conduct a stealthy search until someone made contact, then we'd identify ourselves, surround, and apprehend Weber. At point it didn't matter who took him into custody. No one cared about getting credit, we just wanted to get him.

I asked, "Any questions?"

Only Molly spoke. "Just one thing. Even though these guys usually just give up and cave, he could be very different. He has a complete psychotic disconnect with what we'd term "normal" feelings. As long as he is armed and sees the possibility of escape, he will say or do anything he thinks will help him. Only when we have him in custody will we be able to relax. Until then he may do anything. Just because we have him at gunpoint doesn't mean that he will behave like other suspects we've arrested. When I was with him I saw his demeanor shift in a heartbeat." She pointed at me. "He will try to play to you, Dan, try to manipulate you. You need to be prepared to hear things you've never heard from a suspect."

I reached into my pockets and pulled out a pair of special earplugs I always carry and stuffed them into my ears. Each one has a piston inside that allows normal sounds to pass but will slide into a sound-blocking position when loud soundwaves hit it. They were designed to allow you to hear but shut out the sound of gunshots at indoor ranges which is what this tin-roofed building would be if Weber chose to shoot it out. "I'm ready for this mutt," I said. We all gave each other one last look and split up.

The plan was for Will and me to take the doors on either end of the building. My feeling was that since they were the most likely entrances, they would be the most likely to be observed by Weber. After giving us about a minute to move to the left away from the doors the women would slip in and go right. That way, if either of us had been seen by Weber, his eyes would still be on us. They would work to the right along the wall until they were about halfway up the side wall. We had gone through the exercise of synching our watches. At the appointed moment, I opened my door.

Chapter Eighty-two

Inside the building

Weber heard a confusing sound. It sounded like a door opening, but he couldn't determine which one. He quickly looked and thought he saw the east door swinging shut. That was the main door, the one he expected them to use. He thought he heard something else but needed to concentrate on what he had seen. He drew his pistol and crouched down in a cubby created between tires on shelving. The space was just big enough to tuck into.

His eyes had adjusted enough that light coming in through a window about ten feet from the door allowed him to see the shadow of someone creeping toward the corner of the building. Weber didn't want to shoot yet. He needed to know who it was, and how many people he was up against. He'd attended SWAT briefings and knew that you had to know how many you were facing before you engaged them. How else would you know when you got them all?

He sensed movement over his shoulder and saw a shadow moving. It was a woman. As she slid past the window he could see she was carrying a pistol. He waited, letting her pass him, then, as quiet as an owl swooping from a perch, he stepped out and struck her sharply on the base of her skull with his pistol, stunning her. She fell with a thud, her gun clattering across the floor. He quickly bound her with cuffs— hooking the cuffs around a compressed-air line that ran along the wall. He grabbed a pre-ripped piece of duct tape and slapped it over her mouth. As she turned around he recognized her as his primary target. A rush of success surged through his body and a broad smile spread across his face. He looked her in the eyes and whispered, "Hello, Maria."

Across the building, I'd seen Maria enter and move off to the right. I waited as she moved along the wall to the midpoint. There were sounds of a little commotion, but nothing unexpected. Maria was in the building. I looked toward the opposite wall window and saw the shadow of Molly crouching behind a boat on blocks. I heard a very light scuff of feet on the floor. Without tactical radios, we had no way to communicate silently. Normal procedure would have been to use a series of microphone clicks that would tell others on the team where you were without any noise escaping. But nothing about this was normal.

Will was through the rear door and moving forward to his right. The plan was for Will and Molly to provide a base of cover to the rear of the building. I would hold the front door and Maria would move to act as a driver, pushing him into the open. After the five minutes allowed for Will and Molly to get into position, Maria would start and then Molly and Will would join in a noisy search intended to drive Weber toward the front door, where I would apprehend him. According to Molly and everything I'd ever read about serial killers, he would peacefully concede defeat, fold up, and start singing.

Maria had the furthest to go to get into position, so she held the trigger. We waited for her to start the search. I checked my watch as three minutes ticked by. No Maria. I was concerned. At five minutes, I could hear Will and Molly start their sweep. Still no Maria. I was worried. Maybe waiting for the cavalry was a better idea. We had gone in on pure emotion and testosterone, never a good idea.

Something was wrong.

Weber waited. In his mind, he had the upper hand. He had Maria. He knew the others were in the building and approximately where they were. When Will and Molly started their move, he heard them off to his right. He set down his gun and picked up an old outboard motor prop that was lying nearby and sailed it like a Frisbee across the room toward the sound. It hit with a clatter, missing the pair but making a lot of noise. The sound of movement stopped.

Will and Molly looked at each other. Out the corner of his eye, Will had seen the prop come flying in. He whispered to Molly, "Did that come from Dan or Weber?"

Molly paused and answered, "I'm not sure. It seemed to come from where Maria was supposed to be, but she shouldn't be there anymore. She should be moving with us."

Their plan was based on the belief that Weber would be in the middle of the building, or one of the corners. What if he wasn't? What if he was along a side wall? They reassessed and made a tactical decision to move silently toward the front door. If Maria had been surprised by Weber, she might be out of the game already. But if Weber had captured Maria, he would be handicapped in his movements since he'd have to move her too. Molly said, "He'll want to take her with him; he won't just kill her. He wants both Maria and Dan." She hoped she was right.

Well, that's got them thinking, Weber thought to himself. He looked into Maria's eyes, expecting to see the fear he'd seen so many times before but was greeted by a look of determination. She was far from cowed.

"You don't seem to be too worried yet," he whispered. "That'll change. I guarantee you'll be scared out of your pretty little head before our relationship is finished. Maybe we should have some fun now."

Weber moved right, away from Maria, picking his gun up as he passed the table. He was excited to hold it, to know that it was the same gun that Dan carried. There was a certain irony in that, he thought, that Dan would be killed by the same make and model gun he himself carried. The same gun he'd recommended Weber buy.

I heard the sound of something metal hitting the floor and bouncing into a half-dozen other somethings. Will or Molly must have bumped into something that was on the edge of a cart or table and knocked it onto the floor. I silently cursed them for their clumsiness.

With Maria still missing, I was getting what special-forces guys call "apprehensive."

I was moving. I thought I'd heard movement to my right, but wasn't sure if it was Maria, Will and Molly, or Weber. I couldn't fire indiscriminately at shadows. I might hit one of my own people, a problem Weber didn't have. I had to do something to flush Weber out, at least to localize him for the others.

We were running out of time. I had to act. I stood up and yelled, "Weber. It's Dan Neumann. I know you're in here. Show yourself. You're completely surrounded but you can still get out of this alive."

Weber considered the offer. He believed he'd get out with or without Dan's approval. The only question was how many of them would still be alive. He had Maria. He really wanted to take Dan with him too. Will and Molly would be fun to have along, but they were expendable.

He needed to level the playing field a bit more, and that meant someone had to die. If I can get it down to two, I'll make it, he thought. Given the choice, he'd rather take out Will first and, perhaps, recapture Molly. He had some very special plans for that bitch. Yes indeed. It was her fault he was in this predicament.

How to do that?

He left Maria and low-crawled toward the middle of the room. Technically, it was a tactical error, since it left him open on all sides. But he wasn't thinking defensively. He knew he had the advantage. He knew how many he was facing. No other backup had entered the building—a huge mistake on their part. The correct thing to do would have been to wait for support and then sweat him out, maybe assault the building with a little tear gas. But they had not waited. Were they operating on their own, he wondered. Hmm, that was a real possibility. If no one knows they're here, no one knows I'm here, Weber thought.

The belief in escape grew strong. He'd have to take at least one of them out, but that was of no consequence. He began to focus on the shadows and the gun.

Will and Molly had reached the spot where Dan should have been. No Dan, no Maria. Will's strict FBI training told him to be pissed at Dan for deviating from the plan, but Will was much more flexible than the typical fed. He liked to quote a character from a Clint Eastwood movie, "Adapt, improvise, overcome," the gunny had said. He tried to remember that in situations such as the one he was in.

He looked at Molly and whispered, "Split up. You go back the way we came; I'm going up the center of the building. Dan and Maria must be sweeping around this side," pointing to the right. "That, or something's wrong, like Weber's got Maria."

Molly nodded and started back. Will blinked twice, trying to get better night vision, and headed into the darkness.

I was moving slowly, feeling as much as looking. I listened as hard as I could, trying to keep from just stumbling over Weber. This was going to be a knife fight in a phone booth, and I knew I was getting too old for that crap. I'd be happier with a good old twenty-foot shootout. My foot struck something and I looked down to see an old carburetor. I picked it up and hefted it.

I had another thought. Maybe that clank I heard was Weber chucking something at Will and Molly. Maybe Weber had tossed something to see if it would bring a reaction. My turn. I wound up and heaved the carburetor toward the rear of the building as hard as I could. It hit the far wall eighty feet away on the fly.

Weber heard the crash behind him, whirled and fired. It was pure instinct and he realized immediately that it was the wrong thing to do. "Damn," he whispered. Someone had done the same thing he'd done, but he'd reacted and they had not. Oh, well. He spun back to the front of the building and fired twice along the reverse of the probable line of flight. No idea if he'd hit anything. A return shot missed him.

"How'd I do, Dan?" Weber yelled. "Get you yet?" He flinched as a round came back his way.

I'd gotten the reaction I wanted. Weber fired at the carburetor. But, he surprised me by turning and firing back along the line of flight. The round whizzed past my head, inches away. I felt a rush as I realized I hadn't been hit. Churchill was right. I took a chance and returned fire in the direction I thought the shots had come from. I heard the round hit something hard and zing off in a ricochet. Not a good idea. I heard the sound of movement.

"Not yet, asshole," I yelled. "How about me? Am I in the paint?"

Well, that was a surprise, thought Weber. Someone had fired back. The round had struck about a foot from him and bounced off into the darkness.

"Missed me!" he hollered. He scrambled back toward Maria, who was tethered to the wall. He'd need her now.

Chapter Eighty-three

I moved toward the sound. There were more sounds now, movement all around me. I needed to know who was who. I yelled, "Will, Molly, Maria! Sound off!" I heard Will holler "Yo." Molly said "Yup." I waited. No Maria.

"You won't be hearing from Detective Fernandez, Dan. She's my guest, but she's a little tongue-tied at the moment."

I spun toward the sound. I knew where he was, but not what he was doing. He could have been waiting for me or covering Maria. If I did the wrong thing, he could kill her. I'd kill him too, but that was no trade. I heard movement behind me—Will or Molly must be coming around. A shot came from the mover. Weber returned fire in that direction. I made my move.

In that environment, the effect on a shooter's ears from the sound of a high-powered pistol round going off within a few feet would render the shooter virtually deaf for a few seconds. I was familiar with the effect and had prepared to deal with it by using my earplugs. But Weber was a new shooter; he didn't have the experience to function in that kind of tactical situation. I fired high and got the response I wanted, two shots in reply. I had two or three seconds during which he'd be deaf. I moved.

As I moved toward him another shot rang out. A dim shaft of light coming in through the window let me see Weber's movements. He was sitting behind an overturned desk; I saw him take a quick look in the direction of the last shot. I carefully stepped toward him. He was reloading the pistol. Again, his lack of experience played into my hands as he had to look at the pistol while reloading. He didn't have the experience to know how to reload while keeping his eyes on the tactical situation. Slowly, with the deliberation of a novice, he pushed the magazine release button on the side of the frame as he pulled the empty magazine out of the gun's grip and set it on the table. He pulled a new magazine from a pocket and carefully slid it into the well at the bottom of the grip. I heard rather than saw the mechanical snap of the slide moving forward.

Another shot was fired his way. I saw him move to face it and raise his pistol to fire. Then he pulled it down, apparently changing his mind about the shot. In the beam of light, I could see him looking at his pistol, turning it over in his hands. Then he pointed it at his face. There was a flash.

The 9mm hollow-point +P cartridge sent the 124-grain jacketed hollow-point mankiller down the barrel. With just a three-inch run to accelerate it, the bullet was traveling at a little over 1100 feet per second, fast enough that Weber never knew what happened. The human brain just can't register that fast.

The bullet entered just under Weber's right eye, the hollow-point round performing exactly as designed, expanding to nearly three quarters of an inch in diameter. It pushed anything loosely defined as solid tissue ahead of it and created a pressure wave that traveled through Weber's brain and impacted the upper left quarter of his skull ahead of the bullet, blowing about a third of his head off. Included in the debris was his medulla oblongata, the part of the brain that runs all the automatic systems. He was dead before the spent bullet left his head and struck the wall behind him. He was down and dead. I yelled, "Clear!" and rushed toward Maria.

I carefully peeled the duct tape from her mouth and kissed her. She broke off the kiss and said, "Get these fucking cuffs off me."

Chapter Eighty-four

The lights came on in the building. I freed Maria and hugged her as Will and Molly rushed up, saw Weber, and eased back from full-on tactical. They holstered their weapons and Will checked Weber. He was most truly dead; half his brains were on the wall and his face had a blankly surprised look. Will said, "Nice shot."

"I didn't shoot him; he shot himself. I don't think it was on purpose." I looked at Maria, who'd had a better view.

"Did you see anything?"

Maria picked up the gun, cleared it, tucked it in her pocket and said, "Yeah, I saw it. Let's get out of here before we mess up the scene. BCA will be here and I don't want Judy Loveless mad at us again."

Chapter Eighty-five

We moved outside and Will called his boss. He filled him in on what had happened and where. We filed over to a handy picnic table to await the onslaught of feddieland.

Within minutes, the sounds of sirens could be heard. Lights started coming on in the houses around us and, even though I couldn't see them, I guessed that anyone on the boats in the marina were standing on their decks wondering who the hell had shot off fireworks, ruining their last night aboard before they had to face the coming week.

As the dozens of sirens got nearer, I said, "I was right behind a cabinet. The light was dim and all I could see were shadows. He shot the gun out. I could see the slide locked back so he dropped the mag and loaded a fresh one. Then he turned to shoot. Must have changed his mind because he pulled the gun down. I guess he'd had enough because he pointed the gun at his own head and pulled the trigger."

Maria corrected me. "He didn't mean to shoot himself. He shot the gun out and reloaded. Then, instead of racking the slide, he just dropped the slide release and the thing had a misfeed. I could see that the slide hadn't seated, there was about a half inch of barrel sticking out of the slide. He was looking at it, had his finger on the trigger, looked down the barrel and the slide released. It slamfired and he blew his own head off."

I rolled my eyes and head and said, "Oh, jeez. Of all the stupid . . . ."

Molly asked, "What do you mean by slamfired?"

I reminded myself that, even though she'd been through the Bureau's firearms training, she wasn't what I call a shooter. Like most people in law enforcement, she considered a firearm a tool no different than a car or a radio or a computer. She'd been trained in its use, qualified annually, and carried one with the hope that she'd never need it. She wasn't an expert.

I'd seen it a hundred times at the range. A shooter has a malfunction, tries the slide a couple of times, nothing, so he looks down the barrel. What is it with people? I'd seen experienced shooters at competitions do it. If the safety officers hadn't been there to grab their gun hands, they might have done the same thing.

I looked at the gun. It was a CAB 9c, just like mine. "This thing is brand new. I'll bet it hasn't had fifty rounds put through it. No wonder it misfed."

The others knew as I did that a high-quality firearm is a precision machine. It is built to very tight tolerances and it needs to be broken in. The only way to break one in is to fire it. As it's fired, the slide, ejector, firing pin and myriad other tight-fitting parts wear in and become reliable. When I bought my 9c I put three hundred rounds through it before I felt comfortable carrying it. During the first hundred rounds it "stovepiped" or mis-ejected twice and misfed three times. After the two hundred sixty first round, it has never malfunctioned again. And I've shot thousands of rounds since.

Molly asked, "Can hand racking make that much difference?"

"Sure," I said. "Think about it. When the gun is fired, the slide runs the spring back 100 percent of its travel length. So it's got 100 percent of its tension pressure to push the slide back into battery, But when it's locked open, it still has to have some travel distance so you can move the lock button up to hold it open. It may only be one-eighth of an inch, but that's enough to diminish the strength of the spring. It's a small gun so the springs are short. They need full compression to do their jobs. Some small pocket guns don't even have slide release levers. You have to hand rack them. If the spring is fighting the added resistance of an unbroken-in gun, that leads to misfeeds."

Will, who is a bit of a gun guy for a fed, said, "Typical collection of mistakes that ends in an AD."

AD is an accidental discharge. They are almost always the result of a series of errors usually committed by someone who had no business holding a firearm. In the law enforcement world, they are something to devoutly be avoided. They can be career-ending.

I looked at Maria and we silently agreed to break protocol and demonstrate affection publicly. Just a quick kiss and hug. Sirens surrounded us and the night was filled with flashing lights.

Maria and I stood and walked toward Selma's Ice Cream. The lights were on. No surprise. Almost all the lights in the town were on.

"A maple-nut cone or a hot fudge sundae?" I asked Maria as we left the feebies behind.

Epilogue

Over the next week the federal machine went into action. It went through Weber's RV, car, and home with several fine-toothed combs and discovered very little of value. They interviewed everyone who knew him, had business contact with him, had ever seen him, and came up with nothing but, "I can't believe he'd do anything like that!" They researched him and found the crumb, the diamond, the needle in the haystack that unraveled Weber's entire existence. They found the key.

The key was to a safe deposit box in an Indianapolis bank. In the box they found everything.

The box, one of the biggest the bank had, was nearly full of records, photos, videos and souvenirs. Weber had even transferred his old VHS recordings to DVDs to preserve them. They found evidence of other identities, and properties in at least three locations across the country.

He provided a complete history of the women he had murdered. The feds estimated the treasure trove would close cases all across the country, maybe as many as sixty or seventy.

I couldn't figure out what the "#35 for Dan" meant. He had killed many more than thirty-five by then. The answer came when a high school photo of me was found in the box. I was wearing my hockey jersey with my number, thirty-five.

For those of us involved, finding the answers was a cathartic experience. We were at once both relieved that it was over and astounded at the find. The only bright sides to the whole mess were that there would be no trial and there would be closure for many families whose daughters, sisters, mothers, and wives had been missing, some for more than twelve years.

It was easy for the feds to track down the families, though it didn't make the notification teams' jobs any easier. Personally, I was glad for the find and for Weber's death. I recalled how Ted Bundy had bartered more information for continuing delays in his execution. There wouldn't be any of that this time.

I wondered about the ping I had with the artist. A cursory background check found nothing. I recalled a story an old buddy, Mark, told about spending hours with an artist who was painting a portrait of Mark's family. He described the guy as a troll, a weird little guy with no sense of humor. A truly odd fellow. I must have pinged on Conner Fulbright's oddness. But I'll be watching for his name.

A bigger curiosity was why I hadn't pinged on Greg Weber. Neither had Maria and I trust her senses as much as my own. Something was different about the guy. He was so in front of us, so obvious and noisy. Like living in the approach lanes to an airport, his noise turned into background and he was just a distraction, a cloud obfuscating reality. His good looks, smarts, pleasant nature, and ease in dealing with us completely took him off my screen. He didn't give off the nervous cues that, until now, I thought criminals *always* give off.

I was so focused on looking around him that I didn't see him standing right in front of me.

Will received a commendation for closing the case the same day he received a letter of reprimand for disobeying orders by staying on the case. Gotta love the feds.

Molly was given one of the country's highest law enforcement awards for her part in the finale. In part, the citation read that, while being held hostage, she had kept her head, obtained information from the suspect, and managed to escape and ultimately locate, surround, and defeat the suspect in the final shootout.

That he had died from stupidity wasn't mentioned.

Point of discussion

The firearm used by Dan and the killer in this story is fictional. It's a conglomeration of several popular conceal carry-type guns now on the market. It's chambered in 9mm parabellum, which is the most popular caliber and least expensive ammunition, therefore cheapest to practice with and large enough to be considered powerful enough for defensive use.

Like any modern semi-automatic pistol, it is a well-engineered, finely crafted, tightly machined mechanism. As such, it has a break-in period. During this break-in period, malfunctions can and will occur on even the best most expensive pistols. Once properly broken in, it is virtually impossible for them to malfunction except due to lack of maintenance or ammunition problems. And, it is virtually impossible for them to "just go off." They can be dropped, stepped on, run over with a car, frozen, cooked, and drowned in water. The only way to make them fire "accidentally" is to violate one or more, usually more, than one of the Four Rules of Firearm Safety.* In the story, the killer violated one, two, and three. You could say he followed or violated number four, too, depending upon your point of view.

The malfunction I describe in the story is absolutely credible. I've seen it, as have many range safety officers and firearms instructors. I talked to many of them to check this out and they universally agreed that it's more than possible. It's the result of failure to properly break in a precision piece of machinery.

Phil Rustad
USCCA and NRA Firearm Instructor
Certified Range Safety Officer
IDPA Competitor
NRA Life Member
Sheepdog

*1. All guns are always loaded. Treat them so! 2. Never point the gun at anything you are not willing to destroy. 3. Keep your finger off the trigger until your sights are on target (and you have made the decision to shoot). 4. Be sure of your target and what is beyond it.

Acknowledgments

Once again, a story like this can't be told without help from a lot of people. I'd like to thank some folks for their help and patience. The writing took much longer than expected due to life, and sometimes death, getting in the way.

I first met my editor, Pat Morris, at the Bloomington Writers Festival in, I believe, 2005. The first words I heard her say were in her presentation to a batch of writer wannabes. As I recall, she said, "As you write your story, enjoy yourself. Dwell in the creative moment. Because when your editor tells you to rewrite it for the sixth or sixteenth time, you may not enjoy it as much." With *Judges Choice* I discovered she was right.

She wouldn't let me go to press until major portions of the book were redone. It was necessary because of the time it took to write. Life kept interfering. The result was a manuscript that was choppy, with repeated or missing parts. She sent one section back saying, "I know you know how the story got from there to here, but you didn't tell me." Hopefully, her whip-cracking has produced something readable. If it is, it is completely due to her efforts. If it is not, it's on me.

I must also thank the legion of pre-readers who kept this process going, first by reading the drafts as they progressed and, finally, by reading the manuscript in its more-or-less finished state. My dad, brother Pete, and his wife, Tam, read early versions and kept me going. My good friends Dan Olson, Steve Hinrichs, and Jeff Munson were along for most of the trip. Steve Ganz, Kathy Patregnani, Marque Nelson, Verlene Goodall Birger, and Stephanie Morris all read the near-complete manuscript. All added needed corrections and appreciated encouragement. There must be some I missed, so I apologize in advance.

Thanks to Steve Schulz, the retired sheriff of Kanabec County. I had the pleasure of visiting with Sheriff Schulz early in the development of this book. He gave me a tour of his offices and we talked about what he'd have to do if faced with a homicide like the one in the story. He retired in January 2015. Frankly, I thought I'd be able to give him a copy of the book while he was still in office.

Friend, pilot, and fellow Dog Agility competitor Steve Holmseth is a crop duster. Steve met me at his airport and showed me the ropes of crop dusting. He even took me on a few runs in his beautifully aging Cessna 172. There's nothing quite like 140 knots ten feet above the corn tassels. He even let this old pilot wannabe handle the landing. One of my best ever.

Special thanks to Patti Kleven who lent me a treasured Best In Show ribbon for the cover photo. Thirty years of showing dogs and I don't yet have one of them.

I never met him but I owe a thank you to John Douglas of the FBI. He's one of the founding fathers of profiling. I read several of his books. If you want to know what profiling really is, not what they show on TV, read *Mind Hunters*.

It's hard to believe but I have fans, after a fashion. For the past four years I've been repeatedly asked, "When's that new book coming out?" The persistence of friends is as responsible for this book as anything else.

All the characters in this story are fictional and the story is a product of my occasionally paranoid mind. Any similarity to real people or events is completely coincidental. Except for you, Doug. You know who you are.

Finally and mostly, I need to thank my partner and wife, Cindy, for patience for all the time writing takes, time away from other activities that she could share, we could enjoy, or would actually produce money.

Thanks, Cindy. I still do.

Phil Rustad's

insatiable curiosity and "What if?" imagination have led him into multifaceted experiences ranging from making stained glass windows to being an international AKC dog-obedience judge to working with companies "that make things go boom!" His natural storytelling ability led him to write the Dan Neumann mystery series.

Phil and his family (including the four-legged ones) live in Minneapolis.

Watch for the next Dan Neumann mystery.

Next . . .

Narcotics—the biggest ticket item on the American law enforcement's must-stop list. Everyone's life has been touched by them.

In revenge for her work on a drug task force in Arizona, Maria, Dan Neumann's almost-fiancee, has been targeted for assassination . . . in Minnesota. In a thrilling series of actions that take the reader through Minnesota, Arizona, and into northern Mexico, Dan and his team of modern-day avengers wreak havoc on the drug trade and its leaders, start an inter-gang drug war in Mexico, and attract the attention of the DEA, Border Patrol, the FBI, and the CIA because they don't follow the rules—no one's rules.

Alamo

Semi-retired Minneapolis homicide detective Dan Neumann is happy to hear his best friend's voice until he hears Pete's words: "I need your help, buddy. Grams is dead." Dan's shock at the news about his surrogate grandmother turns to outrage when he learns Grams was murdered. He assumes it was a random break-in until Pete and the rest of his family are also targeted.

Finding out who and why becomes Dan's mission. The puzzle becomes even more complicated when the investigation reveals a professional hit man and a lethal gas from the Balkans of all places, which is an invitation to the FBI to take over the case. No matter. Jurisdiction means little to Dan. This is personal.

Following the evidence into a land of multi-billion-dollar mineral rights contracts, Dan learns about the Bakken Oil Field and a complicated, ugly world of fraud and conspiracy inhabited by men whose greed respects no one, not even family.

As nature's winter fury swirls around him, Dan faces the killer in territory he never expected to find himself — "about thirty miles from the middle of nowhere"—Alamo, North Dakota.

Dart

Nearing the end of a successful career, Minneapolis homicide detective Dan Neumann was looking forward to retirement and a relaxing summer riding his Harley, woodworking, and writing another textbook on ballistics. But Neumann's leisure plans go up in smoke when law enforcement calls on his expertise to investigate a murder involving a weapon so sophisticated, so lethal, it's never been seen before.

Realizing he is up against intelligence and formidable skills equal to his own, Dan pursues the Shooter around the country, determined to crack his last case. Always one step behind the killer, Dan follows an ever-bloodier trail from Alaska to Arizona, murder to murder, enlisting the help of a particularly interesting deputy sheriff along the way. The chase leads to the shores of Lake Superior, whisper-close to the murderer. But is it close enough? And where is the "real justice"?